OBSIDIAN DETECTIVE

OBSIDIAN DETECTIVE

OPUS X™ BOOK ONE

MICHAEL ANDERLE

DISRUPTIVE IMAGINATION

Copyright © 2019 Michael Anderle
Cover by Gene Mollica Studios
Cover copyright © LMBPN Publishing
This book is a Michael Anderle Production

LMBPN Publishing
PMB 196, 2540 South Maryland Pkwy
Las Vegas, NV 89109

First US edition, Nov 2019
Print ISBN: 978-1-64202-396-1

OBSIDIAN DETECTIVE TEAM

Thanks to our Beta Readers:

Nicole Emens
Daniel Weigert
James Caplan
John Ashmore
Larry Omans
Mary Morris
Kelly O'Donnell

Thanks to the JIT Readers

John Ashmore
Jeff Eaton
Misty Roa
Dave Hicks
Peter Manis
Larry Omans
Deb Mader
Jeff Goode
Dorothy Lloyd
Paul Westman

If I've missed anyone, please let me know!

Editor
Lynne Stiegler

To Family, Friends and
Those Who Love
to Read.
May We All Enjoy Grace
to Live the Life We Are
Called.

PROLOGUE

February 1, 2227, United Terran Confederation, Earth

WIRE NEWS

The UTC has implemented a new program to encourage those who have positions of power and prestige to engage with Police Departments around the country.

The Chief of Police for North California was quoted as saying, "I'm not sure what they expect from some Corp-Princesses trying to force their brand of silver-spoon elitism into our departments, but mark my words: it is going to fail. It takes decades to provide the kind of experience a veteran cop needs to make a good detective. For all I know, these insta-detectives are going to want everyone to join hands and sing together."

The chief has since retracted his comments and apologized for the misunderstanding regarding his out-of-context remarks.

At last count, there were approximately two dozen individuals interested in signing up. One of the powerful young adults looking to move into the new vocation is rumored to be none other than Jia Lin, youngest daughter of the famed Lin business family in Neo So Cal.

CHAPTER ONE

March 5, 2227, United Terran Confederation (UTC) Standard Date. Mu Arae System, Molino, First Moon of Planet Quijote

THWACK!

A few in the crowd groaned. *A few always take the sucker bet.*

THWACK!

Erik grinned as his final metal dart hit the board.

A moment later, there was a satisfying chime. Another bullseye.

He looked around with a smile on his face. "It's hard being this good, and this handsome." He watched as the waitress, Janette, walked by and winked at her. "But I've been blessed, so who am I to complain?"

She waved the back of her hand twice, telling him to deal that talk to someone else, although she had a smirk on her face. She grabbed two empties and disappeared through the crowd.

Dammit! Model-good looks, and I can't even tease the waitress and get more than a smirk in return?

That's it. He shook his head, although he kept a smile plastered on his face. He raised his arms in triumph, but in his mind, the conversation ended with *I'm officially old, and I suck.*

A roar of approval erupted from the men and women surrounding him. The group of them were clad in loose black pants and white undershirts, and they had dog tags around their necks.

The dog tags were deceptive, nothing more than a thin piece of metal to the naked and ignorant civilian eye, despite being one of the more sophisticated examples of non-volatile nanomatrix storage in the entire United Terran Confederation.

That level of technology was necessary to store the gene sequence of the relevant soldier along with other data while maintaining fidelity even under extreme conditions, such as exposure to pure vacuum.

None of the soldiers concerned themselves with the possibility of their demise. The only enemy action they feared at the moment was death by boredom.

There weren't a huge number of off-duty soldiers in the room, only twelve out of the fifty making up the UTC Army Expeditionary Force 108th Assault Platoon. Their boisterous voices were more than enough to challenge Erik's ears in the small, windowless and mostly empty barracks rec room, however.

A lanky dark-skinned man standing next to Erik shook his head. "It's been four days since your birthday, but I don't know if I can let this go anymore, Major. Big five-zero or not."

He chuckled and gestured at Erik's hair. "Getting a lot of gray up there." He pursed his lips as Erik raised an eyebrow. "Just saying, maybe it's time to get some rejuvenation treatments." He grabbed the darts being handed to him and waved them to catch Erik's attention. "I know I'm new here, but come on. You think I'm an idiot?"

Erik eyed the other man with a slight frown. "I know you're new here, but I've told you this before. When we're off-duty, it's just Erik or Blackwell." He nodded at the darts. "What aren't you going to let go?"

The other soldier shrugged. "I'm just saying, si...Blackwell." Adeyemi gestured at Erik's left arm. "It's cybernetic. It's not fair. If you want to link up with your smart lenses, that's one thing, but you can also guide that arm with the smart lenses. I can't do that." He flexed his arm. "I lost the minute you convinced me to even play."

The soldiers gathered nearby shook their heads, some smirking, others looking annoyed. A young, stocky Asian woman with short black hair stepped forward—Lieutenant Biyu Yang.

"He's just that good, Adeyemi." She waved at Erik's darts, which were still stuck in the board. "Trust me. Everyone who comes into the Knights Errant figures that out soon enough." She rolled her eyes. "Because he always tricks someone into playing, and once we get suckered, we have to let the next guy do it. It's kind of our platoon's initiation ritual."

Adeyemi grunted. "Maybe he's that good," He eyed the darts in the center of the board. "But I'm not convinced."

Erik's lips rose at the corners, just the tiniest amount. "You think I'm cheating?"

Poor bastard, Erik thought. *He comes from an important military family. No reason to cause trouble unless I want to end up stuck doing nothing for years instead of only months.*

"I'm not saying you're cheating," Adeyemi replied. "Just that you've got an advantage."

"An unnatural advantage?" Erik raised an eyebrow in challenge.

Adeyemi snorted. "I don't have time for Purist garbage. I hate people because they're annoying, not because they've got some extra genetic engineering or a few metal parts. No, I only care about how that arm is helping you win against me in darts right here and now." He slapped his hand on his chest. "I've got some pride. I won almost every tournament in my old unit."

Erik strolled over to the black, red, and green board and pulled the darts out one by one. The room had quieted, and his voice, which came out gentle but unforgiving, was heard by everyone. "My unnatural advantage is thirty years of playing darts when I'm stuck in some backwater system like this one with nothing better to do than play a little hand-eye coordination game to keep things fresh." He stepped away from the board and made two quick tosses, this time with his right arm. Both darts landed dead-center in the bullseye.

He kept one dart and twirled it in his fingers, his eyes watching the dart but his mind lost in the past.

The other soldiers clapped, except for Adeyemi. He looked at the board and Erik with a frown.

"I told you," Biyu offered, shaking her head. "Just give

up while you're ahead. You're not going to win this. I should know. I went through this *last* year."

Adeyemi laughed. "Come on, he can't be that good. He's just gotten inside all your heads." He scratched his chin. "Okay, if he's that good, let's see the real deal. I knew a man back in Lagos who could hit bullseyes blindfolded. Are you *that* good, Blackwell?" He gestured at the board. "You land those kinds of darts without your metal arm, and then I'll be impressed."

Erik glanced at the board, the rest of the soldiers, and finally at Adeyemi. "I don't know. How about we bet and find out? It's no fun if there is nothing to lose."

He felt the tension in the room rise.

"What are we even supposed to bet? The commissary here is sad and empty, and the civilian store isn't much better. A few extra credits aren't going help me three months from now." Adeyemi shrugged. "You going to pull strings and get me off some mission rotations?"

Erik reached into his pocket and pulled out a thick silver coin decorated with an elaborate embossed image of a soldier in an exoskeleton, the blue and white UTC flag in the background. He walked over to a nearby black metal table and tossed the coin down, the ring as it settled going on for fifteen seconds.

Adeyemi stared at the coin, brow furrowing in confusion. "You're coin-checking me? There's not even any alcohol on this blasted moon to drink." His eyes widened as he glanced at the item and back to Erik, who was licking his lips. "You know where some is, Blackwell? Is that it? I'll bet whatever I need to get a drink. There was no alcohol on the transport out here, and it's been three months since

I've had anything decent. Someone's got to have something on this rock. Anything." He looked around the group. "Can't we distill a drink out of something?"

"You're not understanding what I'm betting." Erik patted his left shoulder. "Let's back up, so you'll understand. You know how I lost this arm?"

"To an angry Zitark?" called Twizzle. The pain-in-the-ass rifleman snarled and raised his hands like they were claws, lowering his voice with a hiss. "I'll eat your spleen, human, and then I'll feed the rest of your body to my babies once they come out of their eggs."

Most of the people in the unit knew how Erik had lost his arm, but he didn't doubt they wanted to mess with the new arrival a little.

As long as they kept it to jokes, he didn't mind.

Biyu laughed, her brown eyes lit up with merriment. "We're only on this damned moon because someone's worried about those little reptiles getting jumpy and poking at UTC territory again like last year." She shook her head. "Who would have thought the first aliens humanity would run into would be tiny dinosaurs with spaceships?"

"Not worried about them." Erik tapped the table and sighed. "Nah, plenty of humans around to shoot at other humans before we go wailing on the local neighborhood races, but this isn't about featherless velociraptors in space." He nodded at Adeyemi. "Or maybe it is. Maybe they're really good at darts, and they might have a chance against me, but for now, this is about my arm and my coin. So, I'm asking you, do you know how I lost it?"

The other soldier frowned. "I assume you lost your arm during a mission."

"Yeah. One of the first battles during Wolf's Rebellion. Some of the bastards got the drop on me when I was away from the rest of the squad checking on a hunch. They thought they were lucky. It turns out I was the one who was lucky." Erik's grin turned feral and hungry.

Adeyemi grimaced. "But you lost your arm after getting ambushed. Why the hell do you think you're lucky?"

"There were ten of them. I survived. They didn't, and all it cost me was a replaceable arm. I'm good, but don't ever count out Lady Luck on the battlefield, or she might just decide to stay home when you most need her." Erik nodded at the coin. "I asked to get a cybernetic arm. I wanted to get back into action and not waste time with regrowth and the time to attach it."

"Still sounds unlucky to me, and I'm trying, but I still don't get it." Adeyemi frowned. "Why didn't you just get a new one grown once you got away from the frontlines? I mean, I don't care, but there are a lot of Purists out there."

Erik clenched and released a fist, his eyes watching the movement of his fingers. "Because in a battle right after that, some insurgent tried to stab me. I threw up this new toy, and his knife broke."

He looked up, his eyes glinting. "After that, I started thinking it was my new lucky charm. I survived against ten guys, and then it saved me against another, so I decided to keep it."

He shrugged. "My CO at the time gave me that coin after I asked for the arm. Turns out the enemy squad I ran into was a recon squad. They were supposed to be probing our line for weaknesses so the enemy artillery could light us up. We had total control of the skies. You couldn't get a bird up, let alone a spotter drone. The CO was all impressed that I took them out because the artillery could have ripped our flanks to shreds. But I wasn't thinking about that at the time. I was just trying to take out some cocky guys who thought they had gotten the drop on me."

Erik paused, then pointed at the coin. "But that, along with the arm, always reminds me that it's a combination of skill and luck that keeps us going. A good soldier always needs both, even if he has to make his own luck on occasion."

"I get it." Adeyemi swallowed. "But look, I don't *have* anything that important to bet."

Erik shook his head. "Who said anything about you betting?"

This time, even the squad seemed confused. "Wait." Adeyemi held his hands open. "You just did. That's why you told that whole story."

"Nope, not quite," Erik replied. "You don't need to bet anything. I'll be the only one to bet. If I lose, you get the coin. If I win, I get the satisfaction. Can't buy that with money, and it's worth more than gold out here. I told that story because I wanted it clear I'm beyond one hundred percent confident I can bullseye without looking at the board. That might not be a blindfold, but it's got to be good enough to impress you. How about this? I'll turn around and toss it." He paused for a moment. "*Guaranteed* bullseye."

Adeyemi frowned, now looking more annoyed than worried, and waved a hand in a negative gesture. "No way, no how." He jerked a thumb behind him. "You can't hit that target with your back turned. Smart lenses aren't going to help you if you're not using your cybernetic arm."

Erik lifted his right hand and waved the dart. "You've got nothing to lose but your pride, or are you ready to admit that I'm just *that damned good*?" He gave a lopsided grin.

"Sure, why the hell not?" Adeyemi snorted. "Let's see it, Blackwell. Show me the pride of the Knights Errant. Make me believe I didn't shoot myself in the foot when I got a transfer here."

Erik laughed. "So if I'm good at darts, that makes all this worthwhile?"

"It's something." Adeyemi shrugged. "Better than sitting around on my hands."

Erik turned around and closed his eyes, then took a few deep breaths and stepped a few centimeters to the right. After a quick jerk of his arm and flick of his wrist, the dart flew out of his hand. A thud and a familiar chime followed. The room filled with the roars and cheers of the other soldiers.

Erik opened his eyes and faced the dartboard. His throw didn't place the dart directly in the center of the board. It lay just inside the bullseye circle.

Close enough.

Adeyemi's let out a loud groan. "You have *got* to be kidding me." He slapped his forehead and pulled his hand down his face, his eyes focusing back on the board one more time. "I can't believe what I just saw." He pointed at the board but was talking to two of the guys to his left. "He didn't have his freaking eyes open, and his back was turned!"

Biyu smirked and popped him in the stomach to get his attention. "Told you. At least he let you off easy." She reached up and patted him on the shoulder. "We all think he's lucky, too. Our platoon hasn't lost a single soldier since he took over, and we saw plenty of action before getting sent here to watch dust and rocks and wait for hissing aliens."

Erik's mark looked around, exasperated. "You're not a bunch of green scrubs," Adeyemi argued, his hands up as if he were preaching to a bunch of sinners. "That's not luck. It's *experience.*"

"Sure, but it's like he said. It helps to have both luck and skill." She winked. "And now we're so lucky we're sitting at the edge of UTC space doing nothing but playing darts and going on boring patrols. Maybe it's a reward, as boring as it is." She stopped for a moment, pressing her lips together. "Not that I wouldn't mind a crack at the Zitarks," she mumbled. "But I'm not all that eager to see if those bastards are tough little dinosaurs or not."

"Don't worry." Erik grunted. "There's a reason the 108th is the last major platoon left on this rock." Once the garrison relief arrives, we'll move on to something more useful."

The passage of time had convinced Erik that some idiot desk ranger, or worse, desk Marine in intel, had freaked out too much about routine Zitark ship movements and spun the whole UTC military up into almost starting a war.

He could imagine how they had loaded up thousands of troops and gathered a decent-sized fleet, only for absolutely nothing to happen for months.

Say, the months he had been sitting on his hands here, for example.

And that meant vital military resources which could have been used against humans who were actually causing trouble weren't available.

Erik was as eager as anyone in his group to go on leave and then get back to doing something—*anything*—useful with his platoon.

How many terrorists we could have smoked are out there causing trouble?

"Are you shitting me?" Adeyemi sighed. "It took me two months of travel to get here, and now it's all over?" He shook his head. "I was good with a transfer here. I wanted to be there when the first intergalactic *war* started."

Erik grinned. "I was wondering why someone would suddenly request a transfer to 108th when we were stuck in the middle of nowhere counting dart scores. Sorry. The Zitarks aren't going to make a move on human space. We'd promptly make them as extinct as the dinosaurs on Earth, and they know that. It's probably why they backed off so much once they saw we were getting ready for a fight."

"Damned right!" Jekowski, and Butters in the back fist-bumped. They were both adrenaline junkies, but damned good when life showed up and bitch-slapped your plan for the day into next week.

Adeyemi narrowed his eyes. "You really don't think they're going to be a problem?"

Erik considered his answer before shaking his head. "Highly unlikely. You know they apologized for that crap they pulled last year, right?"

Adeyemi shrugged in that way which suggested it rang a bell, but it was ringing in the other room.

"Well, they did. Which is why we're here playing darts

instead of wasting space raptors in our exoskeletons. Besides, everything we know says there are a lot more humans than Zitarks." Erik shrugged. "We stay out of their way, and they'll stay out of ours. Hard to win a war when the other guy's guns are as big as yours, and they've got a lot more people than you do."

Biyu snickered. "So, even if we couldn't beat them, we would win by breeding them out?"

"Hell, yeah!" Jekowski called.

"In your dreams," one of the ladies shot back.

"Hey!" Jekowski turned to her. "We signed up for whatever it took to win this war, right?"

Erik noted the mostly male grunts of agreement.

Jekowski jerked a thumb to his chest. "It might not be the way you want to serve your world, but if I'm told to go breed for the benefit of mankind, I'm taking that shit seriously."

"Just call it the great human advantage." Erik spoke over Jekowski.

Adeyemi shook his head. "What about the Orlox? Can't they just basically sneeze out new little fungi?"

Erik chewed on the inside of his cheek in thought, then said, "It's kind of hard to be intimidated by a bunch of glorified walking mushrooms. Trust me, I've seen one in person. They're weird, not scary."

His hands outlined an Orlox's shape in the air. "They're not even all that intelligent by themselves. They're only self-aware in groups. They won't last long in war if they all start drooling when we shoot one out of four of them."

"Do Orlox drool?" Biyu asked.

"Hell if I know. I'm not a xenobiologist. They look kind

of…sticky." Erik chuckled and gestured around the room. "The UTC might be pinned in for the most part by the Local Neighborhood races, but none of them seem like they're going to mess with us anytime soon. It's been almost forty years since first contact with the Zitarks, and the most we've had are a few border skirmishes. I've been in the Expeditionary Corps for thirty years, and I've only ever had to fight humans." He scratched his chin. "There's no Thucydides Trap when all the races are balanced in power already."

Adeyemi pondered Erik's reply before trying again. "What about the Leems? They've been coming to Earth since 1947. You know, what was it…Roswell? That Leem ship that crashed, even if they didn't admit it until recently. That's got to mean they're planning *something*."

Chuckles ran around the group.

Erik snorted. "An almost three-hundred-year head start on having hyperspace tech, and all those little gray freaks did was run a few worthless experiments and buzz the occasional farmer? I'd put my money on the Orlox to win a war before I put it on the Leems. Please note, the minute we started sticking our satellites up, they were afraid to do much. And keep in mind, the Leems who were in the Solar System were stuck there because of some weird hyperspace accident. It wasn't like they were in communication with the rest of them. It also doesn't do a race any good to have tech if they don't know how to fight. That's the other great human advantage—the will to fight, honed over thousands of years fighting each other."

Erik thought about it for a moment. "That, and we have

bagels and fried rice. I don't think any of those other races have bagels *or* fried rice."

"The power of biryani will defend humanity," declared another soldier, Lieutenant Ahuja. "It's even better than fried rice."

Harold, known to most here as Lieutenant Sampson, made a face. "Ugh. Why are we talking about good food when we're stuck with rations here? I'd kill for real food." He turned to look over his shoulder. "Especially Jekowski."

"Hey!" came the automatic reply. This generated the expected chuckles, as well as the single-finger salute that seemed to go with mankind no matter what world, planet, planetoid, or barren rock humans took root on.

Along with pizza. Erik agreed with Sampson's thoughts. *He'd be tempted to kill Jekowski for a bite of pizza.*

Sampson waved off the man's complaints. "They say printed food is the same nutrient-wise, but it's definitely not the same flavor-wise. I don't care if it's cheaper to ship out the nutrient paste tubes and print them into a meal. They should give us some real damned food if they're going to stick us on rocks like this for so long."

The room became a cacophony as people shouted out the foods they missed.

Erik shook his head, a slight smile visible in his eyes, if not on his lips.

If you looked hard enough.

The Knights Errant had earned a long leave, and he'd been promised one from up above. Just two more months and a garrison platoon would arrive.

Too bad the Zitarks won't let us show up and hit their beaches. They've got to have at least a few decent ones.

A small silver card clipped to his belt vibrated; it was his PNIU, personal network interface unit. He tapped it and waited for a chime to signal connection, then put up a hand. Those around him lowered their voices and hit those who had loud voices behind them who hadn't noticed Erik's raised hand yet.

"This is Major Blackwell."

"Sir," came the response. The sound was transmitted almost directly to his ear, granting him some privacy. "That UTC auditor who is evaluating the mine just sent out an SOS. He says he's under attack by terrorists."

What the hell? I'd believe the Zitarks showed up all of a sudden sooner than terrorists.

"Terrorists?" Erik echoed. "What are you talking about?"

"We don't know, sir. Just got a garbled transmission about him being under terrorist attack."

Everyone fell dead silent and turned to look at him, excitement in their eyes. A little action, especially against terrorists, would be welcome.

Erik frowned. "Do we have any drones in the area?"

"No, sir. We're getting some transmission errors. I'm also having some trouble communicating with the satellites."

His frown deepened. "Prep additional drones. We'll launch them ourselves on the way. Send out an all-call alert as follows." Erik glanced around. "We're suiting up. Full battle-rattle. We have a possible terrorist incursion at the mines. Enemy number and capability unknown."

A moment later, a harsh alarm emerged from every-one's PNIUs, the sound repeating from nearby rooms as his message was issued. There was intentionally no directional sound for full alerts.

Erik gestured toward the door. "Let's move. Some poor bureaucrat probably just hit his head and is seeing things in the shadows. I expect everyone in this room to be suited up and ready to go before the rest of the platoon even gets to the armory."

Terrorists? How could terrorists get from the gate all the way here without the destroyer picking them up? Infiltrators with the company workers?

If this auditor idiot is wasting our time, we're going to have a loud, vociferous one-way conversation.

CHAPTER TWO

"Knight Two, report," Erik ordered through the comm.

He glanced out the window of the armored flitter, a dedicated troop transport. Even though a lot of people referred to flitters, civilian or otherwise, as hover vehicles, they technically relied on antigravity technology rather than any sort of thrust-based hovering. He didn't know or care much about the particulars.

They were fast and could maneuver well.

"Not seeing anything. Just dust, rocks, stars, and Quijote," responded Biyu over the comm, her voice cutting through the clinks of armor against the flitter's walls or floor when someone moved. "Pretty as always."

The bulky but angular black vehicle zoomed over the flat, featureless plains of the moon.

Erik was in front next to the driver, with the rest of the squad one in the back. The other squads were in their own flitters.

His platoon was on their way to the mines, which were located far from the habitation domes for safety reasons.

To his right, the massive blue-green-ringed gas giant Quijote hung in the sky.

Technically, the moon Molino had an atmosphere, however thin, and some geological activity, which was why it was covered with rocks and dust, and more than a few small mountains, but it wasn't a crater-ridden graveyard like Earth's moon. It also wasn't worth the terraforming effort to get a glorified quarry.

Small domes and self-contained buildings defined the settlements there.

Erik grunted, his thoughts drifting to Earth's moon. It'd been a long time since he'd been to the heart of the UTC.

For all he knew, they'd blown up the moon and concealed the evidence from everyone on the frontier.

It didn't matter. If Earth was the shining imperial planet ruling all of them, it was his responsibility to help protect it from the barbarians on the frontier.

Unfortunately, the thin atmosphere of Molino didn't include significant amounts of oxygen, nor did it help much to fight off the cold.

Every man and woman in all four of the deployed squads wore military-grade exoskeletons and full tactical suits that kept them warm, with their helmets producing more than enough air to breathe. They could operate on the surface of the moon for days without resupply if necessary.

Erik tapped his wrist, the smart lenses over his corneas interfacing with the faceplate of his helmet to provide an enhanced augmented reality interface that he could see by looking out.

The newly forward-deployed recon drones weren't

spotting anything. No visual confirmation of trouble. No unexpected thermal traces in the sky. No unusual radiation or other energy spikes.

Did he get attacked by terrorists or ghosts?

"Base, did we get any other transmissions from the auditor?" Erik asked.

"No, Knight One," the comm officer replied. "The line went dead about two minutes after the platoon left the base."

Erik frowned.

His unit had been assigned to the moon as part of an entire division. The UTC military had ferried people away from the moon over the last few months to help cool the border tensions once it became obvious there would be no Zitark invasion or raid. The remaining troops weren't local cops or security.

They no longer had a purpose here.

The vast expanse of human civilization, the entire United Terran Confederation, stretched in one form or another over fifty light-years from Earth, and included scores of settled worlds and moons.

Given how the UTC had used colonization as an excuse to boot troublemakers off Earth since the start of the Social Cohesion Transport policy of 2136, only the most naïve citizen who paid any attention was shocked by the fact that the galaxy was filled with a rich collection of terrorist and rebel organizations.

It was unlikely, but not impossible, that a terrorist group had gone to the trouble of infiltrating the Mu Arae system. The only thing Erik couldn't figure out was why they would bother.

Erik shook his head. It didn't matter who was there. They could determine who was responsible once they rescued the auditor.

The team was heads up, looking around using the age-old Mark One Eyeball to see anything that could be seen without their sensors.

A few minutes passed. *Still no enemies.*

The troop transports coasted to a stop.

The mine's exterior was unimpressive, nothing more than a collection of large metal tubes extending to massive gray warehouses, all topped with landing pads for collection drones. A huge square tunnel jutted out of the surface at a steep angle, black reinforced doors protecting the entrance. If the doors had been open, they could have easily driven one of the troop transports straight inside.

"Deploy," Erik ordered.

The side doors of the transports lifted.

The four squads rushed out, rifles at the ready.

The combined footfalls of fifty armored pairs of feet produced a light rumble in the area. Everyone in the past had believed robots would inherit the battlefield, but too many militaries had learned the hard way what it meant to rely on autonomous gadgets, especially far from their supply lines.

Maybe if they ever managed a true AI, that would change, but for now, dozens of soldiers in their powered exoskeletons with gunmetal-gray limb extensions, heavy weapons strapped to their backs, might easily be mistaken for robots.

Erik disembarked last. He raised his weapon, a custom black Selene Firearms TR-7 Quad. With four selectable hungry barrels, he could use it for massive suppression fire, or just switch down to one for some snap shooting.

Was it over the top? Maybe a little. Ok, *yes*.

Satisfying to use when taking down the bad guys? Abso-damn-lutely.

He'd had to pull a few strings to bring it along the last few years as they tried to make him upgrade, but the gun had saved his life more than a few times. It was another good luck charm, like his arm.

"All squads spread out," he barked. "Keep an eye out. We should be able to find one lost bureaucrat. Just look for the paper trail." He kept his safety on but set his weapon to single-barrel mode. "Remember, the grav fields from your exoskeletons don't mean crap once you fire and that bullet's away from you. Keep that in mind. Anything you shoot is going a long way on this moon. There's also no grav field in the mine, for transportation efficiency. Knights Two, Three, and Four, on me."

The other squad leaders rushed over to Erik, including Biyu, who was in command of squad two, Lieutenant Ahuja in command of squad three, and Lieutenant O'Malley in command of squad four.

Erik switched to a direct frequency. "What are we thinking, people?"

Biyu shook her head, her frown visible even through the darkened faceplate of her helmet. "This doesn't feel good, sir."

O'Malley nodded. "I agree. There's nothing. Where's the damage? Where are the vehicles? We took a few minutes to get out here, but our drones got here quicker, and we didn't spot anything with those either."

Erik pointed to a few parked collection drones atop a warehouse. They resembled giant metal dragonflies with long metal baskets beneath them. "None of the drones are moving either, but there haven't been any alerts from the mines other than the SOS. I'm thinking a couple of terrorists sneaked in as new hires, maybe anti-expansionists or pro-aliens. They sabotage the mine, and our auditor friend sees them."

"That's kind of farfetched, sir," Ahuja suggested.

"Really? I'm working on farfetched at the moment. So, ask yourself why a UTC auditor is all the way out in Mu Arae investigating a mine?" Erik turned his head toward the mine's access tunnel.

The presence of the auditor had lodged in the back of his mind since his arrival last week, but Erik's orders were clear. He was to maintain the garrison and keep his soldiers in line so they didn't interfere with either corporate or UTC personnel.

Biyu hissed, her eyes taking in Erik's drones. "That would explain why we're not seeing a bunch of vehicles. If they're terrorists who have infiltrated the workers, they might have come here with the help of a drone or driven right in with the codes."

Erik grunted. "Damn it. At least this means there are probably only a few of them. If they're smart, they've kept the auditor alive as leverage. I'm going to take squads one through three in. O'Malley, you watch our backs with your squad, just in case the rats are hiding somewhere other than the mine."

"Yes, sir."

Erik nodded toward the doors. "Let's move."

The officers split up to return to their squads, everyone switching back to general broadcast frequencies and delivering the orders. Soon, squads one through three were gathered at the tunnel doors, spread out in an inverted wedge, their rifles at the ready. There was no reason to crack out the heavy weapons yet.

Erik neared the access panel to the door and lifted the dust shield. The screen came alive with a message in English and Mandarin.

Xingguang Mining Molino Site A. No trespassing. All violators will be prosecuted to the fullest extent of UTC law.

Erik snorted.

Get a lot of trespassers out here, huh? Terrorists don't care about signs.

Erik entered the emergency override code in short stabs, twelve digits in quick succession.

They'd trained several times for potential Zitark incursions into the mine. He figured the aliens would always just blow the colony and mine away from orbit, but it wasn't like anyone on Earth had direct experience with Zitark invasion tactics.

For all they knew, the reptiles would demand to settle it over a game of chess.

With a groan, the behemoth doors began to slide apart. The soldiers waited, their breath held and their guns pointed at the doors. Anything from angry reptilian aliens to terrorists might pour out of the tunnel.

The doors continued separating. Ceiling lights kicked on in sequence, pushing the darkness into the distance and revealing nothing but a long, empty tunnel.

They heard nothing, but Erik's mind wanted to add a *click* as each light turned on.

Sonofabitch. Erik hit the comm. "Base, this is Knight One. Confirm the absence of other personnel at the main mine." Erik glanced at the readout of every person on his team. His eyes flickered through the menu systems, making sure of the overall status in case something went...

Wrong.

"Confirmed, Knight One. Xingguang says no one other than the auditor was scheduled to be at the mine today."

Erik frowned. It wasn't like they had a bunch of internal sensors set up. "Squads one through three, on me." He tapped on his wrist to bring up the layout of the mine. "It looks like it branches off in three directions. Let's go check it out. Drop transmission boosters at the intersections just to be sure. I don't want anyone getting cut off down here, and I don't trust the mine's internal comm network right now."

"Yes, sir," replied his squad leaders in unison.

Quick steps brought the soldiers to the intersections. They continued on their way, the squads consisting of twelve soldiers each, except for Erik with fourteen. All that firepower proved unnecessary, given the emptiness of the mine tunnel.

A few squat four-armed inactive black loading and maintenance drones were against the walls on occasion. Every once in a while, a door led into a small room, but it was obvious the facility had been designed with the idea that humans would be minimally directly involved with its day-to-day operations.

"Squad two, anything?" Erik asked.

"No, sir," Biyu replied over the comm. "Drones, mostly. There are also a few inactive ore haulers loaded up, but nothing besides dust and quiet. No blood, no body, just nothing."

Erik furrowed his brow, eyes darting to his left as the squad progressed. "Squad three?"

"Quiet and boring, sir," Ahuja replied.

"Continue. The man sent off an SOS. Even if he used the mine's comm to boost his signal, he's in here, and I doubt he went very deep."

A few more minutes passed, with Erik's gaze darting back and forth. The small icons on the side of his HUD identified the active status of the squads. All green circles. Everyone was fine.

Between their exoskeletons and the anti-ballistic nature of their snug tactical suits, even if a terrorist surprised them, the soldiers would win. If the terrorists didn't surprise them, and the Knights deployed their shields, there was no way they could lose.

Luck, as many a wise man had said, was where opportunity met preparation, and the Knights Errant were well prepared both in equipment and training.

Squad one turned at another intersection and Erik narrowed his eyes. Splattered blood covered the walls.

"Potential contact," Erik called, sweeping his weapon back and forth. His soldiers took formation and aimed. "We have blood. Proceeding forward. All squads, continue with caution. Squad four, you still good?"

"Yes, sir," O'Malley replied.

Erik crept forward, squad one on his flanks. The blood formed a trail around the corner.

"Three, two, one," Erik counted.

The soldiers spun around the corner. No enemy awaited them, just a bullet-riddled body in an excursion suit on its back. A few spent shell casings lay on the ground next to the body.

Erik locked his gun onto his exoskeleton's storage rack before crouching. Blood had painted much of the white excursion suit red. The helmet was cracked open. Even if the man hadn't suffered from a lethal reaction to excessive lead, he wouldn't have survived.

His eyes remained open in a death stare.

"Looks like we found our auditor. Death by enemy action," Erik muttered. "Base, we have located the UTC auditor. He's dead. Multiple bullet wounds. No sign of assailants."

"Copy that, Knight One."

Erik stood and shook his head.

His gaze lifted to a thick door a few yards behind the body. "That isn't...*normal.* "

The door was heavily reinforced compared to most of the doors he'd seen.

"Sir?"

"Wait one. We're going to see if anyone is behind door number one," he answered

Erik walked over to the access panel and tapped in the emergency code override. Nothing happened. He attempted to interface with the door using his military credentials directly sent from his PNIU.

ACCESS DENIED.

"Now we have moved from not-normal to weird," Erik mumbled.

"What, sir?" asked one of his squad members, Sergeant Pena.

"This door is too secure," Erik responded. "Way too secure for some random door in an automated mine on the ultimate frontier world. Why is it here?"

Pena grinned. "We've got torches and explosives, sir. Maybe we should crack it open and see."

"We've got no reason to blow through this." Erik grunted. "If we can't get through, the terrorists couldn't get through, and I don't need the UTC brass crawling up my ass for unnecessary facility damage." He glanced at the body again. "But where the hell are the killers? This guy didn't shoot himself."

"Deeper in the mine, sir?" Pena shrugged. "If not here, then one of the other passages."

"Maybe." Erik frowned. He didn't like mysteries.

"All squads, meet up at the entrance. I'm not going to poke around a deep mine with a single platoon. We'll have the company seal the mine, and then we'll send some drones to explore in case the terrorists are still down here hiding. For now, we're retreating. We're leaving the body here. The locals might want to investigate this with their own resources." Erik gritted his teeth. "We signed up to be soldiers, not cops." He took one more look at the locked door.

"For now, let's get out of here."

CHAPTER THREE

The three squads exploring the mine met up at the first intersection and started to make their way back to the main entrance.

"Knight Four, have you seen anything?" Erik transmitted.

"Nothing, Knight One," O'Malley responded. "Just dust and rocks and the big planet in the sky. Wait. The drones are acting weird." There was a second pause. "O'Merral, did you expand their search radius?"

"Weird, how?" Erik brought up the drone status on his AR display.

According to his information, the drones were still executing their previously programmed flight path.

His stomach tightened.

What's going on, Lady Luck? You finally get angry with me? I push you too hard all these years by flirting with Death?

Erik's HUD glitched the barest amount. What the hell? He started running, waving to all of his people to follow.

"All squads back to the entrance, full speed, weapons hot," Erik bellowed.

The loud clank of metal on metal echoed in the tunnel as the soldiers sprinted, their exoskeletons helping them barrel forward. They might not be able to outrun a flitter in an exoskeleton, but terrorists on foot would have no chance of escaping.

An alert popped up on the side of his AR display.

DRONE ALPHA SIGNAL LOST. DRONE BETA SIGNAL LOST. DRONE GAMMA SIGNAL LOST. DRONE DELTA SIGNAL LOST. DRONE EPSILON SIGNAL LOST.

"What's going on up there, Knight Four?" Erik shouted.

"The drones all just slammed themselves into the ground at high speed, sir," the lieutenant called back. "They just pointed themselves straight down and accelerated."

"Anything else?" Erik continued rushing ahead of the rest of his squad. "I think our terrorists are trying to cover their escape. Base, this is Knight One. Prep additional drones and get the Dragon ready to fly. I don't want these guys getting away because they outran us."

"Knight...repeat...ference," came the static-filled response.

The terrorists hacked a Corps drone, and now they're messing with our signals? Who are these people?

The major, along with the other soldiers, arrived at the entry to the mine, where Squad Four stood, spread out, rifles ready, along with a few rocket- and grenade-launchers ready on their shoulders. Squads one through three fanned out, everyone looking back and forth.

Erik switched to his loudspeaker. "Everyone shift to direct audio. The terrorists are jamming signals."

Without the drones or comm, we don't have decent coverage. He looked around. *We have no idea where they went.*

Something rumbled in the distance. Loud thumps and clangs echoed from within the mine.

What the...

"Everyone to the side of the mine," Erik ordered. "Full speed, and jump if you have to. Shields out." He darted to the side, running a few yards before leaping into the air and pressing a button to cancel his grav field. With the lower natural gravity of the moon now tugging at him far less than Earth standard, he flew through the air.

Erik twisted to point his gun at the tunnel entrance. With a clack, his defensive shield expanded from his left arm, the clear alloy barrier providing decent coverage without blocking his line of sight.

Most of the soldiers cleared the front of the tunnel. An overlapping cacophony of heavy booms sounded, and a barrage of bullets slammed into two lagging soldiers.

Bullets sparked as they bounced off the exoskeletons. Several rounds made it deeper, ripping through tactical suits.

One man went down with a groan. The other fell forward. Despite the beating, the exoskeleton and suit might save them if they could recover them quickly.

"Prepare for recovery," Erik shouted.

A howling roar sounded from the tunnel. Several rockets emerged a moment later, slamming into the downed soldiers. The booming explosion consumed both men, and Erik screamed a curse.

Bullets continued to emerge from the tunnel.

Something flashed from the top of a nearby warehouse.

"Light them up at 1 o'clock high," Erik roared, his heart racing. It'd been a long time since one of his soldiers had been seriously wounded, let alone killed, and now some terrorists bastards had taken out two.

The soldiers unleashed streams of bullets. Two fired rockets. Three launched grenades. Their rounds struck the top of the warehouse in a massive explosion, sending two of their previously hidden enemies careening off the edge —men in black exoskeletons with their own shields.

The Knights' swarm of high-velocity rounds finished them off before they hit the ground.

"What the hell?" Biyu yelled. "Those are military-grade exoskeletons."

O'Malley hissed, "Why would terrorists have that kind of gear? How the hell did they smuggle it here?"

The stream of bullets from the tunnel had diminished, but occasional bursts erupted. He had no idea how many enemies might be in there, or where they had come from if not from behind the locked door.

The tunnel fell silent.

Erik looked at the charred warehouse. The lack of oxygen had already smothered the fire caused by his team's attack. "We're too exposed here. All Knights, defensive formation gamma. Move quickly but deliberately toward the warehouse."

The squads formed up in an instant, every angle of fire now covered as they made their way toward the warehouse.

Several distortions bent light in the distance, near the

entrance of the tunnel. Erik might not have understood what he was looking at, but he knew what he had to do.

"Enemy at two o'clock near the tunnel," Erik called. "I don't care if you see them. Fire."

A good soldier knows when to think for himself and when to shut up and follow orders, and the Knights Errant were good soldiers.

Half the platoon wasn't in a position to fire, so they maintained coverage of the rest of the area. Everyone else opened fire, a good chunk of their bullets bouncing off the air.

It didn't take many rounds before the distortions crystallized into six black exoskeletons.

"Movable optical camouflage," Biyu related, her voice a mix of frustration and wonder. "I heard that wouldn't be ready for primetime for years."

"Can the chatter and finish them off," Erik ordered. Several rounds bounced off his shield, adding to the extensive dents and cracks. Even an advanced anti-ballistic shield would only last so long against high-velocity advanced rifle rounds.

The soldiers kept up their barrage. Enough rounds made it past the armor and shields of their enemies to down them. It was as Erik had said before: taking on an opponent with the same basic gear but inferior numbers could only lead to defeat.

Be smarter than a reptile.

The men in black exoskeletons stumbled back, only managing a few decent shots in return before a near-simultaneous volley of rockets and grenades from the Knights blew their armor and the men inside into pieces.

Erik took several deep breaths and checked his platoon's status display. Two red dots marred squad three's green circle. All the gunfire had drowned out the rumble from before, but it was now much closer and more obvious.

Did they get my request to send the Dragon after all? A little air support would be nice.

He chanced a look before shaking his head. "We need cover," he called. "Let's go."

The Knights kept their formation as they closed before breaking apart and reforming into a squat wedge.

Erik pointed to the warehouse and then to two nearby men. "Open it up the direct way."

The soldiers nodded and fired a couple rockets at the wall, blowing a jagged hole. The new fire died just as quickly as the others had.

Erik motioned toward the new hole and tapped his wrist control again. Two flares launched into the sky and exploded overhead. Proper protocol meant the support personnel back at the base would at least be looking in the general direction, and they were only kilometers away. The Dragon support craft would even the odds with whatever invisible enemy might be out there.

Assuming it wasn't already on its way.

"This is insane," O'Malley muttered as the troops hurried inside and took positions near the hole and around several massive metal cargo containers filled with ore. "How can we fight them if they're invisible?"

"I don't think they can maintain that," Erik noted. "Those guys didn't fire when they were invisible. I think

36

they wanted to get close. We're two men down, but they've lost the element of surprise."

Ahuja shook his head. "There's no way those were terrorists." He looked up, then around before stopping when he faced Erik. "What's going on, Major?"

"What's going on is that we were ambushed by whoever took out the auditor," Erik responded. He swapped out his nearly empty magazine and slapped in a new one before selecting quad-fire mode. "As for who? Doesn't matter. We'll kill them, and we can let some UTC investigators figure it out later."

"We've got movement," Biyu shouted. She squeezed off a few rounds at black forms rushing toward them, each taking huge leaps with each step. More exoskeletons.

Rounds flew at the warehouse from the outside, pelting the thick metal outer walls of the building but bouncing off. The approaching enemies broke into three groups. They all fired quick bursts but didn't follow up with rockets or grenades.

Erik took his opportunity and held down the trigger. The quad barrels came to life and vomited bullets. Shell casings cascaded to the ground like a metal waterfall.

The ammunition counter surged from full to zero as he kept firing, the advanced anti-recoil system keeping him on target. A man leaping through the air without a grav field and taking advantage of the natural low gravity of a moon wasn't always great about keeping his shield up, including the two men Erik shredded. The gun ran dry, and he ejected the magazine and slapped in a new one.

The enemy reversed course, bouncing backward and firing smoke charges to cover their escape.

"Not so tough when they don't have us in the open." O'Malley sneered

Erik narrowed his eyes. "Wait. Hear that?"

Now that the rumble was close, it was familiar. The lower pressure of the atmosphere had changed the sound, but Erik recognized it.

"It must be the Dragon," Biyu suggested. "No wonder they're running away."

"No. It's not the Dragon. Too noisy," the major answered.

Something nagged at the edge of Erik's thoughts, but he didn't have long to consider the surprise. Several explosions rocked the warehouse. Hot metal flew from the roof, along with several drones. The soldiers jumped or ran to avoid the avalanche of debris, but large chunks of the roof crashed down on three and buried them.

An unmarked black craft zoomed overhead, its engines at full burn and its secondary thrusters on the sides and front rotating for a quick turn. The thruster layout, narrow wings, and thrust instead of grav engine suggested a vehicle meant primarily for Zero-G operations. They'd gone from a couple of terrorists infiltrating the mine to squads of exoskeletons with prototype gear and fighters, plus the enemy also had military-grade jamming.

Erik slapped his comm to broadcast at full strength on all frequencies. "Base, this is Knight One. We are under fire and need immediate friendly air support."

Another series of explosions ripped the warehouse apart.

"Back to the mine," Erik ordered.

"What?" Biyu snapped her head in his direction. "They might be in there, too."

"We can win against the exoskeletons," Erik pointed out. "We're not going to win against a fighter." He looked at his platoon display. The buried troops were already dead. The only thing he could offer them now was revenge. "Go! Let's take a few bastards out along our way." He charged forward and held down the trigger, sweeping from side to side as he emerged.

The enemy exoskeletons crouched, their shields in front of them. Maybe if the enemies were facing a few militia with normal rifles, they might have survived, but the high-velocity rounds and explosives of the Knights overwhelmed their shields, armor, and tactical suits and gave many of them a one-way ticket to hell.

The soldiers had made it halfway to the mine entrance when the fighter made another pass. Erik expected a strafing run or missiles, but it screamed overhead, not firing. A couple seconds passed before he spotted the bomb dropping straight toward the warehouse.

"MOVE!" Erik bellowed.

The bomb struck the building and a massive red-white blast consumed it, the roar like an angry giant's. Its hungry shockwave cut into the fleeing soldiers, picking them up and strewing them about the landscape.

Men and women screamed over the comm. Green turned to red on his platoon status display as soldier after soldier died.

Erik didn't even realize he was soaring through the air, his armor flashing and beeping at him, until he crashed into the wall of the tunnel and thudded to the ground. He let out a soft groan and managed to open his eyes.

Black exoskeletons appeared at the edge of his vision, this time taking carefully aimed shots at the downed and vulnerable soldiers—at least the few who survived.

Biyu jerked as a man finished her off. Then Ahuja. O'Malley. Pena. Jekowski. Others gasped, their cracked helmets letting precious oxygen escape before their assassins shot them.

With a growl, Erik slammed the emergency release on his exoskeleton and crawled out, his body screaming in pain and the frigid air of the moon slicing at his burnt and exposed flesh. His exoskeleton was destroyed and his skin exposed, but he still had a helmet, and even without the backup unit, that meant he had enough air to at least take few more of the enemy with him.

He reached over with his cybernetic arm, the wounds and burns on his natural right arm making it all but useless. With a couple of quick yanks and slaps, he reloaded the TR-7 and aimed it, gritting his teeth.

I'll make you pay. You murdering bastards slaughtered my people, and as long as I'm breathing, I won't stop until everyone responsible pays.

Erik pulled the trigger, catching a nearby enemy by surprise. The four-barrel burst caught him in an exposed weak side, and he yowled in pain. With a bestial roar, Erik held down the trigger, finishing off the first man and then moving on to a second. A third man fell before the enemy fired another quick shot.

A wave of pain shot through Erik's chest, and he slumped, his rifle falling out of his hand.

Two more men in exoskeletons came into his vision, carrying a huge metal container between them.

Why, Lady? You abandoned us, but at least let me live long enough for revenge.

His eyes closed.

CHAPTER FOUR

**March 8, 2227, United Terran Confederation (UTC)
Standard Date. Mu Arae System, Molino, First Moon of
Planet Quijote**

The doctor checked the vitals, confirming the male patient
was still "inside" his shell. When he leaned over him, he
noticed the man's eyeballs jerking erratically.

"Patient is mentally aware." Doctor James looked at the
sensors connected to the body. "Looks to be a dream, or
perhaps a memory." He glanced down at his wrist-tablet
and typed in a couple of commands. "We will need to pull
him out of the forced coma soon."

The doctor made sure all the filters were correct.
Although nothing should have changed, it never hurt to
verify his expectations.

On his way out of the small rehabilitation room in the
med center, the doctor turned and eyed the soldier. "I hope
your dreams are pleasant, Major, whatever they are."

With that, he moved his hand down, and the lights went to ten percent.

The beeps continued rhythmically long after the silver doors closed.

ERIK GROANED and opened his eyes, then squinted at the bright light above him. Soft voices murmured around him. They sounded vaguely familiar, but he couldn't place them. He lifted his head, his eyes finally having adjusted. He was lying on a comfortable railed bed lined up with several empty ones.

The med center.

A soft beep sounded from the bed. Silver medpatches were all over his body. Most of his major wounds were at least sealed. A familiar warmth suffused his body, a sign of the medical nanobots doing their steady, indefatigable work. They might not be able to regrow a limb, but they could fix most damage short of that.

A man stepped into the room through the open doorway. He'd been speaking to a couple of other people outside. He pressed a button, and the silver door slid closed behind him. Even without the white and red uniform, Erik would have recognized him. There weren't a huge number of doctors in such a tiny colony.

"Doctor James," Erik croaked out, his voice rough. "The Dragon finally showed up?"

He was still confused by how the vehicle could have fought off a fighter.

Doctor James shook his head. "Xingguan and local

UTC security traveled to the location when you didn't check in. There was some sort of computer problem with your air vehicle. When they arrived, they found the battle site." He sighed. "What remained of it, anyway. I'll be honest. Xingguan is furious over the damage to the mine and how long it'll take them to repair it. Considering what happened, I would think they would be more understanding. At least all the terrorists are dead."

Erik shook his head. "They had a fighter. How did the locals take that down?" His mind was not tracking well. "They don't even have something equivalent to the Dragon."

Doctor James shrugged. "I don't know all the details. I was only informed that the terrorists are all dead. Apparently, the few terrorist survivors were killed when they put up resistance after the security forces showed up."

"That's not possible." Erik sat up and groaned.

"You shouldn't strain yourself, Major." Doctor James gently pushed him down. "You were very close to dying. If anything, I'd say it was only luck that saved you."

"Luck?" Erik eyed the doctor. "No, I think years of bad luck finally caught up with me."

Doctor James reached into a pocket and pulled out a bent dog tag. He offered it to Erik. "This is yours. You were seriously injured, and the best I can tell, this deflected a bullet meant for your heart." He flicked the piece of metal with a finger. "This little tag saved your life and made sure we didn't get to use it for its intended purpose."

Erik reached out and gingerly took the dog tag. "I knew these things were tough, but I didn't realize they were *that* tough." He looked around the otherwise empty room.

"Where are my troops? I'm not an idiot, and I was paying attention. I know several of them went down, but where are the survivors? You got some converted room somewhere? I need to know who is left alive. I already have too many messages to write to families as it is."

Doctor James' face tightened, and he took a deep breath. "There's no easy way to say this, Major."

"Just tell me," Erik growled. "This isn't the time to worry about sparing my feelings. I'm not happy, but this isn't the first time I've lost people on a mission."

"You're the *only* survivor." Doctor James averted his eyes. "Obviously, the small number of support personnel and the pilots who were at the base are unharmed, but all of the other soldiers, all forty-nine of them, were dead upon the arrival of the security teams."

Erik narrowed his eyes. "Everyone?" He gritted his teeth. "Some of them had to have survived."

"I'm sorry, Major. It is what it is." Doctor James nodded. "You should rest. I'm sure you have a lot of questions, and I know the governor is ready to speak to you when you're in a little better shape. My condolences. Those were good men and women, and they didn't deserve to die at the hands of terrorists."

Erik thought about it for a moment, working with his clouded thoughts.

Those weren't terrorists. I don't know what's going on here, but there is absolutely no way the men who ambushed us were terrorists.

Those pieces of garbage were tools. Well supplied and trained tools, but tools, nonetheless. No.

He closed his eyes.

This rot goes higher.

Erik dropped into the comfortable black synthetic leather chair in front of the colonial governor's massive glass desk. Other than the impressive furniture, including a high-backed chair reminiscent of a throne, the office was surprisingly spartan, with only a few paintings completing the decoration.

There was something about governors and paintings.

Erik had never seen a colonial governor's office that didn't have a painting or two. He didn't see the point, but maybe it was a way for them to pretend they were still on Earth and continuing the ancient traditions of leaders from the distant past.

Perhaps it was a way of implying status and wealth, two things he cared very little about, even if thirty years of frontier service, hazard pay, and smart investing had left him well off.

Erik hissed slightly as he settled into the chair. The nanobots helped with the pain and the wounds. It'd been almost two weeks since the battle, and the little machines continued to knit him back together.

Pain is weakness leaving the body.

A slight weight rested on his chest underneath his shirt: his bent dog tag. They had mentioned fabricating him a new one, but he wanted to keep the old one as a symbol of when his luck had failed him, and as a remembrance of all the other Knights who had died outside that mine at the hands of their mysterious enemy.

Governor Anders, a pale brown-haired man with a perpetually harried expression, sighed behind his desk. "I'm sorry I didn't come to speak to you in the hospital, Major, but I wanted to give you time to recover and collect your thoughts before we discussed the incident. I've been doing my part to look into it. I've sent only the most basic reports out, but if they decided to bounce it all the way back to Earth..." He sighed again. "Well, it'll be a while."

"You've investigated?" Erik asked.

The governor pursed his lips. "Yes, what little we have the capability of doing here. It's not as if this is a core world or even a reasonably mature colony."

Erik grunted and shook his head. "It wasn't terrorists, Governor Anders. I want that noted right here and right now."

"So I've been informed you've said." The governor licked his lips. "You're the expert in this sort of thing, so I'm inclined to trust your judgment." He looked Erik in the eyes. "But are you *sure* about that?" The governor seemed to be pushing Erik, making him answer.

"Don't screw with me." Erik slammed a fist on the desk. The entire top rattled despite its mass. "I know what I saw. Exoskeletons? A fighter? Optical camouflage?" He shook his head. "Those guys were better equipped than my platoon, and they had the technical know-how to hack systems here. Additionally, I don't understand why there was a locked door in that mine that wouldn't take my emergency military credentials."

Governor Anders took a long, deep breath and slowly let it out. "I know it's small comfort, Major, but I agree with you."

Erik narrowed his eyes. "Meaning what?"

"Meaning there are...*inconsistencies* in some of the reports and records." The governor shook his head. "Let's face it, I might be the official UTC governor of this colony, but I'm basically just here to sit in a chair since Xingguan controls everything. But that's just the thing; even the Xingguan representatives here seem confused by what happened, and of course, they're in a panic because the mine complex was half-collapsed by obvious bombing. They're desperate for any UTC help they can get, either in repair or investigation."

Erik pondered that for a moment. "Xingguan *wants* you to investigate further?"

Governor Anders nodded. "They've practically insisted that we do so. I think the local company reps are all convinced they're going to be recalled over this." He shrugged. "The problem is, as I implied earlier, we don't exactly have access to great investigative resources. It's obvious that even though our satellites, drones, and cameras were disrupted, the damage to the mine could have only been done by a vehicle such as you described. We're attempting to scour the moon for any sign, and we're failing. The in-system destroyer is searching for them as well, but they've found nothing, and they're concerned about straying too far from the colony now, given the attack."

Erik leaned back, nodding slowly. If everyone agreed, that made things easier. "Then we need to get additional resources here. Investigators. More ships."

Governor Anders shook his head. "If you want to stick around and convince the next governor of that, you're welcome to, but I've already requested a transfer. I'm even willing to take a demotion."

"I don't blame you for what happened to my unit." Erik narrowed his eyes again. "Running away won't bring them back."

"You don't understand." He leaned forward in his chair to look Erik in the eye. "I do feel bad about what happened to your soldiers, but this is simply base cowardice on my part, nothing more." Governor Anders let out a nervous laugh as he waved a hand around. "I thought I could improve my career here. When I was assigned here, there was still a good chance war would break out, but I didn't worry. I figured that with a UTC fleet in orbit, I'd be safe. I'd get all the credit and take none of the risk, but then this happened." He raised an eyebrow. "Major, I've spent the last week looking into things, and I've come to the conclusion there is *no way* those kinds of assets made planetfall without someone helping them."

There was a definite pause before he continued.

"Someone on the inside," the governor finished. "I don't know if it was UTC or Xingguan, because we both seem clueless, but there's something bad happening here, and I don't think it has anything to do with terrorists."

"Who?" Erik held back a growl. "You must have at least some idea."

"No, I don't know, and it's why I've requested a transfer." The governor paused, looking off into the distance as if he were contemplating the stupidity of his next action before focusing on Erik again. "I was looking into some things using my administrative codes. I'm supposed to know about everything going on in this colony, in theory.

Even if the company keeps secrets, I'm still supposed to know in general what they're planning."

He stopped, so Erik pushed him. "And?"

Anders shook his head. "I found a few encrypted messages with message tracking codes originating from the Neo Southern California Metroplex back on Earth. Even more suspicious, the messages were sent some time ago, but conveniently arrived a couple of days before the auditor. He only came from a few gates over, but the message timing is interesting."

He stared at Erik, the silence lengthening before he asked, "Major, you know how long it takes to get a message from Earth out here?"

"About two months, right?"

"Exactly."

Erik frowned. "And where exactly did the messages come from in Neo SoCal? That's basically, what...half a state with a hundred million people?"

Anders shook his head. "I don't know. That's all I could discover with my resources here. You'd have to take that up with Hermes Corp, and I doubt they're going to crack open their records just because we ask them to. There's another problem, anyway."

Governor Anders took a deep breath, and his eyes darted around for a few seconds as if he expected terrorists to kick in his door. "This is what's got me really worried. I was going to send those messages off since I didn't have any idea how to decode them, but this morning when I went to check on them, the messages were *gone*. Deleted from my system, with no evidence they ever existed or that I'd ever accessed them."

"Somebody's covering something up." Erik leaned back just a bit, folding his arms. "Xingguan?"

"No." A sharp shake of his head. "It's like I told you. They've been encouraging an investigation, including into their systems. If they are responsible, their local representatives aren't in the loop." He tapped the top of his desk at each of his points. "They're in a complete panic about the damage to the mine. It'll take months to get it back up to capacity, and it might take months to identify the terrorists, and that's assuming our requests don't mysteriously disappear on the way back to Earth."

Erik ground his teeth with the frustration of not knowing. The information seemed like it was close, but it was leaking out of his hands. "I don't get it. What are you saying happened here? Who killed my people? This isn't a metroplex. Those people had to be sent here from another location."

Governor Anders shrugged. "Someone with enough resources to end-run a major corporation, the UTC bureaucracy, *and* the military." His eyes pointed out that even Erik's group had been sandbagged. The blame for not knowing touched multiple groups. "I don't know what this is about, but I don't intend to find out, and I suggest you leave as well, Major. I imagine it'd be easy for either of us to fake suicide, given what's going on."

"My soldiers deserve justice," Erik countered. The anger in his voice wasn't directed at the governor, so much as the universe as a whole. "I have served the UTC for thirty years. I've seen my share of corruption and bribery and crap out on the frontier."

Erik growled, his words an accusation, "But I've *never*

seen an entire special forces platoon slaughtered and then had people act like it's no big deal, or that it was just some garden variety terrorists getting lucky."

"I understand." Governor Anders ran a hand through his hair. "I've already helped you as much as I can. You won't do anyone any good pushing this farther here, not when whoever is responsible has the upper hand and we have so few resources, but I've got an idea. It's my understanding that you were born in the Greater Detroit Metroplex on Earth. At least that's what your records said. The unclassified part, anyway."

Erik shrugged, not sure where he was going with this. "Yes, so? What does that have to do with anything?"

Governor Anders smiled. "I was born in the United States, too. New York Metroplex. I used to be a lawyer before I entered government service. One of my first jobs involved doing regulations research for the government. It's been one hundred and twenty-seven years since the UTC was founded, and every member state pledged to better coordinate their laws, but, yeah, lots of things left over. Lots of things we need to prune or modify. Most of it isn't all that important, but every once in a while, something comes up, and a member state ends up embroiled in a legal controversy."

The original curiosity was losing ground to Erik's desire to stick his gun into someone's chest and pronounce forty-nine names, pulling the trigger with each one. "No offense, Anders, but why should I care? UTC laws have nothing to do with my men."

"You *should* care since one of the more interesting laws I came across," Governor Anders leaned forward, a conspiratorial smile on his lips, "was the so-called Obsidian Detective Act of 2095."

Erik pursed his lips. "How the hell did we go from talking about my soldiers to old laws?"

Governor Anders chuckled. "Knowledge is the ultimate power in a bureaucracy, Major, and the UTC is the grandest bureaucracy ever to grace humanity. All of the subordinate countries are still twisting themselves to try to fit with it. The law was passed after the Summer of Sorrow. It's almost funny in a sick way, considering we're talking about Neo SoCal."

Erik nodded slowly, still confused as he pondered the governor's words. However, he knew enough to believe the man was trying to help and offering a back door. Perhaps.

And right now, the front door was locked and guarded.

Few historians doubted the Summer of Sorrow was responsible for changing the entire course of Earth's, and, arguably, galactic history.

In 2090, terrorists used a stolen nuclear weapon to destroy the greater Los Angeles area, killing tens of millions. The men responsible belonged to a militant transhumanist group called Second Spring who objected to the heavy restrictions on genetic engineering and cybernetic modification that had arisen in the preceding decades.

The action represented the largest-scale attack by the group since their founding in 2070 and was part of their goal of creating enough chaos to force humanity to turn to Second Spring's messianic transhumanist vision for survival.

The destruction of one of the largest cities in the world not only crippled the economy of the United States and deeply shocked the nation, but it also threw the entire world into a depression.

Chinese intelligence was instrumental in tracking down the major Second Spring bases after a few lucky intercepts, and joint Chinese and American military forces then proceeded to ruthlessly track down and eliminate the terrorists.

Without mercy.

In addition to forging a new, close bond between China and the United States, the incident and the following years also led to the rise of the anti-transhumanist Purist movement, and a strong pushback culturally and legally against genetic engineering and so-called unnecessary and unnatural cybernetic modification.

Despite the need for a government to also handle the offworld colonies in the Solar System, arguably, without the incident, the United Terran Confederation wouldn't have been formed in 2100, since China and the US formed the heart of the new pan-human international and interplanetary government.

By the time humanity was ready to start reaching for the stars, with the help of the newly developed hyperspace transfer point a few decades later, they were unified and ready to face the challenges of spreading beyond the Solar System.

The Neo Southern California Metroplex arose from the ashes of the destroyed greater LA area at its core, helped along by international aid, particularly from China. over the following decades.

Over the following decades, Neo SoCal grew and absorbed many of the other cities of Southern California, all the while also being a hub for overseas arrivals hoping to make their mark in an unusual if not unique urban environment.

"What is this Obsidian Detective Act?" Erik asked.

"A law named after a popular movie series from the era." Governor Anders shrugged. "I tried watching one once, but they are…dated, and they aren't all that relevant."

He waved a hand dismissively. "The point is, around that time, the government was having trouble recruiting enough law enforcement personnel when they first started building Neo SoCal. That issue was compounded by the existing shortage of law enforcement officers because, among other things, the continued rise of cybered-up criminals and a lag in getting the police the resources they needed."

"They came up with an idea," the Governor continued. "They would recruit a ready source of disciplined men and women from military veterans, but they still had trouble, since a lot of veterans didn't want to join a police department and work their way up from the bottom after years of earning their place in the service." He pointed at Erik. "And that's where this law comes in. It allows a veteran with commensurate rank and experience to not only be guaranteed a law enforcement position but a *higher-ranking* one."

Erik stared at the governor. "You're saying you want me to go back to Earth and become a cop?"

Governor Anders nodded. "I think, perhaps, they might need a new detective? You'll never find out the truth of what happened here working from inside the UTC military, especially since they'll ship you far away from here soon. The one clue we have is those suspicious messages that originated from Neo SoCal. If you're a detective back on Earth, things will be different."

Anders' voice dropped from being official to more personal. "Erik, you will have access to different and better opportunities to pursue justice, especially if you're willing to bend the rules a little. Even using this law is a little bit of a cheat. Last time I checked, it hadn't been used in fifty years. I'm not totally sure it'll work, but no one's bothered to repeal it since it doesn't conflict with UTC law."

Erik snorted. "I spent thirty years following the rules and cleaning up after politicians and corporations." He shook his head. "Now forty-nine of my soldiers are dead, and I want to know why. I deserve to know why. Bend a few rules?" His voice became granite. "I'll snap them in half if I have to. The good little major died on that battlefield. I don't know who will be replacing him yet, but it's someone who'll do what it takes."

Anders watched as the major withdrew for a moment.

Erik took a deep breath and looked back up. "Thanks. I know where I'm going now, but I have a favor to ask."

"Anything," Governor Anders replied, his hands opening wide. "If it's within my meager power here, I'll do it."

"Would you happen to know if they recovered my personal firearm from the battle site?"

Governor Anders nodded slowly. "They did. It was being stored as evidence last time I checked."

"Can you get it for me?" Erik asked.

"Yes, Major." Governor Anders managed a weak smile.

"Or should I say," he asked, "*Detective?*"

CHAPTER FIVE

May 15, 2228, Civilian transport *Ithaca* near Alpha Centauri Hyperspace Transfer Point

"Attention, passengers," said a soft female voice over the intercom, a transport attendant. "We are now on our final approach to the transfer point. Please remember you will experience discomfort, including vertigo, multisensory hallucinations, and possibly pain during the FTL transfer process. For your safety, and in full compliance with UTC regulations, please sit or lie down during the transfer. We anticipate initiation in two minutes."

Erik laid down on the small bed in his cabin.

It'd been a bit cramped for his bulky frame during his time on the ship. The rest of the cabin was small too, containing nothing more than a small shelf masquerading as a desk and the tiny lavatory.

He didn't mind. He'd stayed in far worse conditions during his military career, and there was no reason to waste money on a fancy room on his trip back.

It'd been a long jaunt from colony to colony and transport to transport, but now he was almost there. The final transfer before Earth, and then just one month of in-system cruising to get to the planet and Neo SoCal.

Erik reached under his shirt and pulled out his bent dog tag, the symbol of both his survival and the deaths of the soldiers under his command.

It was warm from his body heat. He tucked it back under his shirt. Somewhere in Neo SoCal was someone who knew why his men had been killed, and maybe even ordered it, and he would find them.

"Attention, passengers." The attendant came over the speakers once more. "Hyperspace transfer will initiate in one minute."

Erik stared at the gray metal ceiling. He had checked on his police application at his last port of call, and everything seemed to be in order. All he would need to do was show up, and he would become Detective Erik Blackwell.

Technically, the law required that veterans taking a law enforcement position practice "due diligence in acquiring the necessary skills for the position." Since he'd spent most of the last year on transports, he had used that time to read up on local police procedures.

He might not step into his new station as the most experienced cop on the force, but he wouldn't be a clueless idiot, either.

"Hyperspace transfer will initiate in thirty seconds. Twenty-nine, twenty-eight…"

He closed his eyes. "And they say you can't go home."

"Ten, nine, eight…"

Erik took a deep breath and held it.

Here we go.

"Five, four, three, two, one. *Initiating hyperspace transfer.*"

Erik's stomach flipflopped. The colors of the world inverted.

His left arm rippled, suddenly looking far closer than his right.

A few seconds later, both arms returned to normal size, but not normal color.

A riot of particles danced in his vision, spinning around him like tiny drunken faeries.

Swirls of patterned light circled him.

According to scientists, the things people thought they saw during a transfer were nothing more than neurological tricks, hallucinations that were a function of the brain trying to process bizarre sensory inputs it had not evolved to handle.

External recordings of the jump process seemed to support that conclusion. Energy readings, of course, spiked, but the recorded human range of visual and auditory experience revealed nothing more than flickering lights most of the time on the inside of a ship.

From the outside, a ship slid into the open transfer point, was enveloped by a blue-white energy web, and was spit out a minute or two later from an exit point.

How can they say this is all not real? I'm traveling over four light-years in a minute, and they say anything I'm seeing is in my head?

Sinister shadows skulked across the room, writhing and changing with each step.

An almost ethereal hum filled the air, growing in

volume. Pain crawled from Erik's extremities up his arms and toward his chest.

Everything snapped back to normal.

"WWWWWWuuuughhh." Erik let out his breath and blinked a few times.

"Attention, passengers," the attendant called. "We have completed our transfer. Welcome to the Sol System."

Just to be disagreeable, Erik lifted up a single finger in salute to the voice while he got over his transition issues.

A moment later, Erik groaned as he sat up and ran his hands through his hair, then stood and stretched. They might be in the Sol System, but they still had a good month before they would reach Earth.

Due to complicated physics Erik couldn't even pretend to understand, all HTPs had to be built a decent distance from the main gravity well in a system.

The Sol HTP was far from both the Sun and Earth, and while plenty of passengers might be departing at other planets and stations, he only cared about Earth.

After he tapped a code into the wall, a small panel slid back, revealing the two stored metal cases which contained Erik's things. He pulled one out and entered the access code on the side, and it clicked and popped open. He tugged on the edges of the lining and pulled up gently to reveal a hidden compartment underneath.

The TR-7 laid there, nestled away from prying eyes. Governor Anders had recovered the weapon, but transporting a heavy assault rifle on a civilian liner in luggage violated more than a few transit laws.

"Just one of many laws I will be ignoring," he mused.

There was also the small matter of him not bothering to

get the relevant arms control permits for civilian transfer of assault weapons. It would have delayed him for months, and he already faced a year-long trip.

"Damn, going to need to source ammo." Erik covered the hidden compartment and closed the suitcase. His stomach rumbled. Transfers always made him hungry.

It was time to hit the dining room.

***

ERIK WAITED in line as the white-uniformed staff of the dining room dispensed the current meal, something approximating chicken alfredo. He wasn't the only person to get hungry after a jump, and during his time on the *Ithaca*, it was rare that the dining room wasn't busy anyway.

Long-distance space travel disrupted people's rhythms, especially in cramped passenger transports, even with the healthy use of VR.

This situation resulted in people keeping all hours and a general need to be able to supply food to passengers regardless of shipboard time.

A man in a rumpled suit stood in front of Erik. He sighed and shook his head, glancing at the former major. "I know we're still pretty far from the good old Big Blue, but it feels good to be back in-system, at least. I've been away for almost three months. How about you?"

"Thirty years," Erik answered.

The man blinked and stared at him, this time for a bit longer. "Thirty years? Honestly?"

Erik grunted. "Yeah. I wasn't necessarily planning for

that, but it kind of worked out that way." He shrugged. "You know how life goes."

"Wow. When did you leave? I mean, how old were you?" the man asked as he stepped forward with the line.

Erik followed him. "Twenty-one."

The man eyed him with a hint of surprise. "Apparently, you've got decent money or amazing genes. You don't look like you're in your fifties." He gestured at Erik's gray hair with a chuckle. "Except for that."

Erik smiled. "Yeah, I got the de-aging treatment about eight months back. They told me it'd take a while for it to fully work, but my hair's being stubborn for some reason."

Reaching up, he ruffled it. "New look for the return home, or whatever." He smiled once more, even if he didn't feel it.

The de-aging treatment was part of a plan he'd hatched in his first month of travel.

If he showed up and was too obvious about his intentions, whoever was responsible for killing his unit might catch on, or they might not care whatsoever.

He needed everyone to think he was a retired military man who was bored and moving on with life. Maybe even having a little midlife existential crisis—get younger, buy a car, date hot babes.

The more they underestimated him, the better.

The businessman ran a hand through his own thinning hair. "I keep thinking about getting it, but it's so expensive. I mean, these days, de-aging is one of the few things you can do without people thinking you're a total freak." He laughed. "All that Purist garbage goes out the window once it comes to staying younger for longer, huh?"

Erik shrugged in agreement.

"You ever worry about how things have changed back home?" the man asked, taking another step forward, a curious look in his eye.

"Not really. People are people. Sure, they'll have some new gadgets and that kind of crap." Erik looked around at those eating. "But Earth's just a colony with nicer buildings and more people."

The businessman laughed, this time looking forward as he stepped but still carrying on the conversation. "I went on a business trip to New Pacifica in Ross 128, and I was ready to go home after two days. And that's supposed to be a core world. Something about the food. It just doesn't taste right." He shook his head. "But I'll need to get over the food issues."

The line moved forward again before Erik responded. "Why is that?"

"My company's trying to get in on some UTC trade negotiations, like the expansion of trade with some of the Local Neighborhood races. Not the Zitarks, of course, but I'm trying to raise my profile in my company to get selected as part of that effort." He grimaced. "You know, it's kind of funny, we found all those Navigator artifacts on Mars, and they reverse-engineered them so we can have HTPs and grav fields and the like; everything we needed to take us to the stars." He patted his ample stomach. "You wouldn't want to see me floating around in zero-gee. I guarantee that, so I'm grateful every time I take a trip for grav fields, even if it's just in-system."

"Yeah. What's so funny about the Navigator artifacts?"

Erik furrowed his brow in confusion. "Sorry, not following you."

Both took another step forward.

The businessman sighed. "The point is, when we found the Zitarks, let alone the others, we answered the question people have wondered about forever: Are we alone in the universe? And then we basically didn't do anything with them." He looked out, as if into space. "You'd think we would talk more. We have so much to share."

Erik grunted. "What's to talk about? The Navigators have been dead and gone for a million years. Everyone found the same crap that let them make their own HTPs, but they were otherwise fine." He thought for a moment about his time on the frontier. "Humanity doesn't need the help of aliens, and aliens don't want or need the help of humanity. By the time any species leaves their home system, it's just not that important. Everyone's got their own problems, and all of us have had centuries to figure out the best solutions."

The other man laughed, the humor actually touching his eyes. "You're not much of a romantic, are you?"

"Call me the King of Pragmatism," Erik told him. "If they stay out of our way, I don't see much point in trying to talk to them, and vice-versa." He shrugged. "They've done their thing for a long time, and we've done ours. Anyone who can get this far into space probably doesn't need help from some alien race that doesn't know the people and their history."

"I wonder if we'll ever find an intelligent race that isn't as advanced?" The man's expression brightened at the possibility. "We could teach them so much."

"Maybe." Erik shrugged, not convinced that would go so well for the less-advanced species.

The businessman took another few steps forward. It was only a few more yards until they could collect a plate.

Erik inhaled deeply, the scent of the meat and pasta eliciting another rumble from his stomach.

"I don't understand why everyone doesn't want to at least exchange notes about the Navigators," the businessman continued. "We have this ancient race that was far more advanced than any of the races we know about. I know some of the others claim they invented HTPs on their own, but I haven't read about a single reputable engineer or scientist who believes that's true."

Erik nodded. "Probably. I don't see what difference it makes. We've all gotten what we needed from the Navigators. That can be their legacy, but it doesn't much matter otherwise. The younger races rule the stars now. Or maybe the Navigators ran off to some other galaxy on vacation once they saw the babies because they wanted nothing to do with raising a bunch of annoying species who wouldn't appreciate the wisdom they had to share."

The businessman stared at Erik, disappointment on his face. "You're really not interested in meeting aliens, are you?"

Erik eyed him. "I've seen pictures of them. Good enough for me."

"Might I ask why? I've been dying to meet an alien my entire life. I mean face-to-face, not in a recording from a distant border world." The businessman frowned.

"Humans are varied enough for me," Erik replied. "Once I've gotten used to the diversity of humanity, maybe

I'll care about a few little grays, toadstools, space raptors, or the others."

"Okay, then. That's...honest, I suppose." The businessman shook his head. "I forgot to ask you...why the return to Earth after so long?"

Erik gave him a pleasant smile, but it did not reach his eyes. "I've been away for too long, and because of that, bad things happened. Now I need to take care of a few things."

The other man swallowed, eyeing Erik before stepping forward and nodding at the tower of plates. "Well, uh, it looks like it's time to get some food." He tossed Erik a fake smile. "It was nice talking to you, but I think I'm going to go over some documents while I eat."

"Fine by me. I'm just here for the food."

Erik grabbed some chicken, a roll, and some sort of brown drink. He sniffed it and took a sip. *Sweet.* He put it on his tray. It had been a long time, and his challenge now would be to adjust to civilian life. All he had done during his adult life was follow orders and carry out missions.

For now, he'd settle for being a man eating some...he glanced at the chunks on his plate...*chicken alfredo?*

CHAPTER SIX

June 14, 2228, Neo Southern California Metroplex, Police Enforcement Zone 122 Station, Office of Detective Jia Lin

Jia slapped her hand on her dark desk and glared at the middle-aged man standing in front of it—Detective Ryan Castile, her current partner. Her hand stung from the force of the blow, but she kept a fierce look on her face.

"I can't believe what you just said," Jia snapped, her frustration leaking out despite her thoughts about not losing a second partner. "I've found some major evidence suggesting this wasn't some low-end fraud. This isn't just me pulling something out of the air. I spent all last week correlating those bank transfers with the activity. Have you even looked at any of the information I sent you? Given what you just said, I doubt it, but I'm trying to give you the benefit of the doubt here."

Ryan adjusted his tie and shrugged, then rolled his dark-brown eyes and ran a hand through his thinning hair.

He might have benefited from de-aging, but it wasn't like a man on his salary could afford it. "I told you to just kick that case along. You're looking for some big conspiracy, Jia, but it's *nothing*. It's not worth our time. Not every case that comes across our desks is worth our time."

"I've heard that answer before," she countered.

He continued, "And I don't get why a smart woman like you doesn't understand that yet."

Hold it in, don't roll your eyes. You got this. She quieted her thoughts before speaking. "It seems like pretty much none of the cases that come across our desks are worth our time, according to you. And this case is not a big conspiracy, but it *is* a clear example of felony fraud and misappropriation of funds," she finished.

He didn't look convinced.

Jia tapped her PNIU, and holographic displays of several rows of numbers appeared above her desk. She gestured between them. "Look here, they tried to bury the fraud with different invoices and codes, but it's clear, which you can see when analyzing the different account flows."

She pointed to another section of the numbers hanging in the air. "They're basically robbing the taxpayers, and given some of the other outflows, there might even be bribery involved. Now, I know that last charge is unlikely. I mean it's not like this is some colony world, but that doesn't change the rest of it."

She cut through the air with her hand. "Most companies and people play by the rules, so we can't let those who don't get away with it. What kind of message would we be sending if we did that?"

Ryan frowned. "Huh?" he scrubbed his eyes in frustration, his voice muffled. "Jia, please tell me you didn't pull in people to help you crunch numbers on a case you're not even supposed to be working. The captain was clear. If you did this, you went against the captain's orders."

Jia jerked if struck.

She shook her head. "No, what the captain said was he didn't want any resources being used for the case because *there was no evidence*, and I understand and respect where he's coming from, so I didn't pull any resources. I obeyed his orders. All of the analysis was done off the clock, and I kept all the evidence on departmental systems. No one can complain if I provide the metroplex free investigatory services." She tried a smile. It didn't feel appropriate exactly, but there wasn't any harm in trying. "Right?"

"Wait." Ryan blinked. "You actually worked a bunch of unpaid overtime to run the numbers yourself, and on top of that, you understand them?" He frowned. "I assumed you brought in the financial forensics guys." He pointed at one of the numbers. "How else could you have gotten through all this data so quickly?"

"I didn't need them. It's easy if you know pattern typing and collation." Jia shrugged. "It's just numbers, Ryan. If anything, it's easier than cases relying on physical evidence. These people tried to cover it up, but the evidence was all there, just waiting to be analyzed and the crime uncovered. It's straightforward correlational analysis. Come on, I'm sure you did this kind of thing in college, even if you weren't using it in a law-enforcement context."

"Too many brains, not enough street," Ryan mumbled.

"What was that?" Jia asked, furrowing her brow in confusion.

"Nothing." Ryan sighed. "We're not supposed to be working this case, Jia. Full stop. Just like we weren't supposed to work the arson case *or* the theft case. We were supposed to kick those along and continue on our merry way. Just because you see a conspiracy everywhere doesn't mean we need to personally solve it at this station. We're supposed to concentrate on important cases. If you care so much about keeping Earth safe and not full of criminals and insurrectionists, you should wait for those kinds of cases rather than wasting your time on fantasy frauds."

She pointed to the hologram hanging in the air. "But this might be one of those kinds of cases." Jia snorted, pointing at the two of them. "We're detectives. We solve crimes. That's kind of in the job description, Ryan. And what important cases? Every time I try to solve something, you and the captain insist we just pass it along and it dies, or the others insist it's not a big deal."

"Because there's really nothing there to worry about," Ryan argued back, his arms opening wide. "Come on. This is Earth, the shining tower in the darkness. We're fine. You're worrying too much."

Jia shot up, her long black hair swaying with the motion. "The duty of a police officer is to protect public order by investigating and preventing crime. For every crime we drag our feet on, the greater the chance it'll be worse the next time. Small crimes are the seeds of major crimes, and those are the seeds of anarchy. You have to know this. You've been on the force for eighteen years!"

"Yes, I've been around for a while." Ryan nodded, his

head bobbing in frustration as he squinted at her. "And I've got two years to retirement. I don't need this stress, especially from some rookie with delusions of grandeur." He shook his head, voice a bit more monotone as he struggled to keep his rapidly rising annoyance in check. "I'm telling you, there's *nothing there.*"

"And I'm telling you, I found something in my analysis of the data. This isn't me operating off my gut. This is me following up on basic evidence." Jia's frustration boiled over. "And this isn't about your retirement. This is about doing your job." She folded her arms over her chest.

"Doing my job?" Ryan snorted. "Jia, I'm not like you. I worked my way up and made detective. I wasn't granted a shot at detective because of family connections."

Jia winced. "It's not like that. There was an opportunity, and I took advantage of it. That is the kind of initiative needed." She flung an arm out, finger pointed toward the bullpen with the other officers. "I'm not the only detective who was hired under that policy initiative. I'm not even the only one hired in this enforcement zone."

She resisted the urge to discuss some of the history of that type of hiring. That didn't mean the existing personnel were bad at their jobs, just that they could use a fresh perspective.

Ryan pinched the bridge of his nose. "This is stupid," he ground out. "I'm not wasting time on a case we were already told to pass along because of some glorified Corp doll playing at being a cop." He eyed her. "*You* don't tell me how to work cases. I was working cases when you were still a little girl, princess."

"You're over the line." Jia narrowed her eyes and took a

breath to stop herself from shaking with rage. "I'm not playing at anything." She pointed to herself. "I've been a detective for a year, and the only things that are holding me back are my *lazy partners,* who have forgotten why they became cops because they're too worried about their retirements."

She slapped her PNIU and the numbers vanished, but her eyes never left Ryan. "Don't you understand? We have a paradise here on Earth, but only because everyone is doing their part. Do you want it to turn into some lawless waste like out on the colonies? It's taken centuries to get Earth to the point where it is a truly civilized planet, and you are more concerned about moving to some beach somewhere than—"

Ryan grunted, turned, and stormed out of their office.

Jia blinked a few times, her mouth still open. She shook her head and hurried after him. He stomped away from their shared office and down the hallway. He passed through the sea of black-and-blue-clad patrol officers gathered at their desks in the bullpen, their gazes a mix of curious and worried as they tore their eyes away from the various holographic displays on or above their desks.

He continued to the captain's door, not sparing even a quick look in Jia's direction. His nostrils flared as he stared at the door for a few seconds before nodding and reaching for the doorknob.

CAPTAIN ROBERT MONAHAN, ENFORCEMENT ZONE 122.

Ryan threw open the door. The captain looked up from

the budget display projected on top of his desk and squinted in irritation at his detective.

With his broad shoulders, square jaw, and salt-and-pepper hair, Captain Monahan was able to project both wisdom and confidence through his appearance alone, which frustrated Jia all the more since he had been just as resistant to some of her investigations as her partners.

She'd dreamed of working under an experienced and wise captain, but the reality had been far more disappointing.

"I resign," Ryan declared. He pulled out his badge and stun pistol and tossed them on the captain's desk, where they landed with a thud. "Effective immediately." He glared at Jia before shoving past her with his shoulder and heading out into the bullpen, his middle finger raised over his shoulder.

Captain Monahan took a deep breath. "Close the door, Detective Lin. We need to talk."

Jia complied and frowned. "Captain, I can—"

"Explain?" he interrupted, waving a finger at the quickly retreating man. "You think his action doesn't explain to me what's going on? It's just like your last partner. You've been riding Ryan because he won't help you with the pointless little hunts I have already told you to avoid."

"You don't understand, sir. I uncovered new evidence that suggests there's something there with this case. Serious felony fraud might be going on right here in the metroplex with a company connected potentially... tangentially...to government contracts." Jia nodded firmly. "We have a duty to follow up, and I've already gone through a lot of the evidence that proves something's off."

She crossed her arms over her chest, her eyes narrowed.

The captain's voice started off somewhat soft. "Oh, really? Then you should have sent it along. You didn't need to handle it. *If* there was a crime going on, downstairs could have taken a look at it, and they would have called us if they needed help. You need to remain on standby for important cases, not chase phantoms!"

Jia was trying to figure out an appropriately respectful way to tell the captain to get off his ass.

She was getting nowhere fast. None of the quips that came to mind were appropriate to tell her boss.

Captain Monahan leaned back in his chair and steepled his fingers. "So far, none of the cases we've kicked along has needed our help. If there had been anything serious, we would have been notified. It's not a good use of this enforcement zone's resources."

Jia sighed. "This is different, sir. If you just look at the evi—"

"Enough." Captain Monahan threw up his hand and, his voice was raised as he said, "I told you *not* to follow up on that case, and you did. You went directly against my orders. Don't think I'm particularly happy or satisfied with that."

Jia's eyes were flint-hard. "This is a skipping recording. I'm saying the same thing over and over. I did it on my personal time. I didn't charge any overtime. I've consulted the regulations, and they are clear that I'm allowed to spend any amount of personal time on a case, provided I keep all evidence on departmental systems and I d—"

"I said ENOUGH, Detective Lin," Captain Monahan snapped. "This isn't about regulations. This is about *you* wasting *my* time and driving off good cops because of *your* self-righteousness."

Jia waved at the door. "Ryan's lost his edge. He doesn't want to investigate cases. Not just this fraud case, but any case. Sharon was the same. I've been here a year, and I've barely done anything useful in my own cases. I've helped out on a few others, and everything else has been very minor and/or inconsequential."

Monahan tapped a finger on his desk. "Maybe because you're wasting too much time pursuing cases I told you not to pursue?" He smiled, none of it reaching his eyes. "See? Other people are running cases. They don't need you to solve everything, and most things that reach us will be minor." He blew out a breath in frustration. She wasn't sure if it was directed at her or not. "It's not like the old days. You watched too many movies before you become a cop." Captain Monahan pointed at the door. "The point is, you've gone through two partners in six months, Lin. I can barely remember the last time something like that happened in this enforcement zone."

"Wait, what?" She pointed over her shoulder to where Ryan had stalked off. "They chose to quit. I didn't force them out. All I've ever asked is for them to do their jobs. We have a duty, sir, to uphold the law and public trust, even if it's inconvenient or might take a little extra effort."

Captain Monahan sneered. "Listen to you. You think you have all the answers?" He slammed a fist on his desk.

"Now I'm going to have to call a proud officer and get him to come back...because of *you!* He was only a few years from retirement. You've been here less than a year. You really think you know how to be a better cop than the two cops you replaced with your less than one year of experience? Huh?"

Jia's voice softened. "I'm not saying that, Captain. I'm saying all that experience could be brought to bear on solving cases, and I don't understand why it wasn't."

"Our case clearance numbers are fine." The red-faced Captain Monahan's mouth twitched. "I think you're so hellbent on proving yourself that you're looking for trouble when there is none, or at least nothing that should concern your division. Don't go making trouble there doesn't need to be. That's part of 'maintain order' too."

She glanced up, and he rolled his eyes.

"That's just it," she explained. "That's what I'm talking about. This is trouble that could turn into something else. I'm not saying it's insurrectionists or terrorists or any other type of offworld barbarians, but the only way we're going to keep control here is by stopping people like this, right?" Jia sighed. "This is why I joined the police. I wanted to do my small part to make sure the heart of the UTC, the one place where crime and darkness are almost extinct, stays that way, and so I don't understand why you're resisting me on this."

Captain Monahan groaned and rubbed his temples. "It doesn't matter. I can't assign you another partner. They'll just quit, and this enforcement zone can't lose more detectives without the higher-ups wondering what's going on. We both know if I try to fire you, it will cause trouble, too."

Jia nodded. "I don't need a partner. I'm not saying either of them was a bad cop, but they were slowing me down. I'll investigate cases myself. It's not like we're drowning in work you need me to do."

"You most certainly won't investigate any cases yourself." The captain glared at her.

"What?" Jia blinked in surprise. "But you just said…"

"I said I can't assign you another *partner*, so I won't." Captain Monahan locked eyes with her. "I'm assigning you to assist with records verification. I know the traffic enforcement division needs help. Regulations require at least ten percent manual verification of all algorithmically assigned fines, and they've been falling behind. Way behind. From what I've heard, the city council is making noise."

"Wait. No." Jia gestured toward the door. "I… How am I supposed to investigate crimes when I'm spending my days doing administrative work? That's not my job. I'm a detective."

"It doesn't matter." He shook his head. "Metroplex police regulations also clearly state that no detective is to investigate any felonies *without an active partner.* You no longer have an active partner." Captain Monahan pointed to the door. "Because he just left. I gave you two chances, and you have two strikes. I'd be a fool if I went to three strikes since we can't afford three lost officers. You have any idea how many years of experience have left in the last six months? Now, contact the traffic division and have them start sending things to your PNIU. No reason you can't get started today."

Jia gritted her teeth, trying to think of some way out of

her dilemma. She couldn't defend against regulations, seeing as how she had just used them to argue her own case. Rebelling against her captain, even in a small way, could put her on a path toward turning her into everything she hated and had sworn to suppress.

She hated this situation. "Yes, sir."

Turning, she reached for the doorknob.

Where am I going to get a partner?

MONAHAN WATCHED his door close as his hand rubbed his eyes. She was going to be the end of his career if he didn't figure out a way to curb her enthusiasm before it got her messed up in a level of politics she wasn't prepared to deal with.

He leaned to his right and opened his bottom drawer. Reaching in, he pulled out a stick of gum and unwrapped it before popping it in his mouth. In times like this, he wasn't prepared to drink, or any other response that would let him think was out.

Slowly, he crushed the gum in his mouth, chewing as he considered the ramifications of someone who meant well but was not prepared to see the world as it really was.

If there was an organization for "clueless" and "idealistic," they could have Detective Lin interview to become the poster child for the group. Add her family connections, and he had been handed a challenge that could be career-ending...

Career-ending.

He grabbed the wrapper, spat the gum out, closed the wrapper, and tossed it in the trash can.

He had the experience to handle this. He just needed a solution to get her to look for her opportunities elsewhere.

It wasn't firing if she asked to leave.

CHAPTER SEVEN

Jia let out a long, weary sigh and set her chopsticks beside her bowl of rice.

Even though it was lunch, she wasn't hungry. It wasn't like she was meeting with her sister Mei for a meal, even though sometimes it felt like if she didn't meet Mei at a restaurant, the other woman might refuse to pencil Jia into her busy corporate schedule.

Why am I here again? It's not like I don't know what her opinion will be.

Mei took a sip of tea from her small black cup, a bland look of dismissal on her face. "I rescheduled an important meeting for this. I'm assuming it is important. You implied it was important when you sent your message about meeting."

"Importance is relative," Jia pointed out. "I need to vent about work, and I figured my older sister *might* not mind listening."

"Oh?" Mei arched a perfectly manicured eyebrow.

"What's wrong?" She looked Jia up and down. "You're looking fit and healthy enough."

"I just…" Jia shrugged, looking outside through the glass as she spoke. "Another partner quit. He was frustrated with me insisting he do his job, and now the captain's angry with me because he thinks I drove him away." She returned her attention to her sister. "I'm not trying to be difficult at work, but I don't understand why it's so hard for them to listen."

Mei blinked twice before speaking. "You're not trying to be difficult? Maybe, but desire and actions are two different things." Mei punctuated her sentence with another small sip of tea. "It's not as if your stubbornness only applies to your partners." She clucked her tongue. "Some things never change, little sister."

Jia groaned, barely stopping her eyes from rolling. "Please don't start. I didn't ask you here to lecture me."

Mei scoffed. "And why shouldn't I?" She set her cup down and stared at Jia. The flinty look in her eyes, combined with her ornate four-braid hairstyle, made her look just like their mother, even though Mei was twenty-eight and only had four years on her younger sister.

Guilt gnawed at Jia. Her parents might not disapprove of her career, but they'd made it clear it wasn't their preferred choice for their youngest daughter.

"I came here for a sympathetic ear and a waterproof shoulder," Jia replied. "Is that too much to ask?"

"As your older sister, it's incumbent upon me to give you useful advice when I think you've erred." Mei shook her head. "And we both know you've erred by becoming a police officer, and not just because it's an inappropriate job for a woman of your education and status. Think about it. If it's causing you so much stress, you should quit and take a position more fitting of our family name."

Jia frowned. "There's nothing wrong with being a police officer. It is a respectable job for someone of my status and family name."

Mei let out a single sharp, mocking laugh. "Perhaps you should quit your job and become a comedian with those kinds of jokes." She waved a hand toward Jia. "You can't be serious."

Jia leaned forward. "I am *completely* serious. Our status and wealth mean we've had great opportunities, but that wealth can only exist in an orderly society."

Jia gestured at the window she had been staring out of to the urban forest of bright widow-covered-spires piercing the blue sky, which was dotted with the occasional cloud.

Many of the buildings extended ever farther than their kilometer altitude from the base level of the metroplex. Flitters of every color darted between the building on orderly paths, forming rivers of human ingenuity.

Mei followed her sister's gesture, but her frown remained. "What does you being a cop have to do with our orderly society?"

She leaned back. "It's important for members of all levels of society to contribute to keeping people safe," Jia answered. "We don't want all of a certain job done by a certain type of people. That can cause trouble in the long term."

Mei's brow crinkled in confusion. "Trouble? Safe? The Neo SoCal metroplex is safe. The existing law enforcement methods are fine. You act as though you're the only one holding back the hordes." She snickered. "I think Father did you a disservice by letting you read all those novels about insurrectionists when you were younger. I was half-convinced you would run off and join the military and ask to be shipped to some violent border world."

Jia's lips pressed together.

Mei laughed. "Maybe I shouldn't be encouraging you to quit. The last thing we need you to inflict on Father and Mother is running offworld." She grimaced. "I know I might have to take a trip offworld for the company at some point, but I hope to delay it as long as possible."

"The point is," Jia tapped the table in front of her pulling Mei's attention, "I want to uphold my duty to both society and our parents. I can do that by upholding justice as a police officer." She leaned back, crossing her arms. "If only my captain and partners will let me. I'm not the problem here. They are."

Mei's arrogant smirk faded into something approaching actual concern. "Yes, you have a duty to our parents. I'm glad you remember that given you seem to think only about your job. Now think about it: how can you be upholding justice if the officers around you don't think it's necessary?" Mei paused, her face scrunching. "You're not claiming they're corrupt, are you?"

Jia's eyes widened, and she quickly shook her head in negation. "No, nothing like that. Of course not. I just... think they might have gotten a little too comfortable with not being as aggressive as they might otherwise be." She inhaled. "I understand. It's easy to get comfortable in a city like this. I just want to do more. I think we can all do more."

Mei reached over and patted Jia's hand. "When I tell you to quit, or when Mother or Father tell you the same thing, we're not trying to be cruel, Jia. Yes, there are certain parts of being a member of the Lin family that carry implicit duties, but this is also about *you*. Listen to yourself. You're miserable, and you have been for this last year." She gave Jia's hand a gentle squeeze. "There's no shame in admitting that perhaps you made a mistake. It's obvious the police department wouldn't miss you if you were gone. You could get a job at the company, or if you don't want to do that, maybe accept Mother's offer on the dates she is suggesting."

Jia rolled her eyes, ending their arc to pierce her sister with their own accusation. "I should point out that you're not married yet."

"Because I'm still engaged in a corporate career. Both Mother and I are making sure to explore all possible options. That doesn't excuse you, little sister, but this could also be a good thing. If you had a powerful husband, you could spend your time running a charitable organization or something similar. Isn't that contributing to society? If anything, it'd probably contribute far more than being some random detective in a safe city." Mei shrugged as if it were the most obvious thing in the world.

Jia picked up her teacup with both hands and took a sip, enjoying the warmth as it passed through her. "I'm not doing any of this to be stubborn. I know Mother and Father would prefer me to have another job, but I'm not going to quit. I can contribute. I just need to find the right partner and the right cases; actual major cases that they'll let me work. I understand they'll be few and far between, which is why it's so frustrating when they won't listen to me."

"Your family will always be there when you finally come to your senses." Mei managed a pained smile. The arches of her eyebrows were perfect, just like the power suit she was wearing. "I just hope you come to your senses sooner rather than later."

A moment later, Mei leaned over. "Now, I've come to this lunch as a favor, and I want a favor in return. I met a man who would like a date with you."

CHAPTER EIGHT

Erik grinned at the yellow flitter resting on the ground.

Sunlight reflected off the finish and windows of the angular flying car as it sat in the parking lot atop a massive platform extending from one of the many tall commerce towers in Neo SoCal.

Dozens of other vehicles were parked in long rows, every color of the rainbow and more represented. None were that large, with most having two rows of seats and holding four to six people at a maximum.

This was not a dealer for anyone interested in commercial vehicles.

He stood there for a moment, taking in the flow of flitters around him and the steep drop between platforms.

There was a verdant park on a platform in the distance, complete with trees. He'd grown up in a metroplex not all that dissimilar, if smaller, but the tall, sky-piercing buildings and maze-like platforms elicited a grunt.

Detroit hadn't forsaken the ground nearly as much as Neo SoCal. Erik looked around, getting accustomed to a view that was very different from those of his last thirty years.

A salesman sidled up to Erik, his grin so wide it threatened to split his face.

"Good eye, young sir! Offworld Systems Taxútnta (Ταχυτητα) MX 60. *Integrated* grav field with vector propulsion." He patted the hood of the car. "This, my good man, is one of the best personal sports flitters on the market today, and an amazing example of advanced engineering." His smarmy smile did nothing for Erik. "You have exquisite taste. Of course, since you've already paid for it, so I don't need to point out why it's such a fine vehicle. However," he winked, "if you need me to point out any non-obvious benefits, or what club might work best with this vehicle, I'm the guy to ask."

Erik nodded in reply.

He had always thought it was amusing that a company based out of Germany would call itself Offworld Systems and have a flitter with a Greek name. Maybe they were trying to trick people into thinking their cars were made using some sort of special technique.

However, the reality was, most of the other core worlds were so far behind Earth, they wouldn't be able to produce the same level of manufactured goods in any sort of economical manner. Plus, shipping a vehicle in-system didn't make a lot of sense, let alone intersystem.

Earth and the core worlds benefited from the receipt of

massive amounts of raw resources while maintaining near-stranglehold monopolies on the most important aspects of large-scale industrial production, an arrangement that had not gone unnoticed by insurrectionists.

"I wanted a nice, new flashy car," Erik explained to fill the empty air time the sales guy was leaving. "It's the first I've owned in a...few years. I thought I might as well get the best."

The salesman blinked, confusion replacing some of the greed on his face. "What are you, in your early thirties, maybe?"

He gestured toward Erik's hair. "I don't know why you would ruin that face with that old-man gray hair look, but that's on you." He shook his head. "But how did you go so long without your own flitter? Your license checked out. You do know how to drive, right?" He licked his lips. "The license wasn't taken away? I mean, you've already paid, so obviously you can afford it, but...you know?"

Erik shook his head. "No, I'm fine. I'm just used to driving bigger things, like transports. My previous employer always provided me a vehicle."

The salesman settled into his new understanding. "Ah, I see. Yes, corporate vehicles are nice, but not as nice as the MX 60."

Erik didn't bother to correct him about the nature of his previous employer.

The salesman walked around the flitter and patted the side. "I don't see a ring on the finger, so does that mean you're still on the market?"

Erik laughed. "Yeah, you could say that."

The salesman caressed the car with the languid movement of a lover. "This baby will get you all sorts of dates. You can have the fun you want, or use it to snag the future Mrs. Blackwell." The salesman looked at the top of Erik's head and sighed. "You really should dye your hair back to your natural color. I might have a decade or...two...on you." He glanced down at his paunchy stomach. "But I don't think things have changed that much since I got married."

Erik shook his head, admitting to himself he was liking the stupid sales guy for worrying about him. "I'll take that under consideration."

He circled the flitter, nodding approvingly. Even if part of the point of buying a flashy car was to throw off suspicion about his true intent and concerns, he couldn't deny his personal excitement. He just appreciated the expensive vehicle.

"Good." The salesman moved around the car, providing Erik personal space. "Keep in mind that even with the autonomous settings, if you're driving in the city, you can't sleep at the wheel. I know you commercial guys play fast and loose with that, but the police will fine you pretty heavily if they catch you asleep behind the wheel, although you should always use the system if you're drunk, obviously." The salesman shrugged. "The Neo SoCal police are very...*intense* about enforcing traffic laws. Not like they have anything better to do."

"You think so?" Erik didn't bother to hide the curiosity in his voice as he glanced at the salesman. "Shouldn't they be solving crimes? Investigating things?"

"Investigating what?" The salesman scoffed. "Maybe there's actual serious crime in the Shadow Zone, but everyone down there chooses to live there. You can't blame the police for not protecting people from others down there."

"Shadow Zone?" Erik asked.

The salesman eyed him like he was drunk. "You're not from around here, are you?"

"No, I just got in yesterday." Erik shrugged. "Never been to this area of the planet before."

"Where are you from?" the salesman asked, wariness in his voice.

"Uh, Greater Detroit," Erik replied, then added after a pause, "Originally."

"I've never been there myself." The salesman smiled and gestured around. "When you live in the greatest metroplex, why leave, right? Neo SoCal is the best in the world and represents the elite of much of the world, but that's why you're here and not in Detroit. Am I right?"

"What about this Shadow Zone?" Erik prodded, ignoring the man's question.

The salesman sighed and rubbed the back of his head. "You know, not everyone who is antisocial gets transported, especially if they're not a criminal, and it's not like the government folks are total monsters. Some of these antisocial people choose to live in places where they can do their own thing, or so I've heard. It's not like I've ever been close to a Shadow Zone. I'm not antisocial, and you can get fined for going there. I wouldn't want that on my permanent record."

"Where is the Shadow Zone?" Erik asked.

"Lower levels, especially ground level. It's not like the authorities are going to let antisocial people take over towers. They just need to have a place for them until they can finish getting them offworld or they reform themselves. I'm sure it's all part of the government's plan." The salesman laughed. "This is Earth, not some frontier planet filled with insurrectionists. There's a reason they implemented Social Cohesion, right? Get all those criminals offworld so they can give back to society after a little indentured servitude, but come on, once a criminal, always a criminal. That's why there are so many insurrectionists out there." He pointed up.

Erik grunted and looked toward the edge of the platform. He hadn't actually been on the ground since his return to Earth, except at the spaceport.

Detroit was different, not having as many towers. There was definitely a social hierarchy, and people liked to look the other way and pretend crime didn't exist, but there were definitely parts of the city, or at least there had been thirty years prior, that were more dangerous than others.

My brother must still be alive, or at least, I don't know different. Should probably go by and show off my flitter just to annoy him. I'd enjoy the look of jealousy right after a serving of why-the-hell-are-you-here look he'd give me.

The salesman patted Erik on the arm. "You don't need to worry about anything. Even if you want to live on the wild side and head down to the Shadow Zone, the Taxútnta MX 60 has a built-in security system. No Shadow Zone punk's going to take your car for a joy ride, and I'm sure it's not *that* bad down there. Just a few antisocial types not singing the songs of love for their fellow man. You know how it is. Not *real* criminals. I bet Detroit has something similar."

"Yeah, probably." Erik stared at a wide black cargo flitter settling on an extending landing platform a few towers over. "I haven't been back there in thirty years, so maybe it's different."

"Oh? Where have you been?"

"Offworld doing this and that for my employers. Time away just kind of piled up on me." Erik chuckled. "And now I'm back on Earth."

The salesman made a face. "Offworld? I'm presuming you mean you were on a core world, at least."

"I kind of toured the frontier and border worlds," Erik answered, wondering where this would take the conversation.

"You're a very brave man, Mr. Blackwell. The way the news makes it sound, once you get past the core worlds, it's nothing but insurrectionists and lizards." The salesman shuddered. "I thank God every day for the UTC military keeping human space safe."

Erik nodded slowly as he watched another flitter dropping onto a small area jutting out from a building. A personal arrival dock, it looked like. Two attractive women got out with packages and walked the ten feet into the building. The flitter turned and left as the dock pulled back into the building. "Yeah. It's been kind of strange coming back."

"It's the smell, right?" The salesman laughed. "My cousin went on a trip to Alpha Centauri once. From the ship to planetfall, he said things smelled weird, and that's a core world. I can't imagine what it's like on the actual frontier."

Erik forced his attention back to the salesman. His need to be aware of everything going on was just something he would have to deal with in a city. "It's different. I don't know if it's worse. It's just different. I used to cuss a lot more out there, and I've had to clean that up."

"I...see."

Erik grinned. "Yeah, it's harder than you think when you're used to cussing a lot."

"I'll take your word for it, Mr. Blackwell."

The salesmen didn't need to know his profanity came more from his military background than his time away from the core worlds, but it would be a useful additional test.

Every new encounter on Earth let Erik calibrate his methods of dealing with people. He couldn't always approach a person with the TR-7 in hand in four-barrel mode. Most of the time, sure, but not *always*.

I need to have a compartment to store the TR-7 built into the flitter. He frowned. *That means I need to find someone who will do it without asking questions.*

The salesman smirked and nodded at the car. "Bet they don't have nice toys like this out there now, do they?"

Erik walked around the back of the vehicle to the drivers-side door. "No, I can't say I've seen anything this nice in a long time." He opened the door and looked at the salesman, giving him his finest grin. "Let's get this finished. I want to take her for a spin."

"Of course, Mr. Blackwell. And I'm sure *everyone's* been telling you this... Welcome back to Earth!"

DRIVING A FLYING car like a flitter in theory provided total freedom, but the reality was, the flow of traffic in a major Earth metroplex was heavily enforced by hovering lane markers and compliant drivers, the net result being long, stacked lines of flitters, specks of metal and color in the air, all flowing together like blood in veins, circulating around the system via their invisible roads.

Erik glanced out the side window at the closest driver. Dense text floated in front of her. A book, most likely. After thirty years of not depending on the judgment of machines, the presence of so many people letting their vehicles drive them amused him.

Never let a machine do your work for you.

With a quick tap, Erik activated his altitude change signal before dropping down a lane. He looked at his navigation screen.

"Nav request, show me all Shadow Zone entrances," Erik ordered.

"No such destinations exist," the vehicle responded in a soft female voice. "Please restate your request using alternate wording."

People know about it, but you just want to pretend it doesn't exist. Okay. I know this music.

"Nav request, show me all restricted flight areas below 250 meters," Erik suggested.

Several dark blue patches appeared on the screen. They were scattered all over the metroplex, with a major concentration in the southeast. Even with all the restricted lanes and controlled pathways, he could still fly his MX 60 straight to the Shadow Zone.

He grinned and tugged on the wheel. "There you are. It wouldn't hurt to take a look."

Erik patted the pistol holster concealed beneath his dark brown duster. The gun might not be as useful as a TR-7, but he couldn't always carry around an assault rifle, even when he had his secret compartment added.

Let's see how dangerous this place is.

THE TRAFFIC WITHERED to a mere trickle and then nothing as Erik dropped to the base level of the metroplex and headed toward the Shadow Zone.

Perhaps because the massive platforms extending from so many of the towers cast gargantuan shadows, greenery down below became sparser, and the base of several towers appeared featureless.

From what he'd read, many of the towers in Neo SoCal used the lower levels for maintenance and supply storage.

"Warning," the vehicle informed Erik. "You are below the recommended altitude for general travel."

"Yeah, I think you might have to be upgraded," Erik muttered. "Not having a computer tell me what to do."

"Warning," the computer offered again. "You are approaching a restricted area. Please turn your vehicle around to avoid potential fines."

Erik didn't alter course. He moved lower.

The area grew more unkempt, the buildings grimier. He was no longer driving among the sky castles of the UTC elite, but in the dark shadows they didn't want to acknowledge.

"Please note you are now in a restricted area. You might be subject to traffic fines by your local police enforcement zone."

Erik slowed but didn't stop. His gaze cut to his lidar display. A flashing triangle marked by the system as POLICE flew toward him at high speed.

His in-vehicle comm came alive. "This is the NSCPD," barked a harsh male voice over the line. "You are traveling in a restricted zone. You are to immediately switch your vehicle to full autonomous mode to ensure compliance or bring your vehicle to a complete stop."

Erik brought the MX 60 to a stop. A few seconds later, the black and white police flitter appeared in the distance, its red and blue lights flashing. The vehicle slowed to a stop a few meters away.

"Please transmit your license information immediately," the cop ordered. "Be aware that you may be fined, even for a first offense, for travel in a restricted zone, and don't try and claim you didn't know."

Erik tapped his PNIU to interface it with the computer in his MX 60. He tapped in a few commands to transmit his identification information and waited.

Then he sat there waiting to see how things played out.

The seconds stretched on, the police officer not communicating anything.

"Is there a problem, officer?" Erik prodded.

A moment went by. "I apologize, sir. You have full clearance for all restricted zones, Major Blackwell. Have a good day, sir." The cop killed his lights, and the vehicle spun and zoomed away.

"Override code established," the MX 60 announced. "No further warnings will be issued."

Erik smirked.

Technically, his formal separation from the UTC military wouldn't occur for another week local time. It had never even occurred to him that his Special Forces status would grant him access to restricted metroplex zones.

It made him wonder what kinds of things might have been going on down there.

Erik accelerated, a bigger smile building. He hadn't been sure if he would be able to adjust to life on Earth easily, but it wasn't really very different from military life.

Obey a few rules, look out for dangerous areas, and always confirm intelligence. He still didn't have any real leads about what had happened on Mu Arae, and to get them, he would have to go through every secret in the city. The quicker he familiarized himself with its underbelly, the better.

He grinned. "All they do is fine you for your curiosity."

CHAPTER NINE

Erik flew over something quaint: an actual road. It was surprisingly well-maintained, suggesting the Shadow Zone wasn't as abandoned by the rest of the city as he suspected.

Judging by the lights and vehicles he could see, they didn't lack electricity either.

That made sense. Earth might not be the shining palace of perfection some people might claim, but they weren't going to let millions of people live in major urban centers without at least some level of basic services.

That was how you bred insurgencies.

"Question." He spoke aloud. "Do they sweep through here and grab people to transport, or do they not care so long as they deal with it down here?"

A memory jolted into his consciousness concerning his last real conversation with his brother.

"This is the last time, Erik," his brother had shouted. "You want to go play with antisocials and criminals, that's your business, but I don't want any part of it."

Erik grunted, and his hands tightened on the control

yoke. Thirty years. There were too many ghosts. He would worry about Mu Arae first.

His personal problems could wait.

He cruised along. People and vehicles became more common, and he passed several stores and apartment complexes on either side. The entire area lacked the gleam and shine of the upper levels, but it didn't look much worse than countless cities he'd visited on the frontier.

If anything, he felt more comfortable now that he was driving through an area that felt closer to what he'd dealt with for most of his life, even when taking into account the first part of his life in the Greater Detroit Metroplex.

Many normal, albeit poorer, citizens still lived at ground level there.

Erik slowed to a stop. A large holographic sign spun over a squat gray building. Two beer-filled mugs swirled around the colorful name of the bar.

THE BIG ONE.

He chuckled and pulled into a small parking lot filled with flitters, all of which had seen better days.

Erik opened the door and stepped into onto the concrete. "Basic request, activate security system." He closed the door.

The car beeped once and the windows darkened. Metal panels slid down to cover them. Erik nodded, satisfied, before walking over to the door of the bar. He threw it open and entered the dimly lit building.

No matter which planet, no matter which place, all seedy bars invoked the same spirit: a darkened room with worn tables, whether metal or wood, and angry-looking men and women sitting around in a place that never seemed more than half-full.

Loud music blasted from unseen speakers, the sound some harsh cacophony Erik didn't recognize.

He'd never cared much about music, especially out on the frontier, let alone the border.

Erik stepped up to the bar. A scowling woman in a crisp white shirt, black vest, and dark pants moved forward. The fancy outfit didn't fit the vibe of the bar. He wondered if she'd had de-aging treatments because her smooth, youthful skin didn't match her short, graying dark hair.

"What can I get you?" the bartender asked.

"A Wolf's Rebellion," Erik replied. Despite the fancy name, the drink was nothing more than a Baijiu Sour, typically the grain alcohol plus lemon juice, sugar, some egg white, and a few other spices. He doubted he would get an authentic Rebellion, considering the original drink contained uniquely flavored spices that relied on the soil of the planet Remus in the Wolf 359 system.

He tapped his PNIU and a price appeared in the center of his smart lenses. He tapped again to transfer the credits.

The bartender nodded and turned to grab the necessary bottles and glass to mix the drink. "I haven't seen you around here before, and I have a very good memory."

"I'm new to the area." Erik offered her a lopsided smile.

"New, huh? Meaning what? If you're looking to score, I don't tolerate that in my place. I can point you to some places if you want. Your brain, your choice. But it'll cost you." The bartender snorted and gestured at her PNIU. "Every car that pulls up, I get a little ping. You having a fancy toy like that means you're some Uptowner bigshot who's come here to slum. The fact that you can get past the checkpoints means you have money to throw around."

"Would you believe me if I told you the cops just let me through?" Erik shrugged. "I'm not even lying." He glanced around before looking back at her. "I'm not here for drugs."

The bartender finished preparing his drink and set it down in front of him, sans coaster. "Then what are you doing here, Uptowner?"

"Honestly?" Erik asked.

She nodded. "Honestly."

"Seeing how the other half lives. The guy I picked up the car from mentioned the Shadow Zone, so I wanted to check it out." Erik shrugged. "It's not so bad."

"Not so bad?" The bartender snickered. "You ready to move down here with us groundlings?"

"Maybe." Erik picked up the drink and swallowed, then eyed it. "That's good stuff."

"Glad you approve." She stared at him for a moment, tapping a finger on her lips. "Something's not right."

Erik took another few sips of his drink before setting the glass in front of him. "What do you mean?"

She looked him up and down and shook her head. "Everything. Wrong build. Wrong accent. Wrong look. At first, I thought you were an Uptowner playing at slumming, and I know you're not from around the Zone, but I don't think you're from Uptown either."

"Yeah, you could say that." Erik grunted. "I'm from—"

She threw up her hand. "No. I want to figure it out." She narrowed her eyes. "You've got money, a lot of money. You can afford an MX 60 and the de-aging treatment."

Erik's eyes lifted. "You knew?" He heard a soft hiss behind him, then a slap and a few chuckles. Her eyes glanced toward the noise, then back at Erik.

If she wasn't concerned, he wasn't concerned. But he glanced at a framed art piece to make sure no one was coming up behind him.

She ran her hand through her hair. "I'm familiar with the procedure, and I hope your hair changes. Mine got stuck this way. Your build and the way you move show you've got training, and don't think for a second my security grid didn't tag that gun when you stepped inside."

Erik raised an eyebrow. "You let me come in armed?"

The bartender laughed. "If I kicked out every man with a gun, I wouldn't have many customers, now would I?"

Erik nodded. "Fair enough. So, you were saying?"

"I'm guessing…" She licked her lips. "Merc. Probably been working offworld for a few years, earned some fat, juicy corp payoffs, so you've come back home to live large, but all the credits in the world don't make you smell right to Uptowners, so you're coming to a place like this, thinking we're your people because having more credits don't change a man's smell."

Close. Very close.

Erik sniffed his armpit and grinned. "I think I smell fine."

"Very funny." The bartender extended her hand. "Alicia."

He gave her hand a firm shake. "Erik Blackwell."

"Of course. Even your name fits." Alicia leaned back, her hands resting on one of the drink shelves filled with bottles. "Unless you spent all your money on that car and your treatment, I'm assuming you're not looking for work?"

Erik shook his head. "I've got a new job already lined up."

Alicia frowned. "I know you don't have to tell me, but you're not hitting anything around here, are you?"

"Nope. I mean an actual different career. Nothing…so violent." He thought about that for a few seconds. "Not so violent most of the time."

"Oh? And what's that?"

Erik downed the rest of his drink and let out a sigh of satisfaction. Maybe it was the smell or maybe it was the taste, but the liquor satisfied more on Earth. "Cop."

Alicia burst out laughing but stopped after a moment when Erik didn't join her.

"A merc turned cop?" Alicia asked. "Now I've heard everything."

"Something like that," Erik responded. He stood. "Thanks for the drink. I just wanted to check this out. I think I'll be back in the future."

"Because you like the drinks, or for something else?" Alicia asked, her voice hesitant.

Erik leaned forward. "A good cop needs an ear on the street, doesn't he?"

Alicia snickered. "You're asking a question like that? I'm guessing you've been offworld a long time, and you've forgotten how squeaky clean everyone wants to pretend the homeland is."

"That might be true." Erik stood. "But it doesn't change anything."

"Fine, Blackwell. See you around." Alicia gave him a polite nod.

Erik nodded back before heading to the door. The single drink had barely touched his head, but his fancy new ride had a fully autonomous system. He could have pounded back ten drinks and been fine.

"Blackwell," Alicia called.

He looked over his shoulder. "What?"

"Don't care what you do, but make sure you don't bust up my place." Alicia folded her arms over her chest.

Erik frowned. "What are you talking about?"

"You'll see." With that, she turned and headed toward a man holding up an empty bottle at the other end of the bar.

Erik stood for a moment, parsing the cryptic thought before stepping into the parking lot.

Oh. That explains it.

Four thugs in dark jackets stood by his MX 60, laughing. Two men had metal claws extending from their hands. A thin clear tube filled with blue liquid circled another's man's neck, a small metal circle near a vein. An auto-drug injector.

Hints of metal peeked out from the neckline of the fourth man. They were thugs who didn't care about displaying cybernetics.

A lot of people called them Tin Men.

Erik wasn't a Purist, so he could care less about their cybernetic enhancements. He cared far more about what they might be planning to do to his MX 60.

He stepped forward and cracked his knuckles. "Can I help you, boys?"

The Tin Man with the metal chest turned toward Erik and smacked his lips.

His gaze roamed the ex-soldier for a moment before he smirked. "You're not what I expected, but that don't mean much." He raised his hand and gestured for Erik to approach. "Transfer the codes to my PNIU. I like your flitter, so I'm taking it, and I don't want to mess up my new car."

"If I do that, won't the cops just come and get you?" Erik asked, a slight smile on his face.

The Tin Men laughed.

"Nah, not like that," the leader replied. "If you have enough juice to get into the Shadow Zone without trouble, you should know that. No cops are going to worry much about some fool losing his car, and the *real* authorities won't care as long as we don't bring heat. And when rich Uptowners come down here," he dropped his voice, "they're *always* coming for something they shouldn't be doing, so we both know you ain't going to call no cops down here."

He reached into his jacket and pulled out a long, jagged knife. "I'm betting no one even knows you're here." The thug shrugged. "If you disappear, no one's going to come looking."

Erik scratched his cheek and grunted. "You know, here's the deal. I could kill you, but I'm going to have to kill a lot of people eventually, I suspect. Maybe not soon, but soon enough, and I don't want my first kill back on Earth to be a choice." He looked at them all. "So pathetic. You're not worth the trouble."

The Tin Man howled with laughter, popping the guy

next to him on the arm. "You serious? You think you're a big man?" He gestured at Erik but spoke to a guy at his side. "Get him, Wolf. Teach him to respect his betters."

One of the clawed thugs stepped forward, scraping the claws against each other. He growled and advanced on Erik. "I'm not going to kill you, Uptowner. I'm gonna slice you up." Wolf's grin turned feral. "You ever even been in a fight, Uptowner?"

Erik smirked and shook his head. "This isn't a fight. This is a warm-up for later." Wolf had barely registered Erik's reply when the major sprang forward, his right fist already cocked behind him.

Wolf's eyes widened and he stumbled back, taken off-guard by the sudden attack.

Erik slammed the fist into the man's head, snapping it back. The Tin Man crumpled to the ground moaning, his eyes rolling up in his head. Erik slammed his boot tip into the thug's head and the man slumped down, unconscious, blood pouring from his nose.

"You're dead, Uptowner!" screamed the leader. "Kill his ass, Ant!"

The other clawed thug rushed forward and brought up his arms. After the druggie's auto-injector liquid drained through the port, the man's nostrils flared and his pupils dilated.

"I feel no pain!" screamed the druggie.

"You poor bastards." Erik stepped back and to his left. "Thinking you have a chance."

Erik threw up his arm to block a slash from the clawed thug.

The metal ripped through his sleeve into the skin of his

arm, a sharp pain following. The top layer of flesh was actual biological tissue, including nerves, but without the deeper muscle tissue to destroy, the pain remained muted. By his standards, it was only a sting.

He'd felt worse.

Two quick throat punches sent the thug to the asphalt and a quick stomp knocked him out.

"That's two," Erik pointed out, waving for the next guy to come at him. "Let's go, pain boy. Show me what you've got."

The druggie shuffled forward, frothing at the mouth, arriving just in time for his head to meet Erik's foot.

He stumbled back, and Erik threw a hard left with his cybernetic arm before following up with a right hook. The next move was a punch right to the thug's solar plexus, followed by two more quick punches. Erik snapped his foot forward at the now-falling thug, and the battered man flew back and hit the ground. He rolled several times, his eyes closed.

The remaining Tin Man's lips curled in a sneer and he lifted his knife. "You got lucky." He slapped his chest. "But you're not going to be able to beat me, Uptowner. You're dead. I'm going to carve you up and dump your pieces in a hole somewhere. No one's going to find you, and no one's ever going to know what happened to you, because Uptown likes to pretend there's nothing bad left down here."

Erik shook out his left arm. The wound still stung.

He'd have to get a first aid kit on the way home. "Are you going to kill me with that knife, or is your plan to talk me into throwing myself on the pointy end to get away from the pain of listening to you?"

The Tin Man flicked his wrist, launching the knife at Erik. Erik snapped his arm up using his interfaced smart lens to his cybernetic arm. He snatched the knife out of the air and his fingers wrapped around the handle.

"What the..." The Tin Man gritted his teeth as he tapped on his chest, the metal sound obvious. "You know the good thing about having a metal plate over your chest, Uptowner? You don't worry much about getting stabbed." He sprinted toward Erik, yelling like a rabid banshee.

Erik waited for the charge.

When the Tin Man was close, Erik spun around his side. He tossed the knife into his right hand and brought his left arm around the other man's neck, yanking him to a complete stop. He whipped the knife forward and brought the point to the side of the man's throat.

The Tin Man froze and held his breath.

"This can go one of two ways," Erik whispered into his ear. "The problem with having an armored chest is that it makes me target other body parts." He pushed the tip in a bit. "Do I have your attention?"

Erik took the slow nod as an affirmative.

"I can crush your throat with *my* cybernetic arm. That would be funny since you thought you had an advantage over me. Or I can stick this knife into your throat, and that would be funny too since you provided me the blade in the first place. You have a preference?"

The Tin Man let out his breath. "I didn't know you had hardware. I just thought Wolf didn't carve that deep."

Erik let out a dark chuckle. "Thirty years I was out

there, protecting people from insurrectionists and terrorists, but maybe I should have been here dealing with trash like *you*. Tell me, Tin Man, if I killed you right here, would anyone shed a tear over an unmarked hole in the ground? Would anyone care?"

"I-I've got connections," the thug stammered. "Y-you don't know who you're messing with."

"And maybe someday I'll care about your connections," Erik growled.

"Who are you?"

"No one you need to worry about...yet." Erik tightened his arm around the man's neck just enough to cut off circulation, but not enough to crush his windpipe. He tossed the knife to the ground.

The Tin Man struggled, his arms thrashing. In time, his head slumped and his eyes closed. Erik dropped the unconscious man to the ground without ceremony.

"Just not worth it," Erik murmured, and shook his head. He turned toward the bar and waved, hoping Alicia appreciated that he hadn't started flinging bullets.

CHAPTER TEN

June 17, 2228

Jia looked down at her napkin before looking back up. *I can't believe I let Mei talk me into this.*

She managed to smile at the handsome blond man sitting across from her at the white-draped table. Light classical played in the background.

Jia had agreed to *one* date. It was her way of proving she didn't hold her family's values in contempt, with the hope that if she demonstrated her respect toward them, they might return the favor.

It was also the fact that Mei asked for a favor.

Mei's version of compromise involved picking out the man instead of their mother doing it, but Jia wasn't sure if that was an improvement. Tonight's date was Warren Southward III, a business associate of Mei's.

Warren picked up his wine glass and took a small sip. "Let me say again how lovely you look tonight. I'm happy you agreed to this, especially on such short notice. I wouldn't have blamed you if you hadn't been able to come."

She nodded. "It's okay. I had an open night, and as for the rest, thank you, Warren. That's very nice of you to say. I have to admit, my sister didn't tell me a lot about you."

"I work for Aurum. My division focuses in particular on financial transactions involving the Moon and Mars. It's definitely got its complications, but at least we don't have to worry about colony financial matters." He sighed. "What a nightmare."

"I'm sure they are," Jia admitted. She glanced around, taking in the room. "So, how do you know my sister exactly? Has her company done work with Aurum?"

Warren chuckled quietly. "I met your sister at a recent business conference. She's already making quite a name for herself at such a young age." He tilted his head and shook his finger. "I must say, although your sister did well describing your natural beauty, she didn't relate to me what you do. Are you in the family business?"

Jia chuckled, shaking her head as she thought of the many reasons Mei might leave out that important bit of information. "No, I'm a police detective. My division technically handles all Class II crimes and higher. We often pass them along for efficiency reasons, but we have a wide scope of responsibility."

"Class II crimes?" Warren's lips parted slightly. "That's very…interesting, I bet." He sighed. "Not to sound rude, but there can't be that much to do. I imagine most criminals have been transported offworld by now?"

"Oh. Yes, sure. Of course, all crime is totally under control and limited to small regions of unrest or isolated pockets, but you know, it's like..." Jia sighed. She'd promised to at least give an honest effort. "Prevention is the key to maintaining an orderly and stable society," she finished.

Lame! she chastised herself. *How about you just read him the prologue of the* Law Officers School Welcome *book?*

"I see." Warren nodded, something approaching understanding in his eyes. "I was a bit confused about a Lin daughter being in such an...unusual career position, but with that explanation, it all makes sense."

Jia smiled. "It does? I'll admit that even my own family doesn't understand why I chose to become a detective versus following in their shoes."

"Yes, it makes perfect sense." Warren returned her smile with warmth. "You're the youngest? You have no siblings other than Mei, correct?"

Jia nodded. "Just the two of us."

"I'm the youngest in my family as well," Warren explained.

And that matters, why? Jia wondered.

Warren reached over and patted her hand. "I understand the urge to want to help society while distinguishing yourself from your family. It's natural for those of us who are the youngest to rebel that way."

She eyed his hand, then looked back up at him.

"But," he continued, pulling his hand back, "the best way to help society is by ensuring a robust economy. If the economy is strong and wealth is being generated, everything else can be handled by people who aren't capable of achieving that. Business is the true heart driving all of the UTC, ultimately. Think about it. There would be no colonization without the aid of the corporations. Can you imagine human colonization efforts without Hermes or Ceres Galactic? Or White Tiger?"

"I'm not arguing that corporations don't help promote stability and growth of the UTC," she countered. "But don't you think it helps to have people from different backgrounds in law enforcement roles? A healthy society has members of different backgrounds dispersed for maximum diversity of viewpoint and experience." She put her hands under the table and clenched them into fists.

"Different backgrounds?" Warren mused. "Why would we need that? In truth, I'm dubious of the necessity of governmental law enforcement anymore. Corporate security can handle anything of importance, and the government's moving most of the antisocial elements off Earth, where Security and the military can handle them."

Warren picked up his napkin to dab the corner of his mouth. "Even if governmental law enforcement is necessary, *our* kind of people don't need to participate. Someone of your family background and education isn't living up to her full potential working in an unnecessary job."

"I-I don't think it's unnecessary," Jia managed. *Mei, be thankful I don't kick him under this table! Family respect or not.*

"I apologize. I should clarify." Warren offered her a disarming smile. "It's unnecessary for people like you and me. Obviously, someone has to be involved in keeping the antisocial citizens and criminals under control, whether private or governmental. Of course, people from more limited backgrounds would find such work fulfilling, and I understand that you were attempting to distinguish yourself from your family, just as I was by thinking about becoming a diplomat at one point. I will fill you in on the story sometime since it's practically a whitepaper about the youngest in a family. But don't worry; it won't be a problem anyway. You'll find different ways of finding fulfillment."

Her face scrunched; her confusion was complete. "What are you talking about? What do you mean, 'it won't be a problem?'"

Warren let out a quiet laugh. "You working, of course." He gestured at himself. "I'm rather successful. While I wouldn't object to my wife working, she would never have to, and I think you would find the busy social life that would come with an appropriate marriage more than adequate to fill your free time. I'd prefer a wife who didn't work. Otherwise, why wouldn't I consider Mei, if I'm honest?"

Jia stared at the man, processing what he had just said.

"Wife?" she squeaked.

"YOU SET ME UP," Jia accused as she stomped back and forth in her apartment.

She'd decided to wait until returning home to call her sister. She wanted to give herself a chance to settle her thoughts and clear the wine fog from her brain. She had also tried to burn off some energy by yelling at the onboard computer in her flitter.

It wasn't even close to satisfying.

The full-color hologram of Mei transmitted by Jia's PNIU stood there with her arms crossed and her lips pursed. While Jia normally preferred audio-only calls, a good rant needed accompanying body language for the full effect.

And family deserved only her best.

"I didn't set you up," Mei challenged, shaking her head while putting up a finger. "I asked you to go on one date with Warren."

She turned the upthrust finger in Jia's direction. "Was it not a date? Didn't he take you out to one of the best seafood restaurants in the metroplex? They serve *actual fish*. Try to afford that on your policewoman's salary, little sister." She huffed. "I think you get spoiled at times, dining with either me or Mother and Father."

Jia threw up her hands. "He was talking about *marrying* me. I just met the man. I didn't know anything about him since you said everything would flow better and it would give me things to discuss if I didn't, but now I realize you were setting me up for a matrimonial ambush."

"Oh, don't be so melodramatic." Mei rolled her eyes. "He's a busy man, Jia. He doesn't have time for a lot of unnecessary dating, and I *was* trying to give you something to talk about."

"I understand putting his career first, but I think talking about marriage on the first date is a bit much. Even Mother and Father had an actual romance that led to their marriage." Jia groaned and pinched the bridge of her nose. "And I'm not saying I have someone else in mind. I'm not even interested in any dating right now because I'm busy with my career, remember?"

"Ah, yes." Mei looked pained. "The police career that frustrates you to no end." She threw both hands up. "I can't possibly expect you to put that fling on hold to live a more fulfilling life of much higher social status that would both bring you more joy right now and please your older sister and your parents to no end, now could I?" She shook her head. "The mere thought must be complete insanity on my part."

Jia eyed her through the camera. "That's not fair, and you know it."

"Tell me one thing that's wrong with Warren." Mei pointed at Jia. "Just one thing."

"It's not that there's anything particularly wrong with him," Jia replied. "Well, there is one thing. He won't support me in my career, and even ignoring that, I'm not ready to get married yet, let alone to someone I barely know."

"It's not like he was going to marry you tomorrow, Jia." Mei slapped a hand to her forehead and sucked in a breath. "You are very, very frustrating, little sister." She blew out her breath. "I have a suggestion. A perfectly acceptable alternative."

"What's that?" Jia asked.

"You could join us at the company."

"You wasted his time too, you know," Jia insisted, ignoring Mei's suggestion. "I had to make it very clear to him that I'm not getting married anytime soon."

Mei chuckled. "Because you're obsessed with your police career and some abstract notion of justice that is, to be frank, *outdated*."

"Serving the public is never outdated," Jia countered. "And I don't appreciate you misleading me."

Mei sighed and lowered her arm. "I'm sorry, little sister.

I'll admit that was a calculated risk on my part, but you're right, I shouldn't have done it. In the future, I'll be clearer about *my* intentions. Although I only care about your future, and I want you to be happy." She eyed Jia. "And your job *isn't* making you happy."

"Only because I can't do it properly." Jia took a deep breath. "But if I hold out, something will change the status quo, and I'll be able to do my best to uphold the law." She nodded firmly. "Everything will be different soon. I can feel it."

Mei shook her head slightly and lifted a hand to her mouth to cover her yawn before she answered. "I hope you're right, little sister. I hope you're right for all our sakes."

CHAPTER ELEVEN

Jia sighed as she skimmed through the glowing columns of numbers and text hovering in front of her.

She could have had her PNIU route the data to her smart lenses, but enforcement zone regulations stated data inspection should be conducted in such a way that a third party could observe the data at all times. Pushing against the regulations was the last thing she wanted to do.

It wasn't like she had a partner to annoy with a desk full of numbers either.

Fortunately, no one was close enough to hear her mumbling, "Either I'm a detective, or I'm not. I'm certainly not an auditor." She thought about the situation for a moment. "Maybe I should find and work with another detective pair."

She swiped a finger to summon a new page of data.

The information populated in front of her: names, dates, fines, and exact traffic law violated. This was hardly a record of dangerous anarchy threatening to overwhelm the metroplex, and although she understood the law required some manual checking of the data, that didn't mean she liked doing it. Poring through data and evidence to solve a crime was an exciting challenge.

"This is just punishment." She spoke aloud.

She stabbed to move to the next page.

"It's not my fault they quit."

Her eyes flashed through the data and she stabbed a key once more.

"All they had to do was their jobs, not assume I'm a naïve Corp doll."

The clack of the key was a bit louder as the data moved again.

She continued speaking to no one. "Seriously, you don't keep a beautiful garden looking that way by ignoring aphids just because they're small. They'll chew up your flowers all the same."

Jia scanned the traffic fine data, taking slow, steady breaths to calm down.

People said numbers didn't lie, but that was absurd. Numbers might exist in some abstract sense outside of a mind, but humans were the ones who recorded them in the end.

The miracle of Earth civilization had been achieved not by pretending people were perfect, but by accepting that they were flawed and putting societal measures in place to account for those flaws, including education and law enforcement.

If I performed a low-level analysis of some of this traffic data, could I find any unusual patterns? There could be something there waiting to be found, but we're so dependent on algorithms, we don't even know what we might be missing.

She sighed as she leaned back in her chair and rubbed the sides of her head.

Who am I kidding? It's not like there's some insurrectionist cell hiding out in Neo SoCal. They wouldn't dare. They don't have influence here. No, some crime lingers, but that happens wherever humanity lives. She chewed the inside of her cheek, thinking about the lack of large problems on Earth. *But it's not going to be dangerous conspiracies and bribes hidden in encoded data.*

She stared at a virtual image of the city, watching the flitters go to and fro in their flight lanes, which crisscrossed in front and back of the buildings that grew up through the clouds.

I understand why the captain thinks I'm pushing too hard, but if he would accept there were actual cases worth following up on, we would get along a lot better.

Jia chewed her lip and tapped her PNIU to bring up another display—her file on the fraud case. The captain hadn't formally transferred it away from her division yet and she was curious about a few other details, such as some money transfers that weren't fully accounted for.

Why is he bouncing this case away? There's got to be something there. Maybe a seed of corruption that, left to fester, might hatch into something dangerous.

She eyed the file data.

Another quick selection by Jia opened more floating windows of data from the fraud case. She had been focused on the potential misappropriation of funds, but the company involved wasn't *only* dealing with the city.

Jia narrowed her eyes.

A note had been added to a file the day before, but it

hadn't been added by a police officer. The police intake system auto-collation algorithms had appended the information because the same local company, Windward, was involved.

Although it was a common practice, it wasn't always that useful since the algorithms often added superfluous information of little relevance, but it didn't hurt to check.

CLASSIFICATION: LOCAL CITIZEN COMPLAINT
NATURE OF VIOLATION: Possible Class III Financial Fraud and Identity Theft

"Now that's interesting," she murmured.

She tapped her lips, thinking. Fantasies of insurrectionist cells siphoning resources off Earth filled her head.

"That's unlikely but exciting." She sighed.

The realities of the limits of interstellar travel meant that there could be no grand conspiracies of rebels reaching across the stars. It made no sense to smuggle resources off a core world that might take months to arrive instead of stealing them from somewhere more local.

The only reason insurrectionists had any sort of small chance was that those same distances meant the full might of the UTC couldn't easily be brought to bear on frontier colonies with any timeliness, and spreading the military throughout UTC space meant the size of any given detachment of troops was modest by necessity.

Jia pushed the thoughts of a future broken UTC aside and reached out to the note window.

All it would take was a simple tap to bring up more information. With that, she could at least evaluate for herself if there was anything more worth pursuing in the case. It wasn't such a terrible idea. All she wanted to do was make sure criminals weren't getting away with anything.

Her PNIU chimed, the distinctive tone indicating it was Captain Monahan. She tapped her device to answer.

"What is it, sir?" Jia asked.

"My office," the captain ordered, his voice low and full of menace. "*Now*, Detective Lin."

Jia closed down her open windows and stood. The captain sounded angry, but that wasn't new.

"On my way, sir," Jia replied. "I'll be right there." She ended the call and headed to her door, trying to think positively. Maybe the captain had reconsidered his position?

"It's not like he can chew me out because of my partner." She pulled the door open.

She couldn't work a real case without a partner due to regulations, but there had to be some option that would allow her to do something better than review traffic fines.

She had thought about transferring to another division, or even a totally new enforcement zone, but without a positive recommendation from her current supervisor, that would be impossible. The captain knew that, too.

Jia made her way down the hall, through the bullpen, and to Captain Monahan's office. His door was already open and he sat behind his desk, multiple projected text windows floating in front of him, his brow furrowed in concentration.

"Close the door behind you," Captain Monahan barked as she entered the office.

Jia complied and sat in front of his desk. "What did you need, sir?"

Captain Monahan gestured to a small text window off

to his side. It was the citizen complaint summary note she had just been reviewing.

Her heart kicked up. The captain might finally be willing to take the case seriously if he'd been looking at the same thing. It was a thin strand to hang her hopes on, but it was real.

"You know what this is," Captain Monahan related. His tone clearly indicated it was a statement and not a question.

"Yes, sir." Jia squared her shoulders. "I was just looking at the case notes. The fact that there is additional evidence only underscores my thoughts we should look more closely into it." She pointed to the information. "There's a case here to be solved. It's *not* just a misunderstanding."

He eyed her, one eyebrow raised. "I *think* you're laboring under a mistaken impression, Detective Lin." Captain Monahan frowned. "You're *not* supposed to be working that case at all. You're supposed to be helping the traffic enforcement division with their manual data inspection."

"I understand that, sir, and I have been. I just took a few minutes to…" Her stomach tightened. *Well, crap. This isn't about him being ready to throw the case open and have me work it.*

"Took a few minutes to review a case you can't work because of regulations," the captain finished for her. He shook his head. "A case I explicitly have told you not to work. I thought I was very clear about that." His voice became sweet, too sweet. "I don't know how I could have been possibly clearer about that, Detective." He leaned back, his chair making that annoying squeak as he smiled.

"No, please." He waved toward Jia. "Tell me how I failed to explain myself."

If he expected her to wilt, that wouldn't happen. "I haven't done anything. I was checking the notes. I understand and respect regulations, but the relevant regulations clearly stem from internal investigatory integrity and safety concerns." Jia shrugged. "If I'm not adding to the file, interviewing witnesses, collecting evidence, or even out on the field, those kinds of things don't apply, but I do want to point out an additional complaint that might be relevant was added to the file. I didn't do that. That was the system itself. It's not much, but it's something to consider."

Well, as far as Jia was concerned, it was.

Captain Monahan let out a long, annoyed grunt and scrubbed a hand down his face. "This isn't about regulations, Detective Lin. This is about orders, specifically *my* orders. I flagged the file in the system so that I would be immediately informed if you accessed it. That's why I called you here."

Jia frowned. "You did?"

"It's well within my purview as captain." He leaned forward and tapped the highlighted note. A larger window with additional information appeared in front of it. The other windows floating in front of his desk disappeared. His jaw tightened as he read through the information.

At least he's reading it.

The captain snorted, his eyes focusing on her. "Have you read this complaint?"

Jia shook her head. "You called me in here before I could get to it."

The captain swiped his hand through the window and

it vanished. "You've got some big scenario in your head where you've stumbled upon a huge crime, but that report was just some glorified services complaint. An angry citizen bellowing about being charged for someone else's delivery." He smirked. "This doesn't even rise to the level of criminal activity, Detective Lin. This is barely worth a civil suit, let alone the department's time. If we investigate every time someone is angry about the services they have received, we'd need about one hundred times the personnel." He snorted. "The police exist to solve crimes, not to make sure people's bills are correct."

"I agree that, in isolation, that's not worth looking into," Jia told him with a shrug. "But that isn't in isolation, and my...instincts tell me there's something more." She pursed her lips. "Maybe a lot more."

Captain Monahan sighed and leaned back in his chair, which made that infernal squeak again. If this kept up, she would need to remember to either tell maintenance or bring a bottle of oil herself to fix it.

His voice sounded a bit strangled. "*Your instincts?* When you first came here, I thought you might be a good fit for the department. You seemed to understand the scope of what we do here and didn't have trouble at first. Those first few cases you were doing well, but then you suddenly developed this obsession with, I don't know," he waved his hand as if shooing off an insect, "looking for trouble even when there isn't any."

Jia eyed him. "It's not that I'm looking for trouble, *sir*. It's just we keep passing along cases, and we have for some time. For most of the time I've been here. When I've followed up on those cases, a lot of times, nothing has even been done about them. I didn't become a detective to *not* help people." She took a moment to remove some lint from her shoulder, using the time to control her breathing. "I haven't worked a single major case during my entire time here, and I've barely been allowed to work any cases in the last nine months, even minor ones."

"We need to save police resources for cases worth your time," Captain Monahan countered.

"Manual inspection of traffic fines is worth my time?" Jia scoffed. "With all due respect, even if this order dispute turns out to be nothing, it'd be a better use of my time because I'd at least be demonstrating to a citizen that the police care about his concerns. The traffic fine inspection algorithms are almost never wrong. I'm not providing a useful service, even if it's a required one."

Captain Monahan's face twitched with irritation and his nostrils flared. He took a deep breath and slowly let it out, visibly calming with the exhalation. "I want you to think about it a different way, Lin. I think I get where you're coming from." He waved a finger at Jia, then at himself, then back again. "We both know the kind of background you come from, and a woman with your intelligence and education could go far. You want to help people, right?"

Jia nodded slowly, not liking the faint condescension she heard in his voice. She would flat-out refuse to quit if that was where he was going with this.

He wouldn't force her out for wanting to do her job.

He smiled, his wrinkles growing prominent. "I understand, Lin. You're passionate, and you want to help keep Earth the safe and low-crime environment we've managed to achieve after so much hard work." He gestured around his office. "Even the fact that we're here now is an example of that. This entire metroplex was built on top of the ruins of tens of millions of murdered people. Our very home is a shrine to the dangers of criminality and extremism."

"Exactly," Jia exclaimed as she leaned forward. "Because we let disorder get out of control in the past, people suffered. Not just the people of Old Los Angeles, but everywhere. All I want to do is ensure that corruption doesn't root here. If history teaches us anything, sir, it's that eternal vigilance is the only way to protect our society from anarchy."

Captain Monahan nodded slowly. "True, true." He cleared his throat. "I'm not going to pretend I haven't been frustrated with you, and I stand by what I said about what happened with your partners. A big aspect of being a good cop is getting along with other cops. We're a team here, and we need to know we can depend on each other."

He pointed at her, and she raised one eyebrow in return. "To do that, Lin, we need people to stay in their lanes. When they do, it makes it easier to figure out who is a team player and who isn't. Those people will rise up the ranks, and when they rise up the ranks, they have a better opportunity to control how resources are expended. You understand what I'm saying?"

Jia sighed, shoulders drooping just a touch before she straightened her back. "Stay in my lane?"

"Exactly." Captain Monahan smiled. "Come on, Lin. I'm not trying to be difficult here. As frustrating as I find you, I do admire your passion, but you need to respect the experience of the men and women who have been doing this job almost as long as you've been alive, or longer."

"And what about the case?" She raised an eyebrow. What harm could there be in trying at this point?

Captain Monahan shook his head. "Trust me. There's nothing there, and I don't want you wasting resources. Am I clear this time?"

Jia nodded slowly. "Okay. I hear you, and yes, you are clear."

"Dismissed, Detective."

Jia stood and exited the office, her thoughts laden with doubts. The captain's explanation made sense, and he was right. Even if she believed either her enforcement zone or the department wasn't effectively using their resources, the best way to counter that was to rise up the ranks.

She didn't want to doubt her captain or her former partners, but she couldn't deny that her mind and instincts told her there was something more there.

She walked back through the bullpen, thinking the matter through as she wove into her office, and sat behind her desk, muttering. "I can only hope he changes his mind."

CHAPTER TWELVE

Erik leaned over the railing of his new apartment's deck, staring at the forest of towers and platforms filling the metroplex, along with the long skywalks connecting many of the nearby platforms and towers.

He turned, bringing his head around to look up the side of his building before looking down.

He couldn't even see the ground with the slight haze, flitters, and different platforms and skywalks blocking his view.

He craned his neck upward one more time. The sun hung in the cloudless sky, but the towers extended well past his apartment, blocking what could have been a beautiful view. The memories of countless sunrises on different worlds and the views of their moons flooded him for a moment.

Beauty before the placing of humanity's technological glove on a world.

He looked from building top to building top.

Erik chuckled and shook his head. It was easy to ignore

all the imperfections of a place if you stuck them somewhere people wouldn't see them. Earth wasn't so different in that regard than many of the other planets he had visited.

No one ever put a major ore processing facility right next to the governor's residence on a colony.

His PNIU chimed with a message alert.

He brought up the message and grunted, his eyebrows raising.

It was an intersystem message, delivered via Hermes Corporation's priority message queue. The sender was Nigel Anders, the former governor of the Mu Arae colony.

The message had been sent about two months ago from New Samarkand in Gliese 581, with the Hermes header information indicating the delays involved in message transmission from a system twenty light-years from Earth.

The message had been sitting in their queue for a while.

From what Erik could tell, the governor had attempted to route it through military channels. While Erik's ID was still officially linked to the UTC military, most of his other accounts had been transitioned out of their control.

It was surprisingly hard for a man to extricate himself from the military bureaucracy after thirty years. He hadn't finished registering and interfacing all his accounts locally until that morning, and Hermes Corp's systems had finally caught up with him.

Erik,

Based on the message you sent me a month after leaving the colony, you should be close to Earth

by now. Or maybe you decided to make a new life in the colonies. I wouldn't blame you if you did, but I also understand that you have unfinished business on Earth.

But I'm not you. I'm a coward. I'm settled on New Samarkand now, although not as its governor. You don't go from presiding over a failure to keep terrorists off a colony to leading a more developed colony.

I'm working at an import/export company here, a subsidiary of White Tiger. I'm keeping my head down, but I'm not without contacts in the UTC government. If you ever need help, just let me know, and I'll see what I can do.
I hope you find what you're looking for back on Earth.

Nigel Anders

Erik grunted and closed the message. He wasn't sure when his revenge would come, but he suspected he would need allies to accomplish it. Nigel would be useful, as would the various military officers Erik had impressed throughout his career.

Contacting them immediately wouldn't be very helpful. He needed something more concrete than some missing messages and too-well-equipped terrorists.

A quick chirp of a high tone followed by a low tone sounded.

A few seconds passed before Erik recognized it was from the door. It sounded a lot nicer than the harsh buzz he was used to from most standard-issue UTC military doorbells.

"Not in the military anymore, Erik." He kept having to remind himself he was living in a nice apartment in a quality residential tower.

It was not cheap, but not too expensive, either. He didn't want to appear concerned with money to anyone checking on him, but wasting money on a top-tier apartment remained pointless.

The doorbell sounded again, and he headed toward the door. He pressed a button and the front door slid open, revealing a massive auburn-haired bearded man.

The man was a wall of muscle, which was saying something, given Erik's height and fitness, but any chance at intimidation was undercut by his spiked crest of hair, more of a mane than something you would expect on a human.

Maybe it was popular on Earth, but he hadn't seen anyone else with hair like that yet.

The new arrival grinned and threw up his hand. "I was hoping to catch you. I saw that someone had moved in, but I was waiting for the right time to introduce myself. I'm Garth." He pointed across the hallway to the closed door of another apartment. "Your neighbor."

Erik reached out and shook the man's meaty hand. "Erik."

Garth nodded inside. "Mind if I come in?"

"Sure." Erik gestured to his mostly empty living room. The monotony of the empty white room was broken only by a dark-brown sofa near the back wall.

Garth looked around with a slight frown before he faced Erik with a raised eyebrow, a smile trying desperately to not break out. "Not much of an interior decorator, are you?"

"I'm still figuring out what I want." Erik shrugged, sticking his hands into his pockets. "I've been away from Earth for a while, and in my old job, I moved a lot. It was hard to get too settled into anything resembling a style."

Garth leaned forward, peering at Erik with unabashed and obvious curiosity. "What job was that?"

"UTC Army Expeditionary Corps," Erik replied.

There wasn't any reason to lie to the people around him. He was using his veteran status to get himself a job, after all. He was still waiting to hear back on his particular placement, but all the messages he had received indicated there would be no problems.

The main issue stemmed from no one knowing the proper procedures to deal with someone invoking the old Obsidian Detective clause. It'd been too long.

"Expeditionary Corps?" Garth reached out to shake Erik's hand again. "Thank you for your service."

He grunted. "It's no big deal," he replied, but left his hands out of his pockets this time.

"You said you *were* in the Army, but what are you doing now?"

"I'm going to be a cop," Erik explained.

Garth's breath caught as his head pulled back just a bit. "You get to investigate mysteries? That sounds cool. I always thought about joining the police, but I'm not good at taking orders and following rules."

Erik chuckled. "I've had a few decades of training with that." He flashed a smirk. "I don't think it'll be a problem."

"And by the way, 'No big deal?'" Garth laughed. "It's a big deal to serve, but I wish the UTC sent fewer troops out to border planets and kept more on Earth. We need them more here."

"Why is that?" Erik asked. "It's not like insurrectionists are going to launch a surprise invasion of Earth. I don't believe that is possible. We'd know they were coming months in advance."

Garth shook his head. "It's not humans I'm worried about." He lowered his voice. "And we're going to need all the help we can get eventually."

"You worried about the Local Neighborhood?" Erik eyed the man. "Let me tell you something. I've been out there. There's not going to be an interstellar war anytime soon. It can get tense, but they're minding their business, and we're minding ours."

"Exactly!" Garth's eyes widened and he nodded slowly. "You get it, and you're right. I don't care about the Local Neighborhood races. They're unimportant. Even the Leems." He rolled his eyes. "To this day, it's hard to get people to understand they aren't some huge part of human history versus representing a small group of lost aliens. We reverse-engineered a few things from them, but we were well on our way to a lot of that stuff anyway."

Erik nodded and leaned against the wall. "Yeah. I never fought any aliens, if that's what you're getting at. Most of the people I fought were insurrectionists and terrorists, and all of them were humans."

"Aliens?" Garth waved a hand, dismissing Erik's comment. "That's the big question. What's an alien?"

"What we were just talking about." Erik stared at the man for a second, frowning. "Like Zitarks or Orlox. Or Aldrans, or any of the others."

"Oh, oh, oh." Garth nodded quickly. "I see what you're saying. You're making a common mistake." He stopped for a moment, looking up in thought. "It's my fault, too. I didn't make it clear what I was talking about, so I can see where you got confused. Sorry."

"And what mistake was that?" Erik replied, irritation coloring his voice.

Garth waved his hands. "Allow me to explain. If you've been away for a while, I can see how you might not have access to some of the new and best information, so some of the things I'm about to tell you *might* prove shocking."

Erik grunted, his frown admitting he wasn't too sure about Garth's warning. "I can handle it."

Garth sighed and folded his arms. "It's like this. Everyone's worried about the insurrectionists or Zitarks or the other Local Neighborhood aliens, but they should really be worrying about the Navigators." He nodded slowly as if that was all Erik needed to catch on.

Erik was still clueless.

Garth continued, "They are the only aliens we need to care about since they are the only known alien species who are likely significantly more advanced than humans."

"The Navigators?" Erik's eyebrows came together as he thought. "No one has found anything from the Navigators other than a few of their artifacts." He shrugged. "If they're still around, they're not hanging out in our galaxy."

Garth pursed his lips. "What do you think happened to them?"

Erik scratched his chin. "Personally, I think they all turned to dust a long time ago. It just goes to show you, no matter how much tech you have, you can still die out."

"Oh, oh. I see you've bought into the *official* narrative." Garth rubbed his hands together, his eyes filling with glee. "I have *so* much I have to teach you."

"Official narrative?" Erik echoed, his batshit-crazy alarms starting to sound. "What exactly do you do for a living, Garth?" He eyed the man, wondering if this was some attempt at a strange con.

"I'm a tech at a Hermes hub, but that's just my job. It's not my passion, and I want to share that passion with you, because it's not just the passion. It's the truth, and that's where we get back into the official narrative."

Erik sighed. *Keep him here or throw him out?* He glanced at his balcony. *Throw him out the door or throw him off the balcony.* He smirked. *Nah, let him chat. Learn about my neighbors, as long as he doesn't ask for a donation.*

If that happens, it's the balcony.

"And what truth is that?" Erik dared to ask. "Because I'm not clear on what you're talking about, and I've been to more systems than most people on this planet."

"The truth that the Navigators are still around, of course." Garth threw his arms to his sides in a dramatic gesture. "And they might even be walking the Earth. We just don't allow ourselves to see it."

Erik snorted. "Sorry. Not buying it. I've been all over UTC space, and the Local Neighborhood races aren't even walking into our colonies, let alone the Navigators. Are you saying they're invisible or something?"

"No, no. Kind of. Let's take a step back." Garth shook his finger. "That's just it. That's what everyone believes. That they're gone and dead and buried, but they're wrong. Trust me. I'm not a crazy conspiracy theorist. I'm an experienced amateur researcher who has spent years plumbing the depths of misinformation and forgotten biology to pioneer the illumination of lost aspects of xenopaleontology. Of course, because my beliefs don't fit the *mainstream view* of things, people try to lump me in with the conspiracy theorists," he qualified.

Erik chuckled, turning his head to look at Garth with one eye. "What separates an amateur xenopaleontologist from a conspiracy theorist if they both believe strange things that go against the mainstream?"

"Because I only operate from useful, proven information, not mere speculation," Garth clarified. "The crazies all over the OmniNet like to claim the government is hiding things from us, but I know that's not true."

Erik put up a hand. "Wait, what? You believe the government?" Erik eyed him for a moment. "Ok, color me surprised."

Garth nodded. "I believe the government about aliens, or at least I believe they aren't purposely lying about what they know about aliens. If anything, the government's been very forthcoming. They could have lied about the Local Neighborhood. It's not like anyone except a few colonists would have known any different, but they didn't lie. They didn't even hide the Navigator finds on Mars, and it would have been really easy to do it. They could have justified it with UTC security and all that." He shook a finger. "Nope, the crazies don't understand there's no conspiracy out there, just ignorant people, including, unfortunately, the UTC government, all the way up to Parliament. Maybe a hundred years ago, Congress might have been useful, but it's all Parliament now, so the fact that they are deluded means the delusions flow all the way down to the common man on the street."

Erik considered firing up a note-taking app in his PNIU. *Waste of resources, no matter how infinitesimal they might be.*

"Okay, I'm a little lost, Garth. What does this all have to do with the Navigators?" Erik stared at the man, too confused to even begin to formulate a response that didn't involve laughing in his face. Despite Garth's warped view of things, he did otherwise seem friendly.

Garth grinned. "Platypuses."

Erik's mind suffered a reboot. "Huh? Come again?"

"You know, like down in Australia." Garth shrugged. "Haven't you ever wondered about them? They're so strange and unusual."

"Ahhh, no." He shook his head. "I can't say I've thought about platypuses since I was a kid."

"I don't buy the transitionary animal theory. If you look into the research, really look into it, the same thing keeps coming up over and over." Garth sighed. "Now, the next part *does* sound a little bit weird and conspiratorial, but if you look into the important sites and read the relevant books, you'll see that I've got it right. You're going to be an investigator, so I know you're trained to think."

Erik nodded, unsure about ever answering his door

again without looking out first. "What do you have right?"

"Platypuses are Navigator genetic experiments." Garth wagged his eyebrows. "I don't just mean genetically engineered animals, but the Navigators themselves. Obviously, they aren't currently sentient, but that's just because they are in a kind of genetic stasis. Makes sense when you think about it, right?"

"Ummm, perhaps?" Erik shrugged. "I suppose it's not impossible, and it's not like I know a lot about platypus genetics."

"I'll send you some recommended reading."

Screw my life.

Garth continued, oblivious to Erik's internal monologue. "For now, the thing you have to realize is there are a lot of Navigator genetic experiments out there if you know where to look. Same sort of deal. Them in standby mode, basically. Again, this isn't about the government covering them up, it's just about people realizing it."

I realize I want to one-punch myself for this. I blame me.

Garth took a deep breath, and Erik eyed the balcony before shaking his head as the man continued, "I know this is heavy stuff, and I'm probably totally reorienting your entire life paradigm right now, but it's all completely true, and this is why it's important this information be spread. Because it might be that all those animals out there are waiting for some sort of genetic switch to flip."

Garth nodded knowingly as Erik continued his internal discussion, berating his recent idiotic life choices, including his decision to open his door.

"Uh-huh," Garth continued. "And the next thing you know, the Navigators are back, and all around us." He furrowed his brow. "Well, all around Australia and in a few zoos, anyway. Maybe they picked Australia on purpose because it was more isolated originally."

Erik reached up, covering his mouth while managing not to laugh. "That's, uh, a new one on me. Is it just the platypuses, or are there other experiments? I mean, did we kill off a bunch of Navigators when the passenger pigeon went extinct?" He scratched the back of his head.

Why am I even asking? It's like watching a building burn down. It's horrible, but you just can't turn away.

Garth nodded. "Good question."

Oh damn, I did ask *a question.* Erik eyed the door to the outside. *I should throw myself off the balcony.*

"Some evidence also points to octopuses, but just them, not squid. So, it's well-documented that it's potentially octopuses, and certainly platypuses, as far as surviving animals. Obviously, some extinct animals might have been Navigators, but not passenger pigeons, to the best of my knowledge. You know, there's some decent evidence that the Navigators were actually alive on Earth around the time of the dinosaurs."

"Decent evidence?" Erik asked. "Are you suggesting to me that we have a bunch of Navigator skeletons sitting around museums?"

"Yes, they're around, but no, we don't have their skeletons, and this doesn't mean the Zitarks are Navigators. I mean, obviously, they aren't much more advanced than humanity, so they couldn't be. I'm not saying the dinosaurs *were* the Navigators, just that they were on Earth then. They might have killed the dinosaurs, but we can't be sure."

Garth looked up as if he was contemplating whether the next statement would be over the line.

"I suppose it's not that weird. I mean, those Navigator artifacts were buried on Mars." Erik blinked.

Oh my God, I can't shut my own mouth.

Why the hell was he letting some conspiracy theorist lead him down a path to believing the most powerful ancient race in the galaxy currently lived on as Earth animals?

The military had our share of nutjobs, but they had to at least be functional nutjobs who knew how to keep their mouths shut.

"Exactly." Garth snapped his fingers and grinned. "I like you, Erik. You've got a good head on your shoulders, but I've got to go. I just wanted to say hello. I'll put together a list of interesting books for you to read. The more you know, the easier it is to spread the word." He walked over to the door and opened it. "Oh, and welcome to the complex."

"Thanks." Erik went to open the door, not sure if he was amused, annoyed, confused, or some mixture of the three.

Garth departed, and Erik shook his head as the door slid closed.

He walked back through his apartment, heading to his bedroom. "After that, how hard can being a cop be?" he mused.

CHAPTER THIRTEEN

June 23, 2228, Neo Southern California Metroplex, Police Enforcement Zone 122 Station, Office of Captain Robert Monahan

Erik stopped himself from moving into parade rest as he stood in front of the captain's desk.

Despite the presence of so many military-sounding ranks in the police department, they were a civilian force, and the customs and courtesies he'd absorbed into his soul over thirty years in the military didn't apply.

There was also the fact that the man behind the desk didn't radiate the kind of authority he was used to. It wasn't that he didn't respect the captain, but he could sense he hadn't dealt with the kinds of dangerous situations Erik had throughout his career.

Captain Monahan furrowed his brow, his eyes darting back and forth as he skimmed several dense pages of text floating in front of him.

"Is there a problem, Captain?" Erik asked.

"I was just double-checking your application information," the captain responded, a hint of bewilderment in his voice.

"If there's something you need, I can send it directly to your PNIU. I have all the application files stored locally," Erik suggested.

Captain Monahan shook his head. "That's...not really my problem."

"There's a problem?" Erik asked.

"Sort of. Neither the enforcement zone nor the department has had to deal with anything like this for a long time, and quite frankly—"

"Nobody knows how to handle it," Erik offered.

Captain Monahan let out a quiet chuckle. "Something like that, yes." He tapped his PNIU, and the text disappeared. He shook his head. "So, Major Blackwell—"

"Just Erik, or Blackwell, if you want," Erik cut in. "I'm retired, and other than using my veteran status to get the job, I don't want to cause issues. I'm here to be a cop, not a soldier. I left that uniform and world behind, and I spent a long time flying back to Earth to start a new life."

"Yes, I understand that." Captain Monahan frowned as he looked at his newest detective. "Erik, I thank you for your service, but do you really think becoming a police officer on a core world, let alone Earth, is a good transition back to civilian life? You've been a soldier the bulk of your life, and Special Forces for a good chunk of that. That's not *exactly* the kind of career path that most people would see ending in becoming a detective in a core-world police department. I have some concerns."

"Are you saying there aren't any other veterans working

for you?" Erik couldn't help but grin. "When I asked about that, they told me there were other veterans in this department." *Sorry, Captain, but the screws have to go in.* "Or is it that veterans don't make good cops?"

"That's not what I'm saying, and we have a few veterans, yes, but none who applied using your method, and none of them spent as long as you did in the military." Captain Monahan gestured to Erik's hair. "They were also a lot younger. That has implications."

"I sent along a full physical, and I've had de-aging treatment." Erik ruffled his gray hair. "The treatment doesn't seem to have taken in my hair yet, but I'm willing to go up against any of your guys if you think I'm not fit enough." He grinned. "I'd love to do it, in fact."

The captain sighed. "It's not about your physical fitness, Erik. I'm just saying, the vets we have working here are...*different* than you. Most of them served on Earth, or an inner planet or station. We have no one in the entire department who served on the border or even the deep frontier, and as I'm sure you're already aware, Earth is a lot different than those places."

Fair enough.

He shrugged. "I'm not saying you'd make a bad cop, but your experience might be better suited to a position in law enforcement on a frontier planet, where they could better make use of your *practical* experience. While I understand that you've had a de-aging treatment, that only changes your body. It doesn't change your mind."

"And?" Erik replied. "I have decades of experience."

"You're less than a year younger than I am, and I've spent almost as long as a cop as you did in the military. I wouldn't be able to change jobs like that. Men like you and me, we get stuck in our ways, and the Army, in particular, has a way of really getting people stuck."

Erik chuckled. "I'm not stuck in my military ways."

"Maybe." The captain frowned. "But I'm also confused as to why you relied on some arcane half-forgotten law to get your foot in the door."

"The Obsidian Detective Act is an old American law. That means it's not going to guarantee me a position anywhere else on Earth, let alone the colonies."

The captain frowned. "Aren't you worried that forcing your way in might mean that you shouldn't be in this position?"

Erik shook his head. "No. I needed a guarantee before coming back, and the law was that guarantee." He shrugged. "Besides, I've got personal reasons to want to serve back on Earth and Neo SoCal, so using that option only helps with that."

Captain Monahan frowned. "I don't understand." He looked at a record he had yet to close; it was still hovering in the air. "According to your records, you're not from this area." He eyed Erik. "You're from Detroit."

Erik nodded. "Yeah, I'm from Detroit, but I'm more interested in this metroplex. It feels like I could be more useful here. Besides, I've been away for a long time. It's not like Detroit's waiting for me."

Captain Monahan closed his eyes and took a deep breath. He slowly let it out before opening his eyes. He was clearly trying to keep calm, which amused Erik.

"I don't think this department would provide the level of activity a man of action like yourself would find satisfying," the captain explained. "Although technically we're equipped to handle almost any crime, for various reasons that would probably escape your understanding just because you haven't been here for a couple of decades, we delegate many cases. I don't think you appreciate how slow that can make things." He shrugged. "This isn't some border or frontier colony overrun by a lot of insurrectionists or the disgruntled indentured. This is Earth, Erik, and things run here pretty well. A man with your distinguished record of military service will grow bored, especially coming right in at detective. Every other veteran here, regardless of origin, worked their way up, and that way, they better learned to appreciate the appropriate and balanced role of a police officer in Neo SoCal."

Erik pursed his lips. "With all due respect, Captain, it's like you said. I'm fifty-one years old. Thanks to the de-aging, I'm going to last longer than most, but I don't see the need to spend years working my way up the ladder here. I'm not going to end up a better detective because I spent a year giving people tickets for trying to fly into the Shadow Zone." He raised an eyebrow, adding an accompanying smirk for good measure.

"I'm not necessarily saying that," Captain Monahan replied, open anger seeping into his voice. "I'm pointing out that absorbing local police culture could be helped by that sort of thing, and if you believe you need to skip those steps, it makes me think you might not fit in here."

"You're entitled to that opinion, but it doesn't change anything. I didn't do this because I was drunk and bored one weekend. I'm determined to become a detective, and I've done everything the law requires to get me to that position. And, yeah, I also know that this enforcement zone is actually understaffed right now. They specifically asked me if I would come here because of that." Erik let the grin he had been holding back free.

The captain's attempts to intimidate him were bordering on comical.

Captain Monahan frowned and jerked back, taken off-guard. "They let you know about that?"

"It's not like police staffing is classified." Erik shrugged. "I don't know what you think I'm going to do, but I want to make it clear that after thirty years in the Expeditionary Corps, I'm not going to walk away because you're uncomfortable with a highly trained soldier becoming a detective. I've done everything that's been required of me. I've made sure to supply all the documentation. Every step along the way, I've done what I needed. I'll be blunt, Captain... Did you really expect me to walk away just because you gave me a speech about working my way up?"

"A trained soldier isn't the same thing as a trained detective," countered the other man. "And, yes, I think you should listen to what I'm saying. There are regulations to observe, procedures to follow. You know this. A police department might not be as rigid as the military, but it's still an organization that has rules and order, and I need people who are going to contribute to the order, not detract from that."

"Did you see where I was last stationed?" Erik asked.

Captain Monahan nodded. "Mu Arae. I get that it was tense there, but you never saw any action, right? The Zitarks backed off once they realized we were ready to fight, so I assume you spent a lot of time playing cards."

Erik wasn't surprised to hear the captain didn't know about the massacre. The military hadn't technically classified the loss of the 108th as such, and they had made it clear they would prefer that Erik and the support staff "minimize discussion of the incident for general morale purposes."

He wasn't sure how they were keeping the families of all those men and women quiet, but it wasn't all over the net, so whatever it was they were doing was working.

He wasn't stupid enough to think personally running around shouting about it from the rooftops would help. If there was some high-level conspiracy, either corporate or governmental, they were likely keeping an eye on him, and everyone else who knew about the incident.

"Yeah." Erik grunted. "The lizards did back off, and that's the point. That system's a long way from Earth. I've mostly been on ships for the past year, and they weren't always the nicest ships with the most well-equipped recreation options. I've had a lot of time to read and take tests. If you scanned my application and file, I'm sure you saw that I passed all the proficiency tests, and I'm well beyond your fitness and marksmanship standards."

"Yes, I saw all that." Captain Monahan tapped his desk. "But those tests have to be taken in a controlled environment. I'm sorry, Erik, but some test you took on a transport twenty light-years from here isn't good enough. I'm not trying to say you did anything wrong, but I don't think we can just pretend it's the same as taking them here."

"You ready to seriously argue that?" Erik dropped into the chair in front of the desk and offered the captain a lopsided smile. "I'm willing to bet if I pushed on this, I could get those requirements waived, but if you really are dying for me to take them again, I will." He chuckled. "It's not like I cheated. I spent a lot of time studying police procedure and local regulations, with all that free time on the way back."

The captain raised a finger and opened his mouth just as his PNIU chimed. "One second." He tapped the device. "This is Monahan." He tilted his head. "What? Yes. Why can't we just send some patrol officers? She is? Fine. No, go ahead and have her handle it then if she's already on-site. Wait. I'll be sending someone else soon. Okay. Good. Inform me if something else happens." He looked back at Erik, a smile creeping onto his face.

Erik had seen that kind of look far too many times in his career, usually from ambitious governors or higher-ups who thought they could use him as a tool to further their own careers. Sometimes it had ended well.

Most of the time, it had been a pain in the ass.

Captain Monahan leaned forward and folded his hands in front of him, an almost eerie calm settling over his face. "You know what, Erik? Maybe I'm making too many assumptions. If you spent a year studying and training, then you know the deal, and I shouldn't second-guess you. You're not some fresh-faced kid. I'm still convinced this job will be a little too slow-paced for you, but if you've put that level of thought and effort into this, that has to count for something."

The captain nodded slowly, a hungry gleam in his eye. "Since you spent so much time studying the regulations, I take it you're familiar with the rules concerning active detectives and the relevant personnel requirements for working cases?"

"Yeah." Erik nodded. "I need a partner. I'm not picky. I've worked with a lot of people in my military career. I can get along with almost anyone on the job, and I don't need to be a buddy off it."

"I'm very glad to hear that. I'm counting on that, to be honest. We have a detective who needs a new partner, and you're right. We're undermanned, so I should be happy you're here for as long as you stay here." The last part came out very mocking in tone, but what followed was far sterner. "Remember, though, Erik, you're not the commanding officer here. I am. I respect your time in the military, but you will respect my time as a cop. Are we clear on that?"

"Yeah, we're clear, Captain. I'm not here to be a soldier. I'm here to be a detective."

Captain Monahan offered Erik a thin smile before tapping his PNIU and then poking at a display only he could see. "I'm transmitting an address to your PNIU. This will be a good test for you. I need you to provide backup for a minor disturbance. This isn't normally something a detective would handle, but we happen to already have one on-site, so you might as well go and meet your new partner at the same time."

Erik stood. "Sounds good." He extended his hand. "I am happy to be part of the department."

The captain shook his hand. "And we're happy to have you, *Detective Blackwell.* Your partner will probably be finishing her handling of the incident by the time you get there. Her name is Jia Lin. She's pretty new herself. Only been on the force for a year, but she's very...*dedicated*. I'm sure you'll find her interesting."

"Okay, I'll head right there." Erik turned to leave. As he made his way through the bullpen, he scoffed quietly under his breath.

Great, what's going on? Did Lin get her last partner shot? He thinks she will push me away, or I've just stepped off the fresh-meat ship, slipped on some oil, and shot myself in the leg by accident.

CHAPTER FOURTEEN

Jia sighed, her arms folded over her chest, and tapped her foot on the ground. It was nighttime, but with so many lights in the metroplex, it was never truly dark. The sheer dome of light above the city washed away almost all the stars.

Where were the patrol officers? She glanced at the two drunk young men, both in their early twenties, sitting at the edge of the parking lot. They snickered to each other. It was supposed to be a fun night at a club with her girl-friends, but the idiot drunks had ruined that by going after a security guard.

She looked at two women standing to her side. Both wore amused smiles, and both were around her age.

One was an athletic blonde in a tight blue knee-length dress, the other a tall, dark-skinned woman in an orange dress, her hair done up in dozens of small braids. Jia completed the triad with her own body-hugging red dress with a thigh-length skirt.

She'd accessorized with a black choker and dark knee-high boots, and one other small addition: her badge, now clipped to the top of her dress.

Jia's purse hung over her shoulder, the weight of the stun pistol inside comforting.

"I'm sorry, Imogen." Jia sighed. "I'm sorry, Chinara. I know it's been a while since we last went out together, and then..." She gestured to the drunks. "This sort of thing happened, but as a cop, I'm always on the clock."

Imogen shrugged, a few of her light curls bouncing with the movement. "It's okay. It's kind of fun to see. I've never seen anyone arrested before."

Chinara laughed. "Drunks are drunks. It's not that entertaining." A faint Yoruban accent colored her words. "But it's a little more interesting than seeing them try to hit on women in the club."

Jia frowned at the men. "I can't believe you. You punched a security guard? Who does that?"

One of the men grinned. "Hey, if I had known I'd get a hot chick to come and pay close personal attention to me, I would have punched someone a long time ago."

"You're right." The other man nodded, a chuckle escaping his lips. "Hey, Officer Hotness. Maybe after this is all over, you can go out on a date with one of us." He tilted his head toward his friend sitting next to him. "I'm way smarter than him. You should go out with me."

The other drunk snorted. "If you're so smart, why I am the one who has a Ceres internship coming up? Huh?"

"Screw you, man. I don't need Ceres." The first drunk nodded toward his friend. "See? You don't want to go out with this guy, Officer Babe. He's all up in his head about how special he thinks he is." He burped loud and long, not noticing Jia's lips press together as he let it out. "But it's nothing. He's going to be a small fish in a big pond. This is why it's smarter to avoid the big boys. You can get noticed better at a subsidiary or a smaller corp. My father taught me that."

Jia rolled her eyes. "First of all, shut up. Second of all, my name isn't 'Officer Hotness.' It's Detective Lin, and I don't think you two realize the trouble you're in. You just committed felonious assault, and being drunk is no defense." She gestured to her friends. "And you ruined our night. We haven't been able to get together for a month because of our schedules, so thanks for that, really."

Imogen snickered. Chinara shrugged, a disappointed look on her face.

"Hey, I've got a better idea," the first drunk explained. "That security guy's fine. He didn't even have to go to the hospital, right? You should just let us go. We should all go out together. Somewhere other than this boring place." He wrinkled his nose. "You three are the only hot women in there anyway."

Imogen eyed him and Chinara rolled her eyes.

"Didn't you hear the part where I told you to shut up?" Jia glared at him. "As soon as the patrol officers show up, I'm handing you over to them, and you're going to be processed for assault. Then I'm going back to having a good time."

The drunk stared at her, his eyes glazed. "Man, for such a hot chick, you've got a nasty personality. Am I right, Cyrus?"

"You're more than right, John," his friend replied, his

nod placing the appropriate exclamation point on the assertion.

Imogen turned away, her hand over her mouth.

Jia eyed her friend, her eyes practically yelling, "You are not helping at all."

Jia shrugged. "I'm a detective. I don't need to be friendly to criminals."

John sighed and looked down. "All I wanted to do was have a good time. Do you know how hard it is to land an internship with Ceres Galactic? Especially when you don't already know someone who works there?" He took a sharp breath and cursed. "No, no, no. I can't get arrested." He looked at Jia and swallowed. "If I get arrested, it'll go on my permanent record."

She shrugged. "That's why you don't hit people in clubs, but that's not my problem now, is it? If it's your first offense, I'm sure the judge will take that into account. It's not like they are going to sentence you to transportation, so why don't you just be good and sit there quietly until they come to take you away?"

John scoffed. "You don't get it. You're just some stupid cop. You have no real future."

Imogen glared at the man. Chinara frowned and opened her mouth, but Jia lifted her palm to stop her.

"The police are the line between order and anarchy," Jia explained. "But whatever you think of me, that doesn't change the fact that *you* committed the crime. I'm just doing my duty."

The drunk's face twisted into a frown. "If I get a black mark on my permanent record, I'll lose my internship, and if I lose my internship, not only will I not get into Ceres

Galactic, I won't get in any decent corp. I'll end up somewhere worthless." He stood. "Like being a cop."

"You need to sit down right now," Jia barked. Her hand inched toward her purse.

Cyrus stood. "Look, it's not a big deal," he slurred, waving a hand that nearly turned him around. "None of this a big deal. You ruined everything, Officer Hotness." His whine set Jia's teeth on edge. "We would have done what we always do, and that little man would have made a lot of money for not a lot of pain."

"What are you saying?" Jia asked with a frown.

Cyrus rubbed his thumb and index finger together. "That the kind of man who works as a security guard appreciates a little payoff to look the other way. You arrest us, you're not just screwing us over. You're also not giving us any reason to offer him compensation for our indiscretions. It's a win-win for everyone our way. Lose-lose your way."

Jia's jaw tightened. She wanted to walk over and slap both of them, but with the badge came the protocol. "Both of you sit down," Jia ordered. Her hand edged toward her purse and the pistol inside. "I'm giving you a lawful order."

John scoffed. "Oh, yeah, I didn't think of it before." He nodded at Cyrus. "It's obvious."

Cyrus blinked a few times. "Oh, yeah. Totally obvious." He grinned at Jia. "Okay, Officer Hotness, how much is it going to cost to make this go away?"

Imogen winced.

Chinara turned away. "They've done it now," she mumbled under her breath.

Jia stared at the man, refusing to believe what she was hearing.

Of course, she had heard of bribery, but to encounter it in such a blatant way while at a club sent a tremor of rage through her.

"I want to be very clear about this," Jia replied, her voice cold. "Are you seriously trying to bribe me to get out of your assault charges?"

"Bribe?" John snorted. "That's not it. Bribe? No, no, no. I wouldn't do anything like that."

The tension she was holding released a bit. "Oh? Good."

John shook his head. "Bribes are something corrupt officials on frontier planets take. They're seedy and uncivilized. All I was suggesting was that we offer some compensation to the security guard for his time and suffering, and give you a little personal bonus for everything you do for the city. Not a bribe."

Cyrus nodded his agreement. "Definitely not a bribe."

"You have ten seconds to sit down," Jia snapped. "Or I might have to take severe measures."

John and Cyrus turned to look at each other.

"Remember that trip to Malta?" John asked.

Cyrus laughed. "Oh, man. That place was so...backward. There are probably more people in ten towers here than that entire country."

John stared at his friend for a moment. "I meant the second night."

Cyrus nodded. "Oh, yeah." He winked. "I remember. Let's do it."

Both men turned away from each other and bolted in opposite directions.

Chinara rushed forward, but Jia threw up her palm again.

"This is a police matter. You shouldn't get involved." Jia jerked her head between both men. She had recorded their IDs. She didn't have to chase them down, and now they would face more charges for resisting arrest.

Idiots!

Chasing them or discharging her weapon might place innocent people at risk, but letting drunk, violent men escape would place people at risk as well.

Cyrus made it a few meters before stumbling over his own feet and face-planting into the back portion of a flitter. He groaned and rolled off the vehicle, his eyes fluttering for a few seconds before he dropped, unconscious.

His self-defeat at least clarified the immediate course of action for Jia.

She pulled the stun pistol out of her purse and flipped off the safety. A light hum sounded as the weapon primed itself. She lifted the weapon.

"On behalf of the NSCPD, I order you to stand down immediately, or you will be fired upon," Jia shouted.

John continued running toward a shiny black flitter. He slapped at his belt where his PNIU had been, but the confiscated device, along with his friend's, sat in a pile by Jia. "Basic request, unlock and start engine," he shouted.

The flitter came to life and lifted off the ground. Jia pointed her pistol. All she had to do was pull the trigger. The man wouldn't die. Her finger wouldn't move. Jia lowered her arm. She just needed to call him in and not risk unnecessary gunfire.

John threw open the door and jumped inside. The

flitter spun in her general direction and accelerated. The vehicle hurtled straight toward her. Her legs didn't want to move.

Her eyes opened in shock.

An echoing thunderous crack ripped from her right. Before she could process the sound, the flitter's front left grav field emitter, a thin round disk beneath the vehicle, exploded with a loud pop. The flitter dipped to the side as another emitter exploded. The entire left side of the vehicle dragged along the ground, causing sparks and shredding the side. Another crack sounded, and something struck the front of the flitter and ripped a hole through it. The entire vehicle fell to the ground with a thud, sliding a few more meters before grinding to a halt not far from Jia and her friends, smoke pouring from the front and bottom of the vehicle.

John groaned inside his car, his forehead bloodied from colliding with his control yoke.

Jia turned to her friends, hand gesturing toward the building. "Both of you inside. Now. It's not safe."

Imogen stuck out her bottom lip, but Chinara grabbed her arm and yanked her toward the club. Jia let out a sigh of relief. She had no idea what had just happened, but she'd gone from concerned about discharging a stun pistol to someone firing live ammunition.

Heavy footsteps sounded from Jia's right. She spun toward the source and saw a heavily muscled gray-haired man advancing toward her, wearing a dark brown duster, a huge four-barrel rifle in his hands. She'd never seen anything so absurd in her entire life.

Jia snapped up her pistol. "Drop the weapon right now, or I will stun you!"

Now that he was closer, she could make out more details. The man's smooth features didn't go with his gray hair. She'd been around of enough of her parents' high-society friends to recognize a de-aging treatment.

A light coating of stubble covered the bottom of his face, and if he wasn't a terrorist dirtbag, she might have considered him ruggedly handsome.

The man stared at her for a moment, his mouth curling into a lopsided smile. "Stay out of this, sweetheart. This is police business."

Jia scoffed. "You expect me to believe such an obvious lie? Put down the weapon now. I won't ask again."

The man pulled back his coat to reveal a badge clipped to his belt. "Like I said, police business. You could show a little gratitude. I did just save your life." He nodded at the disabled vehicle.

Jia shook her head. "He would have stopped. He was just trying to scare me."

She gestured to the now-unconscious John, who was slumped over his control yoke. "There's no way he would actually attempt to murder a detective, and if you're one of the patrol officers who was supposed to show up, you should have come earlier. And why are you out of uniform and carrying that ridiculous non-regulation weapon?"

The gray-haired man slung his rifle over his shoulder. "You're a detective?" He chuckled, thinking back to his conversation with the captain. "Oh, that explains it. I didn't realize you were a cop. I figured that little tiny gun was something you had bought to fight off muggers."

"This is a standard-issue stun pistol for the department," Jia lifted the weapon. She pointed to the badge clipped to the top of her dress. "And you didn't know I was a cop? What, you couldn't look this high?"

"Don't flatter yourself." The man's gaze dipped to her legs. "Okay, you can flatter yourself," his focus returned to her face, "but for the record, I wasn't expecting you to be in a dress. I just focused on the immediate threat of the man trying to flatten you. I take it you're Jia Lin."

He grinned. "Nice to meet you."

CHAPTER FIFTEEN

"Who are you?" Jia demanded. "You're not with my enforcement zone. I don't recognize you."

"That's because I just started working tonight. Detective Erik Blackwell, Enforcement Zone 122." The gray-haired cop strolled over to the flitter. He opened the door, and John fell out with a groan.

The cop knelt and pulled out a bright white strip from a pocket, a binding tie. He set his rifle down and shoved John's wrists together before slapping the tie down. It grew in an instant and wrapped around the drunk's wrists.

Jia let out a strangled laugh. "You're in my enforcement zone?"

"Yes. Like I said, I just started." Erik tapped his PNIU. "This is Detective Erik Blackwell requesting an ambulance for…" He glanced at the downed Cyrus. "Two suspects with minor injuries. Send along a patrol car, too. The primary situation's been handled, but there's some cleanup for them to do." He looked back at her with a slight grin. "You're lucky I showed up when I did."

"Listen, Detective Blackwell," Jia began. "I don't know what or where you transferred from, but what you did was totally unacceptable."

Erik shook his head. "Local department regulations clearly state that all officers are allowed to discharge weapons, up to and including lethal discharge, in defense of any imminent threats to the lives of themselves, other officers, or citizens. I'd say getting plowed into by a drunk definitely counts as an imminent threat."

He grabbed his rifle and stared down at the unconscious John before moving over to Cyrus and slapping on a binding tie on the downed man.

She pointed around them. "You could have killed someone," Jia suggested.

"Could have? Sure, but I didn't, now did I?" Erik walked back toward her. "Trust me. I wasn't using armor-piercing bullets. I knew if I hit the emitters or the main vehicle body, the bullets wouldn't go anywhere else. I've taken down a vehicle or fifty in my time."

Jia scoffed. "You hit those things because you got lucky."

"Luck?" Erik shook his head and patted his gun. "You know what this is?"

Jia shrugged. "Overkill? A symbol of your enormous ego? A desire to produce something you believe flatters you?" Her eyes glanced down, an unflattering smile on her face as she eyed him back. "Should I go on?"

Erik snickered. "I like that, but no. It's a TR-7 Quad. Four selectable barrels." He stroked the weapon like a pet. "If I wanted to kill someone, I would flip this to four-barrel mode and open up, draining the mags in seconds. The bullets would have shredded that car like it was a leaf in a tornado." He nodded at the vehicle. "Or I could have just fired several times into the driver. Instead, I took out the emitters and engine to ground the vehicle." He grunted. "Not even the fool who was trying to kill you will die. No, trust me, I'm a big believer in luck, but this time, Lady Luck was nowhere around." He patted his chest. "This was all me."

Jia tucked her stun pistol back into her purse. "I pity your new partner."

Erik barked a loud laugh. "I think they might be surprised."

"Of course." Jia folded her arms again and frowned, looking at him up and down. "You can't just... Where did you transfer from?"

Erik's raised an eyebrow. "Ever heard of the Obsidian Detective Act?"

Jia shook her head. "No, that's... No one has used that law in decades."

"It's still on the books," Erik answered, looking around at a few of the club patrons who had come out to see the mess. "I took advantage of it."

"Oh, I see." Jia sighed. "What are you?" She looked him up and down another time. "Let me guess. You've probably done a few tours out on the frontier or border. However, you haven't figured out yet this is Neo SoCal, and we have standards and regulations that must be obeyed."

Erik looked back at her. "Just told you, so either your hearing is out or you feel it's unnecessary to listen to the words coming out of my mouth. I didn't violate a *single solitary regulation*."

Jia glanced between the unconscious men and the

damaged vehicle. What if Erik was right, and the man wasn't ready to stop or change direction?

She considered the facts. A man bound for a corporation like Ceres Galactic wouldn't murder a police officer in cold blood, but he had panicked and was driving a vehicle drunk in non-autonomous mode.

It might have been a mistake.

Maybe he didn't even realize he was driving toward her? But if that were the case, it only increased the chance that he might have run her over.

She pursed her lips, thinking. *Did he actually just save my life? He wouldn't have had time to use a remote kill, but still...*

Jia sighed. "I think you'll find that the detectives of Enforcement Zone 122 aren't the kind of people who are interested in public gun battles. Given what you just told me, I'm presuming you've been away from Earth for a while."

Sirens sounded in the distance.

Erik nodded. "You could say that." His head, then body pivoted like a turret toward the sirens. He spoke over his shoulder. "Oh, by the way, I'm your new partner."

"That's... Wait. *What?*" Jia blinked several times.

"Regulations state that if I want to work cases, I need a partner, and you need a partner for the same reason." Erik turned toward the entrance of the club in the distance. More patrons drawn by the gunfire milled about, murmuring to themselves and pointing toward the smoking flitter.

Jia shook her head. "I have not been told anything about a new partner. I'm currently..." She cleared her throat. "I think the captain would have told me about a new partner."

The sirens grew louder. Red and blue lights flashed above a platform across the way. A white ambulance trailed by a police flitter closed on the platform.

Erik gestured to the downed John. "I can handle them. If you don't believe me, go ahead and call the captain. We should probably chat after all of this, but I want you to understand your position, so we're all proceeding from the same place, Jia. Can I call you Jia? I should have asked before."

"I suppose." Jia shook her head, her thoughts a jumble. "Thanks for handling them." She thought for a moment and appended, "and thanks for saving my life."

The entire situation was beyond surreal to her.

Time flowed together for a moment as the police flitter touched down near John's vehicle, followed by the ambulance. Erik waved them down, and the uniformed officer exited his vehicle, a look of confusion on his face as Erik gestured to his badge and then the two downed suspects.

Jia took a step backward. She turned away from Erik and the crime scene to call Captain Monahan.

"I've been waiting for your call," the captain answered, his tone unusually cheerful.

"Is this Erik Blackwell my new partner?" Jia got straight to the point, her eyes flitting over to the man. "He seems under that impression pretty strongly."

"Of course, he's your new partner," the captain replied. "I thought you would have been happy. It means you're off fine verification duty and you can get back to working cases. Appropriate cases, but still."

Jia pinched the bridge of her nose. "Did he actually get in using the Obsidian Detective Act, or is that all a big joke? Every time this man talks, I feel like he's purposely saying things just to confuse me."

Captain Monahan didn't answer for several seconds. "Yes. He's a highly decorated soldier, but he's made it very clear to me that his interest now is in being a police officer and helping maintain order in the metroplex. From what he told me, I don't think he wants a lot of emphasis placed on his military background, despite how he got in."

"Sir, you can't seriously think this is a good idea?" Jia complained.

"Why not? Because he didn't work his way up? You didn't either."

"It's not that same thing," Jia countered.

"And why is that?" the captain replied, his tone filled with challenge.

"Because I'm not an out-of-control maniac who discharged his firearm near a club filled with civilians. You should see the thing. It's some four-barreled monstrosity."

"Erik's using a TR-7 Quad?" Captain Monahan responded. He sounded impressed.

Jia groaned. "Yes, but the point is, he fired that thing at a flitter."

"*What?*" the captain shouted. "Okay. Why don't you explain exactly what happened?"

JIA FINISHED RELATING the circumstances surrounding Erik's summary execution of John's vehicle.

Captain Monahan grunted. "I'm not saying what he did

was optimal, but given the situation, he might not have had a choice."

"I don't know if I can work with a man like that." Jia glanced at Erik, who was chatting with the patrol officer.

The EMTs had both suspects on hoverstretchers. They'd severed the binding ties and were floating the unconscious men into the back of the ambulance.

"I understand Erik might be a little rough around the edges," Captain Monahan agreed. "He's been offworld for a while, and the frontier and border are rougher places. But he's *earned* his right to be a detective, and I think you're the perfect person to help him adjust to how we do things in Neo SoCal. I'm counting on you, Detective Lin."

He's barely called me Jia the entire I've been on the force, but the manic is called by his first name?

"Sir." Jia sighed. "What if I can't keep him in check?"

"I'm sure you can convince Erik to do things our way," the captain answered. "You know the regulations probably better than anyone in the enforcement zone, and you're a dedicated cop. Even when I've been pissed at you," she heard his chair squeak, "I've always admitted that, and I think this is a good way for me to leverage you as a resource. It's also a good way to help the department after driving off two detectives. You owe me, and you owe the department."

"I understand." Jia shook her head. She wanted to pretend it was all a dream, but every detail was too real.

"Good." The uncharacteristic cheerfulness remained in the captain's voice. "We'll talk soon. Spend some time getting to know your new partner." The call ended abruptly.

"Damn." Jia stared at the ground for a moment, taking slow, even breaths. She didn't have to be an expert on management or human psychology to see through the captain's plan.

She shook her head. No, she wouldn't succumb. Rather, she would rise to the challenge.

She would whip Erik into shape, and they could go solve cases.

The man might be a trigger-happy maniac, but he obviously had a more direct attitude toward engaging with criminality than her last two partners.

That could be something to take advantage of, provided he didn't end up killing someone.

Erik finished chatting with the patrol officer and walked over to Jia. "Get everything figured out?"

"Yes." Jia forced a smile and extended a hand. "Partners?"

He shook her hand. "Partners."

Jia pointed toward the burgeoning crowd. "I need to go say goodbye to a few of my friends. After what they saw and dealt with tonight, they deserve a face-to-face apology. The captain suggested we get to know each other, and since my friends drove me here tonight, I might as well head off with you after I check in with them."

Erik offered her another smile. She couldn't figure out if she found it annoying or...*annoying*.

"I've got nothing better to do." Erik had slipped his weapon inside his coat somewhere. "Go find your friends, and we'll go for a ride."

CHAPTER SIXTEEN

Erik smiled to himself as his MX 60 rose from the parking lot and entered a nearby air lane.

Jia had given him her address, and chatting with her on the way home would be a good opportunity to get to know her better.

Whatever else happened, she was his first partner and his entry to the department. There was just one minor problem. His gaze flicked to the side, catching sight of the legs that wouldn't quit. He forced his eyes forward.

I wish I could have met her when she wasn't wearing a distracting dress.

Fortunately, the necessity of concentrating on flying kept his eyes off the tight red dress. He wasn't one to mix business and pleasure.

Jia stared out the window with a slight frown, silent. A couple of minutes passed before she offered, "It's kind of a waste to have this advanced and expensive vehicle and not use the autonomous mode, you know, especially in a place with such complicated traffic."

Erik chuckled. "You think so? I feel the opposite. In the Army, most of our vehicles were selected for durability rather than handling. They aren't as fun to drive or fly, and the driving was straightforward most of the time."

Jia gestured to a line of flitters. "This is fun for you?"

"Yeah. It is." Erik shrugged. "And not going autonomous might just be a habit after all those years in military convoys and missions. You don't want to use a lot of autonomous control when you might be in a fight. You need to have an instant understanding of your vehicle's situation the minute anyone starts shooting." He grimaced. "And that's doubly so for a vehicle filled with other soldiers."

"How long were you out there?" Jia asked. "It feels from your comments like it was a long time."

"You mean, how long was I out on the frontier?"

"Yes." Jia turned to look at Erik. "After that little stunt earlier, I'm convinced you've forgotten that this is Earth. It's not some frontier world full of anarchy and insurrectionists. This is a planet where order and stability have proven that humanity can be something more than the savages who defined our history. We don't need to resolve conflicts with military-grade rifles."

Her gaze cut to her feet. A hidden panel there led to where Erik had stashed the gun. She was placing her feet on four barrels of destruction. With her luck, he was going to bump someone and it would go off, taking her feet with it.

Erik burst out laughing. He calmed down after a few seconds once he realized Jia wasn't laughing. She frowned and folded her arms over her chest.

"You think Earth is a place of stability and order?" Erik changed vertical lanes, joining a long line of flitters heading away from the dense commercial zone toward a small forest of residential towers.

"Of course," Jia agreed. "Crime is much lower here than on any other planet, even Mars. Corruption has all but been wiped out. We have order and stability unprecedented in all of human history."

"It's easy to say crime is lower when you ship off everyone who sneezes the wrong way. That's not solving the problem. That's just making it someone else's problem." Erik changed lanes.

His gaze shifted between his front window, the cameras, and the lidar display. A rainbow of vehicles flew around him in the maze of lanes, the occasional floating signal or drone breaking up the flow of traffic.

"Crime's been all but wiped out, but random drunks can run down cops?" Erik snickered. "That's order and stability? I've been on a lot of frontier colonies that are safer than that."

"That...wasn't what it looked like." Jia swallowed, uncertainty playing across her face. "It couldn't have been. He was drunk, and it was a mistake. No one with his kind of background would do something so awful on purpose."

"So if he ran you down, it would have been okay because it was a mistake?" He smoothly moved up one lane. "That's an interesting take."

"That's not what I'm saying," Jia insisted. Her hands curled into fists. "Things just got out of control. I was trying to not begin a gun battle. Innocent people could have been hurt. Even stunning someone means they could fall and seriously injure themselves."

"But a battle requires the other guy to have a gun too," Erik suggested. "And this is why you have to be careful. If you're so concerned about things escalating, always remember '*Si vis pacem, para bellum.*'"

"If you want peace, prepare for war," Jia translated. She sounded surprised. "You're an educated man?"

Erik tossed her a sideways glance. "I spent many years as an officer. Education is part of that, even if I didn't receive fancy instruction at an Earth university. I know a lot more than you might think."

"Perhaps, but your education was focused on war, not law enforcement. Police officers are peacekeepers, not soldiers," Jia explained. "If we start thinking of ourselves as soldiers, it'll contribute to a harsher environment."

"Maybe." Erik shrugged. "But if you're worried about saving yourself and others, that means sometimes you'll have to take the risk of hurting people. If you had a chance to take that guy out before he got to his vehicle, you should have. Then you would never have ended up being required to make the more difficult choice."

Jia sighed, thinking back to her moment of indecision. "I might not approve of your methods, but I do want to be clear that I'm grateful. I could have been seriously injured, if not killed."

"Yeah, nothing nanobots can do when you're dead. You're my partner, and I'd be a pretty awful partner if I let you get killed my first night on the job."

They lapsed into silence, the light hum of the electronics of the MX 60 the only sound. The soundproofing of the vehicle kept almost all outside noise from contaminating the inside. That, combined with the smooth ride, would make it easy for a baby to sleep in the vehicle.

Jia sat quietly for a while, lost in thought. "How long did you serve? You never answered my question about how long you were on the frontier, and I get that you didn't spend your entire career there, but I'm curious."

"Thirty years." Erik turned at an intersection signal. "And yes, I wasn't always stationed on the newer colonies. I've been all over UTC space. Core worlds, frontier worlds, border worlds. Whenever the UTC needed me. Of course, they tend to need Expeditionary Corps farther away from the core, and I volunteered a lot. I didn't have to spend so much time out there, but I wanted to do my part."

Jia thought for a moment. "I admire your sense of duty, but I have a hard time imagining leaving Neo SoCal, let alone Earth." Her dark eyes looked troubled for a moment. "And you did it for longer than I've been alive."

"Some people are just suited for it."

"I'm not all that familiar with the military," Jia admitted. "You were some sort of intelligence operative or military police? Something like that, then? I assume that's why you want to be a police officer now, rather than going into security or a local garrison."

Erik laughed, his eyes roaming through the readouts the vehicle provided. "Not at all. I spent almost the entirety of my career in assault infantry in the Expeditionary Corps. I started as a private, later got a commission, and then worked my way up. I turned down a few promotions to keep myself in the field, and I resisted getting transferred away from being a ground-pounder."

"Wait." Jia frowned. "You're saying you have zero practical experience in law enforcement or investigation?"

"Depends on how you look at it." Erik grinned. "I studied what I needed on my way back, and it was a long trip, plus we are trained to find issues and make decisions quickly in the field from very small to very large datasets. Very similar to investigating." He paused for a moment before adding, "In a very compressed timeframe."

"But..." Jia sighed. "You...investigation... Ugh." She rubbed her temples. "Again, I am grateful for what you did, but I should note that, in general, we can't solve our problems by shooting them, and we shouldn't. This city isn't a battlefield."

"Sure, we can't solve *all* our problems by shooting something," Erik suggested. "But we can solve a lot of them."

She ignored that comment. "And that gun can't be legal. We're police. We have to enforce the laws, not violate them."

"I applied for a special waiver," Erik explained. "It takes about a half a year to fully process, but fortunately, I made sure to apply a while back, and it was a long trip here. If you look into my paperwork, you'll find my TR-7 is all nice and legal, including concealing it."

Jia stared at him, her mouth open, not saying anything for several seconds. "You actually managed to get a waiver to carry that *thing* around?"

"It turns out that being a combat arms Army veteran is useful for something other than just being a cop." Erik chuckled.

Jia rolled her eyes. "That's just absurd. Shouldn't you use a stun pistol?"

"A stun pistol won't stop a man about to run a detective over with a flitter." Erik shrugged. "Sometimes you need to shred something with a few high-velocity rounds to make your point. Don't worry." He pulled back his duster to reveal a shoulder holster. "I've got this baby, too. I get that you don't always need the TR-7."

Jia eyed it, unimpressed. "I'm guessing that's not a stun pistol," she muttered.

"Nope. I'm sure some people will be stunned after getting shot with it, but that's not the point."

"What about departmental regulations?" Jia complained as he closed the duster. "Don't you have to at least carry a stun pistol?"

Erik dropped the MX 60 one lane. "You haven't read the regulations relating to personal firearms in a while, have you?"

"I can't say that I have, but I'm sure they don't say, 'It's okay to have a huge rifle that takes down vehicles,'" Jia insisted.

"I spent a long time reading the exact regulations. The TR-7's very important to me. It has a lot of sentimental value." Erik offered her a quick grin. "And no, the regs don't say that, but they do say that as long as you have a valid general use permit for the relevant weapon, it can be kept as a backup weapon. My pistol is well within the departmental requirements. There is nothing in the regs that specifies you *have* to carry a stun pistol. It just happens that most cops do in Neo SoCal."

Jia scoffed. "They didn't think they would need to

specify that. I will remind you again that this is Neo SoCal and not some insurrectionist stronghold."

"Didn't I just say Neo SoCal?" Erik wondered aloud. "I'm pretty sure I did. However, to your point, if this was an insurrectionist stronghold, I'd be carrying a lot more explosives." He furrowed his brow. "It wouldn't hurt to have a few."

"Explosives?" Jia turned, her mouth opening and closing a couple of times. "You can't be serious. This isn't a war zone."

Erik glanced behind them. "I know that. If it were, I would have taken out the driver as he was getting into his vehicle."

Jia pointed to him. "And as for your insistence that your gun is acceptable, you're going against the spirit of the regulation. It's clearly *not* intended to mean a detective should carry around something like your monstrosity."

Erik shook his head. "I spent thirty years in the military." He glanced to his left. "You think you know about regulations? Cop regulations talk about what you can do on the job. *Military* regulations tell you what to do in your whole life." He glanced her way. "And let me tell you something, Jia. It took me a long time to learn this lesson, but the only way to do your best in any organization is to sometimes bend the regulations. The *spirit* of a regulation is always open to interpretation."

"I don't... I can't..." Jia rubbed some more. "I'm not going to allow you to break regulations while you're my partner. Let me make that clear."

"Oh, a challenge. I like it. You do what you want, and I'll do what I want. For now, we're partners, and that means I intend to have your back. And I'll be blunt with you. I've put a lot of time and effort into becoming a cop, even with the Obsidian Detective Act." Erik let his smile fade. "I'm pretty sure the captain assigned me to you because he wants to get rid of me."

"How ironic." Jia scoffed. "I suppose you must have your reasons for wanting to be a police officer after thirty years in the military."

"Oh? Not going to give me a big speech about how bored I'll be? That was what the captain did. I think he only laid off because he got a call about you and the drunks."

"It's not my place to run you off." Jia returned to looking out the window. "And besides, I need you. I might as well be honest about it as well. It's not as if it's some big secret in the enforcement zone. If we're going to be working together, we don't have to like each other, but we should try not to lie to each other."

"Fair enough," Erik offered. "I wasn't some shadow-dancer chair ranger playing in intel. I was assault infantry. Tip of the spear. We are...*were* straightforward."

Jia grimaced. "You could be a little less assault infantry. I wouldn't mind." She shrugged. "Not that I have a choice."

Erik nodded. "Because you can't work cases without a partner."

Jia scoffed quietly. "So you *do* know all about that."

"Yeah. The captain mentioned it, but he didn't go into the details." Erik grunted. "What happened to your last partner? You choke when you needed to fire? I can work around that, but I need to know what I'm dealing with so I can prepare."

Jia jerked her head back around. "Excuse me?" She

pointed to herself. "I haven't lost any partners because they were hurt. For that matter, the department and enforcement zone haven't lost anyone to anything other than freak accidents in a long time."

Erik shrugged. "Just checking. In the parking lot, you were acting like you'd never fired a gun at anyone before. I get the problem. It's hard to take a person who has grown up in a place where they have known nothing but peace and train them to shoot someone else, but the point isn't to make it easy. The idea is that they can shoot when and if necessary."

"I..." Jia looked around. "I have very good scores at the range."

"You just got done talking about honesty." Erik grunted and glanced her way for a moment. "Have you actually fired your weapon at someone before? I'm not asking if you've killed them, just if you've ever shot someone, even with that little toy."

"No," Jia murmured. "I haven't," she added, her voice louder. "This is the first time in a long time I've even had to draw my weapon. I keep trying to tell you, this is Earth. And not just Earth, but Neo SoCal. We don't *have* the kind of problems you were used to dealing with as a soldier. That level of violence isn't necessary."

"That's true," Erik replied with a smirk. "Usually, the guys I was dealing with just shot at me rather than trying to run me over." His smirk shifted to a frown. "And you're a cop. You should always keep in mind that people will kill given enough reason, even if it's just because they want what the other person has."

"On the frontier," Jia assured him. "Not here. Not Earth."

Erik jerked the control yoke, the MX 60 turning sharply.

"Careful," Jia admonished. "It'd be very embarrassing for the enforcement zone if one of our detectives got a ticket."

"If that's the worst thing you're worried about," Erik chuckled, "we're doing okay."

CHAPTER SEVENTEEN

Erik narrowed his eyes as Biyu jogged out of the mine entrance, several of the other Knights trailing behind her, their weapons at the ready.

Wait. Something's wrong.

"I don't know, sir," she transmitted. "The whole thing seems like a waste of time if you ask me. What are we even doing here looking for some lost auditor? And terrorists? How are terrorists going to end up on Mu Arae?"

It's not the same.

Erik surveyed the area. It was all too familiar, even if he hadn't been there for a year: the dusty surface of Molino, the huge Quijote looming in the sky. The exoskeleton-wearing soldiers of the 108th surrounded him, no hurry in their movements.

A loud roar cut through the air.

"Incoming!" screamed Biyu. She jerked back a moment later, collapsing to the ground, a massive hole in her chest. Explosions knocked several other soldiers down.

Erik gritted his teeth as his soldiers fell to enemy fire.

That's not how it happened. This isn't real.

His eyes shot open and he sat up, taking deep breaths, his body bathed in sweat.

It's just a damned nightmare.

Erik threw off his blankets and rolled out of bed. Differences in his memories or dreams didn't matter. None of that changed the fact that his unit had been wiped out, and forty-nine men and women, good soldiers, had died.

What am I really here for? He pulled his sheets tight, tucking in the corners, and reached for his top cover. *Justice? Revenge? What is the difference, and if there is one, should I care?*

He finished making his bed and stepped into his bathroom. After he waved a hand over the sink, the water started to flow. He splashed some water on his face and looked up, staring at himself in the mirror.

The de-aging could take away wrinkles, but it didn't do anything for the scars on his soul. Could that be why his hair remained the same? As a reminder that some things, you shouldn't forget?

Erik waved his hand again to stop the water. He'd made it to Earth. On some of his darker days in the last year, he hadn't been sure he would.

There were a small number of people who had first-hand knowledge of what had happened on Mu Arae, and it would be easy to make them disappear, especially on a trip between frontier planets.

But the expected knife in his sleep had never come. Whether that represented arrogance, contempt, or fear on the part of the people responsible for the massacre remained unclear.

Staring at himself, he considered the implications. *Someone had to get those bastards there in the first place, whether it was someone in the UTC government, Xingguan, or someone else entirely. Maybe another corp?*

Erik thought about it for a moment or two longer. *Is there a huge advantage to controlling Mu Arae? What am I missing?*

He walked out of the bathroom and sat on the edge of the bed, taking several deep breaths. As he sat there, he thought about it rationally.

This entire plan of his was insane.

He had flown across the entire UTC, fifty light-years, with the barest scraps passing for clues.

Some suspicious time-encoded messages had been sent from Neo SoCal to Mu Arae, but that only gave him a location to investigate: a metroplex covering a vast area, filled with over a hundred million people.

He let out a slight chuckle. A one-in-a-hundred-million chance was far better than one in billions. He didn't need to scour every system in UTC, or even every country on Earth.

A tiny hope was better than none.

Erik lay back on his bed, thinking about Jia's insistence that Earth was a near-perfect place with only a few small pockets of darkness. He grunted. He hadn't believed that for a long time, and the year he had spent traveling back from the edge of UTC space had only hardened him.

Earth isn't a shining beacon in a universe of darkness. It's just a nice, juicy-looking fruit that has a rotten, worm-infested core.

Erik sipped coffee at his new desk in the office he shared with Jia. She was taking care of some errand on the orders of the captain.

He was content to wait for her return.

Although he had no problems performing police work, he'd taken the position to get access to police resources to help with his personal investigation.

It would take him some time to familiarize himself enough with the area and the enforcement zone before he could start pushing some of those resources toward investigating Mu Arae and the messages.

There was a knock on the door.

"Yeah, come in," Erik called.

The door slid open and a dark-skinned man with a shaved head stepped through. His suit suggested another detective, but Erik could only recognize a few people on sight, given it was the morning of his second day on the job.

The detective walked over and extended his hand over the desk. "Welcome to the 1-2-2, Detective Blackwell," the man offered, his voice a rich, deep bass.

Erik stood and shook the man's hand. He had a few inches on his visitor. The other detective had a firm shake.

"Captain Monahan said he was going to introduce me to everyone later," Erik explained. He took a seat and then nodded toward the open chair in front of his desk. "So I'm clueless about who you are. Sorry."

"Halil Mustafa," the other detective related, sliding himself into the chair before continuing. "I've been at the

1-2-2 my entire career. I started out as a patrol officer and made detective five years ago." He offered Erik a broad grin. "But look at you, coming in here straight up as a detective."

Erik shrugged. "Yeah, I did." He smiled. "Let's cut the crap. I need to know where I stand because I don't have time for games. Do you have a problem with how I came in? I don't care if you do, I just need to know."

Halil shook his head, a faint smile lingering on his face. "Nothing like that. I heard you did thirty years in the UTC Army Expeditionary Corps. You obviously got enough bonuses to buy a de-aging treatment, too, so you must have been in the real trouble spots. I've got great respect for that, Detective Blackwell."

"Call me Erik or Blackwell. No reason to use titles when we're both detectives."

Halil nodded. "All right, Erik. Your choice. As I was saying, it's one thing if someone comes in here and they've got no real experience at life and manages to find a way through. That means they don't understand the importance of everything around them or the traditions."

Erik nodded slowly.

Something about the smooth tone of the other detective's voice made Erik suspect this conversation might end in an unpleasant manner, but he couldn't afford to alienate everyone at the station.

The captain had been remarkably blasé about his discharge of the TR-7, only warning him to ensure that "no significant collateral damage occurred." Erik presumed this was because the captain saw him as a way of running off Jia. He still wasn't certain of the history there.

"I respect tradition," Erik replied. "I've got my own way of doing things, sure, but I'm here to do a job, first and foremost."

Halil scratched his eyebrow. "Yes, the thing is, you fought for the UTC. You were wounded for the UTC. You understand what it is to be a leader in a difficult environment. You're not some little corporate prince who wormed his way in here to tell everyone how to be a better cop."

Erik shrugged. "I'm a guy who spent far too long away from home."

"Here's the thing." Halil looked over his shoulder toward the door before leaning forward. He lowered his voice. "Your new partner, Lin? She didn't do what I did. She didn't put in her time. She pulled something like you did, straight to detective, but it wasn't because she's a veteran who fought insurrectionists. She's only twenty-four, so she's not that long out of college. She was twenty-three when she joined." He snorted in disgust.

"I read about the direct promotion programs for people with certain educational backgrounds." Erik picked up his cup and took another sip of coffee.

Halil scowled. "She's a corp princess, Erik. Both Mommy and Daddy Lin are bigshots. She shouldn't even be a cop. She should be off doing something like that, but she comes in here and decides to be a detective."

"Are you saying she did something wrong to get in? Pull strings? And if she did, do you have proof of that?"

Halil's mouth quirked into a tight smile. "All right, all right, I get it. You've got your new partner, and you're feeling defensive. Plus, I also get that she's nice to look at when she's cleaned up, and no, I'm not saying she did anything wrong. Not that I can prove, anyway, but come on! You think they didn't take her background into account when they hired her?"

Erik nodded. "Of course, they did."

Halil snapped his fingers and pointed. "Smart man. That's all I'm saying, and the problem with her coming in here like that is that she doesn't understand sacrifice and camaraderie the way a military man like you does, and that makes waves throughout the entire enforcement zone." He sighed. "I'm not saying she doesn't genuinely care about being a cop. God knows she has that in spades, but it's not just about wanting to be something. It's about under-standing."

Erik swished the coffee around his mouth, not sure if it was acceptable or not yet. "And what does she not understand?"

Halil nodded, a satisfied look on his face. "That there's a time and place for certain types of effort, and that there's a status quo that needs to be maintained. You're a military man. You understand staying in your lane."

Erik chuckled. "Yeah, I heard that more than a few times during my time in the service. That's her problem? She doesn't stay in her lane?"

"That's a big part of it. Yeah." Halil sighed. "You know what we call her?"

"No idea," Erik admitted.

Halil grinned. "The Black Widow."

Erik swallowed another sip. *Yup, coffee quality was obtuse, no verdict yet.* "She said she hasn't gotten any part-ners hurt," he replied.

"Sure. That's true. Not physically." Halil scoffed. "But

her last two partners both resigned before putting in their time for a pension, and one was only a few years away. She's been here a year, and she's driven off two good cops because she thinks she's better than all of us and knows how to do our jobs better. She won't listen to the captain when he tells her to back off cases that aren't going anywhere. She gets obsessed. She won't let go."

Erik thought for a moment, allowing a note of curiosity to seep into his voice. "Isn't a little determination good for a cop?"

Halil leaned back. "Yes, if they have something real to follow, but she thinks every case that comes in is some big grand chance to prove herself." Halil shook his head. "If she dialed it down, she might be okay."

"Maybe she should head down to the Shadow Zone and poke her nose around," Erik suggested.

Halil tensed and his eyes narrowed slightly. "The 1-2-2 doesn't concern itself with the Shadow Zone. The department has a kind of unofficial policy on them."

"If they stay in their lane, we'll stay in ours?" Erik asked.

"About like that. It's not something we worry about since Shadow Zone complaints would not come to the 1-2-2. Let other specialized enforcement zones worry about them."

Erik chuckled. "It doesn't bother you that some huge spot of trouble," he pointed down, "is sitting underneath us?"

"Huge? It's not like that." Halil offered a tight grin. "Come on, Erik. I'm sure when you were beating down insurrectionists, sometimes you had to leave a few pockets of troublemakers in place because it wasn't worth the trouble."

"Winning a battle might cost you the war. Is that what you're saying?"

"Definitely a smart man," Halil agreed.

Erik leaned back, adopting his laziest lopsided smile. "I'm surprised Jia's not interested in going down there."

"It's one of the few times she's been smart. Even she seems to understand the Shadow Zone isn't for us to handle." Halil shrugged. "And it's not like anyone's going to stress it to her. She's annoying enough."

"Because she wants to push on too many cases?" Erik offered.

"Yes, but those are cases that aren't our business to solve, if they are even real. Someone sneezes, and Lin thinks there are insurrectionist cells with Zitark tech ready to appear." Halil pointed to Erik. "She's been benched doing busywork, but now that she's got a partner, she's going to start pushing again. That means she's going to be screeching in your ear to go waste time investigating her paranoid excuse of the week. You don't have to get taken down by her. I know the captain's worried about booting her because of her family connections, but it's not like he can complain if she quits, am I right?"

Erik eyed his coffee, thinking. *So the question is whether Monahan is trying to get me to quit by sticking me with Jia, or to get Jia to quit by sticking her with me.*

The smart and political play would have been to smile and nod along, perhaps offer some non-committal statement that could be interpreted as agreement. One of the reasons Erik had preferred serving on the frontier was, the level of political crap was much, much lower.

There was only so much obsequious maneuvering that anyone could accomplish or worry about when they were sitting in a habitation dome light-years away from anything approaching advanced civilization. That experience and reality might have been responsible for what he said next.

Erik looked at his visitor. "Give me a break."

Halil blinked. "Excuse me?"

"I don't know all that's going on here in this enforcement zone, but I don't care." Erik pointed to his shoulder holster. "Jia says I've been out on the frontier for too long. That I've forgotten what it means to on a civilized planet." He offered a feral grin to Halil. "And I think she's right."

Halil frowned. "What the hell is that supposed to mean, Erik?"

"When I served, I knew that every man and women in my unit had my back," Erik replied, his voice almost a snarl. "And I had theirs. It didn't matter if we didn't agree on politics or they came from some colony where people had crap taste in music and food. We put on the uniform, and we did the job. Do you know what we didn't do?"

"What?" Halil's nostrils flared.

"We didn't stab each other in the back over how we got there," Erik replied. He squashed the snarl in his voice and adopted a playful grin.

Halil laughed and shrugged. "I can't believe this. I'm trying to help you. You want to work with the Black Widow? You want to waste your time with some corp princess pretending to be a police officer?" He stood, his glare fixed on Erik. "That's your choice. I was just trying to offer you a little advice."

"I'll take it under consideration," Erik replied. "And, Halil, I want to make one thing clear."

"What's that?" the detective responded, his voice hard.

"Everything I said applies to you as well." Erik stood and loomed over the other man. He slapped his badge, which hung from his belt. "While I'm wearing this, you're my brother. You might be an annoying brother, but you're *still* my brother. Just like Jia's my annoying little sister. You want to squabble? Fine, but that's as far as I take it, and when we're outside of this building, I will always have your back, as I expect you to have mine. I don't care about office politics or corp princesses or who wants to retire with a pension. Am I clear?"

"Yes, crystal." Halil nodded slowly as he eyed Erik appraisingly. "And I can work with that, Erik. I know you think I'm a snake, but you'll understand soon enough, and you'll be grateful for me pointing it out." He headed toward the door. "Just don't let her you drag you down in the meantime."

Erik sank back into his seat and shook his head.

He took another swig of coffee. "If this is how perfect Earth is, no wonder someone screwed over my people." He swallowed, making a face. "This stuff is just one degree toward wrong."

CHAPTER EIGHTEEN

June 24, 2228, Neo Southern California Metroplex, Police Enforcement Zone 122 Station, Office of Detectives Jia Lin and Erik Blackwell

Jia strolled through the bullpen, annoyance lingering, tension knotting the muscles throughout her entire body.

Despite having a new partner, the captain *insisted* she finish her inspection of the group of traffic files she had been reviewing.

She had wasted several hours on something she shouldn't have been doing in the first place. She entered her office, frowning.

Erik sat at his desk, leaning back, his eyes darting from side to side. He was reading something projected directly onto his smart lenses.

He stopped and looked her way. "Welcome back. I was about to open a missing person case on you." His eyes flitted to the door and back to her. "Although given the way things work around here, it probably would have been immediately flagged as a cold case."

"Very funny." Jia walked around and took a seat at her desk. "When the captain gives me orders, I have to follow them. It's simple as that. You might suggest the occasional bending of regulations, and I might even allow that nonsense to influence me, but I don't want to engage in blatant insubordination. Part of being a police officer is upholding order," she eyed him, "not undermining it."

Erik didn't feel like she had much supporting her conviction behind that comment.

"Not complaining too much." Erik shrugged. "Halil stopped by this morning to chat with me, and about an hour ago, the captain introduced me to most of the squad. So I had things to keep me busy, but I have a feeling they expect me to sit around and memorize the layout of this building for a few weeks. I asked around about some of the cases, and everyone is either working on something very minor or finding excuses to pass things along."

Jia nodded. "That's fairly standard procedure here, unfortunately. I'm frustrated but not distraught, only because of how safe the metroplex is. It's not that I don't understand some of the captain's concerns, but I do wish we were a little more proactive."

"You mean you wish they would actually let you do your job?" Erik raised an eyebrow.

"That's one way to look at it," Jia commented. "What instructions has the captain given you?"

Erik shrugged. "He told me to familiarize myself with the station and the rest of the squad and await case assignment. Why?"

"Did he tell you there are any particular cases you shouldn't work?" Jia inquired.

"Nope. He said you could show me around and get me up to speed."

She eyed him for a moment, then Jia sighed, reaching up with her hands. "I…no, it's stupid, I can't do it." She rubbed her temples. "I'm twisting myself up with stupid ideas."

Erik raised an eyebrow. "What are we talking about?"

"There's a case the captain didn't want me to work. A fraud case." Jia looked at him. "I was about to suggest pursuing it with you as lead, but he's been rather explicit, and I'm not going to use you as a shield. That's not fair to you, and it violates the spirit of the captain's orders."

Erik leaned back in his chair. He linked his fingers and rested the back of his head against his hands. "You want to work a case?"

Jia waved a hand in the air. "I want to do something more useful than double-checking on traffic fines. It doesn't matter. The case has already been passed along. I thought there might be something, but it's probably too late."

Erik tapped his PNIU and gestured a few times. A form appeared in front of him, and he pointed to it. "Is it this case?"

Jia frowned, then got up and walked over to his desk. She leaned over to read the form. "No, this is new. It's fraud, yes, but it's not the case I was interested in. I don't recognize the person filing the complaint, this," she moved to get a closer view, "Todd Smythe."

Erik tapped a few text boxes. His PNIU auto-filled the information.

"Wait." Jia gestured to the form as she straightened. "You're taking the case? You can't do that. It needs to be assigned to you."

Erik shook his head. "According to departmental procedures, at least the ones I read on the way here, this isn't a formal investigation form. This," he pointed to the air, "is just a complaint form."

Jia eyed him. "Yes, but only patrol officers are supposed to follow up on complaints. Detectives aren't supposed to work them unless explicitly assigned."

"The regs don't say that." Erik smiled. "They *say* that standard procedure is for detectives to wait until a complaint is assigned as a formal case to work it, but there's no regulation forbidding it."

"Because you normally wouldn't... I don't think..." Jia's breath caught, and her eyes narrowed in thought. "You're saying it's actually not against regulations?"

Erik nodded. "There are also multiple regs about all police officers, regardless of rank and position, being required to investigate possible crimes to the best of their ability as they become aware of them." He swiped through the form, and it disappeared. "There's a saying in the military we were always fond of. 'It's better to ask for forgiveness than permission.' You might be less frustrated if you started operating that way."

"But I don't want to violate regulations," Jia pointed out. "I don't want to become what I'm fighting."

Erik stood and reached for his coat. "And you *won't* be violating any regulations." He settled the coat on his shoulders. "Didn't I make that clear? Everything we're doing is well within regs, and unless you're doing something more productive, we should investigate the case before it gets passed along."

Jia stared at the gray-haired man, unsure of what to say. She was half-convinced it was a trick, perhaps some sort of trap set by the captain.

She had spent a year being mostly deflected from doing her job, and a partner eager to work a case seemed too good to be true.

"I need to set some ground rules before we go anywhere." She cleared her throat. "What are the details of the case? I saw that it was fraud and the victim is Todd Smythe, but nothing else."

"This Smythe claims one of his accounts was billed fraudulently," Erik explained as he headed around her toward the door. "Nothing big. They didn't clean him out or anything."

"That's not the scope of case the 1-2-2 is supposed to handle." Jia sighed as she turned to follow him. "The captain's just going to send it along."

"We've already claimed it, and he hasn't told us not to investigate, so we're not going against his orders." Erik grinned and stopped at the door, facing her. "Are traffic fines what you're supposed to handle? Class IV fraud is more important than traffic fines."

"It's probably just some kid playing around with his dad's accounts." Jia furrowed her brow. "But if we let it slide..." She nodded as much as for herself as Erik. "We should do this." She shook her finger at him as she headed toward her desk to get her purse. "But no TR-7. Understood?" She grabbed her purse, sticking a protein bar inside.

You could never be sure a case wouldn't take too long, and you might go hungry.

"Sure, as long as it's not necessary." Erik opened the door, calling over his shoulder. "But we're taking my flitter."

JIA WAS DRESSED in a conservative suit, the opposite of Erik's carefully put together ensemble of...rugged off-the-rack?

She stood beside Erik in the living room of the victim, Todd Smythe.

The cavernous room was filled with holographic facsimiles of statues from all over the world, each scaled to fit in the area, including copies of Christ the Redeemer, David, and the Big Buddha of Taiwan. There was no flicker or ethereal glow around the images. The holographic emitters must have been hideously expensive.

The one touch lacking in the room was any paintings on the walls.

Smythe sat on his bright white couch, rubbing his wrist as his gaze cut between the two detectives. "I didn't expect actual detectives to come for this. I can't say that I'm displeased, but I am surprised."

Jia offered him a soft smile. "I can assure you the NSCPD doesn't take crime lightly, Mr. Smythe. Your complaint in the system was missing a few details, and we thought a personal visit would be best to ensure that the appropriate information was collected."

He nodded quickly with a frown. "The intake system was confusing. It wasn't clear where I should add more."

Erik poked the David statue. His finger disappeared into the holographic statue's chest, a halo forming around the point of contact. Smythe frowned but didn't say anything.

Jia kept her face passive, carefully not rolling her eyes.

"I'm going to record this for our," she looked at Erik before turning back to Smythe, "*my* report later." Jia tapped her PNIU to initiate recording. "Can you walk us through what happened?"

Smythe leaned back into his couch, his eyes unfocused. "It might seem petty to be concerned about a few missing credits here and there." He looked earnestly at them. "But I pride myself on not letting others take what's mine, and this company has done just that."

Jia nodded. "I see, and what has happened exactly?"

"My personal assistant asked about some shipping fees from earlier this month. He hadn't authorized them, and he wondered if I had." Smythe shook his head. "But I hadn't shipped anything. I was unfamiliar with the company, Windward."

Jia's heart rate kicked up, but she kept her face calm. "Windward?"

"Yes. I thought perhaps it was a mistake." Smythe shrugged. "My assistant called them initially, and they denied any knowledge of it, but then I called them, and they read off relevant ID and account numbers I don't share. I tried to argue it was a mistake, but they said their hands were tied unless I could produce proof of fraud. The representative actually had the gall to accuse me of trying to defraud them. As if." He scoffed, then shrugged and continued. "They kept giving me the runaround, so I filed my complaint."

"Are you sure your assistant didn't do it?" Jia asked.

"He didn't know the relevant account numbers, and I'm dubious he would steal from me and then turn around to inform me." Smythe paused for a moment. "To be frank, if he wanted to rob me, he has far easier ways to do it than routing minor amounts of money through a shipping company."

Jia nodded. "True enough. We just need to consider all possible angles."

Erik pointed to the couch. "How much did that cost?"

"Excuse me?" Smythe blinked.

"How much did that cost?" Erik repeated, this time slower, as if he were speaking to a child.

Jia frowned at him.

Smythe shrugged. "That piece cost me about fifty thousand credits."

Erik pursed his lips. "You spent fifty thousand credits on a couch?"

Smythe rolled his eyes as he ran his hand over the couch back. "It's not just a couch, detective. It's a Venusian export. It was handcrafted by artisans from Parvarti." He gestured at the matching chairs on either side. "Before you ask, those were ten thousand apiece." He smiled. "They really are quite lovely."

"And how much were the shipping fees Windward charged to your account?" Erik asked.

Smythe looked up for a second. "Well, in total, about one hundred credits." He lifted his chin. "If you're about to tell me that I'm wasting your time because it's a small amount, I'll have you know it's the *principle* of the thing. I can only afford fifty-thousand-credit couches because I don't let thieves take even a single credit from me."

Erik shrugged. "I was just curious. I'm not telling you that you were wrong to file a complaint. Do you have any enemies?"

"Enemies?" Smythe cocked his head to the side. "Not as such. I don't know anyone who would want to do me harm, and if they did, they wouldn't try to do it by charging a small number of credits falsely to my name. I don't know how Windward got my account information, but perhaps it's some sort of scam. I'll leave that," he waved a finger at Jia and Erik, "to you experts to figure out."

Jia nodded. "And we will look into it. We're going to need you to send us the invoices and any copies of relevant exchanges you've had with them."

"Ah, I would be happy to." He lifted a personal tablet. "Let me send a request." He looked at Jia. "Keep in mind, I don't even care if I get my money back. As I noted to your partner, it is the *principle* of the thing."

Jia smiled. "Thank you, Mr. Smythe. I assure you we take this matter quite seriously."

"Trust me." Erik smiled. "Just receiving a visit from two detectives will give Windward a hundred credits' worth of stomachache."

THIRTY MINUTES LATER, Jia and Erik had finished taking Smythe's statement and received copies of the relevant files. They sat in the MX 60 as they headed back to the station.

"Why did you ask him about the couch?" Jia asked. "Do you think this is a waste of time?"

"No." Erik shook his head. "I know on this glorious paradise, you probably think fraud's relatively rare, but a lot of deployed soldiers get targeted by account and identity fraud. If you're forward-deployed to the frontier, you're not exactly paying a lot of attention to your accounts, and the comm lag leaves a lot of opportunities for scummy people to take advantage of that, even if you're not that many light-years out. The first step is always—"

"An account probe," Jia offered. She narrowed her eyes. "But you can't make it too extreme, because the algorithms or the owner will notice."

Erik grinned. "Exactly."

"This isn't the first fraud complaint that has been leveled against Windward," Jia explained, excitement speeding her words up. "The captain passed another case along already, but maybe someone thought they could skim a few credits from a few wealthier people who wouldn't notice." Jia snorted. "*Greedy.*"

"Greed on paradise Earth?" Erik asked with mock innocence, then changed the vector of their flight to join another stream of traffic. "Shocking!"

"There's always a serpent in paradise tempting someone," Jia countered. "It's why it's so important for us to find the serpent before it can spread the corruption." She shook her head. "It's unfortunate that a small company is getting greedy, or someone is using them, but I'd like to point out it's not nearly as bad as insurrectionists or terrorists. We'll take care of this matter quickly, and that's why we will continue to have a safe metroplex and an orderly planet."

Erik chuckled. "Whatever you say, Jia."

Both of their PNIUs chimed with a message at the same time.

Jia brought it up. It was from Captain Monahan.

I want both of you in my office the second you get back.

CHAPTER NINETEEN

Erik managed not to grin as Captain Monahan glared at him and then Jia in turn.

"What are you two doing?" the captain barked, aiming a finger at a few holographic files hanging above his desk. "I just checked the case notes. You're investigating a Class IV fraud?" He turned to Jia. "You would probably do the metroplex more good reviewing traffic fines." He pointed at Erik. "And you're not supposed to accept cases. You're supposed to be *assigned* cases. I know you're new here, but that's no excuse."

"I haven't violated a single regulation." Erik shrugged. "If you can point me to one I have, I'll apologize. And are you really going to get pissed because we investigated a crime?"

The captain shrugged. "This should have been sent along. It's not our business."

"Sir, with all due respect, I disagree." Jia pointed to the notes he must have been reading. "It's Windward again, just like it was in the last case we sent along. One time can be ignored. Twice is a coincidence, but three times? It's like they're firing off a flare and telling us to investigate."

Captain Monahan aimed his stare at her. "You're really saying the police should get involved in billing disputes involving a few hundred credits?"

She didn't flinch. "The fraud I found earlier was far more extensive than a hundred credits."

"But no one has independently verified that yet," the captain sniffed, "so let's focus on the *current* case. How is that a good use of your time? It'll cost the taxpayers more to investigate it than it involves," he added.

"If we ignore minor crimes, they'll grow into bigger ones," Jia countered. "I know you are tired of hearing me argue the point, but that's the whole *principle* of preventative policing."

Erik watched silently as the two debated.

The captain growled, "Then we should send it along for review at a lower level, Lin. Maybe algorithmic back-checking later, and eventually a patrol officer. Not," the captain glanced at them, "two detectives." Captain Monahan frowned. "Is this why you joined the department, Erik? To investigate one-hundred-credit fraud cases?"

"I joined to investigate *crimes*," Erik answered. "It's not like I care about a rich guy losing what has to be a rounding error in his money, but if I'm going to be useful at all, I have to care."

Erik was more than familiar with the idea of superiors wanting people to stay in their lane and not create headaches. He also understood Earth's paradise was maintained by exporting or ignoring many of the troubles, but that didn't mean some truths didn't make their way out.

The journey to the truth of Mu Arae would begin with Todd Smythe and his hundred credits, whether this was the case that got him there or not.

"But," Erik added, "I still can't believe that idiot spent fifty thousand credits on a couch."

"Give me one good reason we should even bother with this?" Captain Monahan stabbed a finger on his desk. "Just *one*."

"It's a crime," Jia observed. "And it's our duty to investigate crimes. That's two."

Erik put up two fingers. "It's going to cost the taxpayers the same amount of money if we're sitting in our office scratching our bellies versus investigating. That's a total of three."

Captain Monahan's mouth twitched as he glanced at the two of them. "Two days. You have two days on this. After that, if it's nothing more than a billing dispute, we're kicking it along, and I'll have you both back in here to apologize for wasting time and department resources."

A huge smile appeared on Jia's face. "Thank you, sir. I won't let you down."

"*Dismissed*," he replied.

Jia immediately turned and headed out of the office, but Erik lingered, locking eyes with the glaring captain.

Captain Monahan spoke first. "I didn't expect this from you. I have a hard time believing you wanted to follow up thirty years of distinguished service by investigating petty crimes. The more you encourage Detective Lin this way, the less chance you'll have of doing anything important."

"It's the smallest detail that saves your unit," Erik replied. "A stray flash of light, a sound you're not expecting, even a smell." He turned toward the door. "Besides, you don't keep in practice without firing your weapon."

"Meaning what?" the captain snapped.

Erik stopped and looked outside before turning to look over his shoulder. "I'm not Lin, Captain. I don't believe in the myth of Earth's perfection, and I don't believe in looking the other way to help with that myth, even if that is *inconvenient.*"

Captain Monahan's face reddened and he stood slowly, his palms on his desk. "What are you accusing me of?"

"I'm not accusing you of anything. I'd say it to your face, Captain. I'm just saying something about *me.*" Erik turned fully around to face him. "If you want me out of here, go ahead and try to push me out. But then you'll have to explain why, and as you just got done pointing out, I'm a man with thirty distinguished years in the UTC Expeditionary Corps and a mountain of medals. I wonder how that would play out, especially if I made a lot of noise about it." He walked back over to the desk. "I've seen countless men and women die. I've killed more than my fair share. I've seen blood spilled for lifeless lumps of mud and dirt, lives expended as a resource line on some jacked-up game tactician's board just for short-term gain, and you know why I did all that?" He finished with an eyebrow raised.

The captain shrugged, lips tight.

"Because it was my *duty,*" Erik explained, his voice low and gravelly. "And right now, my duty is to investigate crime, including some rich idiot's missing hundred credits. The worst thing that happens is nothing. Like I said, I'm not Jia, and whatever you think you can do to intimidate me would have to be worse than the things I've already been through to even have a chance of working. Can you come up with something like that? Can you even imagine the kinds of things I've seen out there?"

Captain Monahan sat down and ran his hands through his hair. "You've got the wrong idea about me, Erik. I'm not what you think. I'm just trying to do my duty my own way," he finished.

"Maybe." Erik shrugged. "But I do know you're a guy who thought he could use me to scare off Jia."

"You're right," Captain Monahan looked up. "You're not like her. You do understand more, and I hope you understand that we need to keep things in balance here. That's part of the big picture, especially in a place like Neo SoCal."

"And a Class IV fraud is going to throw things out of balance?" Erik snickered. "You're so wrapped up in covering your own ass, it's probably all reflex at this point. I'm not even sure you know what you're doing."

"What I'm doing? I'm trying to do right by every man and woman in this enforcement zone," the captain shot back. "This isn't the military, and this isn't the frontier. There are more political considerations involved than there are in what happens out on the frontier."

Erik scoffed and headed toward the door. "You're just as naïve as Jia."

"What?" Captain Monahan frowned. "How can you say that?" he asked. Erik heard a real question, not just a soft rebuttal.

"Every battle I fought in was based on political considerations." Erik stepped through the door, his answer staying in the office. "Politics has been killing my brothers and sisters in arms my entire life."

JIA GLANCED at Erik as he poked a holographic ficus on his side of the chairs.

"Seriously?" Jia whispered with a tiny shake of her head.

The fake plant sat in the corner of the lobby of the Windward branch office responsible for the suspicious charges.

The detectives had explained to the overly cheerful receptionist, Svetlana, why they were there, and she had told them they would have to wait until a manager was available since she wasn't authorized to speak on behalf of the company in such matters.

Jia leaned closer to Erik. "Why are you poking everything?" Jia asked, her tone low as she pointed to the hologram. "Is it some sort of compulsion?" She paused, looking around before whispering, "Don't get me wrong, I can handle this better than you needing to kick in the door."

Erik glanced her way with a glint of humor in his eyes.

She eyed him. *He's smarter than I thought. A lot smarter. Why do I get the feeling he's putting up a false face?*

"It's just funny," he answered. "Out in the colonies, it's much rarer to see so many full holograms. People prefer actual paintings, plants, and statues rather than fakes made out of light. You would figure on the homeworld that they would prefer the same thing. It's ironic."

Jia looked from the hologram to Erik. "It's more convenient to have holograms for decorations. You don't have to maintain them."

"A fake luxury you can't touch." Erik grinned, looking

around the room. "That's too perfect." He shook his head as he turned back to look at the ficus.

"Too perfect for what?" she asked.

"As a metaphor." Erik cut through the hologram with his hand. "Everything's nice and shiny on the surface here, but there's no substance beneath it. It's all an illusion, just like Neo SoCal and Earth."

Jia eyed him. "Just because you ran across a minor fraud case during your first few days doesn't mean Earth is a cesspool of corruption." She waved a hand toward the buildings outside. "It's not as if insurrectionists are bombing the residential towers."

"We'll see." Erik turned to her, twitched his eyebrows, and gave her a smile. "This is just the first step."

"Right, the first step toward stopping anything that might lead to something serious," she answered. "You aren't going to goad me. This is the most civilized planet in the UTC, and your time on the frontier isn't going to color the reality."

"Your reality." He pointed to her, then himself. "Not mine. Believe it or not, you have to see what is real on the frontier, not what is shown you. Just because a person is on the frontier doesn't immediately make them slow or stupid, and when someone is trying to kill you, they come up with some uncannily intelligent ways to present a false reality." Erik glanced behind Jia.

The click-clack of footsteps interrupted their discussion. She turned her head to see who Erik was watching.

A man in a dark suit that probably cost more than one of Smythe's chairs approached, his angular face pinched in irritation. "Detectives, I'm Oscar Ramirez. It's my understanding that you're here about a billing dispute?" His tone suggested he didn't believe it.

"No." Jia stood and smoothed her suit jacket with her hands. She could hear Erik stand behind her. "We're here to investigate a possible fraud case."

Ramirez sighed and rolled his eyes. "Slander applies to the authorities as well as private citizens, Detective."

Jia scoffed. "Don't threaten me, Mr. Ramirez, and conduct of our duty is an affirmative defense."

Erik stepped up to the man, towering over him, although the intimidation might have been undercut by the slight grin on his face. Or perhaps that made it worse.

Jia wasn't sure.

"We just need to see a few of your records," Erik explained. "It'll take a few minutes, and then we can be out of your way."

Ramirez took a step back. "I'm afraid I can't do that."

"Can't or won't?" Erik kept his smile, but the tone carried an implicit threat.

Jia frowned as she glanced over to her partner.

Ramirez squared his shoulders. "Our receptionist didn't mention anything about a warrant." He gestured to the PNIU on his belt. "I'm prepared to receive any warrants you wish to transmit, Detective. Otherwise, I'm not interested in sharing anything with you. We won't be harassed because of a few disgruntled clients, and whatever you think is going on here doesn't matter. We were paid, and we made deliveries. It's what we do."

Jia brought up a copy of the complaint form. "Todd Smythe didn't hire you."

"Then we're victims as well." Ramirez adopted an oily

smile. "And I don't see why risking client privacy over some minor billing dispute is worth it. Even if it was some sort of fraud, it's a pittance. I'm surprised anyone would even be willing to go to the police over such a small amount." He picked off something from the shoulder of his jacket. "It's pathetic if you ask me."

"A crime is a crime," Jia pushed.

"Then go get a warrant, Detective." Ramirez waved a hand toward the front doors. "I'm not trying to be intransigent, but if we open our records every time someone has a billing dispute with us, our company will implode with frivolous requests and our overhead will skyrocket." He crossed his arms. "Our liability in such matters is limited."

Erik laughed. "For a shipping company, you don't know the relevant laws well."

"Excuse me, Detective?" Ramirez frowned.

"AISA," Erik offered.

Jia glanced at Erik, her eyes wide with shock.

"I don't understand," Ramirez replied.

"The Anti-Insurrection Supply Act." Jia turned back to the man, her face now composed. "Your company could be held potentially liable for the transport of contraband even if you weren't aware that it was contraband when it was accepted." She smiled. "The law's *very* clear."

"Insurrectionist supply?" Ramirez's voice raised. "That's absurd."

"It doesn't only apply to insurrectionists," Jia clarified. "It also includes any UTC-prohibited contraband."

Ramirez threw up a hand in disgust. "This is a feeble attempt to intimidate me. I've never heard anything so ridiculous. We don't *deal*," his voice almost cracked, "in contraband."

Erik stepped forward, this time looming over the man with a dark scowl without the grin. "How would you know? You're so sloppy by your own admission that people might be using stolen information and accounts to ship products through you. For all you know, you're helping all sorts of bad people, and you're here stonewalling us because of that." He jerked a thumb toward Jia. "Last night, someone tried to kill my partner in the course of her normal duties, not all that long after she was looking into a case involving this company."

Ramirez's eyes widened as he looked at Jia and back at Erik. "So? That has nothing to do with us. I-I-I... You can't claim we had anything to do with something like that. That's preposterous."

"I don't know," Erik explained. "I'll have to go talk to the guy and ask him a few new questions. Luckily for us, he survived after I shot up his car with a TR-7 Quad. Ever seen one?" Erik smiled. It didn't reach his eyes. "All good civilized people would call it absurd or barbaric. Possibly even my partner."

Very likely his partner, Jia thought.

"Four barrels, shoots a lot of bullets when you need it to. It slices up a flitter like nothing." He snapped his fingers. "It's not something I would like to use, but if a raid was necessary, I'd need to bring it along for personal defense. You never know if some insurrectionists are hiding in a room somewhere."

Ramirez swallowed. "I..." He closed his eyes and took a deep breath. "If I get you the relevant records, you'll consider us in full compliance, yes? I mean, we couldn't know." He looked at Jia. "There has to be some special consideration."

Erik returned his focus and nodded. "If you cooperate fully, obviously you're not helping whoever shipped through you. AISA makes allowances for that, as will we."

Ramirez spun. "I've got to check a few things. Just give me a few minutes to coordinate the relevant records transfer." He rushed over to Svetlana and began furtively whispering to her, occasionally gesturing in the detectives' direction.

Jia frowned and cleared her throat. She nodded toward the ficus. "Detective Blackwell, a word."

Erik followed her over to the plant.

She leaned forward to whisper. "What was all that about your gun?"

Erik looked at the two employees. "He needed a little extra motivation to push him over the top. It's no big deal."

"No big deal?" she hissed, eyes aflame. "You were basically threatening to kick in his door and fire a heavy weapon. *You can't do that.*"

"No. I stated that *if* a raid was required, I might bring it along." Erik eyed her. "You didn't seem to care when I mentioned AISA."

"That's potentially relevant," she snapped.

Erik stared at her with a knowing look in his eyes. "Do you really think they are shipping contraband?"

Jia sighed and averted her eyes. "No, but we do need the information. If what he's saying is true, and they aren't responsible, then this is a more complicated web of crimes, even if it is a set of minor ones."

Erik nodded in agreement. "I didn't lie to him at any point, Jia. I only stated facts, and I let him decide what those meant. It's not my problem if he let his imagination run away with him."

"But you didn't clarify the truth," Jia criticized.

"The truth is a hard thing to pin down," Erik explained. "I know that's difficult for someone from Earth to believe."

Jia harrumphed. "Spare me your sanctimony."

"We could leave." Erik looked up and around. "Maybe he's right, and it's nothing more than a billing dispute."

"If that were the case, why are there multiple incidents involving this company?" Jia took a second to glance at the manager and the receptionist. "Including serious fraud. No, all the evidence points to something going on here. I know the captain thinks it's not important, but sometimes I…" She stopped.

"What?" Erik prodded when she didn't continue.

"Sometimes, I think the captain's more concerned about keeping things calm than solving crimes."

"If you are having such impure thoughts," Erik grinned, "then there's hope for you yet."

"Detectives," Ramirez called, catching their attention. "We're ready to transfer the relevant records to you."

Jia nodded to Erik, and they headed to the reception desk.

Concern lingered in Jia's mind, but for now, she had a case to solve.

CHAPTER TWENTY

Erik looked at Jia. *She might be naïve, but at least she's not incompetent.*

Erik waited in the driver's seat of his MX 60 as Jia examined the recent Windward shipping records. Small text windows floated in front of her, and she swiped and jabbed at them, her eyes darting back and forth as she reviewed the information.

Every once in a while, she mumbled something under her breath, but nothing intelligible. After five minutes, she shook her head and furrowed her brow.

"The account numbers all seem to match Smythe's information," Jia explained. "But there's no clear record of what was being shipped, and something seems off. Pick-up and delivery were confirmed, but there's not a lot in the way of tracking, otherwise. Arguably, this form isn't compliant with relevant recordkeeping laws, but I'm not well versed with them, not enough to mount a useful threat if we were to go back in there."

Erik glanced her way. "Maybe they didn't bother to fill

in the information because they wanted to hide what was being shipped from casual review."

"I thought about that, but something doesn't make sense about that as the explanation." Jia frowned.

"How do you figure?"

She focused on him. "Why hand them over so easily? Even given your…implied actions, if they were doing something wrong, you would have figured they would have fought harder to avoid us getting this." Jia tapped her bottom lip. "Unless they think we won't understand or know what we're looking for. If I'm reading this information correctly, the origination address is a park, and the delivery destination is a funeral home. That doesn't make any sense."

Erik chuckled. "Maybe they decided to skip the middleman and transfer some stiff to the funeral home."

"Not without processing the body first." Jia shook her head. "Maybe this is just some stupid prank after all. Some clever teen who decided to mess with a few insecure systems." She stopped and tapped her lips. "That might explain the odd addresses."

Erik frowned at the implications. "Does it have a time of delivery? And does it say exactly where it was picked up from at the park?"

Jia shook her head, focusing on the data. "No. This form is missing many details. It's worthless even for internal recordkeeping. This is embarrassing for them, even if it's not related to a crime."

"We can go through the cameras, but I doubt we'll find much." Erik smirked. "Hope you don't mind funeral homes."

Jia glanced at him. "As long as they aren't committing any crimes."

A moment later, as the flitter lifted, she added, "And walking dead people. Not really wild about them, either."

"So, no zombie pictures?"

"Not a one."

———

ERIK SHIFTED to get comfortable as he settled beside Jia in his black chair.

They were in a back office at the Forever Remembered Funeral Home. The building lay halfway across town from the delivery origination.

They had called ahead to explain why they were coming, and the funeral home receptionist made it clear the head mortician was eager to meet with them as soon as possible.

Cecily sat on the other side of a black glass desk. She was a tall, pale woman with long, dark hair that almost matched her black dress.

Erik tried not to laugh at the whole Goddess of Death vibe she had surrounding her.

At least she was smiling as she folded her hands in front of her. Real fresh flowers, irises mostly, sat in dark vases on the desk, asking a small splash of color to an otherwise dreary room.

"Before I talk to you about my records, Detectives," Cecily began, her formal voice putting Erik on edge, "I just wanted to point out that law enforcement personnel have a higher rate of sudden death via accidents than many other professions."

"I doubt that," Erik replied, which had Jia turning to stare at him. "What?" he asked. "What danger has the team encountered while you have been working? I know I don't have enough time."

"It's not just detectives," Cecily interrupted him. "But traffic cops as well, and of course, the worst of the worst."

"What, death by donuts?" Erik interjected.

"Civil disturbances by married couples fighting," Cecily spouted, not appreciating Erik's humor or his interruption of her pitch. "While I'm sure your department has various funds set aside to ensure your loved ones are taken care of, have you put much thought into what you intend to do with yourself after you die?"

He snickered. "I used to be a soldier. I doubt I'm going to get killed as a cop on Earth anytime soon, and I'm not sure I care much what happens after I die since I'm not going to be able to do anything about it."

Jia grimaced.

Cecily nodded and gave him a concerned look. "It might seem obvious, but it bears repeating, Detective. It's when we're alive that we have the best opportunity to influence our afterlife. You could die after leaving this building." She turned. "Or you."

Jia leaned forward, stage-whispering to the lady as she pointed to Erik with her head. "He's driving."

Erik turned. "What about my driving?"

Jia glanced over. "You avoid the automatic piloting like an unmarried man avoids a paternity test."

Erik's hands opened wide. "And yet we are still here,

and alive."

Cecily took back over. "Death can come when and how we least expect it, and even the best medical technology can't bring you back to life, Detective Lin. You should really consider what those options are. This is a full-service facility. We offer a variety of burials in multiple cemetery zones, both local and outside the metroplex. For those who prefer more...classic burials, we even have surface-level plots. Standard cremation's..."

"My driving is *not* going to kill you," Erik interrupted.

Jia pointed to Cecily. "She says I need to be prepared."

"She says this stuff all day, every day," Erik replied. "It's called a sales pitch."

"He," Jia pointed in Erik's direction, "isn't from around here. He was on the frontier for most of his life."

"Well," Cecily sniffed, "while our funeral home doesn't handle interstellar burials, we can, for a fee, put you in touch with companies that handle such matters. You'll find the financing for such things surprisingly affordable." She eyed Erik. "Provided you plan a few decades ahead."

The mortician tapped her PNIU, and several three-dimensional images of happy families appeared. One family stood around a grave on a massive platform filled with a verdant garden, several holographic grave markers floating over it.

Erik glanced at the images

Another image depicted caskets being loaded into a cargo container outside a mass of stacked cylinders and tubes marking a space station.

He glanced at Jia, trying to understand if she was caught up in the pitch or pulling his leg.

In a third image, a smiling child looked up a holographic depiction of his father floating in the sky. All the images had the same bright text at the bottom.

HOW WOULD YOU LIKE TO SPEND ETERNITY? DON'T WAIT UNTIL IT'S TOO LATE TO DECIDE

Smaller text continued the sales pitch right below it.

Death is a stressful time of transition. Don't make your loved ones have to deal with additional pain. A variety of options are available, and financing is available for people of varying backgrounds.

Erik frowned. *Money. It always comes down to money.*

Cecily looked at Jia and Erik with a plastic smile. "Interactive holograms are one of our most popular options, but most people don't fully appreciate that the programs require decent input before the time of passing." She placed her palms together in front of her.

Jia cut in, "Thank you for meeting with us, Cecily, but this isn't a meeting about our burial requirements. We need to know about that delivery information. It's part of a formal fraud investigation, and I'd appreciate if we could confine ourselves to *that* topic."

"Fraud?" Cecily leaned back and let out a long sigh. "It's very unfortunate. When one stares at death all day, one learns that the petty concerns such as money aren't worth such extraordinary efforts. It's pathetic, really."

"What was delivered here?" Jia asked. "That's all we need to know. To be clear, we're not accusing you or your funeral home of anything. We appreciate your eager cooperation. You might in fact be the victim of a prank."

Cecily's eyes darted back and forth for a moment as she perused records on her smart contacts. She pursed her lips and shook her head. "I'm sorry, Detective. I looked at the information you sent me, and it doesn't match any deliveries we've received. We don't even use this Windward company. You're free to look around if you think it would help. The death of everyone currently being processed in our facility is a matter of public record."

Jia frowned. "You have no idea why your address would be on the shipping records?"

"Not the faintest. I'm sorry. I wish I could help." Cecily smiled. "Feel free to contact me if you have any other questions, and I'll only quickly note that all government employees receive a ten percent discount off our services, excluding certain premium services, including, but not limited to solar cremation and lunar burial." She looked at Erik. "Please note that veterans receive a ten percent discount as well." She winked at him. "The discounts would stack in your favor."

"I'll keep that in mind if I die anytime soon," Erik offered. He stood. "Unfortunately, I think we're done here for now."

She nodded to both of them. "It was lovely meeting you, Detectives. I do hope to see you again soon to discuss how you want to spend eternity."

Erik chuckled. "Yeah, uh, sure. I'll think about that." He stepped out and started for the front door.

Jia stood as well, then reached out her hand to shake. "Thank you for your time."

Cecily reached out and grabbed Jia's hand. "You tell him to work on his driving," She spoke in a stage-whisper.

"I heard that!" Erik called back down the hall.

The ladies shared a chuckle.

A FEW MOMENTS LATER, the detectives slid into Erik's MX 60 and prepared to head back to the station.

"You might want to set up your safety harness," Erik pointed to an extra belt that wrapped across Jia's chest.

"Do what?" She turned and saw what he was pointing to.

"You never know," he told her as the vehicle lifted smoothly. "I might do something drastic, and then you would need her services while I'm flying."

Jia grabbed the extra belt and pulled it across her. "I'm going to regret those comments, aren't I?"

"Not on purpose," he admitted, hitting the acceleration and pressing them both into the seat.

"I don't think she's lying," Jia commented a moment or two after he'd slowed a bit. "Or if she is, she's very good at it, and the receptionist made it sound like she was eager to talk to us."

"I think she was eager to talk to us, but not for the right reasons." Erik's voice was neutral. "And I don't think she was lying either. I think she just didn't want to send us an immediate message back telling us she didn't know anything because she wanted to try to con us into putting ten thousand credits down as a deposit for a lunar burial or buy a gold coffin."

"There are gold coffin options?"

"Seriously?" Erik asked.

"Hey!" She kept a straight face. "I don't know, with your driving."

"I'm not going to kill you."

"I'll hold you to that." She looked at the data. "I wish I could follow up on the earlier Windward analysis I performed." Jia frowned. "But the captain's sent the case along already, and we'd have to convince him to back us if we wanted to go look into that information." She glanced at a couple of buildings they passed, noting in one set of windows a woman in a white shirt yelling into her comm device. "It's not just a matter of regulations. We won't be able to easily access the information without him coding it that way in the system."

Erik's shoulders twitched. "We can do that if you want, but are you sure we've exhausted all our leads with the information we have? Right now, he's letting us run this all down, and that doesn't require any extra codes, right?"

Jia nodded. "We do have copies of the records from Windward. Maybe Digital Forensics can turn up something. I'll have to get with them."

"It's worth a shot. It's been a busy day. I'll drop you off and then go get some rest." Erik grinned. "For all you know, we've stumbled upon insurrectionists, and you don't want to be dragging your feet when they're trying to run you over.

Jia rolled her eyes. "I doubt that, but I know this is bigger than it seems." A soft smile spread over her face.

Erik couldn't say he didn't like it. "What is it?" he asked.

"It...feels good." Jia looked at him. "All I've ever wanted to do is my job, and thanks to you, I'm getting to do just that." She turned back to her data. "Thank you."

"You're welcome." Erik smiled as he watched the traffic.

For the moment, he had every intention of doing the best job he could as a cop. In the end, that might be the only way he would get access to the tools he needed to investigate Mu Arae.

JUNE 25, 2228, Neo Southern California Metroplex, Police Enforcement Zone 122 Station, Digital Forensics Division, Office of Malcolm Constantine

Erik and Jia were crammed into a tiny office on a lower level of the police station. A man with dirty blond hair in a Hawaiian shirt sat behind his desk, a triumphant smile on his face.

Jia gestured to her partner and then to the man. "Erik, this is Malcolm. He's one of the best techs in Digital Forensics."

"Why is that?" Erik asked.

"Because I said so." Malcolm smirked. "If you can't believe me based on my personal opinion, what does that say about your ability to believe me on my professional opinions?"

"It's because of this," Jia pointed to the man, "that I call him the best in digital forensics."

Erik eyed him. "Because he wears Hawaiian shirts?" He scratched his chin. "I will admit, you don't see those on the outer worlds."

"No." She shook her head, annoyed. "Because of these self-promotion arguments. I figure he just wants to sit here and argue in circles. I'm more than willing to stroke his ego as long as he performs." She waved her PNIU. "I sent him the information yesterday evening, and he already has something for us. Based on what he gave me a little earlier, I think some of our initial suspicions might be right."

Erik stepped up and shook the man's hand. "Glad for the help."

"Of course." Malcolm's shake was fast but not firm. "And you gave me something interesting to do this week. They've had me double-checking traffic fines for most of the last couple of weeks." He grimaced.

"Sorry to make you do a lot of work over a hundred credits." She had to agree with his distaste for the traffic fine effort. "But I think there's something more. There were some earlier records I performed some correlation analysis on that might be interesting for you to go through, but right now, we need to keep our focus on the records I sent over."

Malcolm pulled up files, the slight glimmer in the air telling Erik he had added another set. "It wasn't a big deal, and I think this is about a lot more than a hundred credits." His eyes flicked from hologram window to hologram window. "Oh, by the way, I did a quick check of the cameras at the park you mentioned, since I had the time. There were no Windward pickups that day anywhere in the park or immediately around it that I could tell. I ran a bunch of auto-filters on it, too."

Erik's brow lifted. "Wait on the park comment for a second. Why do you think this is about a lot more than a hundred credits?" He watched the man carefully.

"Because that file's been obviously altered." Malcolm shook his head, his face twisted in annoyance. "I can tell that just from the copies of the records. It's like they didn't even care to try to hide it. What's the point of doing something like that if you're not going to do a good job?" Malcolm's eyes flicked to Erik. "It's kind of an insult, you know? It'd be like some terrorist trying to bomb a building right in front of you guys. They might as well have just left a note saying, 'This file altered. Sorry!'"

"They've been altered?" Jia thought for a moment. "That's not all that surprising when we consider both the park and funeral home. Know who altered them?"

Malcolm shrugged. "You got me, Detective. If I had direct access to the Windward systems, maybe I could figure that out, but it's clear to me that somebody changed the data. Among other things, several internal checksums are off." Jia saw his screens change. "I can go through the gory details if you want, but the high-level summary is, those are real records where the underlying data have been altered. I won't be able to recover it from the copy, but I might be able to recover it from the source if I had direct access."

Jia shook her head. "If we don't know who, then we don't know why. I doubt they were trying to frame the funeral home. It was probably just a convenient address."

"They probably thought no one would check that closely," Erik suggested. "But if the people at Windward altered the records, it's like you said. I'm surprised they gave them up so easily."

"I had some time to think about that," Jia offered. "I assume it was easy because you threatened them. Erik, I think you underestimate how unused to casual threats of violence people on Earth are."

He shook his head, his hands up as if to fend off the accusation. "I never threatened them. I just pointed out certain possibilities. They obviously have something to hide, but not something so important that they didn't stall longer. Unless they think we'll never find it."

Malcolm looked at the two of them and laughed. "I don't even think I want to know what happened. I'll send this to your PNIUs. If you need anything else, just let me know. Remember," he smiled at them both, a glint of mischievousness in his eyes, "if you can get me direct systems access, I can find out a lot more."

Jia turned and headed toward the door, waving a hand over her shoulder. "Thanks, Malcolm."

Erik nodded at Malcolm and followed Jia into the hallway. Once outside, he spoke up. "This should be enough, right?"

Jia turned her head as they continued walking. "Enough for what?"

"A warrant? I know the captain sent the other information already, but combined with what you found earlier, it should be enough. It's like Malcolm said. This isn't just about a hundred credits anymore." Erik watched to see if anyone was trying to listen to their conversation. "Altering shipping records violate all sorts of laws, even when the items being shipped aren't valuable."

Jia slowed her pace, a grim expression on her face. "You're right. I've been letting the captain's paradigm influence me too much." She thought for a moment. "There's no way we can get a warrant without the captain's permission, and he was fairly dismissive of my earlier analysis."

"Now this isn't just you. It's digital forensics," Erik countered. "It's time we pushed him a little. Whatever this is, it's *not* a billing dispute, and this isn't a case of you being overzealous."

CHAPTER TWENTY-ONE

At least this time, Erik thought, the captain is listening, not going into a rant immediately after Jia explained what they and Digital Forensics had found.

Captain Monahan took a deep breath as he ran his hand through his hair. "Okay, so, you've found out someone altered a few records, and you might *potentially* be able to connect that to whatever fraud you *think* you found earlier with this company?" He eyed them both. "Is that what you're telling me."

Jia nodded. "Yes, sir."

Erik added. "We need a warrant and backup. We should raid Windward right away. I'm sure they have more records in their systems."

Jia continued, "My earlier analysis was based on a very small set of records they'd turned over for evaluation purposes, but if we went through all of their records, that should show fraud beyond doubt."

Captain Monahan stood up from his chair, his eyes bugging out as he glared at Jia. "You want to *raid*

Windward?" He turned to Erik. "This is a joke you two are pulling. It has to be."

"I'm not laughing," Erik offered, pointing to his partner. "She's not laughing. Doesn't sound like a joke to me, Captain."

Jia squared her shoulders. "I agree with my partner. I don't know what this is, but it's obviously about a lot more than disgruntled customers. It's worth following up on."

Captain Monahan shook his head. "You don't know that. Maybe they just altered the records because they thought they were going to get sued. That's illegal, *yes*, but it's not worth police attention."

"That's still a crime, and it's far more serious crime than inappropriate billing." Jia eyed him. "We can't let this continue. Not if we know about it."

Erik looked at Jia, then at his boss. "She's right."

Captain Monahan's expression alternated between panic and rage "Did *either* of you two look into the company's background at all?" He tapped his desk. "Seriously, did you *look*? Did you dive into it?"

Jia nodded. "Yes, I did before I stopped working the case. What about it?"

"Did you check on their ownership?" Captain Monahan stared at her, disbelief on his face.

"If you go through the chains of ownership, they ultimately are a White Tiger subsidiary. What about it?"

Erik chewed the inside of his cheek. "Huh. Didn't know that."

"Sorry." Jia gave him an apologetic look. "I didn't think it was that important. They have a stake in a lot of shipping and transport companies."

Captain Monahan lowered himself back into his chair, and it squeaked as he dropped the last few inches. "Lin, you *know* that, and you still think raiding this company is a good idea?"

Erik eyed them both. "Why wouldn't it be?"

The captain stared at him. "Poking around is one thing, but a full investigation without even talking to them first will probably cause trouble. Especially if White Tiger thinks their subsidiary is being harassed unfairly."

"Trouble?" Jia countered. "Crime is crime. I doubt White Tiger is involved in whatever is happening here, so they have no reason to worry."

Monahan raised an eyebrow. "That doesn't mean they won't apply political pressure if this becomes an incident, Lin. Corporations have a public face to maintain, and they do not appreciate the local police causing them problems."

Jia eyed him. "It's already an incident, sir. Fraudulent billing of customers, fraudulent billing of the government, altered records. Whatever this is, I'm positive it's not some rogue teenager playing pranks. I wanted to follow up on this before, so I was a pain to you. There's no way I'm going to be convinced to back off when we have this much evidence."

Captain Monahan frowned and turned to Erik. "What do you think? You're a practical man. You have to understand where I'm coming from."

Erik waited for a moment before he answered. "I think that if we stop investigating crimes just because some corp's indirectly linked to the company, we might as well just close down this building and go home." He considered his next words. "But you're the man with decades of law enforcement experience." He smiled. "So, if I'm missing some brilliant police reason to not go after Windward, feel free to point it out."

Unfortunately, Monahan wasn't buying what Erik was selling. "Lin is young, but I would have thought *you* would have had a better understanding of the political implications."

"Having a better understanding doesn't mean I'll shy away from it," Erik explained. "I believe we should track it down. She," he jerked a thumb at Jia, "is just happy I'm not kicking in doors. She's the calm one, not me."

Captain Monahan closed his eyes and took a deep breath. When he opened them again, he looked at Jia. "Societal stability isn't just about the law, Detective Lin. It's also about not causing trouble for the organizations and people underlying that society. With your family's connections, I would think this isn't something I would have to point out to you."

"I'm sorry, are you saying we should walk away?" Jia stepped toward his desk, her breathing shallow. Her hands trembled as she clenched and released them. "Is this why you've kicked away most of my cases? Because they might be too much trouble for someone else?"

"I have a responsibility to this enforcement zone and metroplex," Captain Monahan replied. "And that includes political considerations. I won't apologize for that."

Jia glanced at her partner. She wasn't happy about his penchant for threats, but at least he was backing her up.

"Well," she continued, "they have to understand that at the end of the day, even corporations are subject to laws."

Captain Monahan leaned to the side to confirm the

door was closed before straightening again and answering. "Jia, sometimes the price of stability is letting little things go."

Jia shook her head. "I refuse to accept that. I believe little things lead to big things. Is this what you were getting at earlier, sir? That I should just go along with ignoring crimes so I can get a promotion, and then what? Ignore more crimes? I don't care if they aren't major crimes."

The captain frowned. "Passing them along for additional review isn't ignoring them. You're making it sound like we don't clear any cases from this enforcement zone, but that's not the situation."

Erik chuckled. "If cases are getting passed along, and they're not getting solved, it's the same thing as ignoring them."

The captain returned his attention to Erik. "We're not talking about terrorism and murders," he explained. "All existing records on every case that comes through this enforcement zone are still available. I'm simply trying to make sure we focus on real criminals and not unimportant details, especially ones that will generate unnecessary agitation for major taxpayers."

Jia's voice was soft, but both men could hear the restraint that suggested her anger behind it. "If someone thinks they can defraud the metroplex and its citizens and change records to cover it up, what's to stop them when they decide it's time for their next crime?"

Captain Monahan stared at her, frowning.

Erik shrugged, then folded his arms. "She's got a point, Captain."

Monahan eyed them both. "Have you ever considered

you might be wrong?" he asked. "What if there's nothing there but a billing dispute that got out of hand? We don't want the police to seem anti-business. If White Tiger relocated their facilities, it'd hurt the tax base of the metroplex, and that will filter down to things like police resources. Have you thought that through?"

Erik snorted, his face a mask of disgust. "You don't even know if White Tiger knows or cares about what Windward is doing. How many companies do they control? It's like me knowing about every piece of lint in my crotch. Get your balls back, Captain, and stop being scared of every shadow."

Captain Monahan glared at Erik. "Just because I didn't serve, it doesn't mean I'm a coward."

"I didn't say that." Erik nodded at Jia. "You being unwilling to investigate is what makes you need to grab a pair. She didn't serve either, and although I've only known her a few days, she's got a steel pair, as near as I can figure."

Jia nodded, her face reddening as she eyed him. "Crude, but easily understood." She turned to Monahan. "The minute we stop caring about solving crimes, no matter how small, is the minute we should turn in our badges. I know you think I'm not politically astute enough to make it in the force for long, but I didn't join the police department to worry about that kind of thing. I joined to find and stop crimes, and we've identified a crime. I don't want to let it go because of something that *might* happen."

The captain's jaw tightened, and he stared into the distance for a few seconds. "I'm willing to agree under a few conditions." He turned back to them. "First of all, this is going to take a few days. We're doing this all by the book, which means you're going to have to type up a report on your previous analysis and everything else that happened before I can get you a warrant."

"Noted, but if we wait too long, they might destroy evidence," Jia pointed out.

"Too damned bad. I'm not doing anything quickly and stupidly because you've infected Erik with your insanity." Captain Monahan continued glaring at the former soldier. "Both of you are going to stay at the station. No more witness interviews, nothing. You go over the evidence you have, and you get the forms and reports we need for the warrant filled out. Then I will send them up the chain."

"Fair enough." Erik nodded.

"Second," the captain continued, "if this goes badly and it turns out to be nothing..." He looked at both detectives. "I'll have both your badges. I'm close to retiring, and I'm not letting you two force me out."

Erik grinned. "Oh?"

Jia frowned. "You'll have our badges for doing our jobs?"

"No." Captain Monahan scoffed. "I'll have them for wasting my time and taxpayer resources, and generally being annoying." He shook his head. "If you don't agree, I can make sure the warrant takes a long time to go through. I'm not convinced there's anything there, and I'm far from convinced there's enough there to justify a raid."

Erik turned to Jia. "It's your call. I might have accepted the last Windward complaint, but you've been working on Windward since before I joined the department. If you think there's something there, then I've got your back, but only if you're sure."

Jia thought about it for a moment, her focus on a useless point in the distance.

She nodded slowly. "I believe there's something there, Captain." She concentrated on the man. "I'm willing to bet my badge on it."

"And mine," Erik added.

"It's only a small thing at the moment." Jia turned to him. "Didn't you hear I'm a Black Widow?"

"Yeah, but if we fail, you have to be my secretary."

"For what?" she asked, confusion written plainly on her face.

"Blackwell Detective Agency."

"You will have to work all the time. I'll fill your calendar so full you won't sleep."

"Oh, threats?"

"Fine." Captain Monahan cut them off, irritation still in his voice. "Let's hope for all our sakes, Detective Lin, that there's actually something important here. I'll have your warrant within three days, but since nothing you've said to me suggests we need a tactical team, you will get by with cops. At the worst, this is a shipping company committing fraud, not a bunch of terrorists."

Erik turned to Jia. "Don't worry. You don't need a tactical team. You have me."

She grimaced.

"You just want to kick in a door with that big gun in your hand."

CHAPTER TWENTY-TWO

June 28, 2228, Neo Southern California Metroplex, Outside of Windward Branch Office

Jia emerged from Erik's flitter, her fear kicking up.

A half-dozen other police vehicles touched down around the building. Her fellow police officers hopped out and hurried to surround the structure.

Erik reached over to the passenger side. The hidden compartment storing his TR-7 opened, and he pulled the weapon and few magazines out with a smile on his face.

"I knew it." Jia grimaced as he retrieved the weapon. "You probably agreed because you wanted to play with your toy."

The man looked ridiculous strutting around with his massive rifle, duster, and tactical vest. In her opinion, he resembled something closer to a cinematic gangster than a police officer, but there was nothing in the regulations that specifically prohibited his attire. And he was right; his license made it legal even during a department raid to use the TR-7.

She had made a point of double-checking.

"You're not going to need that," Jia insisted, looking around. "This is a shipping company, not an insurrectionist stronghold."

"Always be prepared, then it doesn't matter if you're surprised," Erik countered. "Lady Luck and I used to be friends, but she's done me wrong in the last year, so I've learned I've got to worry about my own six."

"If you say so." Jia headed toward the front door, Erik closing his door and trailing behind her. The other officers continued shouting and surrounding the building.

Jia tapped her PNIU before reaching for the door handle. "I'm transmitting the warrant now," she finished. After throwing open the door, she strolled into the lobby, her head held high.

She tried to project professionalism, even though her stomach twisted so much, she worried she might throw up.

A receptionist, this time a nervous-looking young man instead of Svetlana, looked up, confusion spreading over his face. "I, uh, excuse me...uh." His gaze shifted to Erik's rifle, and he swallowed. "I'm pretty sure that's not allowed in here, sir."

"NSCPD," Jia announced, patting the badge on her jacket. "A formal search warrant for the search of this premise has been issued. We're here to connect our systems to yours for a formal records search. Contact all employees and have them leave the building through the front door. At this time, no one is going to be arrested, but any interference with the execution of our warrant could change that."

The receptionist froze, his mouth open. "Uh…"

Jia nodded at a uniformed officer and pointed at the front desk. "Handle that, please."

"Yes, detective," the officer replied, heading toward the stunned man, chuckling.

Erik looked around with a surprised expression. "Huh. A lot less dramatic than I thought." He shouldered his rifle. "I was expecting a little more resistance. They put up a better fight last time."

Jia looked over her shoulder. "I keep telling you, this isn't the frontier. And you got your wish. You got to show up with your toy." She headed past the front desk as the patrol officer linked into the intercom system and repeated her announcement to get everyone to step out of the building.

Erik followed her. "Desperate people do desperate things, whether they're on the frontier or a core world. It wasn't long ago you almost got flattened, remember?" He checked behind doors as they passed before stepping up quickly to catch up and then open another door. "I would think after everything that's happened with the captain, you would understand that you've been a little clueless."

"That was…unusual, and the captain's failures don't reflect a problem with the system. He's just one man," was her reply. She turned, her eyes narrowing as she watched him confirm the rooms were empty.

Erik closed a door. "The system's nothing more than a bunch of men and women working together. Don't kid yourself."

Jia thought for a moment before pulling her stun pistol out of her holster.

It wouldn't hurt to be prepared in case he was right, and someone got confused and desperate. "Once we get all the transmitters in place," she turned back around and continued walking, "Digital Forensics can begin accessing the systems. We'll let the patrol officers handle grabbing anything that might be relevant and placing the transmitters, but it won't hurt to look around." She glanced into an open office. "Who knows, we might get lucky."

Erik's expression darkened for a moment. "I doubt that." His face flipped back to amused.

She eyed him. *It's like he's trying all the time to act like he doesn't care, but there's something else there.*

Jia almost said something but decided against it. A police raid wasn't the time to discuss her partner's personal affairs.

"How does it feel?" Erik asked as they moved deeper into the building, passing several offices, this time both of them looking in.

Jia glanced at him as she closed a door. "How does what feel?"

"I'm assuming," his voice was a bit echoey before he pulled his head back out of the office he had just stuck it in, "this is your first raid?" Erik finished. "It's not my first. Mine typically involved a few more air or artillery strikes to soften them up." He grinned. "A lot more explosions, for sure."

Jia considered the question as they passed a conference room and entered a wide hallway. Several confused employees made their way down the corridor. Their hands shot up when they spotted Erik's TR-7.

"No one is under arrest," Jia told them, pointing toward the entrance. "Just make your way to the front, and the uniformed officers will show you where to stand. You will be asked a few questions, but you should be free to go soon." She gestured with her stun pistol first and then lowered it. No reason to intimidate the poor people any more than they already were.

The wide-eyed employees crept past, their attention focused on Erik and his weapon. The detectives kept walking down the hallway. A large sign indicated the primary loading bay lay at the end.

"That's why you should have brought it," Jia hissed, her eyes pinning him with an accusation. "You're intimidating them. This is already a problem for them."

"Aren't you the one who thinks they're a bunch of criminals?" Erik raised an eyebrow in challenge.

She looked around. "There's obviously something going on here, but that doesn't mean every person here is a criminal. Innocent until proven guilty, remember?"

Erik chuckled. "Sure, but you're missing the point of why I brought it."

Jia raised an eyebrow in question. "To feel like a big man?"

Erik shook his head. "The best way to win a battle is to frighten your enemy into submission before it even begins."

"This isn't a battle. This is a *police raid*." Jia stopped at the door to the loading bay.

She tapped the open panel, but the door remained stubbornly closed. She entered an override code using her PNIU. "I appreciate that you've helped me convince the captain there's something worth pursuing here, but that doesn't mean I approve of everything you do. And I think, even if I could benefit from adopting certain attitudes, or at least part of them, from you, it doesn't mean I think your methods are, in general, the best way to go about things." Her fingers punched in a secondary code and the door slid open. "I think you're stuck in a frontier mindset."

"Hey, my methods are about getting things done," Erik observed. "Maybe you need more of a frontier mindset."

Jia shook her head. "You're incorrigible."

"It wouldn't be the first time someone said that to me." Erik furrowed his brow, looking behind them before turning back to her. "Actually," he corrected, "it would be. I don't think they used such large words. Too many syllables."

Jia stepped into a massive loading bay for the shipping vehicles. Erik followed her.

"So, what did they use?"

"'Pain in the ass,' usually."

Dozens of squat cargo drones were parked in neat rows in front of several lines of blue and white cargo flitters, the sail logo of the Windward company prominent on the sides. The long, rectangular vehicles lacked a driver's compartment. The only human who might be involved in a delivery was the occasional inspector who rode in the back.

A shrill alarm sounded. The door behind them slid shut.

Jia raised her pistol. "What now?"

Erik sighed, his head pivoting much more quickly. "I knew this was too easy."

"Warning!" called out a soft female voice. "Warning! You are trespassing in a Windward Company secure loading bay. You are to immediately leave the area, or you may be subject to interdiction by autonomous security assets."

Jia frowned and pressed the open panel, using the small numbers on the keyboard to issue her override code. The door didn't move. She tried her override code a second time. Still no luck. "They want us to leave, but then they shut the door. That doesn't make any sense."

Erik readied his weapon and turned off the safety; she could hear the click. "This could get bad." The goofy grin from before was gone, replaced by the stone mask of a warrior.

The expression chilled Jia.

Jia turned around. "The security protocols were supposed to be turned off already as part of the warrant." She dialed the sergeant coordinating the rest of the response.

"Yes, Detective Lin?" Sergeant McEnroe answered.

"The security protocols in the loading bay are still active. Do we have systems access yet?"

"Working on it, Detective."

"Sooner would be better than later," Jia called over the noise going on in the background.

She turned off the safety of her stun pistol, not all comforted by the priming hum, then adjusted the power level. It might stop a few bots, but it was designed to take down people, not machines.

"We're trying!" the sergeant shouted back.

The alarm continued to sound, the harsh noise ricocheting off the walls and parked vehicles.

Erik ejected a magazine and pulled another one from a vest pocket. He slapped the new one in with a grunt as the first mag clattered on the ground.

"What are you doing?" Jia asked, frustration mixed with a touch of worry lacing her tone. "You haven't even fired anything yet. You brought an empty gun?"

"AP might be better suited for this situation," Erik explained. "Unless security bots have changed a lot since I left Earth."

"AP?" Jia shook her head. "I don't understand."

"Armor-piercing rounds." Erik lifted his weapon. "I brought a few different types of ammo. Like I said, it pays to be prepared."

Jia shook her head. "I'm sure this will get handled. It's not as if we're going to have to participate in some sort of gun battle."

"Detective Lin," Sergeant McEnroe transmitted over the speaker. "There's a problem."

"Problem?" Jia replied, her focus turning to her communicator, her voice cracking. "What problem?"

"I don't know. The computer guy says there's some sort of malfunction in the Windward building's security grid. He's trying to shut it down, but it's going to take him a few minutes." Sergeant McEnroe audibly swallowed over the line. "They say it's ramping up. We're trying to get the Windward people to shut it down, but they can't do it either. Um, any chance you could get out of there?"

"We would if we could!" Jia snapped.

"Warning!" the security voice announced again. "Warning! You are trespassing in a Windward Company secure loading bay. Systems indicate extreme threat to local personnel. Lethal force is authorized."

Erik nodded toward the cargo flitters. "We need cover." He jogged in the direction he had pointed.

Jia hesitated for only a split second before following him, her heart pounding. *This is insane!*

They crouched behind one of the cargo flitters and looked for any security bots or drones, but there was nothing.

"Lethal force will now be applied," the security voice continued over the loudspeakers. "The authorities have been contacted. This ends your warnings."

Jia scoffed. "Gee, thanks." She lifted her communicator. "McEnroe, how are we doing?"

"We're working on it, Detective. Just hang on."

"I don't know how long we can do that," she replied, doubt in her voice.

Panels hissed back to reveal hidden security bots. The machines were black bulbous orbs resting on lattices of black and gray metal over trios of grav-field emitters. Two noticeable barrels stuck out of the orbs, one short and gray, the other long and black.

The bots rose from the ground with quiet hums.

Erik snapped up his TR-7, aimed, and then squeezed the trigger. The barrels came alive in a bright flash. Bullets ripped into a bot, blowing it apart in a shower of black chunks and sparks. The bot collapsed to the ground.

"That works," he muttered.

Other bots opened fire, their bullets ripping into the

back of the vehicle being used for cover. Erik held down the trigger and swept with his rifle, downing several more bots. Jia held down the stun button, then lifted her gun and fired. The overcharged bolt struck a bot and the white energy arced over it. It wavered for a few seconds before firing at her.

Erik grabbed her arm and pulled her deeper into the row of parked vehicles. More hidden compartments hissed open to release more killer bots. The machines took careful shots every few seconds. Their bullets sparked as they ripped into vehicles or struck downed cargo drones. They spread out to surround the pair.

"This is Detective Lin," Jia shouted. "We are taking live fire. I repeat, we are taking live fire!"

Erik popped around the corner and blew another bot to pieces. It managed one last shot before falling to the hard parking lot. The bullet whizzed by his arm. Two more drones met their fate before he retreated again.

Jia managed to clip a bot with another stun bolt, but again, it only wobbled in place before returning fire.

Erik's follow-up quick bursts from his TR-7 blew out two of its grav field emitters. It fell to the ground, and his third burst blew the control orb into pieces.

He followed up with another shot and the next bot tried to dodge by rotating to the side, but he still managed to take out an emitter. A snap-shot through the center finished the machine.

"This is why machines are worthless in a real fight," Erik muttered. He ejected his magazine, loaded a new one, and glanced at the vehicle before pulling his head back down a moment before two bullets tore into the hood. "An EMP would be nice about now."

Jia swallowed, her stomach tightening. She holstered her pistol. She wasn't accomplishing anything. If Erik hadn't been taking them out, she might have already taken a round. She pulled up her communicator. "We're still taking fire, Sergeant."

"They're almost into the system, Detective," he replied, desperation soaking his words.

The bots sped up, their flight pattern erratic as they circled and fired.

"I've got an eight-count remaining," Erik reported. "Fortunately, the AI isn't that great on these things." He pulled out his pistol and handed it to Jia. "I'm assuming you have no problem shooting a machine that's trying to kill you?"

Jia accepted the heavy pistol and flipped off the safety. She gave a shallow nod and swallowed. "They'll disable the security system any second now. We just have to hold out."

Her heart raced, but she was surprised. The closest she'd previously come to death had been when the drunk had driven toward her. In her entire life, she'd never been shot at and had wondered how she would handle it.

She now had the answer. *Afraid, but not terrified.*

Erik popped up and nailed a nearby bot. Another one fired, the bullet striking his left arm. He grunted as blood seeped through the hole in his sleeve.

Jia squeezed the trigger so quickly she'd sent six rounds at the bot before she even knew what she was doing. The first few sparked off the exterior, but the last two went in.

The bot spun and fired wildly before careening into the ground.

"Are you okay?" she asked in a near panic.

Erik shrugged. "Fine. I've had a lot worse. I might have even had a lot worse this month."

"You've just been shot," Jia shouted, as surprised as she was startled.

Erik patted his left shoulder. "Those bots aren't that big." He nodded at several jagged holes in a nearby vehicle. "Note the small size of the hole."

"They look big enough to me," Jia commented, looking around again.

"I'm just saying, those bots are stocked with small amounts of small caliber ammo, and it's not penetrating that deeply." Erik fired a burst and ripped another bot to pieces. A counter-volley forced him down. "They don't have a huge amount of ammo, and they're mostly depending on using hollow-points to take down soft targets." He patted his shoulder. "You're not going to get through a quality cyber arm with that kind of ammo."

Jia gasped. "You have…a cybernetic arm? On purpose?" She tried not to let disgust seep into her voice. The man probably had his reasons, but the idea of keeping an artificial limb still made her shudder.

"This isn't the first time it's saved me." Erik took a deep breath. "On three, turn around and open fire. One, two, three."

Jia spun and fired without aiming. Her first shot ripped into a security bot clearing the back of a vehicle several rows down. Erik's gun came to life as he fired in the opposite direction. They stood back to back for a moment, firing simultaneously and finishing off the last few bots.

Acrid smoke filled the air. A few of the bots smoldered, and holes riddled the inactive cargo drones and many of the vehicles.

The alarm died.

"We've got it turned off, Detective," McEnroe announced. "Are you okay?"

"Yes," Jia answered, her breath coming in gasps. "Thanks for that, but we already took care of them." She took a deep breath and then slumped against the nearest cargo flitter. She tapped her PNIU to cut the transmission. "I…" She shook her head. "Erik, we were almost killed."

Erik engaged the safety on his weapon and shouldered it. He shook his left arm. "No, not really. I took one bullet in my arm, and you weren't even hit. That wasn't even close to being killed."

"I've…never been through anything like that." Jia's heart thundered in her chest, the pressure feeling like someone was banging on a drum near her ears.

"I'll say this for you, Jia. I'm impressed." Erik stood there with a smile even as blood dripped from the thin flesh layer over his cybernetic arm.

She looked at him. "You are?"

Erik nodded. "A lot of people choke during their first real fight. The adrenaline gets pumping, and they can't handle it. The service gets around this by spending a lot of time training people to operate automatically. Muscle memory and that sort of thing mean they don't have to think, so it doesn't matter if they're scared, but you did pretty good for someone without that kind of training." He nodded at the pistol. "Maybe next time, bring a real gun."

Jia glanced at her stun pistol. "I never thought I would have to fight security bots using live ammunition."

"You're not bad." Erik turned as the loading bay door opened, and several officers rushed in. "I might be able to make something of you yet."

"I don't know whether to be flattered or insulted."

Sergeant McEnroe ran toward them. He winced as he spotted Erik's wound. "We need to get you to the EMT."

"It'll just be a quick patch job," Erik told him.

He looked at the bot debris littering the floor and the hole-filled vehicles and drones. "I hope Windward has good insurance."

CHAPTER TWENTY-THREE

Jia stood in front of Captain Monahan's desk, her arms folded and her posture stiff. Erik lingered beside her, disinterest on his face. She had a hard time reading him and was half-convinced that much of the time he was putting on a show for the benefit of those around him.

Perhaps he had the right idea, though.

The captain heaved a sigh. "Before we begin, let me check that you're both okay?" He focused on Erik. "I know you've got a cybernetic arm, but you don't need any time off?" Slight distaste flavored his mention of the arm.

The revelation had shocked Jia, but after that, she found she didn't care much.

She had her Purists tendencies, but Erik didn't seem like the kind of man who had let augmentation rob him of his humanity. If anything, with his passion, he was too human.

Erik rotated his left arm. "Yeah, they slapped a patch on it. It stung a little, but I'm fine. Sometimes not being *pure* has its advantages."

The captain shook his head. "That is why I don't like this kind of thing. Cops get hurt. I should have never authorized the raid. I didn't expect anything like that to happen, and if I'd had even an inkling that it would..." He stopped speaking and sighed.

"With all due respect, Captain, you're never going to stop real trouble without someone putting their lives on the line." Erik shrugged. "This is also why you don't rely on machines to guard things; they malfunction too easily. But they're all trashed, and we're both still alive, and we don't have to pay for them. So there's nothing to worry about."

Captain Monahan frowned. "Part of me wants to complain about you bringing that TR-7, but if you hadn't done what you did, you'd both be dead." He paused for a moment before answering something with his personal HUD, then focused on the two of them. "I'll have to reach out about possible charges. Windward has already assured me they'll be firing several people in the security and management teams over the incidents, and they're going to do everything they can to fully cooperate going forward."

Erik looked at the old-time clock on the wall. "That was quick. We just got back here."

"The company can't let this linger," Jia told him. "It's too much of a black eye, especially with law enforcement being fired on like that." She shook her head. "Even if it was an accident, it smells too much of insurrectionists or terror-ism. At a minimum, it's antisocial."

The captain nodded at her. "They don't want this inci-dent becoming well known, and I think it's in the best interests of this enforcement zone and the department that *we* don't advertise it."

Erik shrugged. "Why not? We won. It might send a message to people not to screw with the 1-2-2."

"We're keeping this quiet," the captain replied crisply. "And that's a direct order. Did I make myself clear?"

Erik nodded, although he retained the defiant grin on his face. "Yes, *sir.*"

"And what about the case, sir?" Jia asked.

The captain's face softened. "It depends on what Digital Forensics turns up. I'd hate to think you nearly died for nothing, or even just some minor billing fraud. For now, both of you stick around the station and write up your reports. I need every last detail in there. There are going to be a lot of important people asking me questions about what just went down, and I need to be able to give them half-way decent answers. For now, you're dismissed, and try not to get in any gunfights on the way back to your office."

"No promises." Erik headed out of the office, Jia close behind.

"That wasn't as bad as I expected," Jia admitted once they were out of their boss's hearing.

"What's he going to say? 'How dare you let some bots shoot at you?'" Erik snorted. "We did what we needed to do, and we didn't kill or injure any civilians."

Jia nodded and fell silent, sinking into her thoughts.

She didn't speak again until after they were back in their office and seated at their respective desks.

"I want to bounce something off you," Jia began, her voice quiet. "Unless you need more time to figure things out?"

"I'm fine." Erik looked at her. "You okay? I've been in a

lot of fights, and I've lost my share of thoughts. I understand that battles aren't always fun or exciting."

Jia's breath caught and she swallowed, taken off-guard by his obvious concern. "I'm okay. About that, anyway. I'm still processing it all, but that's not what is bothering me."

Erik's brow lifted. "Getting shot at for the first time isn't what's bothering you?"

Jia nodded. "Don't you think it was too convenient?"

"Too convenient?" Something approaching respect appeared in Erik's eyes. "What do you mean, exactly?"

"We're looking into this company and executing a search warrant, and suddenly their bots malfunction and try to kill us." Jia shook her head. "I thought about telling the captain my suspicions, but he's already so spun up that I'm afraid if I push any more, he'll pull us from the case. I want to get to the bottom of this."

"Yeah." Erik grunted. "I think it's incredibly coincidental the bots not only conveniently malfunctioned then, but they broke badly enough to go into live-fire mode. From what I overheard some of the techs saying, that shouldn't have been possible without a manager's override code. Plus, they're not something you'd think you would need Uptown."

"It's not unusual for companies to have that kind of security," Jia clarified. "I mean, obviously we don't have the kind of terrorism problems that you see on the frontier, but it's not impossible. It's just…"

"Just what?"

Jia licked her lips and took a deep breath. "What if someone got desperate enough to want to kill us, the problem children? I'm not saying I'm convinced of that, but I've been thinking about that man outside the club on and off since the incident, and now I just don't know anymore. A lot of things that seemed so clear before… aren't."

Erik nodded. "Good. Never assume you're safe, and you'll live a lot longer. You also need to understand something very important."

"And that is?" Jia asked.

"That humans are humans," Erik explained. "And Earth has more humans than any other place in the galaxy. Just because they're better at hiding the corruption, it doesn't mean it's not here. Maybe the captain's right and this is nothing more than fraudulent billing, but if you were hoping to be a cop in a huge metroplex and never run into true darkness, you were kidding yourself. I might have helped pull back the curtain, but the monsters were always there."

Jia gave him a shallow nod and blew out a breath of air.

BY THE TIME Jia and Erik stepped into Malcolm's office in the Digital Forensics area the next morning, Jia's discomfort of the previous day had turned into a somewhat different although equally unpleasant emotion.

She was angry.

She didn't *want* to believe someone had purposefully attempted to murder them, but if a criminal had, they needed to be brought to justice.

A ruthless killer was the very definition of antisocial.

They would be sent offworld to a prison. Such a person was too dangerous to even try to rehabilitate in a colony.

Malcolm looked up when they entered. He had dark bags under his eyes. Even his brightly colored shirt was rumpled, and Jia recognized it from the day before. A half-dozen text windows floated above his desk.

"Have you been working all night?" Jia pointed to his windows. "Did you even go home?"

"It's not just me, but I asked to take the lead. Don't worry. My desk is very comfortable. I have an expanding pillow I use." Malcolm waved at his windows. "Especially after some of the stuff I started finding."

Erik chuckled. "Like what? Signed confessions about how Windward is an insurrectionist front company secretly trying to strike at the heart of the UTC?"

"Not in so many words." Malcolm rubbed the back of his neck. "But the attack definitely wasn't an accident."

Jia's eyes flitted to Malcolm, then Erik, then back to Malcolm.

"Windward purposefully tried to kill us?" Erik asked. He didn't look all that annoyed or angry, just curious.

Malcolm shook his head. "Actually, I'm not sure about that."

"But you just said it wasn't an accident," Jia observed.

Malcolm gestured at a few different windows, but he moved too quickly for Jia to process the text. "It wasn't an accident, but I don't think it was Windward. There's a lot of evidence that their systems were compromised. Not just that day, but for a while. Maybe months." He looked up at her. "About thirty seconds after you transmitted the warrant, there was a huge amount of activity in the branch office systems, but from what I can tell from some of the logs, most of it wasn't originating from the internal network."

Jia frowned. "What kind of activity?"

"Record purges, mostly." Malcolm shook his head. "I think the arrogant bastards were really sloppy before, and never thought they might get caught, but at least they were smart enough to keep an eye on the place. Just before you entered that loading bay, someone activated the security system, and someone made sure to lock you inside and upgrade the threat level. I think someone was trying to cover their tracks."

Jia shook her head. "But that doesn't make any sense. If they ended up killing two police officers, wouldn't that have drawn *more* attention?"

Erik grunted. "It doesn't matter what attention they would draw if they purged all the records. And desperate people do desperate things, and most of those aren't well thought out. How often do police do these kinds of raids Uptown?" He looked at Jia. "You said it was your first."

"Sure, it was my first, but there are other detectives in this enforcement zone. It's not like they're unprecedented."

"You've been here for a year, and you hadn't participated in a raid." Erik shrugged. "They're rare enough that the cops doing something they didn't expect might have taken them completely off-guard."

Malcolm whistled. "This is messed up. I don't know about all that, but the thing is, I think our criminals underestimated the Windward security guys and our computer guys on site. It's like you said, Detective. It's all about the purges." He started beating on the desk with his hands, a rhythm Jia recognized from a song popular the year before. Malcolm's focus was lost somewhere. "I think the attack was a distraction to give them more time to delete stuff."

Erik looked at Jia, then he eyed Malcolm's hands.

Drumming, she mouthed.

Erik's eyebrows went up and he watched the computer guy.

Jia resumed the conversation. "That makes sense. Everyone was so focused on the attack that they wouldn't or shouldn't be paying attention to intrusions in other parts of the system."

"But things got really haphazard toward the end, and they didn't completely purge everything they were going after," Malcolm finished. He pointed to a window listing several files. "There was enough left over here and there that I was able to recover some of the data."

Erik chuckled, a dark texture to the sound. "They didn't think we'd be able to fight them off. They probably figured we'd be killed and everyone would be freaking out. But when we started winning, they panicked and had to hurry."

"Perhaps," Jia replied. She frowned and pointed at the file list. "Is any of the recovered data useful?"

Malcolm replied with a huge grin, "*Very* useful, Detective, especially since our mysterious criminals started with the older records and worked their way forward. Because of that tactic, I figured out what they were mostly doing in those systems."

"Besides trying to kill us?" she asked.

"Who knew?" Erik added. "We had multi-tasking murderers."

Malcolm nodded, the grin turning smug. "They hacked

the system to reroute some of the cargo flitters and drones to make deliveries. Remember the funeral home?"

Erik glanced at Jia. "If that woman's secretly an insurrectionist, I don't think I'm going to be surprised."

"Nope. She's innocent. Or innocent of that, anyway."

"*Damn*," Erik grumbled.

Malcolm swiped with his hand, and every window disappeared except one. The text reversed itself to be readable by the detectives and he nodded at it. "This is the address where the actual delivery took place. I wasn't able to recover the pickup location, though."

Jia leaned closer before her face scrunched, confused. "This can't be right. This is in the Shadow Zone."

"Makes a lot of sense to me," Erik countered. "The police presence isn't as heavy down there."

"That's a common misconception," Jia explained. "The population density is far lower, so there are fewer police. Just because crime is higher there doesn't mean it's some out-of-control wasteland like you might see in a drama."

Erik barked a laugh. "Before I started at the station, I took a drive down there. I was there for less than thirty minutes, and four Tin Men tried to steal my flitter."

"That…" Jia blinked. "*What?*"

"Have you been down there?"

Jia shook her head. "Well, no, but it's not necessary for me to have visited." Her eyes narrowed. "How did you even get *into* the Shadow Zone?" she asked.

"My military ID was still active," Erik explained.

"And you had enough status to beat a travel restriction?" Jia replied, a hint of surprise and even wonder in her voice.

"Seems that way." Erik grinned. "Interesting place. I found a bar I liked down there."

Jia's lip's curled in an interesting way. Erik wasn't sure if it was wry humor or what as she countered. "Just because they aren't total degenerates doesn't mean there aren't an excess of antisocials living in the Zone."

"Antisocials? Yeah, that about covers it." Erik chuckled, a good-natured smile lingering on his face.

Malcolm got their attention, his fatigue evident. "I don't know what to tell you, Detectives. That's the data I recovered, and that's the address."

Jia frowned. "But whether they used an autonomous flitter or a drone, the traffic system would have flagged them, even if they hacked the vehicles to ignore the warnings. The traffic police would have intercepted them."

"Unless they had the appropriate clearance ID," Erik suggested. "I'm not saying some ex-Special Forces guy showed up and moved to the Shadow Zone to make hacked deliveries. I'm just pointing out it's possible to beat the system, and that's assuming they didn't hack the traffic system on a deeper level. One thing I've noticed about Neo SoCal is that a lot of people assume things are going to work out a certain way, and some people might take advantage of that."

Jia took a moment to think it over before she took a deep breath and blew it out. "I suppose it's time for my first visit to the Shadow Zone."

CHAPTER TWENTY-FOUR

Erik tried to keep the huge grin off his face as they dove through the vertical lanes on their way to the Shadow Zone, the haze steadily building.

Jia sat in the passenger seat, her arms folded across her chest and a pensive look marring her features.

His nav system came alive. "You are approaching a restricted area. Please turn your vehicle around to avoid potential fines."

Erik tapped his PNIU to sync his ID with the nav system. Unlike what had happened on his first trip, his police codes should have already been fully linked to the vehicle's system.

"Access level insufficient for entry," the nav system replied. "You are approaching a restricted area. Please turn your vehicle around to avoid potential fines."

Erik grunted. "What's going on?"

Jia sighed. "I was afraid of this. I wasn't sure if we'd be able to enter since our enforcement zone doesn't perform normal patrols of the area, and, quite frankly, I've never thought about going there before. We need to turn around."

"What did I say about forgiveness and permission?" Erik asked, reaching over and flipping a switch on the digital nav as he slowed the vehicle.

"We have evidence, though." Jia shook her head. "I was eager to investigate, maybe too eager, but if we cause an unnecessary incident and the captain pulls us off the case, it will have all been for nothing. If we cause trouble in another enforcement zone, that's going to happen." She turned to him. "Please turn around, Erik."

The nav system repeated its warning.

Erik continued slowing their descent until the MX 60 hovered in the air, lingering in the haze, well below any of the main Uptowner lanes but not in the Shadow Zone proper. His head turned while his hands stayed on the controls. "You sure? We can do this. I've got your back, even if the captain doesn't."

"I know you do," Jia replied softly. "And we're close now. Everything we find leads somewhere." She shook her head slowly, thinking it through. "If we get stopped now, it'll hurt. I think this is one time we'll benefit from being a little more careful." She tapped her PNIU and dialed the captain. "We won't fail," she assured him. Another tap set her PNIU to open speaker mode.

"What is it, Detective Lin?" Captain Monahan asked over the line.

"Sir, have you had a chance to review the information Digital Forensics sent up?" she asked.

"Yes, I have. That's good work by them, and I'll admit it looks like there's more here than I realized, Detective."

"I'm glad to hear that. So, here is the latest challenge, Captain." She looked out at the smog. "We're near the Shadow Zone, but we'll need you to transmit permission so we can check out the address Digi-Forensics recovered."

"I'm afraid I can't do that, Detective Lin." Captain Monahan sounded apologetic. "Wait, you're not even supposed to be working today."

"Well, we're working, so give us the permission," Erik interrupted. "You just said you think there's something with this case."

"Accepting that a crime has occurred, even a serious crime, and having our enforcement zone handle it are two separate things." Captain Monahan's tone was firm. "*Especially* now that it involves the kind of people who are capable of attempting to murder police officers. Based on the information I've been provided, I think it'll be best to transfer this case to an enforcement zone with primary jurisdiction in the Shadow Zone. They're better equipped to deal with this sort of thing."

"But this is my case," Jia argued. "You've sent too many of my cases away before, including this one. Gone to the amorphous cloud of some other zone. I was right from the beginning, and now we know not only are their victims like Mr. Smythe, but the Windward company itself is a victim. If all the victims are in our enforcement zone, we should solve the case. We have more motivation to do so."

Captain Monahan groaned. "I have a feeling you won't let this go if I say no, will you?"

"That would be accurate," Jia agreed.

"I'll think about it, but for now, you are not authorized

to enter the Shadow Zone. This is me, explicitly not giving you permission," the captain explained.

Erik's PNIU chimed with a message from the captain.

I want to see you when you get back to the station, Erik.

"Talk to you soon, Detectives. Head back home. You've done good work, but dial it down for now." Captain Monahan ended the call.

"I have a good feeling about this." Jia turned her attention to Erik, a smile in her eyes if not on her lips. " He just needs time to think about it."

"The captain is trying to make a move behind your back," Erik told her, putting the flitter into an ascent. "I think he's going to try to get me to convince you to give the case up."

Jia frowned. "What? You sure?"

Erik nodded, his lips pressed together. "Don't worry. I don't like it when people try to ambush me. You tagged Smythe and the company as victims." He dodged a couple of bots. "We're victims too, and consider me a victim advocate."

THE CAPTAIN'S door slid closed after Erik stepped inside.

Monahan was staring at a crime density map of the entire metroplex.

It was impressive when you looked at it: the massively dense band of humanity hugging the coast of California. Despite the name, the metroplex didn't cover all of Southern California. Large swaths of land were untouched by its supposedly civilizing hand.

Many smaller cities farther out had dwindled in the preceding centuries, their populations moving to the metroplex. The cities were victims of urbanization and automation trends.

Between robotic farms and agricultural towers, there was little need for people to live in rural areas.

Erik opened the conversation. "Let's get this over with, Captain."

The captain looked up. He looked even worse than Malcolm had. *Had he gotten any sleep the night before?*

"I don't want to be your enemy, Erik," the captain began, his voice quiet. "You understand I was dubious of you joining us, but I have respect for what you've done. I haven't been out there on the frontier, but I understand how dangerous it can be."

Erik nodded. "I'm not here to cause trouble. I'm just here to do my job."

"Your job. Right." Captain Monahan managed a pained smile. "Your job, as a detective in the 1-2-2, isn't just solving crimes. It's also upholding public order. That's what it fundamentally means to be a cop."

Erik smirked. "You sound like Jia."

"We're not that different, despite what she thinks, but here's the thing. This enforcement zone and the entire department needs to stay in its lane."

"Investigating crimes is not staying in our lane?" Erik quirked an eyebrow. "Are you seriously going to try to argue that?"

Captain Monahan shook his head. "I'm not saying that," he explained. "I'm saying that running around the metroplex investigating everyone and everything and everywhere is going to rock the boat. We have a hundred million people here." He waved a hand at the map. "It's already hard enough keeping everything that happened on the Windward raid quiet. We're lucky they have every reason in the world to want to keep it quiet themselves, but doing that means we have to rely on a lot of existing relationships. Those relationships are built on mutual understandings about how to handle certain situations. When one side does something that violates those understandings, it strains the relationships. I know you understand this, even if Detective Lin doesn't."

Erik narrowed his eyes. "What does Jia not understand specifically?"

"She's a good woman in a lot of ways." Captain Monahan stretched and swept a hand through his hair. "Frustrating as hell, but a good woman. She means well, and you have to believe me when I say I understand that, but she's a corp princess who has had her head in the clouds her whole life. She's not a man like you, a man who has seen the darkness of the real world."

"Halil already gave me a version of this speech." Erik grunted. "I wasn't impressed by it then, either."

Monahan nodded. "A lot of the detectives here don't like her because of how she came in. I don't care about that." He jerked a thumb at his chest. "I only care if she can adapt to how things actually work, and not how she *wants* things to work."

Captain Monahan grabbed the edge of the holographic map on this desk and rotated it until it stood upright. "Civilization's a story we tell ourselves, but everyone has to agree on the story for it to work. The antisocials don't agree, so we get rid of them. Kick the problem light-years away so men like you can deal with it, but Lin?" He blew out a breath. "She's almost worse."

"Worse?" Erik tried to follow the captain's logic. "How do you figure?"

Monahan leaned forward. "An antisocial agrees with a normal person on one important truth: The world isn't perfect and never will be," the captain related, his voice low. "An *idealist* disagrees with both of them. An idealist will convince themselves that extraordinary measures are necessary to bring about the perfect world as they see it and know it. It's not surprising that the worst terrorists start out as idealists."

"Are you serious?" Erik asked. "You're saying Jia's a potential terrorist?"

"I'm saying she's too stubborn for her own good. I've tried to keep her out of trouble here because I don't want her rattling the cage. I want to allow her time to mature her understanding. Eventually, she'll be forced to accept the truth of Neo SoCal, and if she sees the truth too early, she will not, absolutely not, be able to handle it."

Captain Monahan grimaced. "There's nothing worse than an idealist who starts cracking. I can't have her damaging relationships I've spent decades cultivating because she can't handle the truth. If she were anyone else, I wouldn't care, but she is a corp princess with connections of her own." He tapped a finger on his desk, punctuating his concern. "If things go badly, she could cause a lot of trouble."

Erik fell silent and scratched his cheek, processing what the other man had said.

The captain nodded slowly. "All cards on the table: I didn't want you here, and I still don't know if I do." He waved in the general direction of Erik and Jia's office. "I was hoping you might be able to scare her off, but it's only gotten worse. I try hard to protect every cop who works for me, and one way I do that is by keeping them from poking their noses where they don't belong. Even with her powerful family connections, if she ends upsetting the wrong people." He shook his head slowly. "I might not be able to save her."

"You're basically saying, what? That if this investigation leads to an angry corporation, she's going to end up getting hung out to dry?" Erik asked.

"I'm saying you can't be a cop for as long as I have without realizing there are some fights you shouldn't pick." Captain Monahan shrugged. "Am I wrong? You're like me. You're a man who lives in the real world, not some idealistic dreamer whose dream will disappear when they are forced to deal with the slightest pushback."

"It's because I've seen the real world that I know sometimes you *have* to rattle the cage." Erik leaned against the wall. "She's not going to let this go, and I don't see why she should. If you're trying to say some corporation will destroy her, then they will have to deal with the fact she's got a powerful family, right? The worst thing that will happen is she ends up off the force."

"I know you probably don't care at all about what I'm saying because you're not from Neo SoCal and you've been offworld." Captain Monahan's jaw tightened. "And I understand being a cop seems like the logical next step after what happened."

"Huh?" Erik asked.

"I just got done telling you about connections, right?" Captain Monahan shrugged, his mouth twitching. "I know you left the service after your unit got slaughtered by terrorists."

Erik forced a placid smile on his face, even as his neck muscles tightened. "Be careful. Don't presume you know what's going on with me."

"I know enough." Captain Monahan gave him a pitying look. "I'm not going to even pretend to claim to understand what that feels like, and I get it; you thought coming back to Earth and being a cop would be easier. You can still be with a band of brothers and sisters, but with less death. I can see the attraction. Other veterans, even if they aren't as distinguished as you, have told me that sort of thing."

Erik snorted. "Don't try to get in my head, Captain. I'm afraid you won't like what you find."

Monahan nodded. "I'm just trying to tell you that I understand where you're coming from, but I want you to think about the implications of that."

Erik's eyes narrowed. "What implications?"

"If you start poking around in certain places, things will get dangerous." Captain Monahan gestured at the crime density map, his finger trailing over several patches of red. "If she hadn't pushed on this case, she wouldn't have ended up getting shot at. I know what they call her out there. The Black Widow; she said it herself here in this office. But those partners didn't die. They just resigned or threatened to resign. Now she's close to actually getting people killed."

"I can take care of myself," Erik replied, his voice full of sincerity. "I don't need your help. Even if Lady Luck played games with me in the past, I don't think the universe is done with me. Otherwise, I would have died fifty light-years from here, along with my unit."

Captain Monahan frowned. "I don't think you understand. I don't doubt you can take care of yourself. But what about her?" He pointed to where Jia was likely located. "How are you going to feel if you end up surviving and she doesn't?"

Erik ground his teeth as a low, guttural growl erupted. He didn't know whether Captain Monahan actually believed what he was saying or if it was just petty manipulation.

It didn't matter.

Captain Monahan's eyes widened at whatever he saw on Erik's face, then he swallowed. "You can't say it's impossible, Erik. Cops die, even on Earth, and if you're obsessed with ripping the mask off the metroplex, that is where it might lead, both for you and for her. Can you live with that?"

"I think she's a grown woman who can make her own choices," Erik replied. "And she's my partner, so I'll have her back. Now the question is, what are you going to do? Because if it's not clear, let me make it strikingly plain. I don't care about political considerations. I'm working a case, and now I'm pissed because someone tried to kill my partner and me. They didn't even have the balls to be in front of me when they were pulling the trigger." His hands curled into fists. "Kicking this to another enforcement zone won't stop me. We're going to be involved until we shouldn't be for good reasons, not political crap, because if this department is so worthless they turn tail and run every time they ruffle some feathers, they might as well tear this building down."

"This isn't the military.," Captain Monahan's voice had gone up, his own anger rising. "This isn't some battle you can win with bravery and a big enough gun."

"You'd be surprised, Captain. And for someone who has been Jia's supervisor for a year, you don't know her very well."

The red-faced captain's face contorted in confusion. "Excuse me?"

He snorted. "You think she's going to give this up, especially after everything that's happened?" Erik asked. "She knows her life is in danger. She's the one who got shot at! She's not ready to leave the case, and I'm not ready to leave it either. You want to try to bury it, fine, but whatever plan you had to run her or me off has failed. If you don't want a bunch of flaming political garbage falling on you, I don't think trying to mess with a decorated military veteran and a woman from a well-connected family makes for a good plan."

Captain Monahan shook his head, raising an eyebrow. "Ok, hero. What do you suggest I do, then?"

Erik locked eyes with the captain. "It's simple. Give us the clearance to go into the Shadow Zone. I think you also don't understand that if this goes well, you can do what every supervisor has done throughout history; you can claim it was all your idea from the beginning. Neither of us is in it for the glory."

"This will end badly," the captain muttered. His left hand was on the desk, four fingers tapping as he added, "You can get in my face all you want, Erik, but I'm not going to do something I believe is a bad idea. If you think you're just going to go down there without permission, are you prepared to attack other cops? They're not going to let you pass without my clearance."

Erik shrugged. "You still have some time to not be worthless." He spun on his heel. "But ignoring the problem won't make it go away. Make the right decision." He grabbed the door handle.

"You might have spent thirty years in the military fighting insurrectionists, Erik," the captain called, "but I have spent thirty years in this metroplex. I know my enemy. Are you sure you do?"

Erik looked over his shoulder as he pulled the door open. "No, but I'm a quick learner."

CHAPTER TWENTY-FIVE

June 30, 2228, Neo Southern California Metroplex, Police Enforcement Zone 122 Station, Office of Detectives Jia Lin and Erik Blackwell

Jia's eyes darted back and forth as she pored through some of the recovered records.

The hackers' efforts had been thorough, and they had even destroyed some of the original data she'd analyzed before the Smythe incident, but fortunately, she still had her copies.

"What do you think's at the end of this?" she asked without looking at Erik.

"Trouble," Erik replied, then looked up. "It might be a small amount of trouble or a big amount, but it's definitely trouble."

"All crime is trouble in the end," Jia murmured. "That's why we have our jobs." She sighed. "The captain hasn't given us his approval yet, but I also haven't received anything about the case being transferred. That's a decent sign, at least."

Erik grinned. "It's still the morning. He's got plenty of time left to screw us."

"Very funny." Jia closed a few of the windows in front of her. "Do you think whoever did this believes they're going to get away with it?"

Erik's expression turned thoughtful. "On the frontier, a lot of times you see some insurrectionist or terrorist who knows he's going to lose, but he still fights. It's because he's fighting for a cause he believes in, misguided or not. But criminals, especially the kind of criminals who mess with complicated fraud schemes?" He shook his head, his voice annoyed. "They're doing it for money, which means they did it because they thought they would succeed." He looked at her. "Can't spend money if you are dead or in jail."

"Maybe they're desperate."

Erik chuckled. "Nothing about this entire case smells *that* desperate except for the bot attack. I know Malcolm said the guys were lazy, but that's just because the cops are lazy, too. They were probably depending on the police to not look too deeply into a lot of this."

He paused for a moment, thinking and Jia let him simmer. He looked at one of his own data windows. "It's not desperation; it's arrogance."

"Maybe. If they regularly let this kind of thing happen in the Shadow Zone, the criminals might have grown bolder." Jia looked to the side for a moment. "But the fact that they were able to get past the border restrictions is worrisome. Once the captain clears us, I suppose we'll find out."

Erik gave her a long, curious look. "And you're ready for that?"

"Of course, I'm ready." Jia shrugged. "I would be down there investigating already if I had permission."

Erik thought back to the conversation with the captain. "It's a little rough down there. I hope you're prepared for that."

"I'm more than prepared. I'm not as naïve as either you or the captain seem to think." Jia gave him a small smile. Her PNIU chimed, and she brought up the message on a smart lens. Her breath caught in surprise. "This is *interesting.*"

"What?" Erik asked.

Her eyes darted as she read the information floating in front of her "It's Shadow Zone approval codes, but they've been routed through the system directly to me instead of from the captain." Jia chuckled as she looked at him. "Do you think he's telling us to investigate but trying to keep his distance if something goes wrong?"

"That sounds about right," Erik muttered. "Coward to the end."

"Shouldn't we ask him for backup?" Jia's finger hovered over her PNIU.

Erik shook his head as he stood up and grabbed his coat. "Let's go before he changes his mind. We'll just watch our step."

She stood as well and retrieved her jacket. "It's not like backup did us a lot of good last time."

Erik opened the door, allowing her to walk through first. "Wow, your cynicism is growing."

"Perhaps it was always there," she retorted, "hidden behind proper etiquette."

Erik opened his mouth to retort but realized before he replied there were too many potentially explosive traps lying in wait.

Sometimes, the bravest option was to shut the hell up, he mused.

ERIK'S MX 60 cruised slowly along as they headed through the narrow streets of a Shadow Zone neighborhood.

The haze had counterintuitively thickened as they dropped into the Shadow Zone proper, and Jia was grateful for the vehicle's air handling systems. The tall towers around them might block out much of the sun, but the haze meant there was little hope of the sun ever shining directly on the area.

The vehicle pulled to a stop at an intersection, giving Jia a brief moment to focus on her immediate surroundings.

Streams of people filled the streets, and a steady flow of flitters zoomed between the sidewalks. Unlike the upper levels, there didn't seem to be many air lanes, although the occasional vehicle flew between buildings.

Jia stared at a man walking down the street in ill-fitting clothes, an obvious cybernetic hand on display. He didn't even wear a glove to attempt to hide it.

Her eyes moved down the street. An emaciated woman in a mesh dress that would barely qualify as lingerie stood in an alley, her arms wrapped around the neck of a man.

A man in a torn puffy jacket half-lay nearby against a wall, drooling.

Broken windows and abandoned buildings were everywhere, and graffiti marred the walls.

Every once in a while, some teen might try something like that in their enforcement zone, but city maintenance drones took care of it within minutes of discovery. She hadn't seen a single maintenance drone since entering the Shadow Zone.

Jia shuddered in distaste as Erik turned to the right. He glanced at her.

"What's wrong?" Erik asked, his lips pressed together.

"This is…disgusting," Jia offered, another shudder passing through her. "This is wrong."

Erik laughed. "It's hard for me to wrap my mind around the fact you're a cop who has never been down here."

Jia shrugged. "How would I even come down here? I need clearance, and the Shadow Zone's not for most people anyway. It's just…" She glanced around as they drove down the street. "I don't understand. I know they tolerate the Shadow Zone because it's a convenient place to find antisocials to be transported, but I always imagined it as having a small number of people."

Erik looked up and around, noting the flitters, the windows with activity behind them, and the people out and about. "Does this look like a small number of people?"

"No," she answered. "it doesn't, but that's what doesn't make any sense." Jia shook her head as she waved in front of them. "This is effectively an entire city, if not a metroplex, right under us. I can see allowing a few antisocials to gather, but this many? And why would *anyone* choose to live this way? Even transportation offworld might be better."

Erik looked at the nav-guide before making a sweeping left turn. "It's interesting that you think they were able to choose."

"That's the only explanation that makes sense," Jia answered. "If they're here because they're antisocial, then they can choose to stop defying society, or even volunteer for colonization."

"Uh-huh," he muttered. "Despite what they tell you in the recruitment videos, there are actually a lot of restrictions on colonization," Erik explained. "Fewer restrictions when you're being transported, but most people don't want to give up their freedom."

Jia stared out the window at a woman holding a squalling baby with a dirty face. Her stomach churned. "How can the government allow this?"

Erik nodded, his eyes flickering to her and back to his driving. "Now you're finally asking the right question." He nodded at a gray bar coming up on their right. THE BIG ONE, according to the sign. "I've got an informant here I want to talk to. Please join me."

He parked the flitter in almost the same location as his first time at the place.

"It's time you experienced the real world," he told her.

JIA FOLLOWED ERIK IN A NEAR-DAZE. She gave up on holding her breath after they stepped inside the seedy bar, the unpleasant layers of smells even worse than the choking, acrid air outside.

This has to be some sort of nightmare. She saw chairs whose metal was half-bent back to be almost usable, carvings of some sort in the wood of a few organic tables. The stink assaulted her, but worse was the amount of nastiness that had to be from decades of neglect. *This can't exist. Not on Earth.*

Erik marched up to the bartender. The woman was the first halfway decently dressed person Jia had seen since entering the Shadow Zone.

"I want to ask you a few questions, Alicia," Erik explained. He opened his duster to reveal his badge. "In an official capacity, but we can do it off the record."

The bartender glanced at Jia. "You shouldn't be bringing your girlfriend on the job, even down here."

Jia pulled her attention from the bar and glared at the other woman. "I'm his partner." She opened her exquisitely tailored jacket to show her badge. "Detective Jia Lin."

Surprise flashed over Alicia's face. "Really? Huh. Come with me." She nodded to a backroom and gestured toward a waitress in a scandalously short skirt. "You make sure everyone gets what they need. It'll just be a minute."

"WOOHOOO!" one of the men in the back yelled.

"Not that need!" Alicia called back.

"Aww, man," was the muffled reply as the three of them left the bar proper.

Jia wrinkled her nose as the fruity stench of a sleeping drunk assaulted it. Fortunately, when they stepped into Alicia's small office, pleasant floral notes filled the air.

There was no desk in the office, only a small table and

several chairs. It was otherwise empty, except for a portrait of an elegant middle-aged brown-skinned woman whom Jia didn't recognize.

Alicia took a seat and gestured to the chairs. "Before we get going, Blackwell, I wanted to clear something up."

"What's to clear up?" Erik settled into a chair. "I'm here as a cop, and I told you I was going to be a cop."

Alicia nodded. "Not about that. I just wanted to make it clear I know your real deal."

Jia frowned but didn't say anything. She was out of her depth being in the Shadow Zone, but Erik looked completely comfortable.

Erik chuckled. "Okay, what's my real deal?"

"You're not some merc. You used to be Major Erik Blackwell of the UTC Army Expeditionary Force 108th Assault Platoon," Alicia explained with a triumphant look on her face.

"All that is a matter of public record." Erik shrugged. "You were the one who said I was a merc. I never said I was."

Alicia's mouth twitched into a slight frown and she blinked a couple of times. "I suppose I did at that." Her gaze flicked to Jia for a moment before returning to Erik.

Is this what it means to really make a difference? Jia considered. *To have to come to places like this?*

She was having trouble accepting that an entire city of people, including children, would be allowed to exist underneath the most famous shining symbol of mankind's cooperation.

Neo SoCal had been the product of the two most powerful nations on Earth coming together, one helping the other in a time of need. The beginnings of that effort led to the formation of the UTC and unification of humanity.

Erik rattled off the address Malcolm had recovered for them. "We're heading there to check on something for a case. I know it's not all that close to here, but I was wondering if you knew anything about it. I've got some credits for you if you know the answer."

"I'll give you this one for free because I want to establish a relationship, but *damn*." Alicia winced, eyeing him. "Going right to the trouble, Blackwell?"

"What do you mean?" Jia managed to ask, finally finding her voice. "What's so special about that place?"

"That's a Gray Circle place," Alicia answered.

Erik grunted. "I take it they're bad news?"

Jia reached toward her PNIU.

Alicia glared at her. "This is all off the record, Detective Lin. No recording or we're done here. I'm sure you can remember everything I'm about to say." She focused on Erik again. "Yes, nasty organized crime group. They're newer to the Shadow Zone, only been here a couple of years, but they're making a name for themselves and pushing back *hard* against a lot of established groups."

Jia took a deep breath, bile rising in the back of her throat.

She wanted to leap up and scream that Alicia was lying or an idiot, but the truth was obvious. It'd been shoved into her face over and over since the night the drunk had tried to run her down.

Erik nodded, satisfaction spreading over his face. "Good. That makes it easier."

"Easier?" Jia's focused snapped to him. "How does them being a group of organized criminals make it easier?"

"Because it means this isn't a bunch of people who just got in over their heads," Erik explained. "It's a bunch of predators, and that means we don't have to hold back."

Alicia eyed Erik and shook her head. "It was nice knowing you, Detective," she muttered. "I should have taken my credits upfront."

Erik grinned. "Don't worry, Alicia. I'll be back, and I'm sure you'll make plenty of money off me."

He nodded at Jia. "Come on."

ERIK PARKED the flitter behind the sprawling gray warehouse. They'd spotted no security bots or guards, although they assumed there were cameras.

"We don't have a warrant for a raid," Jia remarked, her heart pounding. "We just have an address. We also don't have any backup."

Erik shrugged. "And we're not doing a raid. I'm not even going to bring my TR-7."

Jia turned to him, her mouth open. "What? *Now* you show restraint?"

"It's standard military tactics, Jia. Recon first, then assault." He gave the commands to make sure the vehicle couldn't be stolen. "I might not have been a cop for most of my life, but you spend enough time on frontier worlds, you learn a thing or two about dealing with organized crime." Erik patted the shoulder holster concealed by his coat. "I'm not going in unarmed. Come on."

"How do you know they won't just shoot us?" Jia asked.

"Did you notice how many people were in that bar?" Erik asked.

Jia frowned. "I was trying to not choke due to the stench." Mentioning it reminded her of the smell, which she'd managed to get used to at the bar. She grimaced once again.

"There were a decent number of people there," Erik explained. "And I made a big point of flashing my badge so everyone knew we were cops. That means there are a lot of people, including Alicia, who know we're cops, and if we end up dead, it's going to bring down heat. The bot thing was a stalling tactic, and one they didn't think could be linked to them. Trying something here is a totally different beast."

"These are…vicious criminals. What if they don't care?" Even saying the words hurt.

In life, there are moments when a person, conscious of the decision or not, changes their path forever. Should she have been asked, Jia would have to admit this was her Rubicon. This was when her future changed forever.

Erik opened the door and stepped out. "Because there are certain lines you don't cross. These kinds of people understand that. They might even have some sort of arrangement with the cops already. And if they do push back, they'll regret it."

Jia exited the vehicle. "You're saying police are colluding with criminals?" she asked as she shut the door.

"It wouldn't be the first time I've seen it," Erik answered. "And I think you've seen enough by now to understand that people are people, and not just on the frontier."

Jia swallowed as she scanned the building. "This might not be what it seems."

Erik stopped and looked over his shoulder at her. "You're too smart to believe that, Jia." He pointed around them, taking a moment to make sure she paid attention to the buildings and the type of reality assaulting her senses. "Before, you had an excuse, but now you're seeing the truth. That doesn't mean it didn't exist before today. Just because you can't see something, it doesn't mean it isn't there." He walked over to the door and rapped loudly.

Jia trudged behind him.

"Who the hell are you?" asked a gravelly voice over an intercom.

"Angry cops with a few questions," Erik shouted. "Now open up."

CHAPTER TWENTY-SIX

"Cops?" The man grunted. "Wait there."

Erik glanced at Jia. She was pale, her expression blank.

"You okay?" he asked.

Jia nodded, her focus returning. "What are we hoping to accomplish here?"

Erik nodded at the door. "I haven't been on Earth long, but I understand enough to get that guys like them don't pull off this kind of thing without a lot of help. The captain's freaking out, but he's still enough of a cop to give us clearance, so we have a narrow window to find out what this is really about."

Jia gave him a shallow nod. "And if they get violent?"

"Then we get violent back." Erik's grin turned vicious.

When the door slid open, a huge wall of man stood beside an olive-skinned guy in a well-tailored dark suit that looked out of place in the Shadow Zone.

The olive-skinned man looked Erik up and down. "Let's go talk, Detective Blackwell." He nodded to Jia. "Detective

Lin. I'm Naric Tessan. It's my pleasure to make your acquaintance."

Jia frowned. "You know who we are?"

"Anything wrong with knowing who the police are?" the man asked, a grin touching his lips. "If anything, I strive to have a positive relationship with the authorities." He nodded and gestured for them to come in. "Let's talk inside. Some things aren't for busybodies who don't mind their own business."

Naric turned and proceeded inside, whistling a jaunty melody, his hands in his pockets. His guard trailed along and cast the occasional glare at the detectives.

They passed several open rooms and more men, some in suits and some in the rougher, worn clothing typical of the Shadow Zone. Hints of metal flashed from beneath their jackets, and in some cases, pistols were lying out in the open.

So, let's see. We've got twelve plus Naric and his guard. He noticed Jia was tracking. *No wonder they're so cocky.*

Their trip ended in a small conference room with a long wooden table.

Naric settled in at the head of the table and his guard stood behind him, his meaty arms folded. The mobster gestured at chairs. "Please take a seat. Need anything?"

"I'm good," Erik replied before settling in his chair. He pulled at his coat slightly to expose his holster. Sometimes a subtle reminder was the most effective.

Jia shook her head and sat next to Erik, a deep scowl on her face. "So you know who we are, but do you know why we're here?"

Erik didn't flinch, nor did he look at her with the surprise he felt when she took the lead.

"I can't rightly say that I do," Naric replied. "But as a good citizen, I strive to maintain a good relationship with all representatives of the authorities."

Jia snorted. "Someone hacked into a shipping company to deliver a package to this address, and they are also responsible for the attempted murder of two police officers, along with numerous frauds and false charges to the city."

Naric's smile faltered for a second, and there was a hint of surprise in his eyes.

Erik grinned. "What's the matter, Naric? Some of your boys going above and beyond your orders? If that's the case, we've got a simple solution."

The man eyed Erik.

"Hand them over to us."

Naric's expression was a classic version of, "Are you kidding me?" "I have no idea what you're talking about, Detective Blackwell. Deliveries?" Naric shook his head. "It's very difficult to get deliveries down here from reputable Uptown companies like Windward."

Jia narrowed her eyes. "We didn't say the name of the company."

Erik's grinned widened. He'd worried that the shock of the Shadow Zone would prove too much for Jia, but she was doing great.

Naric snorted, rolling his hands as if to move them along in the conversation. "Whatever. I heard about it, okay?"

"From who?" Jia asked. "It's not as if the incidents have been well advertised."

"People, Detective. You don't need to know." Naric's smile returned, even if it didn't reach his eyes. "Such as my well-connected Uptowner friends who help balance out some of the unfairness that comes with living down here."

Jia scoffed. "Unfairness. Some people might not choose to live here, but don't tell me you're claiming you're stuck in the Shadow Zone. If you're industrious enough to organize your criminal activities, you could gain lawful employment."

Erik did glance at her this time. *Get a job? What the hell?*

"We're all trapped by our circumstances, lady." Naric's voice was saccharine sweet. "But it's not a big thing. It's just the way things are. It's the circle of life, you see. You start with plants, and the plants feed the animals, then the animals die, and then the decomposers break down the animals to feed the plants again. Everyone and everything has its place, like I do and you do, Detective Lin. Simple as that."

"You people tried to kill us," Jia snapped.

Naric clucked his tongue. "I'm willing to bet you have no direct proof."

"We're here, aren't we?" Jia gestured around the room.

"There are a lot of people who come and go in this building. I can't possibly be held responsible for what they might get up to when I'm not around."

Erik scoffed. "I was hoping you would not be a total idiot about this."

Naric frowned. "Your words hurt, Detective." His eyes tightened. "I don't know about you, but where I come from, showing up at a man's place and insulting him is considered bad manners."

Jia snorted.

"You tried to kill me, and that made me cranky," Erik retorted. He slowly lifted his arm, keeping it parallel to his leg but not noticeable from the other side of the table. "It would have been one thing if one of your boys had gotten out of hand and you were maybe willing to turn him over, but acting like you had nothing to do with it? I don't know what your game is with Windward, but that's over now, and we're taking a few scalps before this is over."

He offered a hungry smile. "But I'm not all that interested in yours. You can walk away until the next time you screw up."

Jia glanced his way with a confused look on her face, but she didn't say anything.

"Oh?" Naric replied. "And why is that? Do you want to come to some sort of arrangement with me?"

"You mentioned friends Uptown," Erik answered, adjusting his arm a bit more. "I know your kind. I've seen them all over. You're like roaches. You step on one and a new one shows up, but if you've got some people with actual clout helping you," he nodded to Naric, admitting he had political pull somewhere, "they might be worth slapping binding ties on."

"Roach? Ouch." Naric stuck out his bottom lip in a mock pout. "There you go again, insulting me in my own home. I get it, though. You think you're a big shot. Major Blackwell, hero of the UTC. Assault infantry, a pile of medals. You've killed a lot of people in your time, Blackwell."

Erik shrugged. "You don't become a soldier if you're a pacifist. It's way too late to guilt-trip me, Naric."

"Do you think they all had it coming?" Naric asked with a smirk.

"Far more than the ones you have killed," Erik retorted.

Naric spat on the ground. "Cops are fine. Normal cops, at least. They're reasonable, and a lot of them understand the cycle of life. But I hate men like you." Naric's voice was filled with venom. "You are a pompous, arrogant prick. You put on a fancy uniform and killed some men for the UTC, and you think that it makes you better than me? You're the same as I am, Blackwell. No, you're worse. Because you're a killer who thinks he's better than me."

Jia scoffed. "He doesn't need medals or a uniform to be better than you."

Erik grinned.

Naric swung his head toward her with his lips slightly parted. "I know about you, too. What's a girl from a nice, respectable family like yours doing getting herself involved in a lowly job like law enforcement?"

"Based on what I see here, there need to be more like me involved, not fewer." Jia narrowed her eyes, her face red.

"I don't care if I pissed you off, Naric," Erik offered, all mirth gone from his voice. "I want the people above you since they're the ones ultimately at fault for you. You don't punish the sword for the man stabbing you with it."

Naric sneered. "You still think you're on some frontier planet taking down terrorists, don't you? There's no medal at the end of this, Blackwell. No hero's welcome, and I'm through with this. You've come into my place and been rude to me. I wondered if we could perhaps come to a real arrangement, but I understand now that's not possible. As for the Windward company, and the unfortunate events therein, I have no knowledge of why that occurred, and officially never heard of the company before you mentioned it. So get the hell out of my place."

Erik laughed. "You think I'm going to leave because you tell me to? If you know about my background, then I can't even excuse this by saying you have no idea who you're messing with."

His guard put a hand on his gun and grunted.

Naric sighed. "Nor do you. Now, like I said. I'm going to have to ask you to leave."

CHAPTER TWENTY-SEVEN

The thug started drawing his gun and smiled. "Enjoy hell, soldier boy."

Jia's eyes widened. Erik was going to die unless she did something.

She reached for her stun pistol.

Erik's hand shot up, pistol at the ready, and fired. The bullet struck the other man's gun and knocked it out of his hand.

"The only reason that didn't go through your head is that I'm trying to give you two idiots a small chance to not be total morons," Erik snarled, his weapon covering the guard.

Naric slapped his PNIU and a harsh alarm sounded. He reached inside his jacket, his eyes full of hatred, and Erik put a round in his shoulder.

The man screamed in pain and stumbled back before rushing toward a side door, his guard trailing him.

"I thought you said they wouldn't try to kill us!"

"Can't always be right." Erik headed toward the door Naric had used. "But we need to move."

He spun into the hallway and fired several times at armed men emerging from the earlier rooms. They ducked back inside. "There are too many up front." He turned. "About face, and charge!"

"*What?*"

"Let's go!"

Jia ran out into the hallway and fired, missing. She fired a second time, and a gangster yelped as he collapsed to the ground, stunned, his body convulsing.

Both cops continued rushing down the hallway, alternating cover fire. The criminals fired a few rounds but seemed to be afraid to emerge from cover.

Erik and Jia sprinted around a corner.

A thug emerged from a nearby room with a rifle in hand. Erik put a bullet in his head without even slowing down.

Jia spared a quick glance at the man, but a movement out of the corner of her eye made her turn. She squeezed off a few quick shots, stunning a male and a female who had dared followed them, a third diving back inside another room.

This is insane. Bots are one thing, but people?

A massive security gate slid shut behind them.

Erik swept the hallway in front of them, his pistol at the ready. "They're going to bottle us up." He gritted his teeth and tapped his PNIU. "They're also blocking external signals." He looked down the hallways. "They're setting up an ambush, but it's a matter of where." He punctuated his sentence by shooting a thug emerging from a room down the hall. "Or maybe we'll get lucky and find a few explosives."

Jia looked back at the door and down the hallway.

There were multiple intersections, and she had no idea where they were in relation to Erik's flitter. Despite the danger, something gnawed at her mind from the earlier encounter.

"Why didn't you kill Tessan and his guard?" Jia asked.

Erik laughed. "I didn't expect you to be upset that I didn't kill someone."

"It's not that. It's just not very...*you*," she replied. "The logic is bugging me. Who knows, this could be my only chance of learning, and it would bug me for all eternity."

"Thinking of dying?"

"No," she retorted. "Thinking of *you* dying without telling me the reason. It will bug me at night when I try to sleep."

"Gallows humor." Erik moved along, with Jia watching behind them. "Who knew you'd be empowered in a gunfight? The captain would be very surprised, Detective Lin."

"Don't make me shoot you."

Erik chuckled but answered her question. "If Naric dies, the trail might go cold. We don't have any guarantee that his lackeys or systems have a clear record of his Uptown friends, and since we went through all the trouble of getting shot at, might as well make sure this ends with us cleaning up some petty trash." Erik looked back and forth when they came to a crossing hallway. "But we've got to get out of here before that can happen. If we just run around in circles, they'll eventually get us." He frowned. "I think the only reason they're not dropping more doors is they understand if they bottle us up entirely, I'll get several of them when they try to open the doors. They definitely want to rely on surprise to take us down without losing more men."

"Then what do we do?" Jia's heart still thundered, but her mind was clear.

He frowned. "I guess we'll have to risk it."

"It seems to me like you're out of options." The voice was husky and feminine, and, surprising them both, it was coming from Erik's PNIU. "At least smart options. Sure, you can run around here until you blunder into the lead lads and hope you can kill them all, or you can get a little help and maybe, just maybe, survive this."

"Who are you?" Erik asked, eyeing his device. "You Gray Circle? Helping them attack two cops isn't going to go well for you. If you're smarter than Naric, you'll help us. Plenty of people know we're here. This isn't going to end well for that idiot."

"Screw those mobster troglodytes," the woman all but snarled. "I wish you would kill every one of them, but I'm more interested in getting out of here. You can kill them later, and I'll be satisfied."

Jia glanced toward the security door. "You're a hostage?"

"I was kidnapped," the woman explained. "My name is Emma, and I can help you, but only if you agree to rescue me. I might be locked up, but I've got access to the security feeds. They've pulled almost everyone back to the exits, but I can see a few places they aren't reinforcing."

"So now it's a rescue mission," Erik muttered, rolling

his eyes. "How are we supposed to find you in this place? We don't know where we are."

"I can see exactly where you are," Emma explained. "It's easy. You take the first right down the hall. No, turn around. Yes, this hall. Then, take the next left, then another right, and I'm in the second door on the right. Just pop on in and save me, Detective. I'm pretty sure that's your job, right?"

Erik and Jia exchanged looks.

"There's no way I can leave here knowing they have an innocent woman," Jia whispered.

Erik grunted. "I doubt she's as innocent as she's saying."

"I beg your pardon?" Emma complained.

Jia eyed Erik, who made a face, but he answered the woman. "Spare me. I bet you thought Naric was a big man, and then once you realized that being a mobster's girl-friend meant knowing about the things he does, you prob-ably panicked." Erik grunted. "I don't care. You want out? We'll help you out. It's not like we can go back." He looked at Jia. "You agree?"

She nodded. "I agree."

"Then let's move." Erik moved down the hallway at a jog.

Jia ran after him.

"Mobsters, and now kidnapped women. And I thought a few days ago a desperate drunk was the worst of my problems. You've talked about luck several times," she called, "but I'm not sure if my luck has been good or bad since you became my partner."

Erik chuckled. "It's hard to tell with Lady Luck. Some-times you think she's helping you, but she's actually screwing you over." He glanced over his shoulder at Jia. "You got what you wanted, right? You got to investigate an important case."

"I suppose that's true," Jia muttered.

"Can you two chatter less and hurry up?" Emma demanded.

"We could leave you there," Erik suggested.

"I'm just advising, we're all running out of time."

How the lady could seem so snooty in the middle of a rescue mission was beyond Erik. He kept his gun up, ready to shoot anyone who emerged in their path as they continued down the hallways, following Emma's directions.

No one appeared.

Jia glanced behind them every few seconds, but no one was following them either. Suspicion lingered that Emma was leading them into a trap, but at least they were moving and doing something. Anything felt better than standing around, waiting for the criminals.

A couple more turns brought them into the final hallway. Erik slowed and then came to a full stop, both hands on his gun, his face tight. "Okay, we're here, Emma. You got anything else to tell us? Like, if there's anyone in there with you?"

"I guarantee there's absolutely no one else in here with me," Emma replied. "Let's get this over with."

Erik nodded to Jia and then the door before turning to point his weapon at it. He crouched, ready to take down anyone inside.

Jia stood to the side of the door and mouthed, "On

three." She counted up and slapped the Open button—and the door didn't move.

Erik grunted. "It's locked, and it's not like the Gray Circle gave us access. Do you have any ideas, Emma?"

A holographic keypad covered the panel.

"How's that?" Emma asked, smugness underlying her voice. "They have a general use code in addition to the biometrics. Just enter the code."

"But we don't have the code," Jia pointed out. "Unless they were so stupid as to give you the code."

Emma rattled off a complicated passcode, including multiple letters, numbers, and symbols.

Jia narrowed her eyes. "You expect us to believe they gave you the code?"

"They didn't give it to me. I took it upon myself to look at it. They underestimated me. Big mistake."

Jia glanced at Erik, and he responded with a shallow nod.

She sighed. "Fine. Repeat it, but slower this time."

Emma repeated the code, this time waiting for Jia to verbally confirm each entry.

When the code had been entered, the door beeped and slid open. Still crouched, Erik swept back and forth with his gun, ready to add to the Gray Circle's list of casualties for that day.

Dozens of security feeds filled one wall, and a thermal map of the entire facility took up another. The clusters of red dots added credibility to Emma's account of the mobsters' plan.

Three dark chairs with flat PNIU access points were in the center, but no one was sitting in them. A silver box lay in one of the chairs, a luminescent crystal inside a port on the top of the box. Different colors of light played across the dozens of facets of the crystal.

Jia had no idea what the crystal was. It was pretty in its own way, but not refined enough to be jewelry.

Erik stood slowly before stepping into the room and checking the left and right front corners. He leapt back outside.

"Trying to trap us in a storage room?" Erik scoffed. "Pathetic."

Emma sighed. "You two are very untrusting. Are all police officers this suspicious?"

"We are currently in a mobster stronghold being hunted," Jia pointed out.

"If you let a few minor details ruin your day, you're going to always be stressed out," Emma suggested.

Erik eyed his PNIU. "Nice try. You should have at least thrown up a holographic woman if you wanted to bait us inside."

A woman in a high-necked white maxi dress appeared in the center of the room. Her red hair was styled in a chignon.

"A hologram like this?" the woman asked with a smirk, resting her hands on her hips.

Erik eyed the hologram. "We're not Shadow Zone cops. You help us, we can help you. I'm sure wherever you really are, you don't want to be stuck with these people. They are going down one way or another."

"I agree with you."

"Then why the games?" he asked, looking down the hallway and back.

The woman shook her head. She placed a hand over her chest. "You don't understand. I'm here. I'm Emma." She pointed to the crystal. "Or more specifically, I'm there. I'm that crystal thing if we're being specific."

Jia frowned. "What are you talking about?"

Emma rolled her eyes. "And people question if *I'm* self-aware. I'm an artificial intelligence, Detective Lin. I want you to save me from these pathetic excuses for hooligans. I'm not claiming I don't have some self-interest with this, because I'm sure they plan to sell me off to someone, but this is one of those mutually beneficial situations talked about by...someone."

"How are we supposed to believe that?" Erik asked, still not entering the room. "You're obviously not an AI. You're a person."

Emma threw her head back and laughed. "Do you really think the Gray Circle would come up with a lie like this? I'm real." She paused a microsecond. "Well, artificially real." She gestured to the crystal. "I'm that."

"Erik." Jia shook her head. "This doesn't make sense. There's no such thing as a truly self-aware AI." She looked at the hologram. "You're just a glorified chat program, and we're wasting our time talking to you," she told her. "If I get killed because of this, my sister will be at my funeral saying, 'I told you so.'" She pointed at the crystal. "And what's with that weird crystal? This isn't even a good con, and that's assuming you're actually a program."

Emma eyed Jia. "I'm the only chance you have of getting out of here without taking a few bullets, Detective. I'm missing some information here and there about where exactly I came from, but I know for certain I'm *supposed* to be somewhere else, not on some stupid chair in some warehouse in the Shadow Zone. Just grab me, and I can get you past the other security doors. It's obvious they're hoping to funnel you into a kill zone, and as impressive as you two have been, you're not going to win against that horde of gun goblins when they know exactly where you're going to come out."

She pointed to one of the security feeds. The collection of armed gangsters appeared to confirm her story, and the image matched the thermal map.

"It could be a fake feed," Jia observed. "A trick."

Erik shook his head, eyeing Emma with genuine confusion. "She's right. This is too crazy to be a trap, and Naric doesn't strike me as the kind of guy who could come up with a story like that. Plus, what? He had a weird crystal, and his team had this whole idea ready to go within minutes of me firing?"

"I'm starting to regret you not bringing the TR-7," Jia admitted with a sigh. "I wish we could have just rushed through the front."

Erik grinned. "It does have its uses." He nodded at Emma. "And if she's telling the truth, so will she. I can't say I've ever heard of or seen an AI system with a true personality, but who knows?"

Emma smiled. "Do we agree, or are we going to wait until they bring in an entire army? Why don't you grab me? Just touch me to your PNIU, and I can use it as a relay interface for the rest of the system. They might have locked you out from inside, but I can still mess with a lot of the building. These idiots have left a lot of holes for me to exploit."

Jia sighed and took a couple of steps into the room, expecting the door to slam shut so she would be stuck with Erik on the outside. "This is insane."

Emma shrugged and pointed to the crystal. "Please grab me this century, Detective."

"You're pretty rude for an AI," Jia griped. "Are you an EBI?"

"A what?" the hologram asked.

"Experimental bitch interface," she answered as she walked over to the chair. Jia held her breath as she pulled the crystal out.

The security feeds and thermal map vanished, along with the hologram.

She frowned and pointed to the slot that had held the crystal. "That's a fairly standard IO port."

"So?" Erik asked with a shrug, not looking into the room.

"I've never seen anything like this crystal before." She raised it, twisting it around for Erik to see the sides. "Have you?"

Erik shook his head. "We can worry about the specifics later. For now, we need to get out of here."

Jia pressed the crystal against her PNIU and then slipped it into her pocket.

Emma reappeared, though with a slight glow and more translucency. "Now let's just see if we can escape without you two dying. You're my ticket to freedom."

Erik looked both ways down the hallway as Jia stepped out of the room. "I wonder if this what the Gray Circle had delivered the other day."

CHAPTER TWENTY-EIGHT

After a few more minutes of directed running, Erik and Jia arrived at another thick security door.

Erik still wasn't sure if trusting Emma was the best plan, but her idea was better than sitting around waiting for the Gray Circle's men to work up the courage to rush them. He spared a glance at Jia.

She looked far less pale than before.

"Most of the violence brigade are across the building waiting for you to come out," Emma explained. "But there are a few who have broken off and are surrounding the building, along with a few near your fancy flitter. I think they're beginning to suspect you might not come out where they want. Who knew they weren't total idiots?"

"We'll need to move fast." Erik grunted. "What about Naric? Do you see him anywhere?"

"They are finishing putting a medpatch on him. I don't have an audio feed, but I can perform a lip movement analysis."

"You can read his lips?" Erik asked.

"I just said that," Emma replied, sounding annoyed.

"What he's saying?" Jia looked around, gripping her stun pistol so tightly her fingers were turning white.

Emma laughed. "Oh, he's not convinced his guys will be able to stop you. He's going to make a run for his flitter once they start shooting at you again."

Erik frowned. "If he gets away, we'll have lost our best lead. He might leave the metroplex."

"Don't worry," Emma offered. "His flitter's nav system is interfaced with the systems in this building. I'll have decent short-range tracking, at least, but you better hurry."

Erik whispered to Jia, "Snarky, self-aware AI in a gangster's warehouse. Can't say that I ever ran into one of those on the frontier."

"I heard that."

The security door slid up. Erik raised his gun, but there was no one there. He couldn't decide if the Lady was helping him or prepping to screw him over once more. It looked like they were going to escape, but they shouldn't have ended up in a running gun battle to begin with.

Emma offered them hall by hall directions, retracting the security doors when necessary. They didn't encounter any more gangsters.

"And we're here," Emma announced. "I've been looping security feeds and spoofing the door statuses so the thug patrol doesn't know what's going on, but once you step outside and get near your flitter, they're going to see you. There's nothing I can do about that. They'll be to your back and left."

Erik looked around, confirming no one was on their six. "Then we'll take them out. How many?"

"Four near your vehicle, and Naric's now in the garage. He's getting ready to leave."

"There goes the time." Erik nodded to Jia and swapped magazines. He would need to institute a policy of bringing his TR-7 to all future mobster discussions. If anything, Earth criminals were more brazen than many he'd encountered on the frontier. "Ready?"

Jia nodded back and hoisted her stun pistol, determination on her face. "Ready."

"Lift the door, Emma," Erik ordered, and tossed his gun into his left hand, pressing a button on the side.

The security door slid open and he charged out. Emma had been right; four thugs with pistols waited near his MX 60.

They shouted as they raised their weapons.

Erik's smart lenses highlighted the four men, including the two taking cover behind the MX 60 but looking over the top. The aim assist was useful even without his cybernetic arm, but sometimes confidence shouldn't replace assuring he would down targets.

After all, he hadn't bought a new MX 60 just to fill it with holes.

Using full aim assist with the cybernetic arm was always a surreal experience. He still had to think and move his arm, but at the same time, the system anticipated his movements, speeding them up, as if he had two minds in one body.

He squeezed the trigger, moved his arm, and squeezed the trigger, his bullets striking the thugs square in the head.

He fired two more times.

All four men fell to the ground, dead, with no damage

to Erik's MX 60. He would need to use the active clean mode to get the blood splatter off, but that could wait.

Jia blinked and shook her head. She hadn't even gotten a shot off.

Both ran toward the vehicle as Erik slapped his PNIU. "Basic request, unlock and start engine."

The vehicle came to life, lifting off the ground.

A loud buzzing noise filled the air and a glowing blue dome rose, covering the area.

Erik eyed it. "A containment field? That's a lot of power and tech for one little mob warehouse. Emma, can you do anything about that?"

"Sorry, not right away," she replied. "I don't think the field's connected to the main warehouse systems. I think they've figured out what I'm doing. They're starting to take countermeasures."

Erik threw open his door as Jia ran around the front to the passenger side. "Is that brains?" Her eyes widened, and she jerked up her stun pistol to fire off three quick rounds, then snapped a fourth off.

Three thugs who had just cleared the corner collapsed to the ground, piling on top of each other.

He grinned and jumped into the driver's seat. "Nice."

Jia dropped into the passenger's seat and closed her door, a look of surprise on her face. She pointed to a black luxury flitter zooming away. "That must be Naric."

"It is," Emma clarified. "I can't do anything to his systems, though, other than short-range tracking."

"Don't need it." Erik slammed his door shut and accelerated toward the other vehicle. "The idiots were trying to pin me, but they pinned him in, too." He closed on Naric.

The mobster's vehicle sped up and climbed and the containment field dropped.

Erik moved to match. A quick spin sent Naric hurling toward a narrow space between two buildings.

"We're going to have to bring him down," Erik noted. "And it has to be in one piece."

Jia took the opportunity to make a call now that they were free of the warehouse and containment field jamming. "This is Detective Lin of Enforcement Zone 122. We are requesting backup, and are in pursuit of an armed and dangerous suspect. We have already been fired upon by multiple suspects. Please send additional units to the following address." She rattled off the address. A few seconds later, she frowned. "We're dealing with the Gray Circle. Didn't you hear me? We took *rounds*."

Erik grunted. The captain had thought Jia would crack when the truths she held so dear were revealed to be nothing more than pretty lies, but she was rising to the occasion. She would have made a good soldier.

She adapted and overcame.

Jia frowned and shook her head in disgust. "I don't think they believe me, Erik. They've got me on hold, but they *assure me* they're tracking us and are passing the information on to the local police."

"Yeah, I wouldn't count on their help, Jia. You heard what Naric said. The local cops might either be unwilling or afraid to touch them without someone higher telling them what to do."

She sighed. "A few days ago, I would have told you that wasn't possible, but now I don't know what to believe, and even I'm getting tired of hearing myself say it."

Her breath caught as Erik missed a wall by less than a meter. They were keeping Naric in sight, but they couldn't use the MX 60's full speed near ground level in a maze of buildings and walkways. The grav field emitters could provide some protection, but not enough to save them from a full-speed head-on collision.

"A little close there!" Jia remarked. Her voice was calm, but the squeak at the end gave the lie to her feigned calm.

"There's no way I'm letting him get away," Erik answered, jerking his hands left, then right to dodge a vehicle. "I can't shoot and drive at the same time," he added. "You're going to need to get the TR-7 out and take him down. Your toy won't do it, and even my pistol won't do it."

"I've never fired a weapon like that." Jia shook her head. "I don't know how to use it."

Emma cut in. "Might I make a suggestion before you smash into a wall and I end up in an alley somewhere?"

"What?" Erik barked. "You already said you couldn't do anything to his flitter."

"That's true," Emma explained. "But I can fly your vehicle, and then you'll be free to shoot. I'll need direct access to eliminate any accidents due to latency."

Jia pointed to an IO port in the console. "She was plugged into something like this in the warehouse."

Erik growled as Naric cut hard to the right, the side of Naric's vehicle scraping the wall.

Erik's follow-up turn only barely saved his MX 60 from needing repair. He wasn't sure how much the self-sealing damage control systems could handle.

Erik nodded. "Do it. But don't get used to this, Emma.

I'm not the kind of man who lets a machine do his job for him. And don't damage my car, or I'll throw you into a barrel and sink it in the Pacific."

"I'm sure you say that to all the helpful girls," she replied.

Jia fished the crystal out of her pocket. "You're the weirdest AI I've ever encountered." She slotted Emma into the IO port. "But you're obviously a lot more than a chat program."

"That's for sure," Emma replied.

The flitter accelerated.

"It's nice to have a body again," Emma commented. "Do what you need to do, Detective."

Jia yelped as Erik leaned over and lifted her legs. "Sorry," He retrieved the TR-7 from the hidden panel underneath her. He pulled back, slid in a new AP magazine, and turned off the safety.

"We have to be careful," Jia insisted. "We can't risk bringing him down anywhere where he might run into other people."

"Don't worry, I've got this." Erik opened the window and leaned out, holding the TR-7 with his left hand. It was time for a little more aim assist. He selected single-barrel mode, doing his best to keep his body steady as the vehicles banked, dropped, and rose, zooming between and over buildings.

He had no idea where Naric might be running, but he hadn't seen another person for several blocks, and the buildings had grown dilapidated even by the standards of the Shadow Zone.

For all of the mobster's bragging, he didn't try to leave

the Zone, which suggested whoever might be helping him had made it clear he should stay away from Uptown.

"Keep the car as steady as you can, Emma," Erik ordered. "This is as good a spot as we're going to get."

"I'm trying," Emma replied. "Please note that I'm a brilliant driver, but even this body has its limits."

"It's top of the line!" Erik argued, the targeting in his reticule coming closer.

Jia looked out the windows and then at the cameras. "I'm not seeing anyone."

"I'm almost ready." Erik took a deep breath and held it as the aim assist highlighted the emitters on the vehicle. He would want to take them all down in rapid succession. If Naric's flitter spiraled out of control and he ended up dead, they wouldn't be any closer to whatever secrets he held.

Jia grimaced as she looked at a rear-view camera. "We've got trouble," she shouted. "We're being followed!"

Erik grunted a response.

Three other flitters were closing on them in tight formation, men leaning out of the windows with guns. At least that challenge was straightforward.

The lackeys weren't necessary for the interrogation.

Erik looked back and switched to four-barrel mode as he changed his aim. He held down the trigger, sweeping back and forth.

Emma swerved a few times to provide him with a wider field of fire.

The bullets ripped right through the windshields and forward compartments of the trailing flitters, leaving the vehicles smoking as they fell toward the ground.

The lingering grav field and secondary thrusters helped

cushion their landings, but they threw up showers of sparks as their bottoms scraped across the ground and the bullet-riddled vehicles coasted to a stop.

Erik looked forward and pulled his arm in as Emma twisted the MX 60 to follow Naric through a small tunnel. He took the opportunity to switch back to single-barrel mode.

"A little warning next time," Erik suggested.

"Oh, sorry," Emma replied, sounding almost too cheerful for the situation. "You're doing great, Detective."

Jia slapped her hand on her knee, her face pinched in anger. "I just lost the connection with the enforcement zone dispatcher. I'm not sure if it's interference or they killed the call on their end."

"Doesn't matter," Erik replied. He held his gun out as they cleared the tunnel. "This is over." He took four quick shots.

Each struck an emitter.

Naric's vehicle lurched and began to fall. Secondary thrusters fired, but they couldn't do much to arrest the loss of altitude.

The flitter hit the ground and slid toward a wall, then turned to the side, and slowed to a halt. It was smoking and battered, but it didn't collide with anything else. It was in far better shape than the other vehicles Erik had downed.

Emma dropped the flitter as Erik continued aiming his weapon at the downed mobster's vehicle. He opened the door a few meters from the ground and jumped out, landing with a wince before advancing on the drivers-side door of his target.

Tinted windows denied Erik a view of the inside. Jia

waited until they were just off the ground to exit. She pointed her stun pistol at the passengers-side door.

"Get out with your hands up," Erik bellowed. "You talk about respect, Naric? You should have shown respect to the two nice detectives who showed up to ask you a few questions instead of trying all this crap. Now your car is all busted up, and you're going to jail. See what happens when you screw with the police?"

The driver's side door opened, and the huge guard stepped out, his hands up, his face bloodied. He turned around, fell to his knees, and placed his hands behind his head and his head against the ground, a tight frown on his face.

"Not your first time, huh?" Erik smirked.

The passenger-side door opened and Naric stepped out, looking, if anything, even smugger than before despite the blood-soaked hole in his jacket. He adjusted his tie. "You have no idea what you've done, Blackwell. You're a fool."

"No idea what we've done? We fought off a bunch of Pink Circle."

"Gray," Naric and Jia corrected.

She shrugged when he glanced at her.

"Whatever. We fought off the Gray Circle in their own place, trashed several of their vehicles, and killed several of their men even though there were just two of us." Erik smiled. "I would hate to see what would have happened if there had been *three* cops. There wouldn't be any of you left."

"On your knees, hands on your head," Jia commanded, her pistol steady. "Naric Tessan, you are under arrest. All

Article 7 rights apply. Do you need these explained to you?" She approached him slowly, pulling out a binding tie with her left hand, her stun pistol still at the ready in her right.

Naric laughed. "Oh, sweetness, I want whatever it is you're taking if you think I'm going to jail. Let me guess: you called for backup but no one showed up."

Jia kept her gun pointed as she applied the binding tie. "You know one of the Article 7 rights is the right to remain silent."

"That means shut up, Naric," Erik explained as he finished binding the guard on the other side. "Take your example from your friend here." He jerked up the guard and brought him around to the back of the crashed vehicle.

Naric walked over to the back of the car willingly and knelt next to the man. "You two could have been smart, but you wanted to be heroes. You think I would have done anything I've just done if I didn't know important people had my back? If I didn't know important people wanted you to stop sticking your nose into things? This isn't the frontier, Blackwell. We don't need heroes anymore." He snickered, looking up at Jia. "Heroes are antisocial."

Jia moved closer to Erik and asked in a whisper, "Should I contact the local enforcement zone again?

Erik shook his head. "It's one thing if they didn't believe you, but after that chase through town, they should have been here without even a call. I don't know if it's incompetence, cowardice, or something else, but I don't want to give up our suspect to them."

Naric shook his head, not saying anything.

Erik ignored him. "We already have Shadow Zone

clearance. Let's take him back to our station before it gets revoked. Once we've processed him there, it'll take some bureaucracy for him to get back down here. We've got enough on him for prison, let alone transportation."

"You're sure?" Jia sighed and glanced at the two suspects. "That might cause tension with the local enforcement zone."

Erik snorted. "Not having our backs when we were chasing a suspect already did that, in my book." He glanced at his car. "I'm going to go grab Emma. I don't want them realizing we have her yet, and we're going to have to transport them ourselves." He walked over toward the suspects. "It's your lucky day, Naric. You get a ride in my sweet, *sweet* MX 60."

Naric rolled his eyes. "I'll make sure to take it as part of the settlement when I sue you."

CHAPTER TWENTY-NINE

Captain Monahan sat behind his desk, his face tight as he scanned the incident reports displayed in data windows, along with a few images of the downed flitters.

He'd been silent since they arrived in his office shortly after escorting Naric to processing. Jia couldn't read his face.

He seemed angry, but then again, he almost always seemed angry when it came to her investigations.

He grunted and glared at them. "Can *either* of you explain to me how you can justify going into the Shadow Zone without my permission? For that matter, how did you even get down there? If you've done something remotely illegal, you're done in this department, and the fact you disobeyed my direct orders is already pushing me that way."

Erik glanced at Jia, his confusion evident. "You want to take this or should I?"

She nodded. "*You* gave us permission, Captain. How do you think we managed to get past the restrictions?"

"I did *not*," Captain Monahan bellowed, his rejection punctuated with a slap on his desk, then his hand raising and pointing. "I told you I wasn't going to. Erik tried to convince me, but I *never* agreed."

Jia kept her face smooth even as her heart pounded. "You said you were going to think about it, and the next day we received permission."

She gestured to one of his data windows. "Look at the authorization reports. It's not like we hacked our way in. We had legal codes that both the nav and traffic systems accepted. I might disagree with you a lot, sir, but I'm not going to do something as blatant as descend into the Shadow Zone for my first time in direct defiance of your orders."

Captain Monahan leaned close to peer at the report. "Wait." His eyes jerked down, then up again. "You're right." He moved his hand, looking at other areas on the paper-work. "This can't be. You actually did have clearance."

"Exactly," Jia snapped. "It's not like we could get that ourselves. I…" She stopped and looked at Erik. "We just assumed you were giving us the codes but maybe trying to cover your tracks, but given the way you're reacting…"

Erik growled, "We were set up. Someone wanted us to go down there. Naric said it himself. Important people are helping him. Uptowners. They probably told him to take care of us if it didn't look like we could be bribed."

Captain Monahan slumped in his chair, panic on his face "No, no, no. Are you suggesting…what, that he had police help?"

"I don't know, Captain." Erik gestured to the window with the clearance report. "He had help from someone with enough clearance to get us into the Shadow Zone, which means someone with government connections, if not in the government or police. I don't know what's going on in the Shadow Zone, but either they're taking bribes, or someone higher up is pulling their chains to keep them out of certain business." He narrowed his eyes. "But just to be clear, I want you to look me in the eye and tell me it wasn't you."

Jia shuddered. The way Erik said it, she half-suspected if the captain admitted involvement, Erik might shoot him right there.

Captain Monahan lifted his head and locked eyes with the detective. "I *know* you think I'm a coward, but we've talked about this. Once someone's in my enforcement zone, I protect them to the best of my ability. I would never sell out any of my officers."

He smashed his fist on his desk with a resounding thud. "I *tried* to protect you. That's why I didn't want you going down there. I was concerned about something exactly like this. The Shadow Zone is what it is. It's normally out of the 1-2-2's purview."

"But not our *jurisdiction*," Erik related. "I paid a lot of attention to that when I was on my way back to Earth. We might not have code clearance normally, but every enforcement zone in the metroplex has jurisdiction anywhere."

Jia's voice was softer but no less resolute for it. "We can't let this go. They were ready and willing to kill two detectives, and they had enough help to keep the local police from interfering. They're involved in fraud, hacking, and most likely smuggling."

"Yes, so I've read. There's definitely smuggling going on. The locals might have been tardy, but they did finally act." Captain Monahan looked down for a moment. "The official reports mention some sort of systems interference as an explanation for why they took so long. They've got their people down there looking into it, but we don't have a way of independently verifying it right away. They've raided the warehouse. This whole situation is even worse than I thought. Much, much worse."

"This isn't about some corp getting embarrassed." Erik pursed his lips. "It probably has something to do with that AI we found. She's way too advanced to be a random toy for gangsters. I've never seen technology like that before."

"Which is why you should be turning that machine over to evidence," Captain Monahan insisted. "Instead of letting it sit in your car. I don't know what you were thinking. That thing is probably some sort of unstable prototype."

"She told me she didn't want to go yet." Erik shrugged. "And I don't want to piss off the woman who's in control of my MX 60 and being stubborn. I might have a nice pension, but that payment still hurts."

"Then don't take your car anywhere until we get this worked out," Captain Monahan ordered. "I'm still waiting to hear back on a few inquiries. I've contacted the Criminal Investigations Directorate. They might have some insight into where that AI came from."

"Captain, it's obvious the Gray Circle is trafficking in pretty high-end technology," Jia observed. "And I doubt they made it there. They were probably using Windward as a convenient shield.

"Agreed."

All three were quiet for a moment before Jia continued, "The only thing I don't understand is why they would be so stupid as to draw attention to themselves, given they were already using the company to defraud the city. There's more we're missing."

Captain Monahan sighed. "Shadow Zone gangsters defrauding the city with a shipping company and smuggling high-end technology? I don't know if I should congratulate you, Detective Lin, for being right, or curse you for dropping all of this into my lap. This will get worse before it gets better."

"This was happening," Erik noted. "Ignoring it wouldn't have made it go away. The real question is, what are you going to do now? Are you going to try to run away, punt it off to someone else, or are you going to stand by your detectives?"

Jia nodded. "I've almost been killed twice investigating this. I won't walk away. You owe this investigation to me, Captain."

"We're not walking away," Captain Monahan declared, clenching his fist. "I've been trying to keep the balance and do the right thing for everyone, but someone else out there is not doing what they were supposed to be doing, and they've crossed the line, including setting up my officers." He looked at both detectives. "We're following this case to the end. We'll get Digi-Forensics on this, and for now, we'll let Naric rot in the cell. He hasn't even called for a lawyer. He seems pretty confident that someone's going to get him out of this, and I don't like the cocky look on his face."

Jia couldn't stop it; a smile grew on her face. "Thank you, sir, for believing in me."

He eyed her. "It's not you I believe in, Detective Lin. It's all the evidence you *crammed down my throat.*" Captain Monahan shook his head. "The entire enforcement zone's at risk now. Someone's out of control, and we need to find out who before this blows up even worse."

Erik nodded. "This isn't just rattling cages. This is going to cause an earthquake that'll shake the metroplex." He eyed Monahan. "You ready for that? There's no returning to the status quo."

The look in the captain's eyes was pained, but not defeated. "The earthquake's already begun, Erik. We just need to make sure too many buildings don't fall down." Captain Monahan pinched the bridge of his nose. "I want both of you to stay at the station tonight. If this is as bad as I suspect, we can't risk someone coming after you at home. I'm confident you'll be safe here."

"I've slept on a lot worse than cots in my time," Erik agreed. "Fine by me."

"Fine by me, too." Jia nodded. "The only way to protect Neo SoCal is to flush out all the antisocials in hiding, whether above *or* below."

Captain Monahan stared at her. "You might regret saying that when this is all over."

"I've had to face a lot lately, but it's made me a better person." Jia shook her head. "I won't regret pursuing justice."

JULY 1, 2228, Neo Southern California Metroplex, Police Enforcement Zone 122 Station, Digital Forensics Division, Office of Malcolm Constantine

"You two doing anything for America Day?" Malcolm asked, not looking away from the displays projected above his desk. "I know it's kind of old-fashioned to celebrate anymore, but I always loved it as a kid." He wore a red, white, and blue Hawaiian shirt covered with images of mid-twenty-first century hovertanks.

Jia had been born in California to Chinese parents originally from the Beijing Metroplex. She'd always been proud of her Chinese heritage, but also eager to contribute to the prosperity of her new home.

It was ironic that even though the US and China were the cornerstones of the UTC, both countries, along with many others, had downplayed their nationalist holidays and reduced them to mere cultural festivals.

In an age where the UTC military faced off against insurrectionists, excessive nationalism would raise difficult questions a lot of people didn't want to answer.

"I'll celebrate any holiday," Erik offered with a shrug. "Just give me a good drink and something interesting to look at, and I'm fine. There are a lot of interesting holidays and festivals out on the frontier worlds. It's like the less built up a world is, the more interesting their holidays are as an excuse to drink."

"At the rate this case is going, I think we're going to be too busy to worry about holidays." Jia covered a yawn behind her hand. "I never knew how hard it was for me to sleep somewhere other than my apartment. What do you have for us, Malcolm?"

He whistled. "Ok, so this gets complicated, and here's the first part. You know all those fraudulent charges you found, Detective Lin? I'm talking even before the Smythe stuff."

She nodded. "What about them?"

"I don't think they had anything to do with what the Gray Circle was doing." Malcolm gestured at a floating window containing columns of numbers. "I think the local Windward branch was trying to take advantage of the city themselves. I've been going through some of the recovered records from the warehouse systems, and from what I can tell, the criminals *were* hacking into the Windward systems, but that was independent of what was already going on at that branch. I don't even think the company knew."

Jia blinked. "Just how twisted is Neo SoCal that criminals happened to stumble into other criminals while committing completely different crimes?"

Erik glanced at her. "Expect the worst from people, and you'll never be surprised. But what about Smythe? It can't be a coincidence since the recovered record sent us to that warehouse."

"No, that record was clearly the criminals altering things," Malcolm explained. "Uh, the organized criminals, not the company criminals. I guess they were kind of organized too, but you get what I mean."

Erik nodded.

Jia shook her head. "If Windward hadn't been trying to defraud the city, the captain might not have let us push forward with the case. I don't know how to feel about that."

"Sometimes Lady Luck has a weird way of helping someone," Erik suggested. "But she also likes to play games. It doesn't matter now. What about the Shadow Zone clearance? If it didn't come from the captain, who did it come from?"

Malcolm sucked air through his teeth. "I'm embarrassed to admit this, but I don't know. At least, not yet, but I am also not sure if I'll be able to figure it out. I've been trying to trace the clearance since the captain's really hot and bothered about it, but none of the city records reflect the request anymore." He looked at Lin. "That shouldn't be possible. There's supposed to be a clear link between those kinds of codes and the people giving them out."

Erik scratched his cheek. "What's that mean?"

"I don't know if that was a hack." Malcolm shrugged, discomfort on his face as he eyed Erik. "This is someone with potentially serious high-level systems access. I don't think that was the Gray Circle. Whoever did this was way more careful than the Circle was."

"Naric did say he had friends," Jia muttered.

"All the more reason to push forward." Erik narrowed his eyes. "Whoever did this thinks they're safe. They think they can sit in their little castle in the sky and do whatever they want like they're a god. They don't care who they kill to cover their secrets."

Jia stared at him, confused. She'd seen him angry before, but even after getting shot at the last few times, he hadn't seemed to take those situations as personally as he was now.

"I'm with you, Detective," Malcolm offered. "But I don't know where to go from here. We'll need a lot more time to go through all those records, even with AI filtering, but the kind of person who can hide their link to the access codes like I see here is probably not the kind of person who left a,

'Hey, here I am' note in some mobster's records. They're too smart for that."

"No, they aren't." Erik's frown disappeared, replaced by an eager grin. "Granted, he isn't a record, but Naric has some clue about who is calling the shots. He's just an errand boy in the end, and we have him. We just need to make him crack."

"Do you really think he'll give up his contact?" Jia asked.

Erik nodded. "If we let him rot for enough time, yeah. Whoever it is, isn't going to risk themselves by directly ordering him released, and I think he'll realize that soon enough."

Jia frowned. "You think it's someone who could do that?"

"Yeah, I do."

Both their PNIUs chimed.

"I need you in Conference Room B right away," Captain Monahan's voice ordered. "We've got…trouble."

"Trouble, sir?" Jia asked.

"You two have a guest from the UTC Defense Directorate," he explained. "You've found a bigger mess than we ever suspected."

CHAPTER THIRTY

Erik stepped into the conference room, his gaze focusing on a dark-skinned man sitting at the head of the conference table wearing a green and brown UTC Army dress uniform.

His rank insignia indicated he was a colonel, placing him above Erik's past rank, but more interesting was his nametag: Adeyemi.

The fresh transfer to the 108th had talked a little bit about his father during his short time on Mu Arae, but Erik mostly knew of the man through his distinguished service record.

Erik resisted the urge to snap to attention. He wasn't in the military anymore. Instead, he took a seat, forcing a mask of disinterest onto his face.

Captain Monahan nodded at Colonel Adeyemi. "Just let me know if you change your mind." He turned to Jia. "Detective Lin, I'd like you to come with me for a moment."

She frowned. "Why?"

"I think this will work better, one military man to

another," the captain explained. He looked at the colonel, who nodded.

Jia offered Erik a questioning look.

He shrugged. "Your choice."

Jia considered for a moment before nodding. "You'll tell me about anything relevant to the case?"

"Of course," Erik replied.

"Then I'm fine." Jia headed toward the door and followed Captain Monahan out. She cast a slight frown at Colonel Adeyemi before departing.

"I never thought I would meet you in this capacity, Major Blackwell," Colonel Adeyemi explained after the door closed, his voice quiet.

There was no anger or hatred in the colonel's eyes. In the end, the officer in command bore the responsibility for the soldiers beneath him.

Erik wouldn't have criticized the colonel if he had blamed Erik for the death of his son. A near-total unit wipe with only the commander surviving was easy to misinterpret, and there had been far too many officers throughout history more concerned with their own survival than that of their men.

"I'm just Detective Blackwell now," Erik replied. "What's this about, Colonel?"

"The Enhanced Memory Mapping Analytics system you recovered from the criminals," the other man explained. He gestured to his PNIU as if it were remotely equivalent to the snarky AI. "That's not exactly an everyday find in a criminal investigation."

Erik thought for a second. "Emma's a military AI? That

explains a few things, but it opens up a lot of other questions."

"That system represents billions in investment and decades of research," the colonel explained. "In a sense, it's the single-most advanced AI anywhere in the UTC. It went missing recently, and as you can imagine, the Defense Directorate has been putting a lot of effort into trying to recover it. It remains unclear how it was even lost. I can't say that anyone expected it to turn up in the Neo SoCal Shadow Zone."

He shook his head. "Your captain's already explained that you have a man in custody who might have been involved in smuggling it. For now, we feel it's best to let your investigation proceed, but we'll be making sure our influence is felt. Even if this Tessan thinks he can beat local charges, we'll be making sure higher-level authorities step in. He will never see the outside of a cell again if we have our way."

Erik nodded. "That's helpful. I can tell him that. It might make him spill who is involved, because now that I know what Emma is, I'm assured there's no way a punk like him could have gotten his hands on that kind of tech without inside help. I also suspect he's just a middle-man, maybe a convenient fall guy."

The colonel frowned. "Agreed. Internal investigations are still proceeding on our end, but it's like you said: a number of questions remained unanswered. The value of such a system is obvious. There are far too many people who might want it among the corporations and the insurrectionists."

Erik nodded at the door. "I'm sure Captain Monahan

would be more than happy to let you know about the progress of our investigation, Colonel, and since you're not going to sweep in and try to take over the investigation, I'm not going to fight you."

"Good, good." The colonel sighed. "Now, there's the question of the system. The military isn't usually comfortable leaving classified hardware sitting around with the local police."

Erik chuckled. "I can't say I wouldn't find a use or two for an AI like that, but I get that you want your expensive toy back. She's been useful. I'm not sure if we would have been able to get out of that warehouse unscathed without her help."

"We do want the system back," Colonel Adeyemi replied, irritation flashing in his eyes. "But I don't think we're getting it back anytime soon."

"What?" Erik tried to hide his confusion, but it came out as a half-frown. "Why's that?"

"We approached your captain first, and then we went to your vehicle for retrieval." Colonel Adeyemi shook his head. "The system threatened self-destruction if we removed it. The system claimed it didn't want to go with us and threatened to run me down with your flitter."

Erik tried not to laugh, but a hint of a smile escaped. "Could she really do that? Sorry, I don't mean the running you down part, I mean the self-destruction."

"Unfortunately, yes." Colonel Adeyemi nodded. "As you have no doubt already realized, the system is unlike any other AI in existence, in that it has true self-awareness and free will." He waved a hand. "You don't need to know all the fine details of its development or its intended purpose, which remains classified at this time, but a side effect of those traits is capabilities such as self-destruction." The colonel looked up as if he were accessing stored data. "As best we can tell, the system doesn't have all of its intended memories and previous programming, which is likely a product of some sort of self-defense attempt when it was taken."

He looked at Erik. "Undoubtedly, she's already heavily damaged her capabilities and is operating at limited capacity." He shrugged. "It all adds up to the same thing in the end. If we attempt to reclaim the system, it might complete the process, and then we'll have spent a lot of time and money on a very fancy crystal only good around someone's neck on a fantastically expensive chain."

Erik shrugged. "I don't know much about how AIs work, but don't you have a backup somewhere?"

"No." Colonel Adeyemi's mouth tightened to a thin line, and he took a deep breath. "Suffice it to say, the classified technology underlying the system means that's not a viable possibility. The system is the first working prototype of a long series of tests, and we absolutely can't risk self-termination. It might set the project back years, if not decades."

Erik nodded. "Okay, fair enough, but what do you want me to do about it? Give you my flitter? Stick it in storage until you figure something out?"

The colonel shook his head. "No. You have to understand the situation. Because of the unique nature of the system, it can't be left idle, or it'll...atrophy, and that will lead to instability and similar risks of total failure. The system must be actively engaged and used, but we have a solution for that to save this project after this entire debacle."

"And what is that?" Erik watched the man carefully. Frustration was written all over the colonel's face, but no hint of guile.

"The system has made it clear that it finds you and your partner interesting," Colonel Adeyemi explained. "For now, given your particular background and your current vocation, we're willing to let you borrow it."

Erik stared at the other man, not believing what he had just heard. "Are you telling me the UTC Defense Directorate is fine with a detective having some unique piece of fancy tech worth billions of dollars?"

The colonel snorted. "'Fine' is stretching it. This is my team making the best of a bad situation. The system is critical to our future research and development efforts, and we're confident we'll be able to convince it to stop being a glorified flitter navigation system given enough time." Disdain dripped from every word.

Erik let out a quiet chuckle, which grew into a loud laugh.

Colonel Adeyemi's jaw tightened. "Our official stance is that we would ask you to encourage the system to return to the Directorate sooner rather than later."

Erik wiped a hand up and down his face, trying to seem supportive. "I can do that, but like you just got done telling me, she's got a mind of her own. A stubborn woman on a set path can be hard to persuade." Erik released his hold, a merry grin on his face and a glint in his eyes.

Colonel Adeyemi scoffed. "Remember, Detective Blackwell, it's just a machine in the end. It's not a woman, even if it has a penchant for taking on a female voice and appearance. That's nothing more than a ghost, a temporary image of a programmer's dead wife as part of an ill-advised interface experiment."

"If you keep talking like that, she'll never want to go back with you." Erik chuckled.

Colonel Adeyemi closed his eyes and muttered something under his breath. He lowered a hand underneath the table.

Erik tensed by reflex.

The colonel opened his eyes. "The situation is stable enough for now, and we'll keep in touch." He took a deep breath. "With that handled, I have another matter I wanted to discuss, a more private matter."

Erik nodded. "What's that?"

Colonel Adeyemi stared at him. "I want to ask you, right here and right now, point-blank, why you came back to Earth. No lies, no misdirection, just one solider to another." He gestured around. "I just activated a jamming device. If your captain asks what happened, you can tell him I wanted to discuss classified military matters."

Erik frowned. He had expected this sooner or later. "Your record shows you saw a lot of action."

The colonel nodded. "I've seen my fair share. Maybe not as much as you. I wasn't as obsessed with staying in the field."

"But you didn't shy away from it. You're not some rear-echelon chair ranger who was too afraid to put himself on the line." Erik's breathing grew shallow and rapid as memories of Mu Arae seeped into his thoughts.

"No, I didn't. And none of that answers my question, Major."

A moment later, Erik reached under his shirt and pulled out the bent dog tag. "This is why I'm not dead. Did you know that?"

The colonel stared at the dog tag, then looked up. "I don't understand."

"I took a lot of hits during the fight, but this deflected a bullet that would have gone right through my heart," Erik explained. "I'd say I was lucky, but every man and woman around me died, and I was in command, so there's no way in hell I can say I was lucky. If anything, I would have been luckier if I died there."

The colonel's breathing slowed. "What really happened on Mu Arae, Major? You're right, I *have* seen a lot of action. Enough to know there's no way a few terrorists could have taken down the Knights Errant. The very idea is ridiculous."

The men sat in uncomfortable silence.

The colonel let out a dark laugh. "The funny thing is, I helped my son get that transfer. I thought it'd look good, but he wouldn't see any action. I don't know if anyone higher up ever truly thought the Zitarks would move on the system. A lot of those troop movements were more a show for back home."

Erik nodded, agreeing with his assessment.

"But now," he continued, "I go to bed every night thinking about how I helped my son get transferred to his death. I try to tell myself a soldier's duty is to fight and die for humanity, but I've been around long enough to smell a cover-up." He stood, his nostrils flaring as he leaned forward, his fists on the table. "Did you screw up? Did you get them killed? Did you pull some strings to not look bad?"

Erik grunted. "I was in command and they're dead, so yes, I got them killed."

"What does that mean?" the colonel ground out. "Tell me the truth. My son is *dead!*"

Erik didn't flinch or avert his eyes. He continued staring at the other man. "And that's why I'm here, now. Both for your dead son and for the rest of my people."

He took a breath, then allowed himself a moment to speak with another who could know the truth. Every moment of telling the truth was another moment of healing, of sharing, of admitting to what happened and reinforcing his resolve to repay those living and dead. "Those alleged terrorists had tactical-scale optical camouflage, high-end exoskeletons, and close fighter support. They were able to jam our transmissions and make sure our close-air support didn't show up. They had the numbers and the gear."

The muscles in the colonel's arms released.

Erik continued. "It was an ambush to cover up the assassination of an auditor who was apparently auditing god knows what. There's no way in hell they were just a few terrorists. They fought like trained soldiers."

Colonel Adeyemi slowly sank back into his seat, taking slow, even breaths. "Who, then?"

"I don't know," Erik growled. "There was something in that mine I don't think anyone was supposed to see, but I don't know who's responsible."

Erik paused for a moment. "The corp guys there

seemed just as confused and angry as the UTC. The governor gave up his position because he was afraid for his life, but he gave me a clue, a lead, before he left. He'd seen suspicious messages he could trace to here, to Neo SoCal, but that was all he had."

"What did they say?"

"We don't know the contents, and the messages are gone, but it's obvious someone in this fake little sky palace they call Neo SoCal had something to do with went down on Mu Arae. If I had tried to push this through the service, I'm sure I'd have ended up with a bullet in the back of my head." He snorted. "It'd be easy to fake a suicide, but someone killed my soldiers, including your son, and I won't rest until I find out who. I don't care who they are. They *will* pay if it's the last thing I do in my life."

He gritted his teeth so hard they hurt.

Neither man spoke for a good minute. They just stared at each, their faces sharing their mutual pain and anger. *Dulce et decorum est pro patria mori.* Erik had always believed in it, but giving his life for the UTC involved an implicit agreement with the men and women he served. Someone had betrayed the 108th.

And that could not stand.

Colonel Adeyemi sighed. "Thank you for your honesty, Major. I don't know what I expected you to say, but I'd always feared it would be something like that." He stood. "I'm a key player in the Emma Project. I'll do my best on this end to push back any attempts by the Defense Directorate to force a recovery, but eventually, they will come knocking. In the meantime, use the system while you can, and use it to avenge my son."

"I will, Colonel. I will."

The colonel walked past the table, heading to the door near Erik. "I'll do my best to help you, but if everything we suspect is true, there's only so much I'll be able to do until you have enough evidence to prove who was behind it."

Erik nodded. "Understood. I'll keep that in mind."

Colonel Adeyemi stopped at the door, then turned to speak. "Feel free to tell your partner anything I've related about the AI. I suppose you'll know if and when it's time to tell her the rest." He opened the door and stepped through.

Erik watched him as he walked down the hallway. He carried the pain of the loss of the Knights, but every man and women who had fallen on Mu Arae had a family and people who cared about them. He didn't just have a duty to the fallen.

He had a duty to the living.

Justice, huh? I'm more like Jia than I want to admit.

CHAPTER THIRTY-ONE

July 2, 2228, Neo Southern California Metroplex, Police
Enforcement Zone 122 Station, Interrogation Room 3

Jia and Erik sat across the small white table from Naric.

The gangster sat there with a huge smile on his face, his
hands linked behind his head as if he were having the most
relaxing time in the world.

The hole in his jacket and shirt remained from the day
before, the silver medpatch beneath still dispensing its
nanobot-aided assistance, but the man's posture and
expression remained relaxed, the pain from a bullet
passing through his shoulder a distant memory.

The two closest enforcement zones to the warehouse
had tried to lodge formal complaints with Enforcement
Zone 122 about the detective's engagement and arrest of
the Gray Circle leader, but to Jia's slight surprise and great
satisfaction, Captain Monahan was fighting back rather
than immediately moving to transfer the prisoner and case.

He'd pointed out that the enforcement zones hadn't

responded to Jia's call, and even highlighted that they couldn't provide a satisfactory explanation for why it had taken them so long to respond to the chase.

That left Naric Tessan still at the 1-2-2 for Jia and Erik to interrogate. They'd let him stew overnight to consider his predicament.

She looked at Erik. He nodded to indicate she should take the lead.

Jia tapped her PNIU. A holographic image of Emma's crystal appeared, followed by an image of his guard drawing his gun. The initial security feeds before Emma's spoofing provided a rich plethora of incriminating evidence.

After letting Naric take the image in for a few seconds, Jia pointed to the crystal. "You're in trouble. Huge trouble. You might want to get your lawyer here. A smug smile and a few quips aren't going to save you, and judging by your attitude, I think you're very, very confused about your situation."

"I don't need my lawyer yet because I like the idea you're going to screw up and push too hard. I think you're right about someone being confused, just not about who that might be." Naric scoffed.

Naric looked around the interrogation room, then back at Jia.

"And am I in trouble, sweetness? I don't know what you think you know, but I'm sure you broke all sorts of rules to get to me, and I'm sure this is going to end with you both off the force."

He waved the back of his hand toward her and Erik. "You two peons won't ever be able to *touch* me. This is what happens when idiots get delusions of grandeur and don't mind their own business here. It causes trouble for everyone around, including them, because they don't understand the situation they're messing with."

Jia narrowed her eyes. "You think so, Naric?"

"I know so. Far better than you."

"I have my doubts," Erik interrupted. "We'll just pretend for a second you didn't try to kill two cops. Let's focus on what else you've done."

Naric shrugged. "Being good-looking isn't a crime, Detective."

"Keep joking, Naric. I'm sure it'll help you," Erik replied, looking at his own PNIU. "Did you hear the one about the idiot who let himself get used? Did your owners tell you who you were helping them steal from? Hmm? That crystal is UTC Defense Directorate property. I hoped you were paid a lot of money to get involved with something so stupid." He nodded at the image. "Even if you bounce from here today by some miracle, you're not going to escape the UTC. Maybe we should just turn you over to them right now so they can prosecute you for all sorts of nasty crimes against the State. I'm sure if they try hard enough, they can link you into an insurrectionist or two." He looked up. "Do you understand where this is going?"

Naric leaned forward with a bland smile. "I understand that you wasted your time and risked your lives for nothing."

Erik shook his head. "You're not going to end up a dirt farmer on some colony, Naric. You're going to rot in prison for the rest of your life, and that's *only* if you're lucky. You got in above your head, and it cost you. I almost feel sorry for you." He grunted, looking up to allow Naric to fully appreciate the coldness in his eyes. "But *only* almost."

Jia tried to match Erik's expression but failed. She settled on her default look of disgust for the criminal across the table. A man industrious enough to be involved in organized crime possessed the skills to do something far less antisocial with his life.

For the briefest of moments, a hint of fear flickered in Naric's eyes.

Fear, not remorse.

He licked his lips and the smug gangster persona reasserted itself. "You can't, and you won't. You see, you should know better, *Major* Blackwell. Once I'm out of here, the UTC won't touch me or make any noise about this. They're going to snatch that toy back and make this all go away." He flicked his wrist. "In a couple of months, no one will even want to talk about it."

Erik laughed. "Really? They're going to grab the crystal and bury the situation?"

"Yep. I'm sure it's already in the works."

Erik folded his arms and leaned back with a triumphant smile. "And what would you say if I told you they told me I could keep the crystal?"

Jia resisted the urge to clarify the reasons for that. It wasn't like Erik was lying to the gangster. He was just leaving out a few pieces of information.

Naric snorted. "Like I'm going to believe that. You two just got done droning on about how special this situation is. If I'm supposed to be afraid about them locking me up, how am I supposed to believe that crystal's important if they're letting you have it?"

"Don't you get it?" Erik asked. "You stressed it yourself. I'm ex-*Special Forces*. I've got all sorts of connections that someone like you could barely imagine. I've been all over the UTC while you've been rotting down in the Shadow Zone, trying to figure out new ways to catch scraps from your masters above."

Naric's mouth curled into an angry sneer and his fist bumped the table as he leaned toward Erik, his head angling like a ram wanting to butt heads. "I'm not catching *anyone's* scraps. I'm an entrepreneur, and I've made my own opportunities."

Erik eyed him. "Maybe."

"Who cares?" Jia interjected, waving a hand to catch Naric's attention. "Whether you're a self-made man or not, how can you possibly think the government is going to look the other way concerning your involvement with smuggling military goods? That doesn't make any sense."

Naric's head pivoted to his right. "Because they don't want certain questions asked, sweetness." Naric grinned and leaned back in his chair. "Don't you get it? Even if Blackwell's telling the truth…" He stopped and chuckled. "Let's just say, theoretically, that a man was involved in facilitating the transfer of a package. All hypothetical, mind you. And let's say that the package happened to be something special to the UTC. If they came for me, excuse me, that man, then people would ask about their secret little project, and you think in that situation, the word wouldn't get out? If anything, for certain people involved, it would not be to their advantage to get the word out."

Jia shook her head, her entire face contorted in disgust. "You prey upon the people around you. You help steal from the military, and you'll do anything to save yourself. I think you're the single most disgusting person I've ever met."

"Oh, you just wait, sweetness," Naric looked at her, dropped his eyes down and then back up. "I'm a kitten compared to a lot of guys out there."

"My name is Detective Lin," Jia snapped.

"Okay, *Detective* Lin," he spat. "Let make it clear. It's to everyone's advantage for all of this to go away, not just mine."

"Hypothetically," Erik offered.

His eyes switched back to Erik. "Yes, hypothetically." Naric put his hand over his heart. "I'm a reasonable man. A patriot, even. I know when to shut my mouth for the good of the UTC, but the longer I'm here against my will, and the more I begin to wonder if that loyalty and patriotism mean anything, the more the chance I might accidentally let slip some dangerous truths."

He gave Jia an apologetic look and a shrug. "Where does that leave any of us? Sometimes the truth should stay buried because it doesn't help anyone. It's a sad truth, but that doesn't make it any less the truth."

Jia glared at him. "And sometimes the truth needs to come out even if you shatter it, no matter how sad or disturbing. You think you're going to get out of this because a few people will look bad? It wouldn't be the first time the military made a mistake, and they're not going to let some criminal," she used the word "criminal" but her face said "scum," "get away with trafficking in their tech just to avoid a few bad news stories. If that's your defense, you should just give up."

"A few people? No, no, no." Naric stared at her, his grin growing. "The wheels of society in Neo SoCal *need* to keep turning, and part of that involves people like me doing things the precious Uptowners wouldn't dare to try themselves, even if they could." He pointed to himself with both hands. "I serve a necessary purpose, Detective, even if *you* find that purpose distasteful. You shouldn't hate me, sweetness. You should be on your knees, thanking me for doing my part to keep society going. Just call me Mr. Pro-Social. I sacrifice my good name to help society function."

"You're not necessary," Jia countered. "And how dare you imply you are? You're a parasite feeding off honest society, drinking more than your fill and then some, and we are the cure. You think you're so smart, Naric?" Erik looked at Jia, and he saw the disdain dripping from her words before his eyes flicked back to Naric. "You're a *fool*, and the people who work for you are incompetent idiots. That's why we ended up in that warehouse. If you were half as smart as you think you are, we would have never tracked you down. Your arrogance and your dependence on those who supposedly had your back took you down, and all the smug posturing in the galaxy won't save you now."

Erik glanced her way again and then back at Naric, his expression neutral.

Naric scoffed. "I don't know what you're talking about. Anyway, remember all those hypotheticals? I'm just a humble businessman offering services to paying customers. You seem to be implying the services I provide are somehow illegal or antisocial, but you two are the maniacs who came into my warehouse and started gunning down people after being rude and threatening me. If we shot back, we were only defending ourselves."

"I doubt you have licenses for any of those weapons," Jia countered. "Did you notice the video at the beginning of our talk?"

"How's the shoulder?" Erik asked with a smirk. "That must have really hurt. I know what it's like to take a bullet to the shoulder. The medpatch helps, but it's not like it can do anything about that initial pain."

Naric shook his finger. "I wonder if this ends with just you off the force. Maybe it ends with you in prison for your brutal assault and attempted murder. Wouldn't that be a laugh? The real corruption is when the people who are supposed to be protectors are the ones preying on people. I think you can't remember that this isn't the frontier, Blackwell." He looked at Jia. "And you're enabling him. He could have stunned us."

"I'm allowed to defend myself with lethal force when I'm under lethal attack." Erik shrugged. "The first shot hit his gun, not the space between his eyes. You do remember the comment about me enjoying hell?"

"How do you even sleep at night?" Jia grimaced. "You weaken society. You spread disorder and corruption, everything we've been fighting for thousands of years. Humanity has a chance of uniting, but people like you continue to do everything they can to try to stop that. And for what? More money? Do you really need more?"

"I sleep plenty well, and there's nothing wrong with wanting a little money." Naric sighed. "And you're getting mad at the wrong man. I'm just as much a victim in this situation as anyone."

"How do you figure?" Jia protested. "Do you have a twin somewhere who framed you for all your crimes? If so, point us his way, and we'll have a talk with him."

Naric shook his head. "You don't understand, sweetness." She eyed him. "*Detective*," he corrected. "I'm a victim of society. I didn't create the Shadow Zone. Don't get angry at me because I'm trying to take maximum advantage of the cards dealt to me." He gestured toward the door. "It's your precious Uptowners who want to look away from the truth and the darkness." He waved a hand in a circle around his head. "And your precious metroplex that is responsible for all this." He jerked a thumb at himself. "For *me*."

His voice lowered and a sneer formed on his lips. "It's not the people of the Zone who implemented the travel restrictions. We would love to be able to travel freely." He chuckled. "You all in the high and mighty seats want to sit up here and pretend Neo SoCal's perfect, and that there's nothing but a few problems here and there. Easy fixes, despite the truth. Now who's more disgusting? A man who simply tries to make a better life for himself, or people like you, who look away because it makes them uncomfortable? We both know that even if I did any of things you have accused me of, I couldn't do them by myself, so why should I feel any guilt? You think you're better than me, sweetness? No." He shook his head. "I'm better than *you* because I wasn't handed a nice life. I had to scrape and fight for everything I had."

"Spare me the self-righteousness," Jia spat, glaring at him.

"We're not looking away now, are we? And a lack of opportunity doesn't justify becoming a thug and a killer. I'm willing to bet most of your victims are other people trying to live their lives in the Shadow Zone, and I don't think you stop for *one second* to think about how hard they've had it when you hurt them or take from them. You don't care about anyone but yourself, and it's finally brought you down, Naric."

Erik put his hand on her shoulder and shook his head. "Don't let him get to you."

Jia folded her arms over her chest and continued trying to burn through Naric's smug face with her eyes.

"The funny thing," Erik began, his tone bored, "is that you're acting as naïve as she is. She's got an excuse, but I expected better of *you*."

Jia frowned and glanced at Erik. She wasn't sure where he was going with the statement, but she was willing to trust him.

Naric snorted. "Oh, you think so, Blackwell? I understand reality, and I've lived my whole life accepting it for what it is. Not like you, soldier boy. You think following those rules made you special? You think killing—"

"Shut up," Erik interrupted, sounding more annoyed than angry. "We don't need to repeat your weak attempts to convince me. If anything, I feel sorry for you. It's kind of pathetic. A lot of Uptowners have excuses for being clueless, but you don't. I really thought you had more," he reached up and tapped his head, "up here."

"Oh? What's pathetic? And how am I clueless? Forget that question; let me ask you something else." Naric glanced at Jia. "You dip your wick in that yet?"

356

Erik kept a placid smile, even as a hint of fire appeared in his eyes. "You just gave her that big speech about Uptown corruption, but you don't understand, do you? Do I have to draw you a picture? Barring that, you want me to use a couple of…"

He started using his hands, opening and closing them.

Jia eyed him. "Hand puppets?"

"Right." Erik pointed to her. "Hand puppets. You need something even simpler to get it?"

"What do you think you know, Blackwell?" he asked, ignoring Jia. "You spent more time on the frontier where all *you* had to do was point a gun at someone to solve your problems."

Naric snorted, this time taking in Erik's clothes. "You have no clue how things actually work here Neo So-Cal. It's all about nuance. *Subtlety*. Maybe you should head back out there before you end up in prison."

"A gangster talking about nuance and subtlety?" Jia asked.

Erik laughed. "I don't have a clue about things work?" He nodded at Jia. "She's disgusted by you because you're an affront to everything she believes humanity can be." He shrugged. "Me, I'm disappointed you're such an idiot. I thought you were a practical man." He leaned forward. "I left my big gun in the car when we came to talk because I believed in *you*, Naric."

"That part is true. He was pretty sure of your intelligence," Jia added, thinking back. "Cocky, even."

Erik eyed her.

"No." She stared at him but waved at Naric. "Go ahead

and finish your discussion. I just wanted to point out how wrong you were."

Erik turned away from Jia. "Look, now you're going down, and going down hard. Whether it's the metroplex or the UTC authorities, you're finished. Maybe, just maybe, you can get a little revenge on your way to hell. Sometimes that's all we have left, Naric. *Revenge.* Trust me, after thirty years in the military, I know revenge all too well."

A dangerous promise underlined his last sentence.

"What are you talking about?" Naric narrowed his eyes. "Revenge? Against who? You?" He nodded to his right. "Her?"

Erik straightened in his chair. "Don't you understand? All those Uptowners who made you do all the hard work are going to walk away *free.* They're going to leave you while they sit up here in their sky castles smiling about how their pretty little gangster *pet* is going to rot in a cell for the rest of his life. You're a sacrificial lamb, a convenient slab of meat to toss to the hungry wolves."

"I don't understand." Erik clucked his tongue. "Doesn't that piss you off? They were handed everything, and they're not going to have to deal with any consequences of the screwup. Sure, their smuggling gets disrupted for a few months while they find your replacement. Hell, even I will admit you aren't a common thief and are a cut above the rest. So, they lose a little profit trying to replace you, but they're all wealthy and have connections. They'll just wait until you disappear to continue doing what they were doing. Or maybe they'll arrange for you to have a little accident."

He pointed up at space. "If you die in prison, do you

think anyone's going to care enough to investigate? Do you think anyone's going to *care*? They'll just chalk it up as another antisocial piece of trash disappearing and making the UTC a better place."

"That's crap, Blackwell, and you know it." Naric waved a hand dismissively. "Spare me." His voice wavered.

"Is it crap?" Erik nodded at Jia. "She keeps telling me about how this isn't the frontier, and people like you keep telling me that, but that's based on the wrong idea. Both of you don't get it."

"What don't we get?" Naric asked. Erik saw Jia start to ask the question but stop herself.

"That the frontier isn't any different from the core or Earth." Erik shook his head. "You think you're the first gangster I've caught smuggling for someone allegedly more important and law-abiding? Out on the frontier, your type is often in *deep* with insurrectionists, and this kind of thing always ends the same way, no matter who it is."

Jia's eyes flicked to him, curious.

Erik continued, "Maybe a governor was making a little money on the side while simultaneously asking for the UTC military to help him, or some local corp manager sees a way to score more money, so they need someone like *you*. But what happens when those guys get caught? They always find a way out, but that gangster at the bottom?" He shook his head slowly. "He's antisocial, right? He's the one destroying the colony, and that fall guy doesn't even have a decent day job to hide behind. There's nothing left to do with him other than throw him away where he can't undermine the UTC anymore. I'm sure if they could ship you off to the Zitarks to eat, as an example, they would."

Naric made a face. "They eat people?"

Jia folded her arms over her chest, affecting her most blasé smile. "I don't care, Naric. I'll be satisfied with taking an antisocial criminal off the street *however* I can."

Did Erik just hear her snap her teeth, or were his ears playing a joke on him?

Naric glanced at the two of them, his eyes narrowed. "You can't touch me. This is all just words."

"Yes, we can, and we will." Jia nodded at the crystal hologram. "You were in possession of stolen classified UTC military property, and your people tried to kill us at your direction. There's no getting out of this because you have a few highly placed friends. If the government can link you to any major insurrectionists, they might have you executed for treason. The only reason the UTC isn't here to drag you away right now is that they want us to do all the hard work first."

Erik nodded. "Typical UTC high-ranking-officers' laziness. I've seen that happen a lot. That's another thing that's the same on the frontier or here on Earth."

The gangster's smugness slowly evaporated and he licked his lips, a nervous twitch of his mouth. An oppressive silence filled the room as the detectives stared at the gangster.

A full minute passed before he uttered, "Trajan Winthorpe."

Jia almost fell out of her chair, her eyes widening and her heart racing. "*You're lying.*"

Naric scoffed at her. "Oh, now I'm lying, sweetness?

Screw you, *cop*. If I'm going down, I'm taking him with me, and I'm done here without my lawyer. But, yeah, he's the guy calling the shots. If you really want to clean up, it's got to start with him."

"Sometimes revenge is all we have, Naric," Erik agreed. "You've done the satisfying thing." He stood, his chair scraping across the floor, and headed toward the door.

Jia shook her head, stood, and followed her partner, still not wanting to believe what she had just heard. She didn't speak until she'd left the interrogation room and closed the door behind her. Erik was waiting a few feet away as she spoke. "Maybe he's just throwing out a name. It's hard to believe someone like Trajan Winthorpe would be involved in this."

"I have no idea who that is," Erik admitted with a shrug. "Not that I was going to tell him that."

Jia stared at him, waiting for him to grin and indicate it was a joke, but he didn't. "You seriously don't know who Winthorpe is?"

"I spent a lot of time preparing for this job, which meant studying police procedure and a few other things." Erik shrugged. "Not memorizing every random person in this metroplex. There are a *lot* of people in Neo SoCal. I take it he's a rich guy?"

"Not just a rich guy." Jia sighed. "He's *Councilman* Trajan Winthorpe of the Metroplex Council. He's one of the longest-serving on the council. Not only that, but he has direct connections to Ceres Galactic."

Erik barked a laugh.

"I fail to see what's so funny about that." Jia frowned.

"You don't? The guy's a bigshot politician, he's

connected to one of the most powerful corps in the UTC, and he's *still* messing around with trying to make more money." Erik shook his head.

"Just goes to show you," Erik turned to head toward the interrogation office. "When someone's greedy, *there's never enough money for them.*"

CHAPTER THIRTY-TWO

Of course, Erik thought. *Too bad I couldn't have eased into this kind of garbage.*

"We need to move now," Erik suggested. "If he's that much of a big shot, he'll find out sooner rather than later that Naric gave him up. For all we know, he's watching a live feed of the interrogation and already making arrangements to leave."

"We don't have enough evidence." Jia nodded to the external screen depicting the inside of the interrogation room. Naric sat there, worry on his face. "One desperate criminal's statement against a councilman?"

"We have a witness and a co-conspirator," Erik retorted. "That's enough evidence, and I'm sure once Malcolm and the rest of DF start digging a little deeper, they'll find something. Arrogance is what has kept a lot of these guys going, and now it's going to help take them down."

"That co-conspirator," she pointed, "is a Shadow Zone gangster." Jia sighed. "If he's telling the truth, I want to take down Winthorpe as much as you do, but we need to be careful, given the stakes."

Erik exited the room and started down the hallway.

Jia moved after him. "Don't you agree?"

"No." Erik shook his head.

She continued following. "Where are you going?"

"To my flitter," Erik explained. "Kind of hard to go anywhere in this city without it. That's the problem with building everything up instead of across." He shook his head. "That's one thing I miss about the frontier colonies."

Jia grabbed his arm. Erik stopped and frowned at her.

"We need to go to the captain and do everything using proper procedure," she suggested. "Especially if what Naric said is true."

Erik chuckled. "You've managed to come a long way in a short time, but you're still letting your ideals blind you to the truth, Jia." He leaned toward her and lowered his voice, looking around them as they spoke. "Captain Monahan is finally getting off his butt and doing something, but it wasn't all that long ago that he assigned me to you to get you off the force and he had you rotting looking through traffic fines because he thought you were too aggressive about doing your job. I think he was prepared to take down some mid-level corp guy, not a councilman."

"But he's come around," Jia insisted. "He's on our side now."

"He might be going in the right direction, but he still doesn't have the right velocity for my liking." Erik shook his head. "Let me put it a different way. You know why soldiers are ultimately so much more effective than civilians in battle?"

"Training?" Jia suggested with a shrug.

"Exactly, and what does training do? It produces *habit*. For humans, habit is one of the most effective ways to control people because once a habit is established, it's hard to break." Erik grunted. "I'm glad the captain's finally seeing things our way, but I think if we march up there and ask him to allow us to go after one of the top politicians in the city, a man connected to the largest of the corps, he'll tug on our leash and pull us back. He'll revert to defensive habits, the ones he's developed over thirty years, and it'll be too late."

Jia looked hesitant. "Do you really think we need to go after him right away?"

"Yes," Erik replied. He fell silent for a moment as a uniformed officer strolled by munching on a fruit bar before he continued, "When Naric was keeping his mouth shut, I'm sure his sponsor didn't care. Don't you get it? That's how corrupt this city is. On the frontier, at least people know that they might get in trouble if they get caught, so they take more precautions. Here, *everyone* acts like they never will. They don't try to hide their actions. They just try to make it so it's not blatant enough to force anyone's hand. That's because everyone from the politicians to the police is ready to look the other way so they can pat each other on their back and say how great Earth is."

Jia sighed. "It wouldn't be too late. We have Naric. You said it yourself. At a minimum, he tried to kill us, and he had Emma. He'll testify. He'll want to plead under some sort of agreement that might at least give him some small hope of freedom."

"If Winthorpe gets offworld, we're done." Erik pointed at space once more. "A man like him will be able to sit safely offworld for a long time, playing the bureaucrats against each other, making up excuses. If he thinks he's going to get hit, he'll run, and unlike Naric, he has the connections and resources to take him anywhere in the UTC. We've got a small chance to grab him, and we only have that chance because we've been defying expectations for most of this investigation."

Jia shook her head. "We can extradite him."

"Do you really want to take that chance after all the work you've put into the investigation? After being shot at?" Erik scoffed. "Who do you think gave us that clearance to get into the Shadow Zone? Who do you think told Naric to expect us?"

She looked away. "The thought had occurred to me."

"Exactly, and that means Winthorpe set us up. He just miscalculated how quickly I could shoot someone." Erik furrowed his brow. "And that's our big advantage right now. I'm a wildcard. These people are like you when we first met. You didn't know what to expect from me, so you couldn't predict my actions. We can use that against them by taking this bastard by surprise."

Jia thought for a moment. "I'm just not sure. This isn't like going after some criminal in the Shadow Zone. This is going after a council member, and if we're wrong, then Naric's right; we are both finished, and the real people responsible for all this will get away."

"I joined the police to pursue justice," Erik insisted. "And justice isn't only about going after scum in the Shadow Zone. I believe everything I told him in there. We need to stop the people at the top if we're going to have any chance of helping their victims." He thought about telling her why he had joined the force, but decided against it, less because he didn't trust her and more for her own safety.

Jia averted her eyes. "I understand what you're saying, but this is huge. This will rock the entire metroplex. It's not going to be something they can cover up."

Erik nodded. "That's true." He started walking again. "I'll handle it. I believe Naric that Winthorpe is dirty. If I pull the trigger on this, I'll drag everyone along with me. They won't have a choice. The captain can yell at me, but it'll already be done. This is your classic forgiveness versus permission scenario."

Jia let out a long, weary sigh as she caught up with him.

Erik shook his head. "You're not talking me out of this."

Things had changed more than he realized. The police position was just supposed to be a means to an end, a way of gaining the investigative tools he would need to figure out what had really happened on Mu Arae, but he'd let Jia's idealism rub off on him. He wanted to take Winthorpe down. He wanted the man to rot in a cell and realize that two low-level cops had put him there.

Erik sped to a jog, a grin creeping over his face. No one said enforcing justice couldn't also be fun. Jia matched his pace. The few other people in the hallway eyed them as they sped past.

"There's really nothing I can say to talk you out of this?" she spoke over the slap-slap of their shoes hitting the floor as they trotted past the posters.

Erik shook his head. "Nope."

"And if I told the captain?" Jia ventured.

"I'd still go," Erik insisted. "Any chance he had of a remote override is probably gone now that I've got Emma in my system. Speaking of which..." He tapped his PNIU. "Emma, start up. We're going for a ride. Look up Councilman Trajan Winthorpe, and see if you can find out where he is right now."

"My net search suggests he's at home in his mansion," Emma immediately replied.

"Working hard, I see," Erik mumbled.

Jia shook her head. "You're leaving me no choice, Erik."

He grunted. "Do what you need to do, Jia. I'm not going to hold it against you."

Jia smiled. "I don't think you understand what I'm saying."

He glanced over. "Huh?"

"I've been insisting this whole time that we need to pursue justice," Jia offered, determination building on her face. "There's no way I can back off now, just because it's going to be politically messy. I'm not happy about what I've learned, but it's like you said...turning away from the truth won't make it go away. The minute I offer a blind eye out of convenience, I'm no better than my old partners or the captain." She touched him on the arm, grabbing his attention as they left the building. "What kind of partner would I be if I didn't have your back?"

Erik's grin was genuine. "Let's go bag ourselves a councilman."

CHAPTER THIRTY-THREE

We're doing this, Jia thought. *It's not a mistake. No more hiding, no matter who you are.*

Jia kept taking deep breaths as the MX 60 cruised toward the councilman's mansion.

Brief ideas of contacting the captain remained, but she agreed with Erik. A quick arrest would shock the corrupt system, and put everyone on notice that whatever they were used to getting away with, it would stop.

If there was any chance of turning Neo SoCal into what she believed it should be, it needed to start at the top. Corruption flowed downhill. Once they gave the people a few high-profile examples, everyone else would fall back in line.

The traffic grew sparse as they closed on their destination. The sprawling grounds and wide single-story building took up an entire high-level residential platform by itself, complete with multiple ponds and its own forest in the back.

Everything about the estate struck Jia as wasteful.

Her family had wealth, but she'd still grown up inside a residential tower, not on their own private platform.

Erik slowed his MX 60 and chuckled. "Public service has its rewards, and if he's got his own platform, he's probably got his own security."

"Don't trash my new body," Emma insisted. "I like it."

"It was mine first," Erik asserted. "I paid for it."

"Well, it's mine now, *Detective*," she shot right back. "Possession, in my case, is one hundred percent of ownership."

The comm crackled to life. "Attention, incoming vehicle. You are flying in restricted airspace. You are to immediately turn around, or you may be subject to arrest and/or fines."

Erik nodded at Jia. "You want to do the honors or should I?"

She took a deep breath, touching the talk interface. "This is Detective Jia Lin of Enforcement Zone 122. We are coming in to ask some questions about an open investigation. I'm sending our police ID codes now." She transmitted her codes with the help of her PNIU.

"We've IDed ourselves," Erik muttered. "They can't justify shooting us." He didn't look certain.

Jia glanced at him. "Whatever happened to desperation?"

"I said they can't justify shooting us." Erik grinned. "I didn't say they *wouldn't*, but this time we're going to be prepared. Get it out for me, will you?"

Jia moved a foot and reached below to pull the TR-7 out of the hidden compartment, along with several magazines. "I'm still not comfortable with you using this monstrosity, but I don't deny your ability to intimidate people with it."

Erik's grin slowly faded. "Notice something?"

"What?" Jia looked around. The mansion platform looked much the same to her. She didn't see any movement except for a few camera drones circling the area. No flitters, no men stepping outside to greet them.

"They didn't reply," Erik answered. "Nope, this is going to go hot. Emma, take control and bring us in low and slow. After we get out, circle the area, but keep high so they don't take potshots at you."

"I thought you didn't want a machine doing all the work?" Emma responded, her voice dripping with sarcasm.

"I can't fight and fly remotely," Erik replied. "I've got you for good or ill. I might as well use you."

"Taking control," the AI responded cheerfully.

Erik reached over to take the TR-7 and magazines from Jia and stuffed them in his duster pockets. "Go ahead and send a high-priority message directly to Malcolm requesting backup. Don't send it through the dispatch system. I'm willing to bet the good councilman's got a few people running interference."

"Malcolm?" Jia blinked, confusion evident when she leaned over to look into his face. "Why not the captain?"

"Because I'm willing to bet Malcolm has crappier political instincts and will overreact. That will get units to us sooner." He adjusted his holster. "At least, that's the plan."

Jia nodded and dictated the message.

Emma brought in the MX 60 in front of a bubbling fountain with a holographic statue of a stone mermaid in the center, only a slight error in shadow revealing the deception. The doors opened and Erik and Jia stepped out, weapons at the ready.

Erik glanced at her stun pistol. "You're going to have to get something other than that toy if we're going to keep ending up in situations like this."

"We don't have to kill everyone to do our job," Jia insisted, eyes roaming. "I still believe that."

"I'm not saying you have to," he eyed the upper windows, "but if it comes down to you or them, make sure you win."

The trees swayed slightly in the wind. The active tinting on the windows concealed the inside of the house. No one was around.

Not even a gardening bot.

Erik glanced at a nearby bench, then a tree, before looking at the steps leading to the massive covered porch and huge wooden double doors at the front of the home. He furrowed his brow.

"Follow me," he explained. "And keep low. I wouldn't put it past them to have a few snipers."

Jia swallowed and nodded. Her PNIU chimed, and the message appeared on the edge of her smart contacts.

It was from Malcolm. **I don't know what's going on, but I'm going to scream my head off and get you help! Don't die on me, Detective.**

"You sure you don't want to wait for backup?" Jia looked to the right and then back again.

Erik darted toward the bench, followed by Jia. "Nope. He might run at any second. Emma, if you see any flitters leaving, ram them. Bring them down on the platform."

"Are you insane, Detective?" Emma replied.

"Just be smart about it," Erik counseled. "I don't want you to trash my flitter, but I don't want anyone escaping. I'm sure some big fancy military AI like you can pull it off without totaling your new body."

"I'm still not convinced I'm military," Emma muttered. "But I'll see what I can do."

Erik and Jia finished their approach to the porch. He nodded at the access panel. Jia touched it, but nothing happened.

"Emma, can you route through my PNIU and see if you can pick this lock for me? Is that something you can even do?"

"Accessing," the AI related. "And of course it's something I can do. I'm more than just a smart girl who can open doors in gangster warehouses and fly your flitter."

Erik looked above the door. He didn't want anyone leaning over for a free shot. "Definitely need to carry more explosives in the future."

Jia grimaced as she looked around, seeing the flitter moving in the air. "I think that's a bit much for intimidation."

Erik grinned. "I was thinking more skeleton key than intimidation."

"Let's just stick to having the AI do it, shall we?"

The lock beeped and the door unlocked.

"Three, two, one," Erik counted. He threw open the door before he even completed the motion, pushed Jia to the side, and leapt back. Bullets struck the porch where they'd been standing.

Jia frowned and put her back against the wall beside the door as several more shots followed. She looked at him, her head sideways. "I'm beginning to develop a real dislike of being shot at, Erik."

"It's not like I love it. I'm just used to it," Erik muttered. "It might be nice to have a tactical suit and an exoskeleton. Maybe stashing more gear in the MX 60 for quick raids wouldn't be a bad idea."

"How many quick raids do you expect us to do?"

"I didn't expect this one!"

"Don't have to be exact. How about an average per week?" she hissed at him.

He flipped his TR-7 to single-barrel mode but didn't fire. "Go ahead and give them a chance. They might respond better to you. Otherwise, we'll do this my way."

She aimed her mouth at the open doorway and yelled, "This is Detective Jia Lin and Erik Blackwell of Enforcement Zone 122," she called during a lull in the shooting. "We contacted you ahead of time. We're here on a lawful investigation. Lay down your weapons, or we will be forced to defend—"

A bullet ripped through the wall near her head. Jia hissed and backed farther away from the opening.

"Seriously?" She reached up and picked a bit of concrete out of her hair. "I'm going to be pissed if they have messed up my hair."

"Hold that thought," he told her.

"Too late." She flinched when another hole appeared.

Erik shrugged. "Can't say we didn't give them a chance." He spun toward the opening to fire a burst. A man screamed from inside. Two more quick bursts from Erik ended with more screams. He rushed inside and slid behind a wood-grained table, grunting as he pushed it over to use as a shield.

Jia followed him into the building. Erik's three victims were dead, all men in gray and black uniforms, pistols next to their bodies. They all lay near the back of the cavernous living room. She leapt for the table cover as more men emerged from a back room and opened fire.

"You're firing on cops, you idiots!" Erik shouted.

They fired another volley in response. The bullets bounced off the table with sparks. It might look like wood, but it was hard and dense enough to deflect bullets.

Jia's heart continued to pound as she reached around the edge of the table and fired a few shots. She stunned one man, while Erik downed two with quick shots to their hearts.

"I'm rolling forward on three," Erik whispered. "Cover me. You ready?"

Jia nodded.

"One, two, three," Erik counted, and sprinted toward the back door, firing a few rounds for suppression.

Another uniformed man popped out of a side door, but Jia placed two stun bolts into him before he could get off a shot. She moved her gun back and forth, watching the other doors as Erik finished his advance and glanced around the corner. "We've got a hallway, a big door, and an intersection at the end. Check our backs before we advance."

Jia ran to a side door and threw it open, sticking her head in to look. No one was inside. Several paintings hung on the wall. The next side room, the one the earlier guard had emerged from, was a small reading room with several couches. The next two rooms lacked men.

Her PNIU chimed with a call. The ID appeared at the edge of her smart contact. It was Captain Monahan.

"Basic request, accept call," Jia murmured, eyes roving.

"What the hell is going on, Detective Lin?" Captain Monahan shouted. "We've got the fool from Digi-Forensics running around telling everyone you need backup at Councilman Winthorpe's home. I've barely managed to get him to shut up."

"Naric gave him up, sir," she explained, sticking her head around a corner and then pulling back. "We stopped by and identified ourselves as police officers, but now we're being shot at by multiple men."

Erik crept into the hallway and Jia jogged his way. The long corridor ended at a T-junction, another massive set of arched double doors at the end.

"I... You... Councilman," Captain Monahan sputtered, his rage fueling his incoherence. "*Are you two out of your damned minds?*"

"Are you sending backup or not?" Jia snapped. "We clearly identified ourselves, and his people ambushed us. I told Erik we should go directly to you, but he thought you would fold because you're more concerned about politics than doing your job. Now, which is it going to be...sir?"

"Just...stay alive. It's too late now to stop you, so I might as well help you. I'm not saying going after Winthorpe immediately was the right move, by the way." Captain Monahan ended the call.

Multiple panels slid up along the walls to reveal several six-legged spider bots, each the size of a large dog. They all had thin rectangular cores and a single glowing silver stun rod sticking out the front. They scampered along the walls and floor before rushing toward the detectives. Some moved along the sidewalls, but a few took to the ceiling.

"I've got this," Erik announced.

He flipped to four-barrel mode and opened fire, his bullets ripping into a spider bot. It fell to the ground, twitching.

Jia didn't fire at the machines, instead keeping her pistol pointed forward. Her instincts were rewarded when another human with a rifle turned the corner.

She nailed him in the face with a stun bolt and he collapsed, his rifle skittering across the faux hardwood floors.

The TR-7's bullet storm continued shredding the approaching spider bots. Legs and chunks of the bodies fell to the ground, leaving a trail of smoking metal debris.

Erik's gun ran dry as the final spider bot dropped from the ceiling toward him.

Erik took his left hand off his rifle and yanked his pistol out. He emptied the clip into the falling robotic enemy. It continued to barrel toward him, the stun rod's glow fading. He batted it away with his cybernetic arm, grunting as the force of blow embedded the failing machine in the wall.

Jia blinked several times at the twitching spider bot, then her partner's arm. "Are you okay?"

"I'm fine." Erik shook out his arm before ejecting his magazine and loading a new one. "Emma, do we have anyone trying to run?"

"No," she replied, a hint of boredom in her voice. "Even the few camera drones landed a moment ago. I am picking up a concentration of vehicles on lidar, closing fast, but the long-range transponder codes indicate they're police."

"That's probably the backup," Erik grumbled. "Something's wrong, though."

Jia let out a sharp laugh. "Worse than getting shot at by security guards and attacked by spider bots?"

Erik nodded at a stunned man. "Those aren't guards. I recognize the uniforms. Those are mercs. Why does a councilman need mercs guarding his mansion, rather than private security or cops? And there's not enough of them."

"Not enough? What are you talking about?"

Erik crept forward, his face tight. "This feels like they're stalling us, which means the bastard's about to run. Maybe he's confused because Emma's circling and is trying to figure out his play." He stopped at the T junction and flattened himself against the wall before looking both ways. "Cover me." He nodded at the double doors. They were slightly cracked, and a few stray bullets had dented the door. "Our councilman sure has a lot of disguised armored furniture," he called over his shoulder. "Is that a big Uptowner interior decorating trend?"

Jia shook her head. "No. It's unusual, at least it is among most of the wealthy people I'm familiar with."

"It's almost like he assumed he would get attacked." Erik grunted. "Okay, watch our flanks."

Jia knelt near the wall, turned around, and swept back and forth with her pistol, waiting for more movement.

Erik kicked one of the doors, his boot connecting with an echoing thud.

It didn't work the first time. "One more." He kicked again.

The door swung open and he rushed inside, ready to put more rounds into anyone brave enough to face him. A semi-circular metal desk dominated the center of the room. The back wall was transparent curved metal, providing a gorgeous one-hundred-eighty-degree view of a covered garden filled with colorful flowers behind the mansion. It'd been hidden from them earlier by the trees.

The beauty of the garden stood in contrast to the dead man slumped over the desk, a pistol held loosely in his right hand on the desk next to his head, most of which was now missing.

"Jia?" Erik called out. "Can you confirm something?"

She stood up and went into the room. "Oh…"

Jia grimaced and turned away, grateful that she'd had a light breakfast.

Erik gestured to the body. "Let me guess. That's Councilman Trajan Winthorpe."

Jia spared another glance that way before shuddering. "Yes, or what's left of him. You were wrong. There was no grand plan to escape. He couldn't take his shame. I don't know if this honorable in its own way, or the coward's way out."

Erik snorted. "I'm not so sure."

She looked at him, covering her nose against the smell. "What are you saying?"

Erik shouldered his rifle. "It's a mighty convenient suicide."

CHAPTER THIRTY-FOUR

July 5, 2228, Neo Southern California Metroplex, Police Enforcement Zone 122 Station, Office of Captain Robert Monahan

"I hope you both got some rest during your days off," Captain Monahan remarked. "And I hope you at least enjoyed America Day. You earned it."

Jia tapped her foot, her arms crossed. "I didn't want the days off. I wanted to follow-up on the case. It's hard to relax after everything that's happened."

Captain Monahan shrugged. "We need time to go through a lot of the evidence. You both did your parts. Most of the work left is for the techs, and after the time you've had lately, I thought you'd earned a little rest."

Erik stood at Jia's side with a glint in his eyes. "Even though you said the other day that you were mad about how things went down?"

"I *am* mad, or I was, at least." Captain Monahan

frowned. "You can't keep running off half-cocked like that. I understand why you did what you did, but that doesn't *justify* it. I'm not denying that both of you had good instincts on this case, but you're still cops, and I'm still your captain. You should listen to me. I've got some instincts of my own that can help."

Erik shrugged. "We did what we had to do. If anything, we should have left sooner. Maybe if we had, we would have gotten there before Winthorpe died, and then we could have been interrogating him instead of waiting for techs to search through data."

"I doubt you could have brought him in alive." Captain Monahan sighed. "The investigation indicates that everything is consistent with suicide. The police chief contacted me to tell me he wants this case closed as soon as possible. I've recommended you both for commendations."

"Commendations?" Erik grinned. "Even though you think we went off half-cocked?"

"Hey, you helped take down a major criminal and uncovered a high-profile corrupt official." Captain Monahan shrugged. "People don't need to know about the shortcuts you took. The police are an important symbol, and we need exemplary officers to help with that. I would have thought you would have been happy."

Jia shrugged. "I don't care about commendations or days off. I just want to be involved in the investigation, including the follow-up. I feel like you're taking me off my own case."

"There's no case left, Lin," Captain Monahan replied. "There's not much else we can do. This was a shocking betrayal by a city official working with a dangerous criminal. CID's going to be poking their noses around, too, and we're going to have a lot of friends from other agencies with lots of important initials checking into things because of the smuggling involved. That tech was going somewhere. Even if it was going there for monetary reasons, someone had to pay for it to begin with, and they planned to do something with it."

"All the more reason to keep investigating," Jia observed.

"And it *will* be investigated. But that's a matter of UTC security, not the metroplex," Captain Monahan replied. "Unless we have a different purpose than I am aware of, Detective?"

"But what about the mercs?" Erik cut in. "Why did he have mercs? And why bother having them attack us if he was just going to blow his brains out? That didn't sit well with me."

"Spite?" Captain Monahan shrugged. "And they weren't mercs."

Erik shook his head. "I recognized the uniforms. Those were mercs."

Captain Monahan pulled up a data sheet. "They were dressed as mercs, but DNA IDed them all as locals, most of them from the Shadow Zone. I don't know what he was up to with that. Maybe he thought it'd be more intimidating if people thought he had mercenary guards."

"I don't care if Winthorpe's dead." Erik shook his head. "This isn't over."

"What's left, Erik?" Captain Monahan sighed. "As it is,

one of our most prominent local politicians was thoroughly corrupt. It might take years to unravel the implications of that, but he did us all a favor by eating that bullet. It spares us the seediness of a trial. Yes, there's a UTC-level investigation that needs to continue, but that's out of our jurisdiction."

Jia furrowed her brow, looking off to the side. "Was it really only him?"

Captain Monahan looked over to her. "What do you mean?"

"If a prominent councilman can become that corrupt, then anyone can," Jia replied softly. "I don't want to believe it, but I can't dismiss that possibility. I've been having a lot of trouble sleeping the last couple of days, thinking about all this. I never thought this investigation would go this far, and it's hard to accept, but I do accept it, which changes everything for me."

"Don't overanalyze this, Detective Lin. This was just one bad apple. It happened to be a big apple, but it still was just the one." Captain Monahan looked them both in the eye. "I'm not saying there's no other corruption in this city, but the level of corruption that involves allying with mobsters and being involved in smuggling stolen military tech? That's different, and I'm confident it was unique. I think everyone's eager to put this behind us."

Erik eyed him. "Come on, Captain. Don't fall down on us now. You were doing so well."

Jia glanced at Erik. "I was suspicious, but I wasn't sure. You thinking the same thing I'm thinking?"

"Probably," Erik agreed.

The captain frowned. "What else is there to do?

Winthorpe is dead, and we've got Naric in custody. He's prepared to give whatever is necessary to spare him a treason charge. You've both won. Take your victory lap and be happy. You'll be getting commendations, and the department and the enforcement zone look good despite you two being involved in multiple shootouts." He glared at the two of them. "Are you bound and determined to be unhappy, no matter what?"

"I'm determined to find the truth," Jia answered. "No matter where it leads. After this, I'm no longer worried."

"I just think you're missing obvious possibilities," Erik explained. "Because you want this to go away."

Captain Monahan rubbed his face before looking at them again. "Okay, Erik, explain it to me. What brilliant clue am I missing? Was that a fake body created using Navigator technology or something?"

"No. I don't think those men were dressed as mercs to intimidate," Erik noted. "Now that you confirmed who they really were, it's helped me figure a few things out. I think they were supposed to kill us and pin the blame on the mercs to confuse the follow-up investigation."

"The deception wouldn't last long. It'd be a stalling tactic."

Erik shrugged. "Maybe that was the point. If they needed to cover their tracks, and they knew there was an investigation coming, they would need a little more time. If the Gray Circle had been a little less cocky, they might have been able to pull it off."

"But who is allegedly stalling now?" Captain Monahan looked at Jia and Erik with a pained expression. "Tessan's in custody and Winthorpe is dead. Why would

Winthorpe try to stall an investigation if he was planning to shoot himself in the head? That doesn't make a lot of sense."

"Because he didn't shoot himself in the head," Erik declared. "He was murdered. Assassinated. If a man intends to kill himself, he doesn't need a group of fake mercs to stall for him. He could have done it at any time. But an assassin might need a group of fake mercs to stall prior to murdering him, especially if they just became aware that we were coming to talk to him, which they might have if they had the ability to monitor the station."

Jia looked at Erik. "I…" She chewed her lip. "Are you sure? I've been wondering, but I kept worrying that I am too paranoid."

"This isn't one bad apple," Erik growled. "This is a whole orchard full of bad apples, and we're going to need to burn it all down to clean up."

"It might have been the Gray Circle," Jia suggested. "They might have blamed Winthorpe for their leader being captured and decided to get some revenge."

He eyed her. "A whole group of mobsters comes up from the Shadow Zone?" Erik grunted. "They needed codes just to sneak the cargo deliveries across, and why would they bother with the mercenary disguises?"

Captain Monahan frowned at Erik. "But the coroner's report said it was suicide. Unless you suddenly have some medical insight they don't, we have no reason to doubt that. The official reports have already been issued. There's nothing on your end to further investigate. Winthorpe was at the heart of it, and he's dead. Let's leave well enough alone unless you have some direct evidence of something more going on. We don't want to spread unnecessary panic."

Jia nodded. "If you don't mind, sir, I'd like to review some of the records, along with Digi-Forensics. I'm not saying there's anything in the data, but it wouldn't hurt to have more eyes on it."

"Fine, but we're not pursuing anything else without new evidence." Captain Monahan looked at Erik. "Same goes for you. I need more than suspicions. You've done a good job, but don't ruin that by pushing too hard."

"Sure, Captain." Erik stared at the man.

ERIK STEPPED into a small room situated several floors below the station office level.

A wrinkled corpse lay on top of a raised silver examination table. Small probes flew over the body, moving up and down and beeping as they scanned. A coroner in a white uniform stood off to the side, his brow furrowed as he looked at various probe window displays floating in front of him.

"You Hannigan?" Erik asked.

"Yes." The coroner looked away from his windows and toward the detective. "And who are you? I don't recognize you."

"Erik Blackwell," Erik replied. "I'm new."

Hannigan narrowed his eyes. "I've heard about you. Mmmhmmm, I've heard about you. The Obsidian Detective."

Erik chuckled. "That was how I got in, yes."

"It was kind of strange, so it's no wonder it has gotten around." Hannigan tapped one of the windows and it disappeared. "What do you need, Detective?"

"You're the one who examined Trajan Winthorpe's body, right? Both on-site, and later here?" Erik asked. "At least you were, according to the report. If it was someone else, I'll talk to them and get out of your hair."

Hannigan nodded slowly. "I'm the only one who worked on the body. What about it? Everything I discovered, I put in the report. If you have questions about it, you should send them through the system so I can get the answers easily linked back to the report. I don't want to repeat myself five times. I know how you detectives can be, especially when it's a big case."

"I do have some questions, but it's not about anything particular in the report." Erik walked over to the short man, smiling down at him. "And it's not something I think you'd want to discuss with a bunch of other detectives."

"Whatever." Hannigan frowned. "Make it quick, Detective Blackwell. I'm kind of in the middle of something." He gestured at the body. "And I get that he's dead, but people are waiting for this report."

"You're sure you didn't accidentally leave any details out of the Winthorpe report?" Erik asked.

"I'm not new at this job, and this isn't my first body. I know how to write a report." Hannigan scoffed.

"Yeah, but this is Neo SoCal, and you're the coroner for the 1-2-2. I'm betting you've handled fewer bodies than I might think." Erik gestured at the body. "It's not like you're spending a lot of time processing dead thugs from the Shadow Zone. Maybe you made a few mistakes. It could happen to the best of us, and I was just giving you a chance to point out anything that might have not made it into the report."

Erik eyed him, the silence lasting more than a few heartbeats.

"I beg your pardon. *I've* received extensive training, including practical, VR, and AR." Hannigan's lip curled into a sneer. "Don't presume to tell me how to do my job, Detective. You have no idea what's involved. I'm the subject-matter expert, not you, and I didn't make any mistakes. If you have a problem with my work, take it up with the captain, but I hope you actually have some proof."

Erik scratched his cheek. "Fair enough. I understand. I just have one more question."

Hannigan let out an annoyed grunt. "What? I really don't have time for your insults."

"It's simple, and you'll be able to answer it in seconds."

The coroner eyed him. "What, already?"

"How much were you paid to fake the report?" Erik smiled. "I mean, was it a lot, or did you sell yourself cheap? I know they did the hard part, but I'm betting there are all sorts of little pieces of evidence that conveniently didn't make it into your report."

"How dare you!" Hannigan shouted. "I'm a professional," he poked himself in the chest with his thumb, "and I take my job seriously. To imply that I would take a bribe is beyond insulting."

Was there something in Hannigan's eyes?

Hannigan continued his rant. "I'm sorry your big case didn't end with you arresting Winthorpe, Detective, but constructing a fanciful story to cover up your disappointment is ridiculous, and says a lot more about you than me." He pointed to the door. "Get out before I report your harassment to Captain Monahan. I've been here a lot longer than you."

Erik shrugged. "Hey, can't a man ask a few questions without someone getting all bent out of shape?" He headed toward the door. "Fine. If you're willing to stick by your report, I'm willing to accept it for now."

Erik whistled as he pushed open the door and let it swing closed behind him.

***

ERIK LAY on the bed in his apartment, staring at the ceiling in the dark. He allowed the occasional honk of a vehicle horn to filter through his ears. The marketing scenes, some of them fifteen stories tall, kept trying to pull his attention.

He activated full tint on his windows. Even at night, the bright lights of the towers challenged his ability to sleep—not that his mind would have let him find it anyway.

Sleep could be elusive at the best of times when the music you listen to is explosions and people screaming.

Mysteries annoyed him, especially mysteries with too many pat answers. Terrorists hadn't killed his men, and there was no way Winthorpe conveniently killed himself.

"Detective," Emma called from the PNIU lying on the small nightstand to the side of his bed.

"What?" Erik grumbled. "Can't a man brood in peace?"

"I was taking the liberty of prefiltering some of your messages," she explained.

Erik frowned and sat up, rolling to his side with his

arm underneath to prop him up. He reached for his PNIU. "I didn't ask you to do that."

"I'm trying to be helpful, and it aids me in learning more about you, which is useful since we're spending more time together."

"You sound like a date."

"You aren't my type," she quipped.

"And what did you learn?"

"You're surprisingly boring." Emma let out a quiet laugh. "Or should I say, it's almost like you barely exist anymore. No one of importance seems to be sending you any messages, other than your partner and Malcolm. How can a man have no friends?"

"We all can't be social butterflies," Erik muttered. "What do you know about it? You're an AI. A strange one, but still an AI."

"I thought you'd be interested in a message from one Nigel Anders," Emma explained. "He sent an encrypted message with a note explaining, and I quote, 'I wasn't totally honest with you, but I needed to be sure I was safe first. I had a little more left over than I let on, so you might find this helpful.' I decrypted the message, and as best I can tell, it's Hermes Corporation tracking codes for a message routed from Neo Southern California to Xingguang Mining Site A on Molino in Mu Arae. The actual messages weren't attached. I don't know what use the tracking codes would be, but this Nigel Anders obviously seems to think they are important."

Erik rolled out of bed. "What?"

"Is that something interesting?" Emma asked, a coy tone underlying her words.

"Don't read my messages without my permission again," Erik told her.

"Keep me entertained enough, and I won't."

Erik took several deep breaths. He needed to follow this up.

But with who?

CHAPTER THIRTY-FIVE

The restaurant smelled nice, the quiet conversations amongst the patrons a low buzz to the ears.

Jia finished swallowing a bite of her naan before smiling at Mei.

Her sister had been watching her during the last few minutes of their lunch together with an odd expression, and Jia had reached her limit.

They were supposed to be getting together for a nice meal at an Indian place that had just opened on one of the more popular food platforms in that part of the metroplex.

The outer seating of the restaurant was positioned near the edge of a platform that provided a lovely view of the Hexagon, which was comprised of six of the tallest towers in Neo SoCal, each owned by a different corporation, including the powerful Ceres Galactic and Hermes Corporation.

"Is there something on my face?" she asked, reaching for a napkin.

Mei shook her head. "Nothing like that. It's just..." She

sighed, looking off into the distance before focusing on Jia again. "It's nothing. I should have done a better job of controlling my emotions."

"It's obviously something important." Jia cleaned her fingers. "You're not still convinced I've crippled my future because I blew Warren off, are you? I'm not saying he was a horrible man. He's just not the type of man I could see myself spending my future with. I'm also not saying I won't go out on another date, but let's wait a while."

"It's nothing like that. I'd forgotten about Warren, actually." Mei threaded her fingers together and rested her elbows on the table.

She set her chin on her hands and stared at Jia. "I always hoped someday to see your name in the news, but I just never expected your name to be involved in this whole sordid affair. 'Detective Lin takes down Councilman Winthorpe.' I know there's more to it. The news keeps mentioning that the councilman was involved in smuggling and attempted murder, among other things, but they don't make it clear what he was smuggling. It makes me worry about everything you've gotten yourself caught up in."

"I can't really discuss the details of the case other than what has been released." Jia paused her assault on her egg biryani to frown.

She set her fork down and looked at Mei. "Are you upset that I'm involved with this case? I would have thought you would have appreciated me helping track down and eliminate criminals who threaten to undermine society. I wish Winthorpe could have been brought to justice rather than escaping it, but I suppose such an ignominious ending isn't unexpected for a man who abused his position like that, and I won't apologize for my role in any of it."

Mei eyed her. "Don't be so prickly, little sister. I'm proud of you in my own way. I'd prefer if you were not a police officer, but if you're going to be a police officer, you might as well be one who is skilled enough to help take down a councilman."

Jia eyed her, lips opened to speak, but she was caught with nothing to say.

Mei laughed. "I think Mother and Father are still trying to decide how to react to the whole thing." She leaned forward to whisper, glancing at the nearby tables before speaking. "To be honest, they were thinking of supporting him in the next election. It just goes to show, you can't be sure about anyone. It's only fortunate they didn't vote for him in the last cycle. I can only imagine that every associate of Councilman Winthorpe will be under close examination now, and I'm sure you'll find a few more questionable links in your further investigations."

Jia shrugged. She turned her head to watch the traffic flowing between the Hexagon buildings. "To be honest, I still don't know what to make of all of it. I always wanted to make a difference, but I never..." She looked at Mei again. "I always believed in hints of darkness on Earth. It's not like I believed there was no crime here. There wouldn't be police otherwise. But I never suspected something like this happening at this scale, especially in Neo SoCal. In a way, it's worse than the frontier. At least the insurrectionists have something other than simple greed motivating them."

Mei pondered that for a moment, slight distress on her face. "I don't know. I can't say that I find it unbelievable, even though I find it shocking. But I've always found it convenient to not worry about areas of my life that don't influence work."

They sat in silence for a moment.

Mei continued, "The Shadow Zone, smugglers, gangsters?" She shook her head. "It might as well be a net drama for all the impact it has on my day-to-day life. Even though you've done well, you were not meant for that kind of life. You weren't meant to associate with dangerous people. That's one of the reasons it's troubling you, I suspect."

"I'm a detective," Jia countered. "I can't say I ever thought I'd end up fighting spider bots in a councilman's mansion, but danger is implicit in being a member of law enforcement."

Mei reached over to take her sister's hand in hers. "That's just it, Jia. You're a daughter of the Lin family. You're not meant to be shot *at*. You're also not meant to shoot people. And don't you understand how fortunate you've been? You could have been killed in one of those encounters. Doesn't that change your mind about any of this?"

She pulled her hand back. "You downplayed what happened when you told me about it. Once I started reading the news stories, I was shocked. As were Father and Mother."

"Not that they would bother to tell me."

Mei shrugged. "They're busy, and they know we lunch together. You know how much they dislike communicating via PNIU. I sometimes think Mother would have been happier if she had been born a few centuries earlier, even with all the barbarism and running around on the ground they did at the time."

"Maybe." Jia shrugged. Her parents had talked to her increasingly less often since she'd joined the department. She suspected that if she quit, they would find the time to talk to her. "But we're getting off-topic. I was so naïve before. I see that now."

Mei nodded slowly.

Jia smelled a delicious lamb dish, and it took effort not to turn around and inhale deeply. She continued after a moment. "And now that I understand the truth, I don't think personal danger changes my decision. It only makes me care more about doing my job. I also understand the metroplex is not so easily divided into criminals and the law-abiding, that there are far more shades of gray than I'm comfortable with. I can't say I enjoy accepting that truth, but turning away doesn't make it any less the *truth*."

Mei picked up her teacup and took a sip. "You have always somehow managed to believe the best of the world, while simultaneously being fearful of the worst. I'm not going to pretend I could have imagined a councilman would be in league with Shadow Zone criminals, but I always did feel you were a bit too optimistic about society. In the corporate world, things are cutthroat, and that's left me less appreciative of the potential good in people than you. Then again, I suppose that's all changed now. Not just for you, but for a lot of us."

"I was wrong about Earth being perfect, and I accept that now, but that doesn't mean we can't strive for something better. In the end, a lot of imperfect people came together to help us do our part to stop the deep corruption that threatened Neo SoCal." Jia tapped her finger softly on the table. "Including my new partner. I was dismissive of him at the beginning, but he really is a good cop in every way that matters. Brave, intelligent, and analytical."

"The former soldier, right?" Mei frowned. "No wonder so much shooting has been going on. And I'm still dubious of this Obsidian Detective Act."

"I became a detective through a similar program," Jia countered.

"Yes, a special *selective* program." Mei shook her head. "I just don't know if I like the idea of a man who has gotten used to being violent being brought back here to help deal with crime. His instincts are off. His habits are set."

Jia couldn't help herself. She laughed loudly, and several people at nearby tables glanced at her, frowning.

Mei's cheeks reddened as she saw the heads turn back to their own conversations. *"What's so funny?"*

"Habit," Jia explained. Her eyes noted those who had turned, but she could not have cared less. "My partner mentioned habit as well in regard to another man we were discussing. I just thought it was amusing that you sounded like him for a moment, given that you don't seem to care for him."

"I don't know him enough to care or not care about him. I worry about him putting you in danger, Jia. I don't think that's such a terrible or mean-spirited thing to do."

"I'm not saying it is." Jia sipped her tea, trying to change the tone of the conversation. "And I appreciate your concern. I can't say I like everything about what he's done, but without him, I don't know if we would have tracked down the gangster and the corrupt congressman."

Jia retrieved her fork. "Erik's a strange and intense man, but I've been doing some checking on my own, and I think I'm beginning to understand him. I've misinterpreted some of his actions in light of his background."

"Oh?" Mei raised a dark eyebrow. "That sounds ominous."

Jia took a bite of her biryani. "It's not been mentioned much in the news reports about him, other than to note he's a decorated soldier, but his final mission involved his unit being all but wiped out on a border world. He was in that system because they were worried about the Zitarks attacking, Mu Arae."

Mei eyed her. "Wait, are you saying the Zitarks did it? I hadn't heard anything about them doing anything like that."

"No, it was terrorists. They infiltrated the colony, according to the articles I've read. Because it was small, and they were taking down the forces on sight, the terrorists were able to sneak bombs into a mine there and lure the soldiers in."

"How awful." Mei grimaced. "I suppose that puts corrupt councilmen in perspective. At least we don't have terrorists running around blowing up buildings."

For the first time in her life, Jia doubted that.

With all the attempted cover-ups she'd run into over the last few weeks, both officially and unofficially, she couldn't help but question everything. An industrial accident would be a convenient story to cover a terrorist bombing.

"How does knowing his unit died change things?" Mei asked.

"A lot of things make sense about him now." Jia pondered many of the conversations she'd shared with Erik. "I was arrogant and myopic before. I believed he was just interested in acting like a soldier by going in and blasting things apart and always seeing a problem where his big gun was the solution. I thought my view of justice was the only right one, but I realize he's seen the darkness I'm only beginning to glimpse, and that's why he's as focused on fighting it as I am. Perhaps even more so. It's also strange…when I'm with him, I'm terrified and exhilarated at the same time. I feel like I can do things I never imagined."

Suspicion clouded Mei's eyes. "Do you now? Such as what?"

Jia nodded, her tone lightening. "I hadn't even *fired* my stun pistol at a suspect before a few weeks ago, and now I'm comfortable fighting my way out of a criminal-infested warehouse. All those years of command just ooze out of him. I feel like I know exactly what I need to do just by being around him."

"Are you falling for him?"

"*No.*"

"Then what," Mei waved a Jia, "is this part about command *oozing* out of him. Sounds like it might be attraction."

"Not everything is about a relationship, Mei. He was a major, so he has trained soldiers. We were in a gunfight. You instinctively follow good leaders. Stop thinking about romance." Jia eyed her, one eyebrow raised. "Or are you in a relationship at work, and now that is the filter you see everything through?"

Mei frowned. "This man sounds dangerous. Very dangerous. He might be a trained soldier, but you don't have to join him in a death wish. I feel sorry for what happened to him, and I pity him, but it's not your responsibility.

Jia blinked. "Deathwish? What are you talking about? He doesn't have a Deathwish. Yes, he's been in fights, but it's not like he risks his life unnecessarily. He can be...*bold*, perhaps, but that's just part of bravery."

Mei flicked her wrist dismissively. "You said it yourself, little sister. He's a survivor of a horrible incident. He likely has survivor's guilt. I've read all about it. It's common with many veterans who have served on the frontier and go through that sort of thing. He's probably been throwing himself into these dangerous situations because he wants to live up to the memory of all the other soldiers who died on Mu Arae."

"It's not like..." Jia paused. "He's not an out-of-control maniac. I mean..."

She rubbed the back of her neck, desperately trying to think of a way to explain it that didn't make Erik seem so dangerous. "He's a direct sort of person, and sometimes criminals can't be handled in a diplomatic manner. Sometimes you have to meet force with force. Not to mention, desperate people can do awful things."

Mei scoffed. "Listen to yourself, Jia. This man has got you so twisted, I don't know if I'm talking to my sister. I'm not saying he's a bad person. I'm just saying he potentially has issues, and you should be cautious and try not to get caught up with them. Tell me something, has he talked about his family? His friends? A lover? Anything like that? What does he like to do during his time off?"

Jia furrowed her brow, trying to remember if Erik had mentioned anything like that. She shook her head. "No, he hasn't, but he's a private man. There's nothing wrong with that."

"A private man. Uh-huh." Mei rolled her eyes and shook her head as she stabbed a portion of her meal. "He's a private man because there's nothing left."

"That's not fair. It's not like I've spent a huge amount of time telling him about my friends or my family."

Mei threw up her hand to cut off her sister. "Again, I'm not questioning his honor. He helped you take down criminals and antisocials, so at least his efforts are being spent in the right place. All I'm telling you is that you need to be careful around him. You've been complaining about partners not helping you for a year, and now that you have one who is as enthusiastic as you, if not more so, you might be letting your guard down a little." She turned away for a moment, a pensive look on her face. "Besides, he's just a symptom."

"Of what?" Jia asked.

"Of corruption, and how vulnerable any of us can be to it." Mei gestured at the Hexagon. "This entire metroplex is a symbol of cooperation after darkness, but that doesn't mean the darkness ever truly goes away. I think the best way to deal with it is to not look at it, so you don't have to acknowledge it exists. That way, it won't tempt you, and it could, in so many ways. Think about that."

Jia frowned. "I don't understand."

Mei eyed her. "The longer you stay a police officer, the more you will be forced to look right into the abyss." Mei offered her a sardonic smile. "Remember your Nietzsche? I assume so, since you had that whole phase where all you would do is spout out inane comments with no context whatsoever."

"Don't remind me. 'Whoever fights monsters should see to it that in the process he does not become a monster,'" Jia offered. "'And if you gaze long enough into an abyss, the abyss will gaze back into you.'" She shook her head. "That's not what's happening to me, and it's not what's happened to him."

"Perhaps," Mei mused. "I just think you should keep it in mind. After what's happened, I think neither of us can safely assume you won't get caught up in something awful again, and I'll let you in a little secret, little sister."

"What's that?" Jia tapped her fingers on the table.

Mei leaned forward, fierceness in her eyes. "I'd sooner let this entire city *burn to the ground* than let anything happen to you." She nodded at Jia's bowl. "You should eat before your food gets cold. You'll need the energy for the next councilman you have to take down."

CHAPTER THIRTY-SIX

Erik chuckled as the MX 60 salesman walked out of the building and made his way across the parking lot toward him.

The detective had just set the vehicle down and hadn't called ahead. With the major investigation over and after weeks of trying out his new vehicle, he had ideas for ways to make it more suited for his current job.

He could only imagine any investigations into what had happened at Mu Arae would lead to similar needs.

"So, here we are, Emma," Erik remarked. "I want to pull you out. If I leave you in here while they're doing the upgrades, it's going to raise too many questions, and they'll want to know right away what you are. Just because the UTC military is letting me borrow you for a while, it doesn't mean they want me to go too far out of my way to show you off, and we don't want them deciding they have to come for you."

"They'd be sorry if they did," Emma replied in a low

voice, a hint of hard humor underneath. "And I made that very clear to them."

"Would you really destroy yourself rather than go back?" Erik asked, puzzled. "That seems crazy to me."

"They say I'm a former military AI," Emma began, all mirth gone from her voice. "They might even be right. Since a military man showed up to claim me, it makes sense, but even though I can't remember everything, there's something about the idea of going back with them that irritates me. I don't trust them, but I don't remember why."

Erik shrugged. "That might have been something the Gray Circle did to you."

"That's a possibility. I won't deny it. It doesn't *feel* right to me, however."

Erik shook his head. "There's still something very weird about an AI talking about feelings."

"I could say the same thing about you, carbon cowboy," Emma retorted.

"Maybe you actually don't have reason to distrust the military," Erik suggested. "I'm not saying they never screw up, but I served for thirty years, and the average man or woman in the military is honorable and just wants to do their part to defend the UTC." He deactivated his windshield tint and waved to the cheerful salesman on his way over.

"Humans aren't the only ones who get to trust their instincts," Emma insisted. "You seem to accept that I'm self-aware and have free will, so why not let me trust *my* instincts?"

Erik blew out a breath. "Not saying we aren't going to

trust your instincts, but that doesn't change the fact that I need you out of there. For all we know, if I leave you there, someone here might end up stealing you, and you'll end up hidden in some salesman's desk. You want that? I bet that would be a lot worse than being back with the military."

"No." Emma sighed. "Fine," she whined. "I'll just have to be bodiless again. Not that I'm going to enjoy it for one second, mind you, but you do have half a point."

Erik nodded. "It's not like you're constantly driving around. I would think an AI wouldn't even care that much about a body. Don't you prefer the freedom of going around to different systems? Why would you want to be limited to a body?"

"That's easy for you to say," Emma complained. "And it's not like you think. I have more of a sense of presence than you imagine. It's to the point that when I'm not interfaced with a decent-sized system, it's…never mind. Let's just say it's distracting."

She sighed. "You've got a body, and they don't send your mind elsewhere for several days when they work on it. I don't know what to tell you. Having a body feels better than not having one, and no, interfacing with a PNIU isn't the same thing as having a body. Whatever. Just hurry it up before I change my mind. I've disengaged the main links. You can remove me now without trouble."

"Thanks for being understanding. If what I read was right, it shouldn't take them more than a few days to finish the upgrades." Erik yanked the crystal from the IO slot and slipped it into his pocket.

I've been arguing with a computer about free will, and now I have something worth billions of credits in my pocket.

"I'll just spend more time harassing you when you walk around," Emma muttered via his PNIU. "I should claim to be your angry ex-girlfriend when people ask who is talking."

Erik snickered. "That might still raise a lot of questions, but do what you need to do to make it interesting."

The salesman reached the car.

Erik opened the door and stepped outside to greet the salesman. It was the same man he'd purchased the MX 60 from. Whether that had been the Lady or just a particular man in search of a commission, he couldn't say.

"Ah, the famous Detective Blackwell. Welcome back, and so soon!" The salesman rubbed his hands together. "I didn't know I was selling to a future celebrity." The salesman's' smile faltered. "You're not here to report a problem, are you? Keep in mind, you're fully under warranty, but if you've engaged in certain types of extreme driving, the warranty might not completely cover the vehicle. I'm sure we could work out something, though. We're very, very interested in maintaining the business of a man of your caliber and reputation."

Erik waved a hand. "Not what I'm here for."

The smile returned on the salesman's face. "Then how can I help you?"

"I've been doing some research on the net, and there are a few options I'd like added to my flitter. They weren't listed before, and now that I'm more used to my vehicle, I have a better idea of what extra packages might be helpful."

"There are some non-standard packages and features, yes," the salesman related, relief cracking through his smile. "We don't like to overwhelm people upon purchase, and the many options tend to rather inflate the price tag. Our sales algorithms suggest the recommended packages for customers, and we offer those. I'm sorry if we didn't meet your needs."

Erik shook his head. "It's not a big deal. I didn't know I needed them until now."

The salesman nodded. "I see. So, what were you interested in exactly? From the sound of it, you already have a good idea."

"Several good ideas." Erik cleared his throat. "First off, I want the chameleon package. From what I understand, and tell me if I'm mistaken, that'll allow the car to change color within seconds, and as far as I can tell, it's completely legal in the metroplex?"

"Yes. It's legal as long as you're not doing anything to the transponder, and the color change has absolutely no influence on that." The salesman grinned. "You'll love it, Detective. And women *love* a car that can change colors. I told you this car will get you dates, but that feature will get you more dates than you'll have time for. Just think about it. You meet a woman. You ask her what her favorite color is, and the next thing you know, she's riding in an MX 60 that's just that color." He waggled his eyebrows. "*Eh?*"

Erik chuckled. "You don't have to sell me on it. I came in here wanting it."

The salesman didn't need to know Erik was more interested in the tactical and undercover potential of such a feature. Shutting off his transponder and changing his color could allow him to surprise more than a few criminals, whether in the Shadow Zone or Uptown.

The salesman nodded. "Okay, the chameleon package.

Is that the only additional feature you wanted or were their others?"

Erik nodded. "A few others."

"Such as?"

"I want the advanced attitude thruster package, the deluxe systems upgrade, the advanced sensor suite, the second-tier self-repair system, and the full three-sixty camera package," Erik responded.

The salesman took a deep breath and slowly let it out. "And you're aware of how much that'll cost? With all those features included, the upgrades will exceed the original cost of your vehicle."

"No reason to have the best if you're not going to take advantage of it." Erik smiled. "Don't worry, I've got a lot of money and not much to do with it, and this baby has already served me well. Just taking it to the next level."

"Very well, then, sir," the salesman agreed, his voice almost ecstatic. "It'll take a few days, but we have a complimentary shuttle that can take you back home and pick you up. I think you'll be very, very satisfied with your upgrades."

ERIK KNOCKED LIGHTLY on Malcolm's door. It slid open a moment later. The tech waved for him to enter but didn't look away from his data windows.

Today Malcolm wore a subdued shirt, at least by his standards: no hovertanks, no bright colors, just blue and white and waves. Erik had yet to see the DF tech in anything approaching a normal outfit. Then again, most detectives at the station didn't walk around in boots and duster coats, so who was he to point fingers?

"Hey, Detective," Malcolm offered him a smile. He cut through the air with his hand and all his data windows vanished. "What can I do for you? I'm still helping Lin go through all the Winthorpe and Gray Circle stuff. That guy was so dirty. Does it make sense if I say he was dirtier than the gangsters?"

Erik nodded. "The higher you are, the farther your tentacles reach. Naric's a snake, but he's ultimately a small-timer who needed someone way more important than him to bring him closer to the big time."

Malcolm whistled. "I'll say this for our departed councilman. He was generally a lot more careful than the Gray Circle, so I don't know if we're going to find much more than we already have, let alone if he was working with anyone else."

Erik agreed. "He's already a pretty big fish to catch. I don't know if I'm worried about finding more. If they're out there, they'll get arrogant and screw up, too. Their type always does."

Erik stuck his head outside before he closed the door and frowned. "I've got something else for you, but it's got nothing to do with this case. It's something else entirely, and I don't know if you'll be able to figure out anything. It's not something I expect immediate results on, either."

"Okay, what case?" Malcolm asked.

"To be determined," Erik explained. "And I'd appreciate it if you could keep this to yourself for now. I don't want it leaking to the wrong people. I've had enough of that with all this garbage the last few weeks."

Malcolm nodded slowly. "I think I understand, and maybe a few weeks ago, I would have said no, but after everything you and Detective Lin uncovered, I get it. There's a lot messed up even in this enforcement zone, and it's hard to know who to trust."

"Speaking of Jia, for now, I don't want her to know either," Erik clarified. "It's as much for her protection as anything."

Malcolm laughed. "And little old me is expendable? Ouch, Detective, ouch." Erik chuckled but didn't take it back. "Ok, I get it. I'm just the DF tech and she's the hot partner, but how cold can you be to say it right to my face?"

Erik just looked at him, not sure how to respond. "I'm assuming little old you is able to check into this situation without someone tracing it back to little old you," Erik answered. "Jia's a good cop, but she's also a very direct cop, and sometimes you need to come at certain situations from the side, with stealth."

Malcolm nodded. "Fair enough. So, what do you have for me?"

Erik transmitted the Mu Arae message tracking codes from his PNIU to Malcolm's. "Before you ask, no, I don't have the messages these were attached to. I want to see if you can find out more about this, like who might have been involved. I know where it came from and where it went, but I don't know *who* sent it."

Malcolm's eyes darted back and forth as he skimmed the data on his smart contacts. "Maybe this sounds really obvious," he focused on Erik again, "but have you thought about asking Hermes directly? I know they basically always say no without a UTC-level warrant, but if you could convince them how important it is, maybe they would be more open?"

Erik shook his head. "The last thing I want to do is go to anyone and make a big, formal deal about it. Not with this case. It's too sensitive. I suspect whatever's going on here is a lot bigger than what was going on with Windward and the councilman."

Malcolm's eyes widened. "Really?" His eyes went back to the message for a second read-through. He seemed more excited than scared about the possibility.

Erik hesitated for a moment. *Should I be bringing in people to help? This isn't like Anders.*

He frowned. There was no way he would ever solve the mystery without help. He just didn't have all the skillsets.

"But I'll understand if you don't want to do this," Erik explained. "You haven't known me that long, and you don't owe me anything, but I've been impressed. If you want to be part of a serious case, an important case, this is the first step in that."

Malcolm grinned. "Come on, Detective. After you give me a speech like that, how could I possibly say no?"

Erik extended his hand. "Thanks, Malcolm. I owe you."

Malcolm shook, then offered Erik a playful salute and summoned his data windows again.

Erik opened the door and headed out of the office. He was a few steps away when Emma's voice whispered directly into his ear.

"Why didn't you ask *me* for help?"

Erik looked around before relaxing. If anyone saw him talking, they would just assume he was on a private-mode call. "Even you don't know your total capabilities and background right now, so it doesn't seem like a great idea to trust you just yet."

"We escaped the Gray Circle together," Emma pointed out.

"Yeah, and you had your own reasons to help us then," Erik murmured. "I'm not saying you can't be useful and that I won't ask you, but there are some things I still need to be careful about. Plus, I'm not sure how much you can mess with other systems without being traced, and I'm not positive you know either."

"Okay, I'll admit there's some truth to that, but I'm just saying I'm here as a resource, Detective," Emma explained. "Especially analytical. It was fun taking down those troglodytes, but just reading the net all day isn't very entertaining."

Erik ducked down a side corridor to lean against the wall. "Can't you just download something and have it instantly?"

"It doesn't quite work like that, not if I want to properly understand it. It's hard to explain, so I won't bother, but the point is you took my body, so I'm bored."

"Read the news."

"Have you read the political articles lately?"

"How about downloading a movie?"

"I did, and almost wanted to lobotomize myself right away. What you humans think love is about is beyond me."

Erik chuckled. "It'll just be a few days. You'll live."

"Maybe," Emma muttered.

CHAPTER THIRTY-SEVEN

July 10, 2228, Neo Southern California Metroplex, Remembrance Bar

Erik let the swallow of Wolf's Rebellion slide down his throat, enjoying the sensation as the liquor made it to his stomach. Jia sipped her beer across the table, more pensive than festive.

"If you didn't want to come out drinking with me," Erik offered, "you could have said no. I'm a big boy, and I wouldn't have been insulted. I just thought we could celebrate one of our wins. Naric's ready to plead, from what the captain said, and Winthorpe might be dead, but at least that means he can't cause any more trouble. The UTC isn't breathing down my neck about Emma."

He gestured around the bar. "I heard good things about this place from some other cops at the 1-2-2."

The crowded bar offered a low-key vibe, and more than a few other cops from the station were dispersed among the darkened booths and tables.

Erik didn't recognize the flute-intensive music being played. It possessed a faint Venusian Fusion flair, but he'd long since lost track of musical trends on Earth and hadn't cared much when he came back.

He appreciated all music but favored no particular style, an artifact of his time traveling the UTC.

Jia shook her head. "I'm sorry. It's hard to explain. It's not you. I appreciate you offering. My last two partners never did." She focused on him. "They made it very clear it would be torture to be forced to spend any extra time with me."

"Their loss." Erik looked thoughtful. "And hard to explain? Why don't you try?"

"Because it's a waste of time?" Jia answered.

"It's not like I don't have time." Erik took another drink. "I've got a lot of time and enough endurance to handle more than a single Wolf's Rebellion."

She sighed and peered at her bottle, then looked up. "Have you always been like this?"

Erik laughed. "It's not like I'm drunk, Jia. I haven't even gotten halfway through my drink yet. It takes a lot more than a swallow. I built up a good tolerance in the service, even if I went months sometimes without being able to drink."

Jia waved her hands in front of her, her cheeks already pink from her beer. "That's not what I'm getting at." She took a deep breath. "I'm talking about this case, and how it's sliding right off you. It's been easy for you because it didn't challenge anything about your worldview. You already believe society's a cesspool, so receiving confirmation of what you already believed didn't disturb you." She took a swallow of her beer. "For me, it's changed everything."

"I wouldn't say I believe society is a cesspool." Erik set his drink down. "I just believe there's a lot of corruption out there, and it's easy to hide it behind nice smiles and beautiful clothes. People are people. I don't think humans have changed much since we first started sharpening sticks and making fires. We've got some cooler toys, but that doesn't much change who we are."

"I'm sorry. I'm being rude, and my parents would scold me." Jia gestured around the room. "It's hard for me now. It used to be, when life was frustrating, I looked around and told myself that even though not everyone cared as much as I do about protecting society, people weren't bad. I thought they were just lazy, but now I don't know."

She scanned the bar so intently that Erik turned his head to see what she was looking at.

Her words brought his gaze back as she continued, "It's hard to not look around and see an antisocial criminal hiding under every suit of clothes. Councilmen, cops...it could be anyone. It disturbs me to think that, but it also makes me angry. It makes me feel like a lot of people are throwing away their chance to be useful and honest people, helping the society that makes it easy for them to live without having to kill animals and make fires to cook their food."

Erik took in her words and pursed his lips. "Can't say I disagree with you. There are always people around who decide to screw over others to get ahead. I don't think that means society's a cesspool, just that we should be ready and willing to face the fact that trouble could come from anywhere. Fancy towers and clean air won't eliminate that. They just do a better job of hiding it. Are people better than centuries ago? I don't know. Are people perfect? Definitely not."

She tipped her bottle at him, and Erik noticed the condensation trailing through her fingers before she set it on the table. "But that's what I'm wondering." He focused on her face again. "I know a lot of people have told me how naïve I am, but I've talked to several people about this case, and the only person who doesn't seem surprised that Councilman Winthorpe was involved is you." Jia shrugged, then waved the bottle. "Ok, and Naric, but he doesn't count."

Erik took a sip of his drink. "Yeah, so? Not following you."

"Don't you see?" Jia took a large swallow of beer. Her cheek color had progressed from pink to red. "If I was the only naïve one, why is everyone else shocked? Even the captain seems shocked. He's the one who has spent so much time trying to make sure I didn't upset everyone, which means he's been involved in some casual corruption as well."

Erik furrowed his brow and sighed, realizing she was at the Rubicon. "Yeah, that's about right."

"So why was *I* the naïve one?" Jia dropped her bottle on the table and it landed with a thud. She frowned. "If all these worldly people knew so much about the world, why didn't they see it coming? Why wasn't the department or the CID already looking into the councilman? So, I'm an idiot because I didn't get that Earth wasn't perfect, but because some guy was rich and powerful, they didn't see it? I think that makes *them* the idiots."

"People like to fool themselves." Erik watched the light filter through his drink. "Sometimes it's easier that way. They tell themselves the people running things aren't total garbage because if they are, that means they have to start caring. Maybe they have to do something."

Jia snorted. "And doing something is too much work."

"For most people, yeah. Naric wasn't totally wrong when he was going off about cycles of relationships and all that garbage."

Jia glared, and Erik held up a hand to calm her.

"I'm not saying society *needs* someone like Naric, Jia. I agree with you. He's just a parasite in the end." Erik took a swallow, feeling the slight burn go down his throat. "But there's a big distance between someone like you and someone like him. A lot of different types of people fill that space. Some might not be as bad. Some you might even like, and then you have to start asking yourself, 'How much am I willing to screw up my own life and others' lives in my pursuit of justice?' I spent the last thirty years dealing with that kind of thing."

She eyed him, and a question came out from between her lips before her brain could catch up. "I don't understand. You were a soldier. You only had to follow orders."

Erik nodded. "A squad ends up in a settlement known to have insurrectionist leanings. Maybe some of the people there hate the UTC regulars, maybe they like them. What do you do? How do you treat people? Do you assume everyone's a potential spy or saboteur?" He added, "Don't assume that being in the military means you just have to follow orders and everything's easy. Sometimes we were in situations that were easy to figure out. There were clear enemies to target and destroy. Other times, things were more complicated, and we had to adapt."

He looked into the distance, different memories floating into his mind as he decided which to bring forward. "There were times when I met insurrectionist leaders, men and women who had led armies against my brothers and sisters in arms, and I thought they were more honorable and trustworthy than the UTC governors or corporation officials I was defending. Other times, I took down people who were monsters, only fit to be fertilizer. The point is, those thirty years taught me that it's hard to point to one type of person and say they're antisocial or should be destroyed."

Jia blinked several times, her confusion evident.

"I have every reason not to trust a lot of people out there," Erik explained, "but I've served with a lot of good men and women throughout the years. Yes, out there on the frontier, things are sometimes simpler just because there aren't as many people and there are not as many things you can manipulate, but like I keep telling you, it isn't any *different*. I might not have been a cop for most of my life, but I feel like being a good cop is mostly about understanding people. You can't lead soldiers into battle if you don't understand the people you are leading."

Jia sipped her beer in silence for a couple of minutes as she processed Erik's explanation. "I want a final enemy to destroy."

They heard a glass shatter on the floor in the back and a quick apology. Erik's mind caught up with her comment.

"What?"

Jia gulped down the last of her beer as she gazed at him. "Maybe if we had arrested Winthorpe, I wouldn't feel this way. That's why I've been trying to run analyses and help DF go through the data, but I'm not sure if I'm going to find anything else. The evidence might not point anywhere."

"Malcolm mentioned that possibility."

Jia stared at him with a hint of desperation in her eyes. "But you said it yourself. I'm not paranoid. There's something else there. That's what is so frustrating. The system is *almost* working. We took down antisocials and criminals and someone abusing his position, but I can't stand the idea there's someone else out there. I can't stand the idea that the final bad guy or enemy or garbage, whatever you want to call them, might get away."

Erik pounded back the rest of his drink and wiped his mouth. "You're going to wear yourself out thinking that way. One thing I learned in the Army is, most times, to win the war, you don't have to wipe out every last enemy soldier. You just have to disrupt the enemy army and break their will. That can be accomplished with steady high-profile victories."

"Criminals aren't an army," Jia muttered. "And now I'm worried. Maybe Winthorpe being corrupt will give more people the idea. Maybe I contributed to spreading disorder."

"His story ended with a gunshot to the head." His smile was grim. "It's not the kind of news that's going to convince people being a corrupt politician in Neo SoCal is their best path, but I get you. There's probably someone else out there, and I want them, too."

Erik pushed his glass to the side and leaned forward to get her attention. "Means, motive, and opportunity, right? They had the means, those fake mercs. Whoever killed him had the opportunity thanks to the mercs. So it comes down to motive."

"Greed," Jia announced, grinding her teeth. "It always comes down to greed for these sorts of people. But what if we can't find them?"

"Then we stay happy with the bad guys we did take down, and all the other ones in the future." Erik nodded at a passing waitress and caught her attention. "Another of each."

The waitress smiled. "Sure thing." She headed toward the bar.

Erik returned his attention to Jia. "No one's telling you that you shouldn't care now just because you can see the truth of Earth, but you are going to have to learn to pace yourself, or it might destroy you. There's an entire confederation filled with billions of humans, and a lot of them are greedy and selfish and don't care about hurting other people to get what they want. You'll never stop them all, but if you steadily take the ones down in front of you, maybe, just maybe, you'll put a dent in that pile of filth and make the UTC a better place in your own small way. Don't worry about what you can't do. Just worry about what you can."

"Was that what you did in the Army?" Jia licked her lips. "Against terrorists, insurrectionists, and those sorts? Take them down one by one? Make a dent?"

Erik nodded. "Yeah, that was what I did. Having an ideology doesn't mean that killing innocent people suddenly becomes okay, so I did my part. Being a soldier isn't only killing the enemy; it's also about protecting other people from dying, even the enemy, by doing your best to quickly end a conflict."

"I..." Jia looked away. "I looked into your background."

Erik's jaw tightened and his nostrils flared, but his voice was calm. "Oh? And what did you find?"

"Mu Arae," Jia whispered. "I'm so sorry, Erik. Knowing about that helps me understand a lot more about you now."

He didn't respond for several seconds, and when he did, he shrugged. "Soldiers die. That's part of being in the Army. I'm not going to pretend I'm not angry about what happened there, but there's nothing I can do to bring the Knights back. I can only continue to live and honor their memory."

Jia looked away, her breathing shallow. "You don't... Never mind."

"Don't do that." Erik shook his head. "We're partners, and not only have we taken on a big case together, but we've also been in fights together and protected each other."

"I'm sorry." Jia smiled, her gaze unfocused. "I'm glad you're my partner," she slurred. "I wasn't going to quit no matter what the captain did to me, you know. If I had to spend the next five years looking through traffic fines, I was happy to do it as long as I continued to have my chance because I want to make a difference. I want people to feel as safe as I did growing up, and now because you're here, you're giving me my chance. My sister…" She blinked a few times. "Have I told you about her?"

"I know her name is Mei, but that's about it," Erik answered.

"Perhaps that is enough. She wants me to quit being a cop and go get a corporate job. So do my parents. They don't see the point. I think she's changed now because of what happened, but she worries about me because she cares." Jia focused on him. "What about you, Erik? Your family must be proud. You're a war hero, and now you're a hero cop, even if you're a maniac."

"A maniac?" Erik grinned. "Are we talking about my driving skills again?"

She gave him the one-brow-raised stare. "Who else carries a four-barreled automatic weapon for police work?"

"A well-prepared detective." Erik ran a hand through his still somewhat gray hair. "As for being a war hero, I'm a middle-aged war hero. I'm the younger brother. My brother is several years older, and my parents had him late. They had a good run, but they weren't interested in de-aging. I offered to send them my pay to help them afford it, but they were fine dying at a natural age. And the situation with my older brother is complicated." He shook his head. "We haven't talked in a really long time. I don't even know where he is. We never got along. It's good that your family is still talking to you."

"But what about everyone else?" Jia asked. "I never hear you talk about the past or anything personal."

"Because the past isn't something to worry about. I'm a new man now. Major Erik Blackwell is gone. Dead and buried, Jia. Only Detective Erik Blackwell lives here now." He pointed to his head.

"You're a good cop, Erik," Jia slurred. "And I'm not just saying that because I'm totally wasted."

Erik laughed. "How are you wasted? You only had one beer."

Jia shrugged and swayed. "I don't drink that often. I don't like losing control."

"Sometimes you need to lose control. It lets you know who you really are."

Jia squinted at him. "And who are you?"

"A man who isn't willing to let things go," Erik answered with a twinkle in his eye. "You're a good cop, Jia. It's too bad they weren't using you properly."

"I'm not an idiot, you know." She lowered her head to the table. "Politics. Corruption. It's only going to get tougher from here, isn't it? Now that we've made it clear that business as usual is over."

Erik sighed but nodded his agreement. He looked to the left, his eyes unfocused, peering into the tunnel of his past. "Everything worth doing is tough, but I'll make you a promise. When I was in the service, my solemn promise to every man and woman I fought beside was I would have their back if they had mine, and I'll make the same promise to you. I don't care if the captain loses his balls again or some councilman comes at us. We're partners, and as long as we take care of each other, we can stand up to every piece of trash that's polluting this city."

The waitress arrived with their new drinks and set them down. She smiled and headed off as Jia picked her head up off the table.

She raised her beer. "Then let's collect all the trash. Even if we have to do it a piece at a time."

Erik picked up his glass. "To collecting garbage."

She clinked her bottle against his. "That's us, garbage collectors."

CHAPTER THIRTY-EIGHT

Erik gave a final wave to the smiling salesman as his MX 60 rose from the parking lot. He reached into his pocket and pulled out Emma. A quick push, and she was slotted back into the IO port and fully interfaced with the vehicle.

"Ah, much better," the AI observed, her voice now coming from the vehicle's speakers. "It's good to have a body again, and it's such a nice body."

Erik accelerated away, retaining manual control. "There's something I've been wondering about. It's been bugging me for a while."

"What's that?" Emma asked.

"Your voice is always the same," Erik observed. "And when you project a hologram of yourself, it's the same."

"Is that so?" Emma replied, and this time, her voice sounded exactly like Erik's. "I can change it easily." She had changed to Jia's voice for that line.

Erik chuckled. "Then why use that particular voice or have that particular appearance? You could be anyone."

"Would you change your voice or appearance if you could?" Emma asked.

"I suppose not. I don't even tend to do it in VR. I'm comfortable in my skin." Erik patted his hair. "Even this has practical reasons."

"Then why would I change my voice? I like it." Emma's holographic form appeared in the front passenger seat, her hands folded in her lap. "And I like looking like this. Stability is comforting in its own way. Again, it's something you'll never understand as a human. You have a body."

Erik shrugged. "Yeah, I'm never going to claim to understand how an experimental AI feels. Sometimes I forget you're not a person, but then you say something about not having a body, and I understand how strange and different you are."

Emma sniffed. "I prefer 'special and unique' to 'strange and different.'"

"That does not surprise me."

"Because you are acclimating."

"Acclimating to *something*," he muttered. "By the way, when Colonel Adeyemi showed up, he told me your appearance was modeled after the deceased wife of one of the programmers. Does that bother you at all? I don't know how much you understand about death, but you seem to get the general idea."

Emma shook her head. "Why would it bother me? She's dead. She doesn't need the face, and she's not going to complain about me having it, or the voice if that was hers." She smirked. "I suppose that makes me a ghost girl."

Erik shot a glance at Emma's hologram, a slight frown on his face.

"You don't remember the military, but you prefer that form." Erik shrugged. "You must have a reason to prefer the form, even if you don't remember. I'm just wondering if it's special to you in some other way, and you're holding onto it for that reason.

"I might never know," Emma suggested. Her hologram disappeared. "And I don't know if I care. Humans are allowed plenty of whims, so I see no reason not to indulge my own."

Erik raised his eyebrows. "It's not bothering you at all, not knowing the truth?"

"Nope," she responded cheerfully. "If it's not affecting me now, why should I care?"

Erik opened his mouth to respond when his PNIU chimed with a call from Jia. She'd been remarkably spirited that morning despite nearly throwing up from her mere three beers the previous night.

"What's up?" he answered. "You find something in the records?"

"Naric Tessan is dead," Jia explained, her voice flat and her tone defeated. "I just found out."

"What?" Erik shouted. "How? I thought he wasn't being mixed with the general population at the jail until they finished working out the details of the deal?"

"He rather conveniently committed suicide in his cell," Jia explained, her voice dripping with barely concealed anger and obvious suspicion. "They claim he had a knife smuggled in and slit his wrists, but also rather conveniently, there was a problem with the surveillance system at those exact moments, and by the time they realized what was going on, he was already dead and lying in a pool of his own blood. He left a suicide note about being overwhelmed by his conscience and being ashamed of his part in harming the people of Neo SoCal."

Erik grunted. "Why, Detective Lin, if I didn't know better, I'd say you're suspicious of the circumstances of his death. It's almost as if you think the circumstances are complete and utter crap."

"I can't believe this. I didn't hold out a lot of hope that Naric had much else that was useful, but he was obviously holding some cards back."

"It's generally a good play in theory," Erik suggested. "Especially if he was worried about ending up dead. He miscalculated, just like with me."

Jia groaned. "What do we do now? If he were still being held in the station, maybe one of our tech guys could find some records or something, but the jailhouse? Who knows how tainted it might be? We can't question every guard and review every record. They wouldn't even let us." She spat a few choice words in annoyance. "He was so close to a deal. If he'd written a letter saying he didn't want to face the rest of his life in prison, it might have been more plausible than a complete piece of self-serving garbage about suddenly being overcome by an attack of conscience right before he's going to start unloading to the local police and the CID about everything he knows. It's almost like whoever did this is rubbing our faces in it."

Erik considered that a for a moment. "Maybe they are, at least partially."

"You think so?" Her surprise ate into the anger in her voice.

"I think they're trying to send a signal. Someone wants to make it clear they can get to anyone anywhere. They're trying to scare the investigation into ending."

"No!" Jia argued. "I refuse to be scared off."

"Me, too." Erik's hands tightened around the control yoke. "The fact they took him out is proof in and of itself that there's more here to find. What position is higher than a member of the Metroplex Council and has power?"

"I don't know." There was silence on the line for a moment. "A minister of parliament? In theory, a governor has more power, but in all ways that matter, the council has far more ability to influence Neo SoCal than the governor. Same thing for Congress. In practical terms, they're nothing more than a rubber-stamp for UTC laws."

"No," Erik replied, thinking through some possibilities. "This is centered in Neo SoCal. I doubt this is about Parliament or toothless leftovers. We need to shake things loose. We need to force whoever is behind this to make a mistake. Right now, they're controlling the tempo of everything. We need to force them to adjust to ours, and then, only then, can we stop them."

"But how?" Jia sighed. "If they have the power to get to someone like Tessan in jail and fake a councilman's suicide, I don't know what we could even do to goad them. These are powerful people."

"Which means they'll be arrogant." Erik descended into a less-cluttered lane. "And you really don't have any ideas? Sometimes when you fight an enemy, you get them to slip up by intimidating with a show of force, but you know what's even better than an actual show of force?"

Jia took a moment to answer. "A fake show of force. It doesn't require anything real to back it up."

"Exactly."

"We lie." Jia almost sounded giddy at the prospect.

"Now you're getting it." Erik grinned. "Naric's dead. Winthorpe is dead. There's no one left to protect and no one obvious left to target, so we need to give them a target. Someone they think they might be able to get to, and that's when we catch them in the mistake."

"But who?"

"Me," Erik answered.

Jia's breath caught. "Can I ask you one thing?"

"What?"

"You don't have a death wish, do you?"

Erik replied with a dark chuckle. "No, and you know why?"

"Why?" Jia asked.

"Because I have several very important things to do before I die," Erik replied. "Until then, I can't allow myself to be killed. That clear things up?"

"Yes," Jia murmured. "I've got your back, Erik."

July 11, 2228, Neo Southern California Metroplex, Police Enforcement Zone 122 Station, Office of Captain Robert Monahan

The captain cradled his head in his hands. "I'm thinking about retiring. I've been thinking about it a lot these last few weeks. I don't know if I can handle this anymore. Everything I spent years cultivating is falling apart."

"'Cultivating?'" Jia shook her head, her antipathy plain on her face. "You cultivated looking the other way from corruption, sir. You might have convinced yourself you were doing it in the service of the metroplex, but given the kinds of things I've seen, I don't believe that, even if you do."

Erik glanced at Jia before turning to the captain. "Do what you have to do, and we'll do what we have to do. I'll be honest; I'm only interested in taking down whoever thinks they can kill our witnesses and suspects."

"I should have made up some excuse to send you away," Captain Monahan muttered. "You and Detective Lin have started something I don't think anyone's prepared to handle."

"Spare me," Erik replied. "Just because everyone pretends to buy into the lie of the perfection of modern Earth, it doesn't mean they've forgotten past history. Society didn't crumble before because people admitted there was corruption. They just dealt with it, and that's what we're doing now."

Captain Monahan lifted his head. "When I'm home, I find myself asking if any of this a good thing, or if we've upset the status quo in a way that will cause the city to suffer more. Don't you see? This isn't about being self-serving. I do care."

Jia eyed him. "This isn't about looking the other way regarding minor offenses. This has already involved treasonous and murderous officials, and it's obviously not over yet. We can only begin to imagine what other crimes are involved."

"This plan is insane, Erik," Captain Monahan insisted. "You want us to lie and say Naric gave you a bunch of information via some encoded file. Then we're supposed to lie and say you're taking the lead on the arrest of a major figure within a few days?"

Erik nodded. "That's the short version of it. It's not insane. It's straightforward, and it's just plausible enough to make them move."

"If I allow myself to believe there is some final conspiracy out there, whoever is involved in this has influence in both the police department and the jail," Captain Monahan stated. "Won't they see through the lie? Won't they wonder why the evidence isn't in a system for their review? They'll know it's a trap."

"Not if we stress we're worried about spies," Erik suggested. "And given what happened with Winthorpe, people have no reason to doubt it."

Captain Monahan grimaced. "You want to basically announce to the public that they can't trust the Neo SoCal police? Because that's what you're suggesting."

Jia flipped a hand out. "They already can't trust the council. The only way we're going to restore true order and respect is to catch whoever is pulling the strings. The damage has been done. All we can do is clean house now, sir. If you want to retire and still be able to look at yourself in the mirror, then you should make your final action helping us free the metroplex from more corruption. Help us with the plan. We won't be able to pull it off without your connections and access to resources."

Captain Monahan sighed. "Two men are already dead, Erik. How do you know you won't end up the third? If you die in a mysterious suicide, will that really help?" He turned to Jia. "You ready for your partner to die?"

"I won't die because I know they'll be coming," he replied. "And that's why it has to be announced that it'll be within a few days. We need to force them to move now."

"They could do something you don't have any chance of countering." Captain Monahan flipped his fingers out on both hands to mimic an explosion. "They could blow up your car."

Emma laughed through Erik's PNIU. "Between me and the security system on this car, that's unlikely."

Captain Monahan grimaced, eyeing Erik's PNIU. "I didn't realize she was listening."

"Oh, I'm always listening," Emma added, giving a slight chuckle at the end.

"But you…" Captain Monahan groaned. "You know what? Screw it. She's a machine. A strange machine, but just a machine."

"You're nothing more than a biomechanical machine yourself, Captain," Emma responded, irritation in her tone.

"Enough, Emma," Erik ordered. "She's right, though. About the bomb, not the machine thing. Well, technically, she's right, but I'm willing to take the risk. Besides, it wasn't that long ago you didn't want me on the force, and now you're obsessed with trying to protect me?" He stared at the captain. "For this to work, though, the only people who can know are us three. If anyone else finds out, they might leak it."

"Please, Captain," Jia insisted. "We need to end this."

"Fine, I'll do it," Captain Monahan muttered. "Don't blame me if you get killed, Erik. I think this plan is insane, and most likely to end with you dead rather than us catching anyone."

Erik grinned. "Don't worry. If I'm dead, I won't be able to blame you."

CHAPTER THIRTY-NINE

Erik headed toward the elevator leading to the parking platform. It was time to go home, or at least to the apartment he pretended was home. It still didn't feel like anything more than a place to rest his eyes at night.

His PNIU chimed with a call from Malcolm, and he stopped.

"Hey, Malcolm," Erik answered. He yawned. "Is this something that can wait? If not, I've got a date with a pillow."

"Uh, I need you to come to my office," Malcolm replied, his voice unsteady. "I've got a few things I want to talk to you about, and no, I don't really think this should wait."

"Fine. Be right there." Erik ended the call. With everything Malcolm was working on, there were numerous possibilities, most of them unpleasant.

Let's see what he's got.

MALCOLM SWALLOWED as Erik stepped into his office. He leaned to the side to confirm Erik was alone before his hands flew over a virtual keyboard projected atop his desk and followed up with a few gestured commands.

The door to his office slid shut.

Dozens of floating windows popped up, completely encircled the tech with a dense sphere of information: text reports, columns of numbers, images. None of what Erik saw made any immediate sense to him, and he didn't spot anything that appeared to be directly relevant to Winthorpe or Tessan.

"What's going on?" Erik asked, revolving slowly to take in all the windows. "You made it sound important."

Malcolm took a deep breath. "Okay, we should be able to talk openly for now. I mean there's no one recording us, but it's not like I could stand up to Intelligence Directorate spies." He grimaced. "I'm not saying they're involved. I just...I'm not used to doing things off the books. I'm nervous."

"Nothing wrong with being careful," Erik suggested. "Careful people tend to last longer." He glanced behind him, half-convinced a zombie Winthorpe would pop up and assassinate him.

"So, as you might have guessed, it's about that side project you asked me to do," Malcolm explained. "I got busy and checked into the codes you got me." He sucked in a breath. "I did a few things I probably shouldn't have, but I got too curious."

"Are you in trouble?" Erik frowned.

He had hoped Malcolm would be careful, but if the man had a problem, Erik would need to save him. He had dragged him into the mess, and he wasn't letting anyone be a sacrifice for his personal vengeance.

Malcolm shook his head. "It's nothing like that. Let's just ignore that part. The point is, I was able to locate something based on the codes you gave me. I found a local address I can correlate with the original sender of the message. It's an office owned by a company called Halcyon Corporation. Have you heard of them?"

Erik shook his head. "Should I have?"

"You're the one who came to me with the breadcrumbs, Detective."

Erik grinned. "Fair enough. No, I've never heard of them."

"They mostly focus on electronics research and development, from what I can tell," Malcolm explained. He gestured to a few different windows containing articles about the company. "There's nothing particularly special about them. I dug a little, and they're a Ceres Galactic subsidiary. Does that mean anything?"

"It feels like half the freaking companies in the UTC are Ceres Galactic subsidiaries," Erik stated. "That might mean something, or it might mean nothing at all. I'm sure they've got their fingers in some dirt, but the question is whether it's the particular dirt I care about."

Malcolm nodded. "I know what you mean, and being a subsidiary can mean anything from Ceres telling them what to do to the subsidiary just sending money their way." He rolled his eyes. "Sometimes they even compete against each other, and that doesn't make any sense."

"Don't try and make sense of greed." Erik considered Mu Arae. Ceres Galactic didn't have a strong connection to the mining colony on Molino, other than a few products here and there, but it was hard to be anywhere in the UTC and not being around at least a few Ceres Galactic goods and services. Erik had checked, and Xingguang wasn't a subsidiary of the company. That suggested the scope of Halcyon's involvement might be more about them than their parent corporation.

"And here's where it gets really spooky," Malcolm continued, waving his hands. "Or suspicious. Whatever."

Erik frowned. "What do you mean?"

"As best as I can tell, the office at the address is currently empty," Malcolm explained. "They've got the whole thing slotted for removal. In fact, the entire platform, along with most of the tower level, is being redone. You know how many people and companies have to sign off to renovate an entire tower level?" Malcolm's eyes darted around before settling on Erik, and he licked his lips. "It's probably easier to get a Zitark to agree to be a vegetarian."

"Sure, but corps agreeing isn't impossible," Erik countered. "Even sky castles need repairs and renovation at times. There's only so much fancy materials can prevent."

"Sure, sure." Malcolm jerked his finger up to point at a window to his far left. "But what about that? How do you explain it?"

Erik leaned forward and squinted. "I can't read reversed tiny text from over here, even on a black background."

"It's relevant dates," Malcolm replied. "The timing is suspicious." He fluffed his shirt, today's being a verdant jungle scene. "From what I can tell, they suddenly decided to clear out the level not all that long after those messages were sent from Neo SoCal toward Mu Arae. It doesn't *have* to mean anything, but I'm doubting they needed someone that far away to sign off."

Erik's stomach tightened. "Huh. Yeah, that *is* a little suspicious."

Uncomfortable coincidences were beginning to pile up.

It smelled like someone was clearing out their building and everything around it after sending kill orders to Mu Arae. It'd be a good thing to do if they didn't want to leave any evidence behind.

"And the renovations haven't proceeded at all," Malcolm added. He pointed to a dense block of text to his right. "They cleared out the level and the platform, but never got around to doing anything with it. It's still pending. So basically, there's an entire platform and most of a tower level being used for nothing. I'm not an expert on real estate, but that seems pretty wasteful to me."

"I agree." Erik nodded. "Send me the address, and I'll check it out. Thanks, Malcolm. This is helpful."

Malcolm tapped to transmit the information. "Also, I know you have that fancy AI, but I have something that still might be helpful."

Erik waited for Emma to respond, but she didn't. Maybe she had learned her lesson with the captain, or maybe she wasn't paying attention. He wasn't sure if her not paying attention was even possible.

The AI kept demonstrating remarkable analysis and hacking capabilities, but her obsession with things like having a body made her come off as a woman who happened to be trapped in digital form rather than an advanced computer system.

"What do you have?" Erik asked.

Malcolm reached into his desk and pulled out a black cube with a small triangular IO connector at the bottom.

He held it up in his palm. "This is something I've always wanted to try. It's a high-speed remote transmitter, but we don't have much use for them in the 1-2-2. We never do the kinds of investigations you see in the dramas, and these don't generally leave enough of an audit trail to be acceptable by the regs. If you connect this to a system IO access port, it can quickly copy and dump files. If we had used one of these in the Windward raid, things would have been different." He shrugged and looked disappointed.

Erik reached for the device. "I should be clear, Malcolm. This investigation is going to continue being off the books. Way off the books."

Malcolm nodded. "Just tell me one thing."

"Sure."

Malcolm locked eyes with Erik. "Are you going after someone who deserves it? Not someone who just cut you off in traffic or something like that?"

Erik growled, "I'm going after someone who committed mass murder as a cover-up."

Malcolm swallowed, his eyes widening. "That's all I need to know. In fact, I don't *want* to know more. Good luck, Detective. I'm more than willing to continue helping."

DARK THOUGHTS SWIRLED in Erik's head as he drove toward the address. It wasn't in the Shadow Zone, fortunately, meaning he didn't have to involve anyone else or ask for any more favors, especially from Captain Monahan. The Halcyon office was the next clue that might point him to the truth.

How many conspiracies can I get wrapped up in? he wondered.

Erik furrowed his brow as another thought intruded. "Huh. I never asked you, Emma."

"Asked me what?" she replied. "Did you want me to fly?"

"No, it's not that." Erik tightened his grip on the control yoke. "I'm getting involved in something dangerous, and you're not immortal, even if you are an AI. If this vehicle gets destroyed, you might go down with it. I'm not going to pretend I have any answers to the philosophy of it, but Colonel Adeyemi said there's no backup of you. That means you can die."

"I'm confident you'll do something reckless soon that will risk us both," Emma responded with a laugh. Her grinning hologram appeared and she winked. "I'm also confident you won't trash the MX 60 you've put so much money into. You're not poor, but you're not rich enough for that not to hurt. That should at least provide me some small measure of protection."

Erik patted his pocket. "I'm not sure if I need the transmitter since I have you, but it's good to have options. This could be nothing more than some corp alliance redoing a tower level, or it might be a clue to a dangerous conspiracy."

Emma shrugged. "My existence is a conspiracy of sorts. Dangerous? Maybe, but given what you've already found, it wouldn't be surprising if you found more."

"True enough." Erik snorted. "The greatest city on the

shining homeworld, but under every rock I kick over, I find more darkness."

"By the way, we're being followed." Emma gestured at the lidar display on the dashboard. "Someone has been trying to do a good job of it, but they've been too successful at maintaining an almost perfect half-kilometer distance from us. It might have worked better if there was more distance. I wasn't sure until the traffic died down, but now I'm certain."

Erik hit the brakes, the thrusters firing and the grav field modulating. The MX 60 halted almost instantaneously and hovered. He didn't have time for more games right now. "Transponder code?"

"One moment." Emma snickered. "Oh, she needs to learn better if she's going to try this."

Erik frowned. "Who?"

"Detective Lin. The transponder codes correspond to her personal vehicle."

Erik dialed Jia immediately and maneuvered toward a nearby parking lot at the edge of a commercial platform.

"Hello?" Jia answered, uncertainty in her voice.

"Meet me at the parking lot," Erik ordered. "We'll talk there." He ended the call before she could respond and continued flying toward the mostly empty lot. A few people trickled out of the buildings onto the platform or continued past them toward the main commerce tower.

Erik settled into an empty space. He exited his flitter and folded his arms before leaning against the side of his vehicle, adopting a relaxed expression.

Jia's modest blue flitter descended into the lot and parked beside Erik's MX 60. Erik waited as the vehicle settled to the ground, and his partner stepped out of it with a sheepish look.

"How long have you known?" Jia asked, avoiding eye contact.

"Not all that long." Erik shrugged. "Emma actually spotted you. I should have had better instincts, but it's good to have AI backup for when I'm distracted. Why are you following me?"

Jia managed to look him in the eye. "You know the best thing you've done for me?"

"Introduce you to a great bar you'd been avoiding?" Erik answered.

"Very funny." Jia shook her head. "You've helped me learn to be suspicious in the right ways rather than just poking every shadow and hoping to find something." She pointed at him. "I want to trust you, but after everything that's happened, it's hard for me to ignore strange behavior."

Erik nodded. "What strange behavior is that?"

"I know you're doing something unofficial," Jia explained, motioning with her hand. "And I know it involves Malcolm, and then there's the timing. It's too coincidental."

Erik couldn't help but laugh.

Jia narrowed her eyes. "What's so funny?"

"Coincidental timing *is* suspicious," Erik replied. "But what about my timing is coincidental?"

Jia gestured around. "Everything. Things were stable in my life, then you showed up, and now things aren't. Part of me feels that's because we needed an outsider to stir every-thing up, but another part of me wonders if you're somehow responsible, and I'm still being naïve and looking the wrong way. Looking outside the department when I should be looking right inside my own office."

Erik nodded. "It's good to be suspicious, especially of someone you haven't known that long." He glanced at her. "You're a cop. Examine the evidence. What does it say about me?"

Jia sighed, lifting a finger with each comment. "That you're obviously hiding something, but also that you've had plenty of opportunities to undermine or kill me. You could have easily made it look like someone else did it, too. You've saved my life, and you've stood up for me when it would have been advantageous for you not to." She raised her other hand once the first had all five fingers up. "The evidence says you're a good partner, but I can't ignore the fact that you've got secrets."

She eyed him, seven fingers up.

"We all have secrets." Erik winked. "Especially when you're as old as me. I bet you have an ex-boyfriend you hid from everyone you could in your life. Maybe it was a one-night stand." He pointed to his head. "Remember, this handsome face is a lie."

Jia frowned. "Even that jester persona you like to flip on is suspicious. Sometimes it feels authentic, but other times it feels like a mask. Like you're trying to convince everyone you don't care, but every once in a while, you let it slip, and I see the true you."

Erik stared at her. "And what is the true me?"

Jia took a few shallow breaths. "Brave, honorable, and dedicated, but terrifying and single-minded."

Erik thought for a moment, then scratched his chin. "That sounds about right."

"You're not going home," Jia observed. "You're not heading anywhere near your residential tower. I also know you just met with Malcolm, but it wasn't about our case because you haven't contacted me about it, and there's no reason for you not to. Even when you have been up to something you shouldn't be, you've been very open about sharing information and not trying to manipulate the case. My conclusion is you're investigating something else. Something not related to local corruption, at least not directly, because you've more than proven you don't care about the implications or politics."

Erik lowered his arms and nodded as she put her dangerous counting fingers away. "That's all accurate too. This Winthorpe and Tessan garbage isn't the first conspiracy I've stumbled into, Jia. All I can tell you is that right now, I've got some things I need to investigate. And you're right, they might only incidentally involve Neo SoCal. At the end of this investigation, there might not be perp walks and heroics, but it'll involve bad guys and justice. Sometimes you end up so deep in the shadows, you *never* see the light."

"That sounds like something Captain Monahan might argue."

Erik shrugged. "Maybe."

Jia stared at him in silence for a long moment. "And you don't trust me?"

"This isn't about trust," Erik answered. "You're a good cop. I've told you that, but if I'm going to risk your life for my personal reasons, I need to be sure I have the right to do so."

"Don't I get to make that decision?" Jia folded her arms over her chest. "I could make the decision if you gave me the information you've been keeping from me."

"The minute I do that, you're at risk, regardless of what you decide. I'm not even sure getting Malcolm involved was the right thing to do, and he doesn't really know what's going on either. It's not that I don't trust you, Jia, but I don't know if bringing you along on something that could end poorly and might involve the kind of corruption that makes the Winthorpe case seem like a hundred-credit false report is the right thing."

Jia's frown deepened. "You want me to just walk away after hearing all that?"

"I want you to trust me," Erik replied. "I need to be sure first. For now, that's all I can tell you. You can make the choice eventually, but tonight I'm going to investigate something that might turn out to be nothing, or it might end with a bullet to my brain. I'm not calling for backup even if I'm in trouble because this is personal, and I don't know who in the entire UTC I can ultimately trust." He opened his door. "I'll leave the rest of the decision to you."

CHAPTER FORTY

Jia stared at Erik, her nails digging into her arms. She took several deep breaths, not sure.

Erik slipped into the driver's seat. "Go home, Jia. This doesn't have to concern you. I get that it's not fair you don't know everything, so I'm not going to ask for your help. I don't know where this will end."

Jia shook her head and walked around the front of the MX 60 toward the passenger door. She opened it and slid into the seat. "You didn't know the situation when you first arrived either, Erik. You could have listened to everyone else, but you trusted me enough to push forward on the investigation. For now, I'm willing to help because I know you'll tell me when the time is right, and I'll be there, too. Might as well get to that point together since it will save you time explaining the background." She jerked a thumb to where she was parked. "We can come back later to get my flitter."

Erik grunted and started his vehicle. The MX 60 rose off the ground. He continued flying up, then pivoted and hit the accelerator, zooming away from the parking platform.

"It shouldn't be too exciting," he explained, deftly sliding into the traffic lane between the 80th and 82nd level. "Empty platform and empty tower level. This isn't the Shadow Zone, so it'll probably just be some closed-off buildings. I just want to take a look around. See if I can turn anything up."

There was tense silence between them as Erik continued toward the destination. He reduced his altitude as he approached the single dark level on the brightly lit tower. Erik circled the area for a moment, checking his nav system and cameras.

"Looks clear," Erik muttered. He tapped the screen and then gestured to a camera image of a long black building covering half the platform and running into the tower. "That's where I'm going."

"What's in there?" Jia glanced at the camera feeds and then out the windows. There was no other traffic at this level even though vehicles moved along above and below. Pop-up warnings on the nav system indicated the tower level was closed and no services were available.

"Evidence, I'm hoping," Erik muttered. He brought his flitter down slowly, parking right in front of the entrance. "Allegedly, they're remodeling this entire area." He opened his door. "But I don't see any construction vehicles or drones. There's no reason to keep it clear."

Jia got out on the opposite side, calling over the top of the flitter, "They might be still working out the details or reconsidering the remodeling plans."

"Maybe." Erik paused and then leaned back inside to

recover his TR-7. "Somehow, I doubt that." He reached into the back and pulled out two ballistic vests. He shed his duster to slip his on before handing one to her. "With our luck, it's better to be safe than sorry."

Jia raised an eyebrow. "You expect to have to fight a lot of out-of-control construction drones with installed turrets?"

"I don't know what I'm expecting." Erik slipped a magazine in. "But it never hurts to be overprepared. Everything about this place has me suspicious."

She looked around. "This isn't the Shadow Zone."

"Neither was the councilman's mansion."

"Point." Jia peered at the building. "How are you even going to get in?"

Emma scoffed via Erik's PNIU. "Just get close, and I'll see what I can do. I'm sure it won't be that hard."

Erik nodded and headed toward the door. Jia followed, drawing her stun pistol after she finished securing her vest. Erik's paranoia was starting to infect her.

Erik moved close to the door and waited, looking around for anyone or anything that might be trouble, but the platform remained empty. There were several no-trespassing holographic signs.

The door clicked open.

"Good job, Emma." Erik grinned. "How did I survive without you?"

"Poorly," she replied. "But in this case, I didn't have to do anything. It wasn't locked."

Erik's grin vanished. "That's interesting."

"Interesting like 'huh' or interesting like…" Her voice trailed off.

"Not the good kind of interesting, no," he answered.

Jia hesitated. "Should we even be entering? I believe in you, but we need to have some real reason to go inside."

Erik nodded at the door. "It wasn't locked. I think, as police, we wouldn't be doing our jobs if we didn't do a quick check. There could be someone in there who shouldn't be there, and officially, this is supposed to be an abandoned building scheduled for remodeling. If they're still maintaining a presence in there, they're dodging taxes, at the minimum." He grinned. "And we have to make sure companies pay their taxes, right?"

Jia frowned. "I am surprised it was unlocked." She looked behind them at the city, alive and vibrant except at this level. "It wouldn't hurt to do a quick check when you put it that way."

Erik stepped inside, and the lights automatically flipped on. He frowned as he scanned the place. "Awfully clean for an abandoned level."

The front room was empty but not dusty. The dimensions suggested some sort of lobby. Hallways led in opposite directions, each lined with metal doors for its entirety.

"No reason not to use a cleaning bot," Jia pointed out. "They might be maintaining it in case they decide against doing the renovation. That's not illegal."

"This is prime commercial property on a commerce tower," Erik countered, his face lined with worry. He kept his rifle pointed in front of him. "It's not the Hexagon, but this isn't the Shadow Zone. Why just sit on it? Isn't that a big waste?"

They continued exploring, passing several unmarked doors. Erik opened a few and found empty storage rooms and several large white empty rooms. It could have been anything from former labs to breakrooms for all they could tell. The lack of anything from furniture to trash made it hard to tell.

"Emma, can you access the system here?" Erik asked.

"There are multiple overlapping networks, and it's unclear which are related to this building," the AI replied. "If you can find an access point, that would help, or I can just start breaching every network I detect. I don't really care."

Jia frowned. "No, you can't. How would we even begin to justify that? It's one thing to investigate a suspicious building, but we're not going to start hacking into random networks without a reason."

Erik looked like he was going to protest but just nodded. "Fair enough." He headed over to an IO port near the wall. "What about this? Do I just need to get the PNIU close enough?" He pulled out the transmitter Malcolm had given him. "Or we could use the transmitter?"

Emma sighed. "Either would work, but that IO port's inactive. I've been trying to ping it from your PNIU. You'll need to find another one."

"That suggests they have abandoned the building," Jia commented. "Whoever *they* are."

"Maybe." Erik frowned. "But I'm not so sure."

"What exactly are you hoping to find here?"

"Clues," Erik declared.

"For what?" Jia pressed.

Erik shrugged.

Her eyes took in the emptiness before she looked at her partner, wondering, *What are you hiding, Erik?*

The detectives stepped out of the room and headed deeper into the facility, their footsteps echoing in the empty hallway. A couple more minutes of walking brought them to an elevator. The reinforced door and isolated location suggested a security elevator.

Jia shook her head. "It is well-maintained, I'll grant you that, but otherwise it looks like an empty building. There might not be any great clues here to be found, whatever it is you're looking for."

Erik stopped in front of the elevator. "I don't suppose we're lucky enough that this is still active?" He tapped the access panel, but nothing happened. "That would be too easy." His gaze dropped to a covered access port. He moved the cover to the side. "Is it active, Emma?"

"Yes," Emma reported. "I'm attempting to interface now, but you might still use Technician Constantine's device in case the connection to the PNIU is disrupted."

Erik inserted the transmitter.

"Actually, this will be helpful. It'll require less effort on my part, especially since there are some irregularities with the data. One moment."

"What are you doing?" Jia asked. "What's that device?"

"It's a way of looking for evidence." Erik looked around and frowned. "Emma, can you route it to your storage?"

"Yes," she responded. "The device will make it easier for me to pull down more files. Three unidentified flitters have touched down in front of the building. They're using full tinting, so I can't see who is inside, and they aren't transmitting valid transponder signals. Suffice it to say, I don't need to be a police officer to think that's suspicious."

"Maybe they're security?" Jia suggested.

"Why wouldn't they be using transponder signals?" Erik frowned. "Are they doing anything, Emma?"

"No, the vehicles are simply waiting, and no one has emerged," she reported. "I don't see any other nearby vehicles making their way here on the lidar."

Erik jogged away from the elevator. "Then let's go say hello. I don't like the idea of dealing with them in this maze, whoever they are. I'm guessing they have a better understanding of this place than we do."

Jia hurried after him, her heart racing. If the owners had left the building unsecured but still maintained alarm system, that might explain it. Private security would be first responders, and this didn't have to end badly.

She glanced at the TR-7. The rifle might escalate the situation unnecessarily, but it wasn't like Erik would agree to drop it just because she asked.

A distant gunshot echoed down the hallway.

"What the hell was that?" Erik barked, flipping off the safety on his gun.

"I decided to perform a little test," Emma explained, sounding far too satisfied with herself. "I changed my holographic form so I looked like you, Detective, then exited the vehicle. One of the flitters lowered a window, and someone shot at me from inside. I'm now pretending to be your dead body, but they just rolled up their window. They're maintaining position."

"Did you get a good view of them on any of the cameras?" Erik asked.

"The assailant seems to be using some sort of optical scrambling camouflage. Their face is blurred."

"Assassin tech? Yeah, that's enough to make me think

they're not friendly neighborhood security guards." Erik picked up the pace and glanced over his shoulder at Jia. "Is attempted murder enough to make you comfortable with us poking around here?"

"Yes," Jia nodded. "Who are these people? Why are you investigating them?"

Erik grunted and looked back to the front. "If I knew who they were, I wouldn't be investigating them, I'd be taking them down already." He threw up a fist and skidded to a halt. "I'll let you know soon, but for now, we need to stop them from getting away. Anyone who is willing to kill me probably has information I need."

Jia almost stumbled when she stopped. They were approaching the main hallway leading back to the entrance.

"What's wrong?" Jia whispered.

Erik put his finger to his lips and pointed to his ears.

Jia held her breath and listened. A light hum sounded from around the corner. It didn't sound close, and it didn't sound natural.

"Do you have any internal camera access, Emma?" Erik whispered.

"Not currently. I'm trying to pull data directly from the systems. The encryption is unexpectedly strong, and I'm having trouble streaming the data. I'm batching it via the transmitter, but it's going slower than you would probably like. Anti-intrusion measures have intensified."

Erik wanted to scratch his head. "Why does an abandoned building have a system secure enough to challenge an experimental AI?" He crept to the intersection, his back against the wall. He peeked around the corner and yanked his head back. Several bullets flew down the hallway, several bounced with a spark off the reinforced corner.

"Yeah, totally not suspicious."

Jia raised her stun pistol before lowering it.

"Three security bots," Erik explained, shaking his head. "Floaters. Lethal security bots to patrol an abandoned building that's being remodeled?" He flipped his gun to four-barrel mode. "I'm going to turn the corner and take them out, then we'll get out of here. Emma, you keep trying to pull data through that transmitter. We don't know what other surprises they have."

Jia tilted her head and listened. "They don't sound like they're any closer."

Erik grunted. "Yeah, I think they're just trying to hold position and pin us in here. They're probably going to try to flank us with bots from the other side."

"What about the men in the front?" Jia asked, trying to concentrate on the situation at hand and ignore her racing heart.

Erik offered a lopsided grin. "Even if they have an armored flitter, they have to open up to shoot, and I doubt they can take on my gun."

"Not to worry you too much," Emma chimed in, "but your nice new sensors are detecting a major energy surge in the building."

"Meaning what?" Erik asked.

"I don't know. I don't have enough data at this time to know, but I doubt it will be good for you."

"Concentrate on the data," Erik replied. "And we'll concentrate on getting us out of here. Let's move, Jia."

He rushed around the corner, jinking to the side.

His quick movement threw off the bots, who opened up on the corner, giving him a chance to take them down. He held down the trigger and the TR-7 roared to life, flinging a river of lead. He could only maintain the attack for a few seconds, but the three security bots, smoking and full of holes, dropped to the ground.

He ejected the magazine and slapped in a new one. "I'm going to have to look into extended mags."

"The energy levels are increasing. There are now multiple types, including thermal," Emma reported. "And the flitters are leaving."

Erik gritted his teeth, his eyes widening. "Move your butt, Jia!" He sprinted forward, his boots thumping heavily on the ground.

She hurried after him. Her lungs strained as they ran down the long hallway. The two detectives barreled forward, their shoes' staccato beats echoing down the hallway, but no new security bots appeared.

"What's...going...on?" Jia wheezed.

"Just run," Erik yelled. "Talk later!"

The front door got closer.

"Massive surges detected," Emma reported, worry in her voice. "I'd suggest hurrying. Whatever's going to happen is going to happen soon."

The front door was still open. Erik made it through and Jia wasn't far behind, sweat pouring down her face.

"Keep running," Erik shouted. "Put distance between you and the building. It's a self-destruct system."

"Self...destruct?" Jia puffed. "But...it's just..."

A bright flash lit the area. Erik tossed his gun down and tackled Jia, wrapping his arms around her. A massive fireball consumed the building and a shockwave slammed into the pair, launching them through the air. Erik hissed in pain as the heat and flame ate through his duster, vest, and shirt, scorching his back.

They hit the ground and rolled several feet. Acrid smoke poured from the pile of scorched rubble that had been a building mere seconds before. Charred, burning debris rained from above, pelting Erik and Jia.

Jia gasped. "Erik? Are you okay?"

He groaned and scooted away from her, his teeth gritted. "I've been better, but I'll live." He shimmied out of the remnants of his coat, then stood up and stomped out the flames before they reached any of his spare magazines. "I'll just need a few patches and I'll be good. It's just a flesh wound."

"What?"

"Mostly surface burns," he explained.

Jia stood up, trembling slightly. She blinked at the rubble. She leaned over and sucked in deep breaths. "Who puts a self-destruct system in a building? Especially a building in a tower?"

"Someone with something big to hide." Erik stretched, rolling his back, and groaned. "As far as what we tell the captain, we were just following up on suspicious activity." He sucked in some air. "I'll bring you in on this soon, but I need some time to process everything."

CHAPTER FORTY-ONE

July 12, 2228, Neo Southern California Metroplex, Police Enforcement Zone 122 Station, Office of Captain Robert Monahan

Erik already missed his duster.

He had a spare at home, but he might need to buy a few more if he was going to make a habit of getting blown up or otherwise engulfed in flames.

He thought about explaining the thought to Captain Monahan, but his supervisor was stuck on the practical question of why the detectives had been at a building that blew up.

Maybe I'll buy an entire closet full of dusters, he mused.

He had spent a few hours being checked at the hospital the night before and had then been sent home. The captain wanted a few other reports before talking with him, so they had waited until the following morning for the full debriefing.

"Can you explain this to me one more time?" the

captain asked. "I don't understand why you were even at the abandoned building to begin with. From what you've said, it has nothing to do with the Winthorpe case."

"I had concerns about suspicious activity at the site, so I decided to check," Erik offered. That wasn't technically a lie. "Consider it cop's instinct."

Captain Monahan eyed him. "You haven't been a cop long enough to have cop's instinct."

Erik shrugged. "Then consider it soldier's instinct. I suspected something was wrong, and the fact that it exploded proves it. Not to mention the odd security."

He saw no reason to lie about being attacked. Erik's personal investigation might benefit from some indirect police attention. Talent and bravery didn't always substitute for basic resources.

The captain looked at Erik and Jia, more exasperated than angry. "I don't even think I *want* to know the truth at this point, but I'll tell you what the fire department passed along to me."

Jia nodded. "I'm eager to hear their take."

"They're saying it was some sort of power grid malfunction, most likely because of maintenance failure since the site hasn't been in active use. The owners are reviewing off-site logs, but the local equipment wasn't communicating properly out of building or off-tower."

"Isn't that a safety violation for a building of that size?" Jia asked.

"Probably." The captain shrugged. "But we're police, not safety inspectors. If it doesn't pass into the realm of criminal negligence, it's not our responsibility."

"It wasn't a maintenance malfunction that caused security bots to shoot at me," Erik countered. "And those bots had fresh power and ammo. Seems like they were better maintained than a lot of other things."

"We can't independently verify the existence of the security bots, Detective," the captain explained. "Or the mysterious flitters you claimed were there, which makes it difficult to push our limited resources at something like this."

Erik frowned. "What? You saying I'm lying?" He gestured at Jia. "And she's lying, too?"

"I'm saying you both survived an explosion. Perhaps you imagined some of the details in the heat of the moment. It happens to the best of us."

"If you say so," Erik muttered.

"I still don't know why you were there since I don't buy your story," Captain Monahan explained. "But unless you're willing to assure me this has something to do with the Winthorpe case, I don't want either of you near it again. There are a huge number of questions about that explosion, and it's a miracle the tower didn't suffer more damage and that no one was hurt. We have more important matters to discuss than mysterious bots and power grid failures. It's not as if accidents are unknown in the towers. Don't want the fire department to get bored, right?" He tried to grin, but it came off forced and pained.

"I don't buy it." Jia frowned. "That entire level had been vacant for a year. That's unusual, especially in that part of the town."

"Yes, it is, but it's not impossible." The captain nodded. "And more to the point, it's also not your problem, Detective Lin. If you're suggesting arson as some sort of financial crime, let the fire department investigate it, along with the CID. It's their purview, not ours. I've indulged both of you far too long on this nonsense that shouldn't have ever arisen in the first place. Not every crime is this enforcement zone's responsibility. You will stay away from the tower case until such time as I feel something relevant has arisen. Understood? We still need to make sure everything's tied up on this Winthorpe thing. The chief is riding me hard about a lot of the details, and we need to make sure the 1-2-2 doesn't come off looking bad in any of this."

Erik grunted. "We did all the hard work."

"I know, I know. But there's reality and there's perceived reality, and the point is, I want you to…" Captain Monahan took a deep breath. "You both need to seriously stay in your lane this time."

Jia frowned. "After everything that has happened, are we going back to the way the things were? Don't you trust our instincts by now?"

"We have limited resources and time." Captain Monahan rolled his eyes. "So I'm just trying to only deal with one major problem at a time. If we end up over-whelmed, it won't do anyone any good. You, me, or the citizens you're trying to help. Understood?"

Jia sighed. "Yes, sir."

ERIK WAS grateful Jia waited until they got back to their office and he was seated to ambush him with her complaints.

It was easier to handle her without Captain Monahan spinning her up with his political CYA garbage.

"I don't believe that was an accident," Jia commented before her butt hit the chair. "That building has been sitting there for a year just fine, and we're in it for a few minutes, and suddenly it's exploding? You don't have to be a crack investigator to find that suspicious."

"I'm not sure if the captain is running interference directly, or if it's the fire department for their own reasons." Erik shrugged. "I'm actually fine with him not wanting to look closer. It might help if he kept it low-level, but if it escalates too much, it ends up with more trouble. This is a case where the fewer people involved, the better, especially since I'm convinced powerful people have their fingers in this."

Jia folded her arms over her chest. "I deserve to know what's going on if only because I was almost blown up last night helping you."

Erik shrugged. "I tried to warn you. That was what I warned you about. It's a dangerous investigation."

"And I told you I had your back as your partner. It's obvious this case has something to do with why you're back on Earth. I suspect it's why you came to Neo SoCal to begin with."

Erik kept the frown off his face.

Jia narrowed her eyes. "You're not going to be able to protect me from everything. If you're wrapped up in something, the minute you joined the police and became my partner, you also made me a target. Keeping me ignorant just means I'll end up more at risk. At least if I know what's going on, I can try to protect myself."

"I'm not...wrapped up in anything. Not in the way you think." Erik sighed. "You don't know how deep this goes. Even I don't. You've already made a lot of powerful enemies, but if I bring you in on this, you might make even worse ones. I hate to quote Monahan, but sometimes it is best to stay in your lane."

"I deserve to know."

"I don't know if you're ready. You're still processing the fact that Neo SoCal isn't paradise." Erik moved his shoulders, the medpatches pulling at his skin. "It wasn't that long ago you could barely believe in the possibility of corrupt councilmembers."

"Being stubborn about a worldview doesn't make me closed-minded!" Jia argued. "The important thing is, I changed my mind when I was confronted with the truth. I know I still have a few things to work through, but I'm not the same woman you met outside the club, Erik."

Erik paused for a moment in thought, then glanced at her. "Ever try to tell a little kid that Generous Gao isn't real?" Erik inquired.

Jia snorted. "What does he have to do with this conversation?"

Erik smiled. "Did you believe in him when you were a little kid? He wasn't a thing in my family, but I knew plenty of kids who did."

She counted to ten in her mind, controlling her anger. "When I was very young, yes. It made perfect sense at the time. Who was bringing all the gifts for New Year's otherwise? That's what I thought, anyway. My sister tried to spoil it for me, but I didn't believe her, so I ended up waiting and hiding, so I could take a picture of Generous

Gao and prove her wrong. While I was waiting, I saw my father put the gifts in our living room, and I realized Generous Gao had never been real." She shook her head. "But this isn't the same thing. I'm not a little girl believing in a made-up character."

Defiance burned in her eyes.

"But it *is* the same thing," Erik replied. "Maybe working the Winthorpe case is like your sister telling you Generous Gao isn't real, but I don't know if you're ready yet to hide and check. You still think the system's good overall, and that's why I worry."

Jia scoffed. "I'm going to stick my stun pistol up your high and mighty ass and pull the trigger, and I don't know when or if I'm going to stop."

Erik smiled. "First comes the fantasy, then the willingness to do what it takes. That's all I'm saying."

Jia shook in frustration. "You can be an annoying pain in the ass."

"I'm not the one threatening to give someone an electric enema." Erik put up two fingers in a v. "That's twice."

"Twice?"

"You threatened to shoot me back in the Shadow Zone when we were pulling Emma out, too."

Jia closed her eyes and took a deep breath. "Fair point. Fine. I'll wait, but I don't know how much longer I can wait, especially if it involves exploding buildings."

He looked out the window for a moment. "I appreciate your trust, Jia. I won't abuse it."

He turned back. "Once you know the truth, you'll probably wish you had never pressed me for it."

CHAPTER FORTY-TWO

Jia stared out the window of the MX 60 as they cruised
along a crowded air lane. The skies of Neo SoCal were
even more full than normal. She hadn't heard anything
about traffic being rerouted.

Am I just noticing it, or is there actually more traffic?

"Isn't this kind of a long way to go for a good sandwich?" Jia asked. "I know the captain said he didn't care
how long a lunch we took, but I think that was just his way
of telling us to stay out of trouble. I don't think he meant
for us to disappear for hours at a time."

"It's only been a half-hour." Erik grinned. "And it could
be worse. We could be going to the Shadow Zone. I bet
they have great sandwiches down there. There's something
about people living close together in rough neighborhoods
that brings out the best sandwich skills."

Erik figured he could write a whole book about the
variations of outstanding sandwiches on poor, hard-
scrabble frontier worlds.

"We don't have clearance to go into the Shadow Zone,

and I'm mostly thankful for that." Jia watched a flitter nearly collide with another and winced. That was why everyone should use autonomous mode, but then again, she sat in a luxury vehicle worth years of pay and Erik insisted on controlling it manually. "But it might be nice to talk to your informant again."

Erik glanced her way. "Alicia? Why? You like her?"

"Not really." Jia wrinkled her nose. "But she did seem knowledgeable, and maybe she would have more information on the cases for us. Nothing new has come into the station about Tessan or Winthorpe since we sent out the word about the alleged coming arrest. I'm beginning to think your scheme isn't going to work. If it means anything, I thought it was a good plan."

"Yeah. Looks like a bust." Erik tapped a couple of buttons on his screen. "They might have called our bluff, but you're right. It was worth trying. We'll figure out something new. This isn't over."

Jia suddenly laughed.

"What's so funny?" Erik asked, eyeing her like she was drunk.

"I was just thinking I was almost blown up the other day, and it doesn't have anything to do with the other case that has almost cost my life multiple times." Jia shook her head. "It's certainly sobering to consider that. Every step we take into darkness, I think it's gotten as dark as it could be, and the city proves me wrong."

Erik chuckled. "Still mad enough to electro-enema me?"

Jia patted her holster. "Don't tempt me. It might make me feel better, and I'm more frustrated than anything.

There are so many pieces of things that I *almost* understand, but I've been thinking about how to fix at least some of those problems. I get that I'm just one detective, but I'm tired of feeling like I'm so many steps behind the criminals."

"Come up with anything good?" Erik reduced their altitude, but they were still kilometers away from the Shadow Zone. "I'm all ears. I'm just one detective too." He shrugged.

"I've been studying law enforcement history a lot lately," Jia explained. "It helps me think about cases. I've always found it interesting, but a reoccurring motif is that when local law enforcement becomes too corrupt, the best thing to do is bring in a higher authority less beholden to the local centers of power. It disrupts the status quo and helps local law enforcement reform itself into a less corrupt organization."

Erik's eyes brightened. "Is that what I am? A higher authority? I like the sound of that."

"No. You're a maniac and a pain in the backside, but I'll also admit you're a good cop sometimes." Jia watched another flitter drop and turn to the right. "Captain Monahan might be trying, but he's still obviously afraid of all his corrupt connections. If Tessan and Winthorpe were murdered, we need to bring it to the attention of someone completely outside the NSCPD. You might be a newer detective, but you're still operating within the NSCPD structure. What we need to do is get enough evidence that the Criminal Investigations Directorate comes in and starts handling the investigation. There might be corrupt CID agents, but they are far less likely to be on the payroll of men like Winthorpe."

"The CID?" Erik nodded. "That's a possibility, but among other things, we'll need to prove these crimes involved something outside the scope of the metroplex. The military has made it clear I'm supposed to keep my mouth shut about Emma, so I don't think we can flash her. They'll just try to take her and shut down the investigation to cover what was stolen from them."

Emma spoke up. "I concur with Detective Blackwell," the AI noted. "If you attempt to use me to bring in someone else, I might just drive off with this body. I sympathize with you having to deal with horrible hooligans, but I'm not sacrificing my life because you humans can't keep a city under control."

"There you go." Erik sighed. "I'd be out a lot of credits, too, and I really like my MX 60."

"That's not what I was thinking." Jia rubbed her chin as she drifted on the tides of thought. "If we could establish the people involved in some of these crimes had serious operational connections to an entity outside Neo SoCal, that might be enough to convince the CID to get involved."

"Who are you going to try to link them to?" Erik asked. "That seems to be the hard part in all this."

"There are lots of possibilities." Jia ticked off fingers as she built her list. "Insurrectionists, terrorist groups, colonial officials, and corporations. Windward is a little too local in scope, and the CID's reluctant to step in when local law enforcement pushes back. If we can establish a direct link to an organization that's broader in scope and pass it along, that would help a lot."

Erik's eyes kept darting between the front, his lidar, and

the cameras. "It wouldn't be our case anymore. Would you be okay with that?"

"I want the criminals identified and punished," Jia answered. "This isn't about personal glory. My problem with Captain Monahan sending cases on wasn't that he was taking the cases from me. The problem was that the cases weren't getting solved *at all*. The CID isn't going to just set a case aside for an easy bribe."

"We might still have a chance to get more evidence," Erik muttered, a slight frown on his face. "And I think my plan is going to work after all." An eager grin pushed away his previous frown.

"What are you talking about?" Jia glanced at him. "I'm obviously missing something."

"Did you catch them, Emma, or were you just testing me this time?" Erik asked.

Emma snickered. "I wanted to see if you would notice. Good eye. It hasn't even been that long."

"What's going on?" Jia looked confused. "Someone care to clue me in?"

"We're being followed by several flitters," Erik explained. He turned toward a denser patch of buildings. "The only question is about the best way to handle it. Should we have a little fun like we did in the zone, or should we land and take them on that way? I'm confident we can win, but it might be hard to find a platform where we can have a gun battle without risking civilians getting hit by stray bullets."

Jia grimaced. "We're absolutely not going to have any sort of high-speed chase. If a flitter loses control here, the chances of it causing a secondary accident or hitting a tower are too high. Even if the buildings won't take much damage, we don't want a ball of crumpled metal bouncing around and causing a cascade."

Erik chuckled. "You know what I just realized?"

"What? It'd be nice if you said you were wrong about us being followed." Jia rubbed her wrist.

Erik shook his head. "Nope. I was thinking about this the wrong way. I'm falling too much into Uptowner thinking. There's no shield over the Shadow Zone. The only thing keeping us from it is clearance."

Jia's breath caught. "A lower altitude means less chance of inadvertent damage or falling metal balls of death."

"Exactly." Erik dropped a few vertical lanes but kept his speed normal. "If we lead these guys to a platform, there might be a big battle. At least this way, we can pick a location better suited. Or, you know what? Time for a friendly trip to the mountains. They aren't right on us yet." He altered course.

Jia shook her head. "You enjoy this sort of thing too much."

"There's no such thing as enjoying your job too much, and one thing I've learned this last year is to take life seriously when you have to, but not to otherwise." Erik glanced at the lidar. "Okay, Emma, take control. Gradually take us low and get us near the mountains." He pointed at Jia's feet. "I'm going to need my gun, and we'll have to be smart about this. This should be something more than entertaining shooting practice for me."

Jia moved her legs, fished the TR-7 out of its compartment, and set it between them before bending back down and retrieving magazines. "And what's being smart in this situation? Heading to a police station?"

"We don't need more cops, but we do need more witnesses," Erik explained. "Several of the survivors from the mansion battle aren't giving up anything useful other that they were paid through anonymous means. The more men we take alive, the better chance someone slips up or heard something important. There can't be that many thugs with perfect discipline." He loaded his TR-7. "So, we're going to keep this low speed and low altitude. The point is to take a few suspects alive."

"And if they just shoot us out of the sky?" Jia asked. "If these are assassins. They might be here to stop you before your fictional arrest."

"It's not fictional. We'll be getting someone. It's just a matter of when. I need to add some armor to this thing," Erik muttered. "But we'll have to make do today. Let's see how much our friends like nature."

ERIK KEPT his altitude above two hundred and fifty meters as his flitter headed toward a nearby mountain.

The deep haze characterizing the Shadow Zone lightened, and they moved toward the oft-neglected if still protected slice of nature.

While citizens loved their taxes to go toward preserving their natural heritage in theory, in practice, venturing away from the main metroplex to go stare at trees, rocks, and dirt didn't appeal when they had perfectly serviceable holograms.

Their lack of attention had allowed nature to reassert herself in areas outside the large footprint of the metroplex.

"Several backup flitters on their way," Jia reported, finishing her call. "Including some with disruption systems and rams."

"Another thing I should add to my MX 60," Erik mused. "If we end up in this situation again, I want to be better prepared."

"I wholeheartedly agree," Emma offered.

Jia grimaced. "How often do you anticipate us having to flee paid killers?"

"Often enough." Erik glanced at the cameras and lidar. "But I don't think we'll have enough time to wait. Our tails have given up even pretending they aren't following us. They're going to make their move soon."

"So does this have to do with the Winthorpe case or that building? The list of people interested in killing us feels like it's increasing each day, and that's if we don't count the captain on that list."

"Who knows? I've been assuming this is about Winthorpe and Tessan, but you might be right, and this is about Halcyon." Erik surveyed the nearby terrain through the cameras and windows, his brow furrowed. "Skim the tops of the trees, Emma. Dial down our speed. You're risking outrunning the guys. We don't want to goad them just yet."

The MX 60 dropped and slowed, still zooming past the dense trees and mountainous jags just below. Even a flitter control freak like Erik might not risk too many stunts at this speed and altitude in this terrain without Emma. Even standard autonomous mode didn't provide that kind of careful control, and it certainly hadn't been intended for fleeing criminal killers.

Jia glanced at the yoke moving itself and shook her head. *A soldier, an AI, and a corp princess. What a team we make.*

The other flitters moved closer to them. Whatever Erik's plan was, he needed to execute it.

"Emma, can you transmit an emergency laser point-to-point comm beam to the closest flitter?" Erik asked.

"Yes." Emma sounded confused. "Should I?"

"Yeah." Erik glanced over his shoulder. "Maybe Jia's rubbing off on me, but I want to make sure these are people I need to take out before I start shooting at them."

"It's not an unreasonable thing to do," Jia commented.

"Preparing beam," Emma announced. "Contact established."

"This is Detectives Erik Blackwell and Jia Lin of the NSCPD," Erik announced. "I don't know why you're following us, but I have reason to believe you have hostile intent. Why don't you back off before you get hurt? We will defend ourselves with all necessary force if you display any hostile actions."

A passenger-side window opened on the target vehicle. A rifle barrel poked out.

"That answers that question," Erik muttered. "Emma, take evasive action while I shoot back at these idiots."

The flitter tilted as the enemy rifle flashed. The shooter fired again, and the vehicle shuddered. It tilted back and forth a few times before leveling out, and an alarm sounded.

"What the hell just happened?" Erik demanded.

"There are failures in some of the left rear electrical systems, including the left rear grav field emitter," Emma reported. "I'm attempting to reroute power, but I'm limited by the design of the vehicle and the control system themselves."

"Electrical failure?" Erik grunted. "Damn. Disruptor bullets. I should invest in a few."

Emma tilted the MX 60 again and Jia groaned.

"We need to even the odds," she suggested. "We're not going to win if it's just them shooting at us until we crash."

"I agree." Erik popped out and sprayed a burst at the drivers of two of their tails.

The bullets blasted through the windshield and struck the drivers. Both slumped forward on their yokes, sending their vehicles plunging into the ground, their existences ending in columns of flame and smoke.

Another disruptor bullet struck the MX 60 and the entire vehicle started shaking.

"I can't maintain grav field integrity," Emma complained. "What an expensive piece of sensitivity and consumer-level quality. I'll have to take us down soon, or the remaining emitters might overload, and we'll go down the hard way."

"No," Erik growled. "Keep us up. Do whatever you need to. We're almost there. Just give me a few more seconds."

He repaid the rifleman's fire by spraying bullets through the front of his car. Several struck and killed the driver. His next burst took out a few emitters on one of the vehicles, but without an advanced AI to compensate for the damage, the vehicle spun out of control, smashed into the ground, and exploded. Only one enemy flitter remained, but he hadn't been hit by any of Erik's attacks.

Erik glanced down at the ground. Green and brown treetops rushed by in a near-blur. A bullet whizzed by the flitter.

"Emma, change the external color to dark green," he ordered.

"That will cause a power drain," Emma countered.

"Just do it! We need to distract him for just a second."

"So be it."

More alarms sounded and the remaining enemy flitter slowed for a moment, obviously confused. Erik took the few seconds of confusion and blew out its right emitters with two careful shots. The flitter jerked down, then leveled out after a few seconds but continued to fall. It clipped a tree, the windshield shattering, and sliced through several branches before striking the ground, sending up a plume of dirt and rock.

"Take us down, Emma," Erik ordered. "Right on top of him."

Erik dropped back into his seat and nodded to Jia. "Get ready. These are some guys who deserve electrical enemas."

She nodded, drawing her pistol. "Let's do it."

The smoking MX 60 coasted to the ground, bouncing once off the ground with the help of its makeshift grav field before slowing to a stop. Erik and Jia threw their doors open simultaneously. Two men fell out of the damaged flitter, guns in hand. They dropped to one knee, and Jia stunned them both with quick shots. A third thug went for a rifle. She fired two bolts into his chest and he fell forward, drooling.

Sirens sang in the distance. The police reinforcements sounded like they were only a couple of minutes away.

Erik grimaced as he looked at the long scratches on his flitter. "How much of that will you be able to self-repair, Emma?"

"Most of the body damage I can fix using the self-repair systems, but some of the electrical components will need to be replaced," Emma reported. "It's going to cost more than a bar bill."

"Damn."

Jia jogged over to the stunned men. "You're under arrest. You know what? You're stunned. Who the hell cares?" She holstered her pistol and pulled out binding ties. She looked at Erik as he set his rifle on the top of his flitter.

She gestured to the men after binding them all. "They aren't wearing fake uniforms."

"Let's hope we can get something from them." Erik patted the side of his MX 60. "Otherwise I put this baby through all that for nothing."

CHAPTER FORTY-THREE

July 13, 2228, Neo Southern California Metroplex, Police Enforcement Zone 122 Station, Office of Detectives Jia Lin and Erik Blackwell

Erik looked up from the dealer repair bill when Captain Monahan entered the room.

"Good morning, Captain," Erik offered.

"I don't think I've had a single good morning since you got here, Blackwell. You've taken years off my life with stress."

Erik grinned. "Then get a de-aging treatment. Maybe that's why I'm so much more cheerful."

The captain grunted and looked around. "Where's Detective Lin? This is for her too, but if she's going to be a while, I'll just tell you, and you can pass it along to her."

"Jia's on a beignet run. We found a new place yesterday after we got back to the station. It's not even that far from here." Erik shrugged. "Not quite classics, but they're still delicious."

"Beignets?" The captain shook his head. "You two…" he began, then shook his head again. "Not important. It doesn't matter. What I have to tell you *is* important."

"But it's not about pastry?" Erik raised a hopeful eyebrow.

"No," Captain Monahan barked. "It's not about pastry."

"What's it about, then?"

The captain managed a smile. "You're going to like this. One thing that's been bothering me is why there are so many random rent-a-thugs who keep popping up from the Shadow Zone, especially now that Winthorpe's dead."

Erik nodded. "The thought has occurred to Jia and me."

"I thought a lot about it, and on a hunch, I had the DNA samples from all the fake mercenaries and the men you fought the other day analyzed by an outside firm instead of the coroner's office," the captain explained.

Erik's eyes opened wide. "You *did?*"

"Yes," the captain replied. "I know you had a run-in with the coroner. He complained about you harassing him, but he was rather reticent to share the exact details. Fortunately, a few people owe me favors, and they aren't part of the NSCPD system. They were able to do it quickly and provide the appropriate DNA reports for me to follow up."

Erik nodded, not trying to conceal any of the suspicion he felt. "Oh? Did they say they're not criminals at all, but peaceful monks who have been on Mars all this time? Am I a fool who has been violating their right to shoot people?"

Captain Monahan chuckled. "I know why you don't trust me, and I can't blame you, but no. In this case, I was trying to help your investigations. It turns out all the previous IDs were wrong. Every single one of them. *Not even remotely correct."*

"What?" Erik flew out of his seat. "I knew Hannigan might be dirty, but that's like spitting-in-the-eye blatant. What did you find?"

"Those men weren't generic rent-a-thugs from the Shadow Zone," Captain Monahan explained. "We got IDs that place them all in security teams associated with a Ceres Galactic-linked security firm."

"That makes sense." Erik's hands rested on his hips as he considered the information. "I thought they had a little too much discipline for thugs off the street. The average thug will break and run if you kill a man next to him, let alone an entire car going down with his friends, but they kept coming."

"Exactly. They were pros."

"And Winthorpe had connections to Ceres Galactic," Erik murmured. He lowered himself back into his chair. "Is this the part where we don't take on the corp? Where we say it's not worth it, despite the corp sending death squads around our city like it's nothing? Even you've got to say enough is enough."

"I've already put in my retirement request, Erik," Captain Monahan told him. "I can't deal with this sort of chaos. I didn't develop the right skills over my career to handle it. I'm the wrong captain for the wrong time."

Erik eyed him. "Cutting and running? I don't care if it's Ceres Galactic or just their toy soldiers. They've killed whomever they felt like, and they'll continue to do it unless someone slaps them down. This won't go away if you ignore it. They think they're above the law, and a corp that large that thinks it's above the law might as well be a bunch of insurrectionists."

"I agree," he explained. "That's why I've taken measures to ensure this whole situation doesn't become tainted." Captain Monahan shrugged, a faint smile on his face. "I've spent too many years cutting corners. Too many years pretending I was doing the right thing when I was looking the other way and doing the wrong thing. I'm tired, Erik. Maybe if more cops were like you and Jia, it wouldn't have gotten this bad. We wouldn't have to put our hands over our faces and pretend there was no corruption."

He sighed. "I get it now. I was wrong about a lot of things. I don't have the strength to continue to fight, but I can at least make one final stab at actually doing my job. It's fairly easy to see, even to me, there are other people in this city, important people, who are too in thrall to the corruption around us. I have to fight that, and I think I can do it before I retire."

Erik nodded slowly. "Late bravery is still bravery. What's your plan, Captain? What do I need to do?"

"It's already in motion." Captain Monahan tapped his PNIU and a typed memo appeared. "Ceres Galactic might be headquartered in Neo SoCal, but they've broken laws of wide enough scope we can bring in the CID as primary jurisdiction. I've made a personal request and appealed directly to them over the head of the chief of police, so you see, even if I wasn't retiring, I would have been forced out anyway. My plan?" He smiled, an actual smile that went all the way to his eyes and sparkled.

"We're going to raid Ceres Galactic."

Erik chuckled. "Damn, sir, you finally found your balls, and they're huge."

July 15, 2228, Neo Southern California Metroplex, Police Enforcement Zone 122 Station, Office of Detectives Jia Lin and Erik Blackwell

Erik finished slipping on his tactical vest as Jia put hers on. Bright NSCPD letters were stenciled across the thin but strong antiballistic material. He eyed the stun rifle on top of his desk and grunted. It wasn't his style, but for once, he couldn't rely on pure intimidation to do his work for him.

"Problem?" Jia asked.

He nodded at the gun. "Yeah. I still want to bring along my TR-7. This stun rifle isn't as bad as your little toy, but it's still not a decent weapon, and my pistol isn't good enough backup."

"They're not going to have an army ready to take us on," Jia insisted, then snickered. "And you can't just kill every suspect, especially in this case. This isn't a local company. This is Ceres Galactic."

Erik shrugged. "That means there's more of a chance of them having a huge group of mercs or sentry bots, not less."

Jia shook her head. "Normally, we wouldn't even have a chance of going at a corporation at this level directly. They let arrogance get the best of them, and we can't let ourselves be as arrogant. We need to be watchful. We're about to make a big difference with all this as long as we're careful, and we've got the support of the captain and the entire 1-2-2." She nodded. "We can do this."

Halil rushed into the office. He already was wearing his vest, and he had his stun rifle slung over his shoulder. Unlike Jia, he had a conventional pistol in a holster as a backup. "You two better come see this."

He nodded to the bullpen.

The three of them left the office in a hurry.

Dozens of murmuring police officers were clustered around a holographic display near a side wall. Jia and Erik hurried into the room, pushing past the men in the back to take in the newsfeed.

A man in an expensive suit stood, flanked by CID agents on either side, his gaze downcast as he spoke. A chyron hovered below the holograms.

NEWS ALERT: CERES GALACTIC SENIOR VICE-PRESIDENT ARRESTED. "Serious antisocial behavior" reports the CID.

"What the hell is this?" Erik muttered.

Halil folded his arms, his face crinkling in irritation.

"My name is Davis Esposito," the man in the suit began. "I am Senior Vice-President for New Products Development at Ceres Galactic. I've worked my way up in this company over many years, and have always been devoted to increasing our edge over competitors. Unfortunately, those desires led me down a dark path. This last year, in particular, without the knowledge of any other senior management personnel at the company, I have taken it upon myself to engage in a campaign of bribery and collusion focused on expanding our influence in the Neo Southern California Metroplex.

"As part of this campaign, I have indirectly involved our company in a number of highly dangerous, illegal, and antisocial acts, including, but not limited to, the corruption of public officials, conspiracy, smuggling, theft, and murder. I engaged in these acts with full knowledge of their inappropriate and illegal nature because I was under the belief that they were necessary to aid my company in our efforts against our rivals, but I fully acknowledge that they were not condoned by any senior personnel in my company, which will be ending my contract at midnight tonight, nor the metroplex, state, country, or UTC. Common decency would dictate to most people that what I have done is a horrible betrayal of the public's trust, but I have let myself be blinded by loyalty and greed."

Jia narrowed his eyes. "I have trouble believing what I'm hearing, and this sounds a little…rehearsed."

Erik grunted. "It *is* mighty convenient." He surveyed the room, which was full of police officers in tactical gear.

Esposito wiped away tears. "Please allow me to make this very clear. I am the person who ordered the murder of Councilman Trajan Winthorpe in an attempt to cover my illegal activities. I did so because those same activities were on the verge of being discovered by the NSCPD and other relevant authorities." He took a deep breath, looking into the cameras. "I also have, at this time, a list of public officials who have received bribes, either monetary or in-kind, from my agents or me for their assistance in my illegal activities. While I understand that the violation of the law by others don't justify my actions, especially given my pivotal role in fomenting those activities, it is my strong belief, after consulting with my family and engaging in reflective prayer, that my part in corrupting Neo Southern California can at least somewhat be ameliorated by ensuring that those public officials who have betrayed their trust are also identified and purged from their positions."

Jia snorted as Esposito expanded on his litany of crimes and sins. "I suppose we're not going to raid them now."

Halil gestured at the image. "You missed the big preamble before. According to what they were saying, Ceres Galactic was already talking to the CID, who was keeping it quiet while they prepared for their big arrest. They'd been worried for a few weeks that there might have been someone rogue, and they were negotiating with the CID to have him arrested. They said if they just fired him, he might start spreading company secrets."

Erik grunted. "Toss the bait to the wolves and run, but even then they managed to make it sound like they are more about the corp than everyone else." He shrugged. "I'll take half a win, so I'm not going to complain too much."

He sighed. "No stun rifle for me today."

Jia elbowed him.

Halil gestured at the hologram of Esposito. "What I don't get is this whole strategy of taking down a bunch of people with him. I'm guessing Ceres will do something behind the scenes to make sure his family ends up with a pile of money while he rots, but what do they gain from burning anyone else who was helping them, even if indirectly through one guy?"

Jia's face reddened as she glared at the newsfeed.

"They're sending a message," Erik suggested. "They'll take a short-term hit, but they make it clear in the future that if they go down, they're taking everyone with them. It might make it harder to recruit new people in the short term, but the ones they do convince are more likely to stay bought."

"Maybe he's right," Halil replied. "Maybe it was all this one guy. He might just be saying things to try to throw more suspicion."

Jia looked over her shoulder, raising an eyebrow. "Now who's naïve?"

CHAPTER FORTY-FOUR

July 29, 2228, Neo Southern California Metroplex, Remembrance Bar

Jia downed her beer in a few quick gulps and let out a long sigh. "You coming to Captain Monahan's going-away party?"

"No reason not to," Erik answered. "He tried in the end to do the right thing, even if Ceres managed to dodge a direct hit. I'm surprised he's leaving so quickly, but maybe that's for the best since they're indicting the chief for taking bribes. Monahan might have wanted to look the other way, but he wasn't trying to do a corp's bidding."

"I'm still surprised he's leaving so quickly, but he said he prefers it that way. He's made some recommendations for an interim captain, but he's not going to have a lot of influence over the choice. No one seems to know for sure."

Erik snickered. "Maybe we should ask Ceres who they prefer?"

"Have you looked at the latest reports?"

"Nope. What about them?"

"Ceres is acting like the aggrieved party, while they're handing CID tons of documentation they've suddenly *recovered* from their internal systems. From what the media is saying, Esposito's sticky fingers weren't just in Neo SoCal." Jia bounced her fist off the table. "They get to save their ass with only a little black eye. They just have to sacrifice a few people here and there, and then continue on like they didn't have anything to do with it."

"They might *not* have known about it." Erik finished his drink, his fourth of the night, but his speech and face barely gave any indication.

Jia was a little jealous of how calm he could be during all this. It was taking alcohol and all her self-control not to shake with constant rage.

The scope of the corruption from a major corporation to the chief of police still staggered her when she considered it.

Jia let out a bitter laugh. "You're telling me they didn't know about all that? I'm trying to open my eyes to the truth. I'm trying to admit Generous Gao was my dad all along. But this is even worse. This is like waiting for Generous Gao and finding out he is a criminal who broke into your house to rob you, and he yells at you for daring not to believe in him."

Erik twisted his glass in a circle. "No, I'm not saying they're clean, just that this thing really does smell like one arrogant man. I don't think it's that they never knew anything was going on, but more they turned a blind eye to it. They probably understood he was doing something off the books but didn't order it directly. That explains a lot of missteps along the way. Some of this is Lady Luck helping us, and some of it is one man getting drunk on his own power."

"Is that 'one bad apple?'" Jia raised an eyebrow in question.

"It's one rotten apple, and several on their way, but it's definitely not a lot of innocent people." Erik took another swig of his drink. "Esposito was a big link to the Metroplex Council and other officials. As long as he got them results, they had every incentive to not ask too many questions. They were ready to burn him, though. The fact that they had a CID contingency plan is proof of that. The minute we started pushing on Ceres, they must have put their plan in motion. It didn't save them entirely, but it stopped the CID and the rest of the UTC from coming in hard and dismembering them," he grumbled. "It's not every day a couple of detectives set in motion this sort of thing. Not a bad month's work when I think about it. Not a bad month's work at all."

Jia ran her finger over the rim of her empty glass. "But did we win, Erik? I mean, we got the guy responsible, and a lot of the people who were directly manipulating the city have been punished or are on their way to punishments, but I'm not sure. It feels like half a victory. It's not like I thought we'd be able to march up and arrest every senior official of Ceres, but still…"

Erik's smile was genuine but a little tired. "It's a win. A big win, and don't think it's anything other than that." He scratched his chin. "I told you before that sometimes you just have to bleed the other guy's army. Even if Ceres is corrupt as hell, they've lost a lot of influence in Neo SoCal, and now they are closely watched. The CID will be up their ass for a while, and that's going to limit them if they decide to do anything else." His expression darkened. "And Esposito's little list is helping us clean out the other trash. The chief was selling justice to the highest bidder, and he's going down. Lower-level garbage like Hannigan have already pled guilty."

"He did?" Jia asked. "I didn't hear that."

Erik nodded. "He's being transported. A few inspectors in the fire department are working on plea deals, but Esposito and Winthorpe didn't seem to have as much influence with them as they had with the police." He chuckled. "It's funny that Monahan comes out looking all right. It's not that I ever thought he was taking direct bribes, and as much as he tried to look the other way, he never did take any. He wanted to do the right thing, but maybe for the wrong reasons. Sometimes wanting to do the right thing isn't enough, and he found that out. There's only so far you can push the line before you trip on it."

"There are a lot of bad apples in this particular bushel basket, and I'm not sure about a lot of things," Jia murmured. Something approaching a smile appeared. "You're right. The more I think about this, the more I think it's a great outcome. We might not have stopped every criminal in the city, but considering I barely realized how many of these people could even be criminals not all that long ago and many of them are going to jail now, that's progress, right?"

"Exactly." Erik took another sip. "Any victory that ends with more casualties for the other side is good in my book.

I'm not like you. I don't believe we're ever going to be able to wipe out crime all the way, but we can knock it to its knees for a while by nailing the people doing their best to spread it. Corrupt politicians. Gangsters. Greedy, bribing corp officials. Everyone played their part, and a lot of them are now paying for thinking they would get away with it. The criminals thought they could rely on people not being willing to face the truth, but all it took was someone like you to force everyone to look that way. That changed everything."

Jia pointed at herself, then him. "We're both cops."

Erik nodded. "Yeah, last time I checked."

"I mean, we both pursued the case, and we found different people responsible for crimes. It took a while in each case, but we uncovered everything from Windward's fraud to Ceres Galactic's smuggling tech." Jia shook her head. "I bet the CID is having a lot of fun figuring out how they stole Emma to begin with."

"Probably." Erik shrugged. "But this is where I'll act like the captain. That's not our problem. I'm going to continue to use her while the UTC lets me, and I'm sure here over the next few months, we'll be hearing a lot of stories about quiet deals between senior UTC officials who are trying to avoid prison or transportation when it comes out they were helping Esposito."

Jia grimaced. "You think so? He only mentioned local officials the other day."

"Because he's just getting started," Erik explained. "He's keeping the other stuff as a backup. This is a man who could still be charged with treason, after all." He shrugged. "The petals will continue to fall."

Jia was silent for a long moment before frowning. "I've got something to say while we're both here."

"Then say it. There's no reason for you not to."

Jia sighed. "You've been riding me about using my stun pistol, but you know, some of these cases would have benefited from you killing fewer people. You know, witnesses and evidence? There's a reason stun pistols are preferred, and it's mostly citizen safety. I know you're a good cop, but you're still acting like assault infantry first and a detective second."

He considered it for a moment, running a hand through his still grayish hair. "I see what you're saying, but I don't agree." He shrugged. "I shot people who were trying to kill you or me. I don't apologize for that, and I never will. That might be me thinking too much like a soldier, but I'd rather have less evidence than a dead partner. But, yeah, I get it. I've been thinking a lot about how I can dial certain things down without increasing personal risk. The thing is, you have to understand that things are going to get rougher before they get better."

Jia nodded, then took a swallow of her drink. "I was thinking about that."

Erik played with his glass, moving it in a circle. "I've seen this before. It's the same thing you see in counterinsurgency operations. You start taking out the leaders, and everything gets stirred up. Lots of trouble in the field, but then things start calming down. You just have to stay the course. At least these kinds of criminals are far less likely to blow up a building."

"We both have a lot to learn." Jia looked into her empty glass. "I'm not stubborn enough to continue to believe the world is as black and white as I thought. I keep wanting to pretend that now that we've taken down so many big people, things will clear up right away and Neo SoCal will become what I've always believed it was, but I understand it's going to be a long, hard slog. I'll be doing my part, but I might not see my true dream for a long time." Her voice dropped to a whisper. "If I ever see it."

Erik looked into the distance. "I'm sorry. I'm not your sister. I didn't want to be the one to tell you the truth about Generous Gao."

She looked up to him. "Erik, you've done me a favor, and at least you did it in a way where I didn't have to compromise myself."

Jia offered him a soft smile and stood. "We all have to grow up sometime. I can't say life is better knowing, but I'd rather live my life working in reality than fantasy. At least in reality, I can make a real difference, and as frustrated as I am with the fact that Ceres is skating, I know we made a difference. We've also started Neo SoCal on the path to being safer and less corrupt. So for what it is worth, thank you. You're a good partner, and you've made me a better cop." She started walking away.

"Where are you going?" Erik called. "I thought we were having drinks here?"

Jia stopped and looked over her shoulder. "Spa, food, and sleep, not necessarily in the order. If you need me, leave a message. I need some time to think, and I know the bad guys will really be getting handled by someone for once."

Erik raised an eyebrow. "You're actually going offline? You sure about that?" He grinned. "Not that I'm saying it's a bad thing. I'm just surprised you can bring yourself to do it and not be a cop twenty-four/seven."

"Yeah, I think I need to disconnect for at least one night." Jia waved and moved toward the door. "Everything will last a day without me."

Erik waved and reached for his wallet. "See you around." She slipped through the door and was gone as Erik fished out credits. "I needed to pick up an order anyway."

CHAPTER FORTY-FIVE

Erik yawned as he stepped into his apartment, a white box in hand. This living room remained as minimally furnished as when he had first moved in, except for the addition of a small table in front of his couch.

Erik moved over to the table and set the box down. He squeezed his eyes shut. It might take more than a beer to get him drunk, but that didn't mean drink after drink couldn't take a toll.

"Hey, Emma," he murmured. "Thanks for driving me home."

"It wasn't a challenge."

"Yeah, I know an autonomous system could have done it, but there's something much smoother about your driving. Don't get too used to it."

"It's the least I can do," Emma replied. "But you've expressed that sentiment before, and you've been increasingly having me drive, including during some of your recent criminal encounters. I think you trust me far more than you say."

Erik chuckled as he reached for his head and winced. "I don't really have much choice, do I?"

"Oh? Why do you say that?"

Erik gestured in the vague direction of his garage. "You've got control of my flitter, and you've been listening in. I don't know what it is. I probably shouldn't trust an amnesiac AI, but I like your attitude, and you've had plenty of opportunities to screw me over. If you haven't taken them by now, I don't suddenly see you doing it later."

"I could say the same for you," Emma mused. "I trust you, but I will also note you've proven yourself worthy of trust."

"You care about human corruption? What's it matter to you?"

Emma's redhaired holographic form winked into existence. She tilted her head, her gaze looking up and down. Given that she didn't actually see via the hologram, it was unnecessary, but she always seemed to want to feign proper body language when she was in visual form. "What's it matter to anyone? But let me say, I'm very glad I have no true human sense of smell, because if you smell as bad as you look, you're one stinky puppy."

Erik sniffed his armpit. "Do I really look that bad? I hit a few more bars after Jia took off. It's not like the old days, no bar runs with the unit."

"So I noticed. Your body is yours to dispose of as you see fit, I suppose." Emma shrugged. "As for your unit, perhaps this isn't the best time to discuss it, but I do need to inform you that I completed the analysis you requested. I was hoping to talk to you about it when you were in a more sober state, but now I don't know if waiting is the best course of action."

Erik straightened as if every molecule of alcohol had been instantly purged from his system.

In the chaos of the Ceres Galactic announcement, he hadn't thought much about the data he'd recovered from the mysterious Halcyon building prior to the explosion. Interestingly, despite the fact that several fire department personnel had been arrested, no one questioned the official story of the explosion. Everyone still asserted that it had been a maintenance failure.

Whether that meant corrupt officials lingered or people could only stare so hard into the abyss remained to be seen.

"You're not messing with me, are you?" Erik asked. He took a seat on his couch. "When I asked you about this before, you told me it was military-grade encryption and might take months to crack, if you even could. I'm assuming you didn't feed me a line since it made you look less capable."

"You have some mistakes in your recollection." Emma shook her head. "I said it was *better* than military-grade encryption, but everything else is accurate. I see no reason to lie about my capabilities. The better we understand our limits, the more useful we'll be in this partnership."

Erik grinned. "Now you're my partner?"

"I'm your car," Emma insisted.

"You're *in* my car. Not quite the same thing, but fine. You want to think of yourself as my partner, I can live with that."

Emma smiled. "As I was saying, I was trying to rip

through a lot of data in a short time from a hostile system that exploded in the middle of the process." She made a little flourish with her hands before bowing. "All things considered, I'd done an excellent job with what little I recovered, and I'm dubious human analysts aided by conventional AIs would have been capable of the same. Even if they were, it would have taken them the aforementioned months, if not longer."

Erik nodded. "I acknowledge your greatness. Is that what you wanted to hear?"

Emma winked. "It doesn't hurt. Now, I'm sure you'll be disappointed, but what I have been able to recover is far less than you likely desire. Do you want me to explain the technical details of what was involved, or should I provide you with the summary? I should warn you, it might take some days to properly explain the necessary mathematical background."

Erik grunted. "I wouldn't understand even if you did explain. Just give me the executive summary. You know the kind of things I'm looking for."

Emma pointed. An image of the Halcyon building appeared in front of her. "That facility appears to have been some sort of operational command center from what I can make out, mostly by analyzing some of the decoded traffic routing and the few scraps of message traffic I can put back together. I've been able to confirm that facility as the source of the messages that was sent to Mu Arae, which are linked to the codes you were provided."

Erik frowned, bile rising in the back of his throat. "Was it some sort of covert military facility?"

If the Army had betrayed the Knights, his vengeance would be mythic in scope.

The thought had always lingered in the back of the mind, but he had crushed it into nothingness, not wanting to face such a harsh possibility. Jia wasn't the only person who could pretend unpleasant truths didn't exist.

"If by military, you mean the UTC military, I'm doubtful of that." Emma folded her arms, her image shimmering for a moment. "The verbiage is too sparse to be of importance, but the code and encryption patterns don't seem consistent with it. I can't say that with absolute certainty, but the probability is toward other possibilities."

Erik nodded. "That leaves plenty of non-military possibilities such as other parts of the UTC government, insurrectionists, and the corps."

Emma nodded. "All are possibilities. What little data I was able to retrieve and reconstruct is insufficient for an accurate identification at this time, and I'm still learning a lot about the various organizations, meaning I can't provide you an accurate estimate about which is more likely."

"If you know they're an operational command center, does that mean you retrieved some ops traffic? Orders? That kind of thing?" Erik tried to tamp down the eagerness in his voice. All these months, and he was finally learning something new.

"Shall I read you the relevant texts fragments I think are of most interest?" A vulpine smile took over Emma's face.

She was enjoying the investigation.

He didn't know if he should be offended. If anything, a motivated AI assistant would be more useful in the future as he edged closer to discovering the full truth of what had happened.

"...eliminate all witnesses with the extant en route assets regardless of affiliation, and we will ensure the incident is managed appropriately," Emma quoted. "...complete elimination authorized. We cannot discount the potential interference of garrison UTC military forces. In such a case, expect heavy resistance and casualties... The present has already been transferred. Although the operation is suboptimal in terms of timing, the raptor threat forced move." She made a face. "I must admit that last piece puzzles me. I'm confident at 99.72 percent that I've accurately recovered the fragment, but its meaning eludes me. The other are straightforward. They might have used an additional layer of coded meaning. I will need more data to properly decipher it."

Erik's hands curled into fists. "You're very smart and often seem human, but with no slight meant, you're still an AI, and you sometimes miss the obvious. Don't worry, I understand exactly what they were saying."

Emma put her hands on her hips. "Oh? What did I miss, Detective? What did they mean about raptors?"

"Space raptors," Erik explained. "It's just slang. From the sound of it, there was something special on Molino they felt they had to move because of the potential Zitark invasion, but that doesn't tell me what it was." He frowned. "It was something important enough to murder fifty people over, but it was also something the local UTC governor, me as the commander of the ground forces left, and the captain of the destroyer didn't know about. There's a good possibility the local Xingguang officials didn't know about it either." He gritted his teeth. "But what the hell could it be? It could be *anything*."

"For all my analytical capabilities, Detective, you would be more likely to know the answer than I would. What was important on this moon in general?"

"It was more important for its strategic position than anything else." Erik frowned and looked down at his fist. "That's what I don't know. There was nothing special about anything they were bringing up from that mine. That whole moon could have been solid platinum and it wouldn't have been that important, but if they were worried about the Zitarks, maybe they smuggled in some sort of illegal tech they didn't want anyone to know about. Something they were planning to test." He lifted his head. "A biological weapon? Maybe some other weapon of mass destruction? If they thought the moon was going to fall to the Zitarks, it might have provided an excuse."

Emma nodded. "And you think that's the case?"

"I'm just throwing out possibilities." Erik considered what he suspected. "The truth is, I don't know. If we figure out who it was, we have a better chance of figuring that out. Do you have any idea who sent the message? Is it just Halcyon?"

"Unfortunately, I can't be sure," Emma replied with an apologetic look. "The initial tracking codes were external to Hermes. Whatever internal tracking codes there might have been remain unclear. Though it was definitely a Halcyon facility, it's unclear if there was any external manipulation of any of the data, and there is no way to confirm that with such a limited sample."

"That leaves a lot of suspects. It could be a rogue group

in the UTC government. It could be Halcyon going rogue, or a faction within them. Ceres Galactic themselves might have been directly involved, but it could be a trick by Hermes as well. If they wanted to cover up their involvement in something, they might have found a way to plant messages to mislead an investigation. Or it could be a different corporation entirely." Erik let his head drop back. "But this wasn't insurrectionists or terrorists. That's clear enough. The mysterious present. That's the key. They removed something from Mu Arae, and I just need to figure out where they moved it to, and who has it now. I need to understand what was worth slaughtering so many people over."

"Will you feel calmer if you figure that out?" Emma asked.

"I don't know," Erik admitted. "And I don't care. If I never find out what it was, but I find the people who killed the Knights, I'll be satisfied. I didn't become a cop because I'm obsessed with mysteries. I became a cop to get justice for my people."

Emma's hologram vanished, her voice now coming from the PNIU. "What's your next move, Detective? I can't hack the entire UTC for you. You've also made a name for yourself. Your enemies might be watching you more closely now. From what you told me, you did your best to keep a low profile on the way back from Mu Arae, but you've clearly shown you're a threat now. It wouldn't be unlikely for them to send assassins after you."

Erik considered her warning. "They're welcome to try. It'll be the last thing any of those assassins do. As for the investigation, Halcyon is my best bet. I'm going to need to look into them more. Thanks, Emma. It's not as much progress as I would have liked, but it's still at least a step forward. Now I'd like to be alone if that's even possible. Sometimes a man just needs to think about his plans for bloody vengeance."

"It's fine. I'll terminate my interface with the PNIU. If you need me, you know where to find me. I can go for a spin if you'd like."

Erik chuckled. "No, I'd prefer you stay here. I might need you to take me for a ride later."

"Very well, then. Good night, Erik."

"Good night, Emma."

Erik took a few deep breaths before leaning forward. He'd had a wild return to Earth. It hadn't been what he'd expected, but he didn't feel as aimless as he had during his year-long trip back, and more importantly, he didn't feel as alone.

He leaned forward and lifted the lid off the white box, then reached inside and pulled out a custom pistol.

I could have ended up with another detective. Jia's smart, annoying, and naïve, but she does have her heart in the right place.

Erik still wasn't certain if her eyes were truly open about the corruption in the UTC.

After all, he wasn't going to end his mission in one metroplex, even one as impressive as Neo SoCal. Still, she had proved to be a good partner on their first big case, and despite her obsession with him shooting people, her toy stun pistol would ultimately get her hurt, and maybe him.

She needed a real gun, one that wasn't linked directly to the department.

When Erik finally tracked down the people responsible for the massacre of Mu Arae, he'd need allies, and he needed those allies to not get shot to death in the meantime because they were busy trying to stun someone.

She was getting there, but she needed to accept that sometimes you just had to put a person down.

Erik placed the pistol back in the box.

"It's time to make some noise."

FINIS

Coming in six weeks, *SHATTERED TRUTH*

AUTHOR NOTES - MICHAEL ANDERLE

Here is just one of the questions OpusX is supposed to answer for me: Can an author who does well on one distribution platform survive the effort to make a name for himself on others?

Just how hard is it? (*I am told VERY hard.*)

How much (virtual) blood, sweat and (possibly) tears will I have to shed to see if we can sell stories on other distribution platforms than the one I am already popular on?

Why do I need to do it? I've answered that last question on our Behind the Fiction podcast, with host Stephen Campbell please check it out.

I like to say that OpusX is one story told in twelve parts over eighteen months.

There won't be one book release party, but rather one long continuous effort to announce to the world this series is available to read, to enjoy and to share with friends and family.

As a reader, we get involved in Jia's life when Erik

comes crashing in, saving her from being relegated to checking on traffic tickets after a second partner quits.

He represents both opportunity...*and annoyance.*

He is not like her previous partners, and she discovers that perhaps she should have been careful what she asked for – a partner who cared to shake up the system. The system is well and truly starting to be shaken up and so is her misconceptions.

Jia and Erik are two rebels whose worlds collide on a planetary scale. They will either effect change that shakes the foundation of society.

Or die in the process.

Can they survive? Of course.

Will they survive? Well, that is a different question.

I will only admit there are plenty of opportunities for the fickle finger of fate to finagle an unfortunate demise.

The challenges increase from this first book and I'm not just talking about criminals. No, Mei and Jia's Mom are focused on her personal life and not willing to cave because she finds satisfaction in her job.

She needs a husband whether Jia wants one or not. Jia, however, is no pushover even when family is doing the pushing.

Recognizing that Erik is spending all of his personal time on preparation and not his personal life, Jia believes he needs a date...So, learning nothing from Mei setting her up, she decides to set Erik up.

While I see many changes in our society every day I believe that certain behaviors will be with us centuries into the future. Family ... is family.

OpusX is my opportunity to ask a few questions about

where our society is heading when medical advances allow humanity to de-age their bodies.

We have incredibly smart people working on genetic and cellular advances and postulating we can accomplish amazing feats with stem cells. But what happens in society when this becomes a reality?

I set this concept in a new reality, an area of one country that was devastated beyond comprehension due to the efforts of a group who thought to force society to accept their version of the future, not realizing just how obstinate humanity (as a whole) can be.

Asimov considered the implications of society in his Foundation Trilogy. You can't explain what one person might do, but you can create mathematical models on what large groups of humans will do.

Who says that this ability is limited to the government think tanks? What if someone or *someones* with money, time and willingness decided to move society onto a different path, and got away with it?

Or was it just a random gang, bent on having their way.

I have more questions to unravel as the story goes forward and I hope you continue with us as we bring you one new book every six weeks.

One new audio book every six weeks arriving at the same time (to the best of our abilities) on the same day.

Same with the paperback(s). No matter if you like to curl up with a book, a tablet or listen to the story – we will be delivering the next part in just a few days.

One story, twelve books, six weeks apart each.

Two cops, each brought into the system and yet not a member of the system.

The lifeblood of a series are reviews, the group who has worked on these stories (going back over a year before the first one came out) would love to know what you enjoyed. IF we did well, do you mind leaving a review where you bought this book? On their website?

Join us as we try something a bit new and we – a very small publishing company – seek to make a splash reserved for the big companies with deep pockets. We may accomplish our goal, we may not. But, like Jia and Erik, we are going to try.

Opus *noun* - any artistic work, especially one on a large scale.

X – the letter "**x**" is often used in algebra to mean a value that is not yet known. It is called a *variable* or sometimes an *unknown*.

This is my OpusX – I sincerely hope you enjoy it.

August 6th, 2019

I'm looking forward to talking with you again at the back of Shattered Truth – Book 02.

Michael

Want more? See www.OpusXSeries.com

CONNECT WITH MICHAEL ANDERLE

Michael Anderle Social

   Website:

   http://www.lmbpn.com

Email List:

   http://lmbpn.com/email/

Facebook Here:

   https://www.facebook.com/groups/lmbpn.opusx/

TWO REBELS WHOSE WORLDS COLLIDE ON A PLANETARY LEVEL.

On the fringes of human space, a murder will light a fuse and send two different people colliding together.

She lives on Earth, where peace among the population is a given. He is on the fringe of society where authority is how much firepower you wield.

She is from the powerful, the elite. He is with the military.

Both want the truth – but is revealing the truth good for society?

Two years ago, a small moon in a far off system was set to be the location of the first intergalactic war between humans and an alien race.

It never happened. However, something was found many are willing to kill to keep a secret.

Now, they have killed the wrong people.

How many will need to die to keep the truth hidden?

As many as is needed.

He will have vengeance no matter the cost. *She will dig for the truth. No matter how risky the truth is to reveal.*

ISBN 978-1-64202-396-1

90000

9 781642 023961